Praise for *IQ*

Shortlisted for the 2017 Edgar Award for Best First Novel, The Strand Critics Award, the Anthony Award for Best Debut and the Macavity Award for Best First Novel

One of the Best Books of 2017 according to the *New York Times*, the *Washington Post*, the *New York Times Book Review* and Amazon.com

'Joe Ide is the best new discovery I've come across in a long time. And Isaiah Quintabe is the kind of sleuth not seen on the mystery landscape before' Michael Connelly

'This is one of the most remarkable debuts I've read . . . Deliciously quirky, written with exceptional panache and a fine ear for dialogue, it introduces the world to an LA private detective who might just become the Holmes of the 21st century' *Daily Mail*

'Fantastic detective debut about LA and rap moguls' *Sunday Times*

'[*IQ*] kicks off what is apt to be a madly lovable new detective series about this smart guy and the vibrantly drawn criminal culture that surrounds him . . . Ide packs a lot of action and scenery into the book's investigation scenes. But he has also built and bolstered Isaiah as a fine, durable character' *New York Times*

'One of the most original thrillers of the year . . . [A] sometimes scary, often whimsical, off-the-wall delight . . . It's a mad world that late-blooming Joe Ide has brought forth from his past, a spicy mix of urban horror, youthful striving and show-business absurdity. His *IQ* is an original and welcome creation' *Washington Post*

'Joe Ide introduces one of the coolest investigators working the mean streets of Los Angeles' *Chicago Tribune*

Praise for *Righteous*

'Witty and confident, with a bustling plot, this is a worthy follow-up to Ide's excellent debut' *Guardian*

'Ide writes with confidence and a sharp wit' *Sunday Times*

'The first new crime writer I have read in ages who truly feels like an heir to Elmore Leonard' *Daily Telegraph*

'Ide's superb ear for dialogue and sharp observational eye make this hum with life' *Daily Mail*

Praise for *Wrecked*

'Joe Ide is one of the hottest mystery novelists at work . . . The wonder of love, the cruelty of war, the black world he knows well, the music he loves (Count Basie, Duke Ellington, Louis Armstrong, George Shearing) – all the beauty and cruelty and craziness he filed away in his mind before he began writing these novels. With *Wrecked*, Ide confirms that he's among the most original new voices in today's crime fiction' *Washington Post*

'*Wrecked* is full of violent action, hairbreadth escapes and poignant life lessons: an unpredictable book written by an author with wizard-like gifts' *Wall Street Journal*

'With writing so sharp you may cut your fingers on the pages, Joe Ide's latest IQ novel, *Wrecked*, is outrageous and laugh-out-loud funny, a page-turner with devastating observations about the dangers of state-sanctioned violence and its consequences. The characters are unforgettable, none more so than IQ himself. Like the previous books, IQ's tender intelligence and his tight moral compass are what make this series so stirring . . . and touching' Attica Locke

Praise for *Hi Five*

The Times Best Crime Novels of the Year
New York Times Best Thrillers of 2020: 'Playful, fresh, full of life'
Wall Street Journal Best Mysteries of 2020: 'Among the most inventive and smartly written books in the genre'

'Savor the freshness, vividness and ingenuity of the author's prose . . . Hit men, henchmen, bagmen – they all wander in and out of a highly diverting book that crackles with life and vividness' *New York Times*

'Engrossing . . . The author is skilled at developing the humanity of every character, regardless of their perspective. It's a hallmark of Ide's evolving style that allows *Hi Five* to stand on its own for first-time readers, even as the series deepens longtime fans' engagement . . . *Hi Five* succeeds on so many fronts as it sets IQ and the series' characters on an uncertain path down darker roads' *Los Angeles Times*

'Stellar . . . Readers will root for Ide's distinctive lead every step of the way. This innovative series continues to show promise for a long, high-quality run' *Publishers Weekly*

Praise for *Smoke*

'*Smoke* bristles with the idiosyncratic invention that is Ide's trademark' *Financial Times*

'Ide manages to keep all the plates spinning with his customary wit and zeal' *The Times*

'If you've read any of his other novels starring the rogue East Long Beach private investigator Isaiah Quintabe, known as "IQ", you know that Ide doesn't write conventional suspense stories . . . In its own idiosyncratic fashion, *Smoke* is superb' *Washington Post*

'Mr. Ide, always a generous plotter, weaves several storylines into this kaleidoscopic chronicle . . . Dozens of other wonderfully sketched minor characters – science-fair whiz kids, pimps and prostitutes, working-class heroes, vengeance-bent relatives, sorrowful junkies and idealistic strivers – flesh out this richly imagined and sharply written saga. *Smoke*, which concludes with a cliffhanging crisis, positively demands a follow-up, and fast' *Wall Street Journal*

'Ide has displayed a rare ability to mix dark comedy and gut-churning drama . . . Mix-master Ide's compulsion to blend light and dark affects the two plots in surprising ways, again producing an emotion-rich form of character-driven tragicomedy, but one in which peril forever loiters in the shallows' *Booklist*

Joe Ide grew up in South Central Los Angeles. His favourite books were the Arthur Conan Doyle's Sherlock Holmes stories. The idea that a person could face the world and vanquish his enemies with just his intelligence fascinated him. Joe went on to earn a graduate degree and had several careers before writing *IQ*, his debut novel, was inspired by his early experiences and love of Sherlock. Joe lives in Santa Monica, California.

www.joeide.com

Also by Joe Ide

IQ
Righteous
Wrecked
Hi Five
Smoke

FIXIT

An IQ Novel

Joe Ide

First published in Great Britain in 2023
by Weidenfeld & Nicolson
an imprint of the Orion Publishing Group Ltd
Carmelite House, 50 Victoria Embankment
London EC4Y 0DZ

An Hachette UK Company

1 3 5 7 9 10 8 6 4 2

A CIP catalogue record for this book is
available from the British Library.

ISBN (Hardback) 978 1 4746 1210 4
ISBN (Export Trade Paperback) 978 1 4746 1211 1
ISBN (eBook) 978 1 4746 1213 5

Typeset by Born Group
Printed and bound in Great Britain by Clays Ltd, Elcograf S.p.A.

www.orionbooks.co.uk
www.weidenfeldandnicolson.co.uk

To Jack, Jon and James
The Ide brothers don't play

FIXIT

PROLOGUE

Grace arrived at the food truck midmorning. She put on a hairnet and an apron and set about prepping for the lunch crowd. Deronda's Downhome Buttermilk Fried Chicken would soon be mobbed. Grace was aware, but not aware, of what she was doing, soaking the chicken pieces in buttermilk, dredging them in the dry ingredients and setting them on the rack to dry. She chopped up the collard greens, fried the fatback and onions and put the stock on to boil. Odeal came in, huffing, groaning, the three steps taxing her weight and her wind. Her grandson Lester brought in the casserole dishes. Grace usually looked forward to it, lifting the tinfoil, revealing the world's best mac and cheese, the top crust golden, the molten mix of cheeses still bubbling. The smells were usually comforting, even heartening, but she was far away, staring into the deep fryer, the first bubbles plinking as they emerged through the amber oil.

"You all right, Grace?" Odeal said. "You don't look well, baby. You comin' down with something?"

"No, no, I'm okay," Grace said. "Not enough sleep, that's all."

"I hope you not out there carousin', young lady," Odeal said, only half joking.

"Not me. I'm a homebody."

Grace busied herself, trying and failing not to think. A few days ago, she broke up with Isaiah, the hurt like a stab wound, bleeding into the void left in his wake. She did it on the phone too. Impersonal, like she was canceling a magazine subscription. Ending their love deserved better than a voice from a cell tower. Isaiah was in Northern California somewhere, unwilling or unable to meet her because he was in another mess. He didn't tell her the specifics; his way of "sparing her" from yet another human goulash of suffering and grief. She couldn't take it, being with a man who invited violence because he couldn't resist risking his life for every victimized person he met. Everyone in the hood knew his rep. The underground PI who helped you find justice when the police wouldn't or couldn't. His cases covered the range of human depravity. He brought down rapists, armed robbers, kidnappers, drug lords, gunrunners, gangsters, con men, thieves, hired killers and pedophiles. Along the way he'd made enemies.

The waiting wore Grace down. For Isaiah to come home, or not come home, wondering what morally compromising, soul-crushing decisions he had to make, or imagining what subhuman cave dweller was swinging at him with a meat cleaver. Grace wasn't naive, she didn't demand tranquility. She wanted to grow as an artist in relative calm, like anyone making their way. If they were a couple, his enemies would be her enemies. She'd be at risk, a target. That was why he didn't ask her to go with him when he left. He wanted her to have peace, be safe. He was Isaiah, after all.

Grace had gone her own way since she was a kid. She was a loner, a misfit, eschewing pop culture for something more meaningful, always with a pencil or a paintbrush in her hand. She didn't know what she wanted in a man until she met Isaiah. Kind, compassionate, loving in his quiet, unobtrusive way, immeasurably competent, and courageous as the three hundred Spartans.

But life with him was so dangerous, so fraught with evil it was, or seemed to be, intolerable.

All she wanted now was something resembling ordinary. There were takers everywhere. Looking for a man? Put on a hairnet, wear no makeup and a shapeless apron, be entirely indifferent to whoever you're talking to and you'll be hit on by every lonely guy in LA. She was saying things to herself like *It's no one's fault, it wasn't meant to be, you're better off without him, things happen for a reason* and a bunch of other fucked-up, nonsensical, bullshit clichés, none of which made one fucking iota of sense.

She missed Isaiah. Every day, all the time. She couldn't have spent more energy thinking about him if he were here. Neither ever said, "I love you," because it didn't matter. Why say something you knew to be true? Why say something that was so obvious it was etched into your retinas? They'd never talked about marriage and they probably never would. Commitment was supposedly a decision. With Isaiah, it was genetic; indelible, like the color of your skin. *Call him, Grace. Call him now. What are you waiting for? Do you think Isaiahs grow on trees?* She resisted. If you were Isaiah, how would you feel? Overjoyed because some fickle artist says she'll cut you a break? Save yourself the effort, Grace. You've lost him once and for all.

She was on edge the whole afternoon; angry at herself and the world that kept her apart from Isaiah. *Be a grown-up, Grace. No tantrums today.*

A bearded man came to the window. Faded T-shirt, pinched face and cadaverous, all ribs, clavicles and elbows. He looked like an unpublished poet.

"What can I get for you?" Grace said.

"Is your chicken non-GMO?" he asked.

"No, it's not," she said. A proselytizer. Cut him short, Grace. "Have you decided? You've got a line behind you."

"If your chicken is not no-GMO you should put it on your sign," he said indignantly. Why do all the assholes end up in this line? she wondered. She felt her temper coming on, like the creaking of a doorknob.

"You mean we should put 'We buy our chicken at Vons' on the sign?" she said. "I'll speak to the management. Could you please order?"

"What kind of oil do you use?" he demanded.

"Pennzoil, 10W-30," she said. "Come on, dude, this is a food truck, not your guru's gluten-free commune. Order or get out of line." The doorknob was turning.

"I'm a consumer. I have the right to say what I think!" the man shouted. He turned to the people in line. "I'd like you all to know, their chicken contains dangerous hormones!" In return he got a chorus of boos and fuck yous. The anger door swung open.

"That's it, asshole!" Grace shouted. She was about to lunge through the window and stab this moron with a plastic fork, but a heavyset Black man in a postal uniform shoved the guy out of line.

"People are hungry, boy. Go home and make your own chicken!"

There was a round of applause and Grace joined in. She went back to work. After serving the postal worker, she realized she felt different. High emotion triggered high emotion, and there was nothing more emotional than her feelings for Isaiah. *What's your problem, Grace? Isaiah's not worth fighting for? You're afraid he'll reject you? The risk is too great? I've got news for you, girl. Love* is *risk.*

She told Odeal she was leaving early and drove home, anxious and eager, her heart bumping, damp palms choking the life out of the steering wheel. First thing she'd do was fix her hair, put on a little lip gloss and fresh clothes—ridiculous for a phone call but she'd feel better. Where should she be when she made this momentous call? There was the chaise in the backyard or the easy chair in the living room but neither felt right. Maybe in bed. Yes, that was it. Talk to your man while you're in bed.

She parked the battered jeep in the driveway, turned off the engine and lifted the door handle. Skip surprised her as she got out of the car, saying her name like he was spitting, gleeful when he hit her in the gut, the breath ripped out of her throat, the pain erupting, doubling her over. The hitman cackled as she fell to her knees. The last thing she saw before the sky went dark was a dog collar hanging around his neck; chrome-plated, shiny and spiked.

CHAPTER ONE
The Message

Isaiah was a patient at the Coronado Springs Hospital, five hundred miles away from East Long Beach and home. He was recovering from injuries he'd sustained during a case—a case he didn't want, need or ask for. To compound his troubles, he was suffering from PTSD. A lifetime of violence, tragedy and suffering had ruined him; his body depleted, his psyche shattered, his emotional self a charred wreck. He was tortured by nightmares and wracked with horrifying flashbacks. He couldn't sleep, he couldn't stay awake, every thought a tirade of self-loathing, doubt and pity. The idea of another case repulsed him. He didn't want to be IQ anymore. He didn't want to make a difference. He wanted to be nobody. He wanted Grace.

He was in this condition when he met a young man named Billy Sorenson, an escapee from the local neuropsychiatric ward. Isaiah came back to his cottage one day to find Billy stealing food from his kitchen. He was in a pathetic state; scared, on the run and friendless. Billy believed a serial killer named William Crowe was coming to Coronado Springs. Crowe's presumed intention was to murder someone, identity unknown. According to Billy, Crowe was the infamous AMSAK killer, so called by the press because he disposed of his seventeen victims at the convergence of the American and Sacramento Rivers. Crowe was on a nine-year killing spree and the police had yet to identify him. Billy wanted help bringing him down.

Isaiah soon learned Billy was not a reliable source. He was an alarmist and had a history of making up stories and crying wolf. The whole town knew about him. Isaiah wanted no part of it. This was exactly the kind of thing he'd vowed to stay away from. No more falling into the sewer with the filth and the vermin, covered in the blood and sludge, never to be clean again. He told Billy no.

He told himself he'd take a look. That was all. Isaiah interrogated Billy at length. He laboriously checked the kid's story and went through a raft of police and FBI computer files Billy downloaded from his mother's laptop. She was an assistant district attorney. Isaiah carefully examined the data, reluctantly concluding Billy's story was true. *Why is this your business?* Isaiah thought. Self-preservation demanded he walk away. But he didn't. Couldn't. The local sheriff didn't believe the story and Crowe would kill another innocent. He had to be found. He had to be caught.

The case was insanely harrowing. Isaiah came close to death several times, closer than he ever had before. He became a fugitive and contemplated suicide. He was kidnapped by outlaws. A gale nearly blew him off a cliff face. He had a knife fight in the middle of a bonfire. He crashed a motorcycle and was nearly crushed by an avalanche, and in the midst of this maelstrom a stinging irony revealed itself. The PTSD symptoms had virtually disappeared. The danger, the adrenaline, the mental machinations and extreme physical demands abated the illness. But when the case ended, the symptoms roared back and flattened him. Now here he was in the hospital contemplating his future. There were only two choices.

To be sick again, or to resume the work that made him sick. "I'll be sick," he said as he lay there on the gurney. He'd never return to the cesspool. He would get out of here and go someplace where there was peace, where no one knew him, where there was no IQ. Where there was no I.

A nurse had just left his room. Isaiah was curled up in the crisp hospital sheets. He should have asked her for more meds. Something to make him sleep and escape his misery while images of Grace strobed in and out of his mind. They'd lived together briefly. In the late afternoons, she'd set up her easel in the backyard. She said the light was warmer and softer when the sun set and rose. Isaiah observed her from the window. She stood at her easel, perfectly still, like an egret waiting in a tide pool. Long minutes passed. She wasn't restless and she didn't fidget. He admired her humility, knowing the world changed in its own good time. They did small things. Cooked, shopped, went for walks, talked about nothing, sat on the stoop and drank cold beers and read to each other lying in bed; things he immediately forgot but that now in retrospect seemed so meaningful and sweet.

Deronda called and stirred him out of his reverie.

She was breathless, like she'd run up a flight of stairs. "Grace has gone missing," she said.

Isaiah sat up. His pains vanished, his stomach lurched. "Missing? What do you mean?"

"I mean she's missing and nobody knows where she's at. Last time I talked to her was yesterday. I texted her a bunch of times, but she don't answer. I was hoping she was with you."

"No, she's not." He was already out of bed and donning his clothes. Deronda said Grace left her handbag behind. Keys, wallet, everything.

"The police ain't doin' shit. They told me to wait seventy-two hours," Deronda said. "It's some kinda policy."

"Do they know who did it?"

"Dodson said it was somebody named Skip Hanson. I asked him how he knew and he said it was the dog collar."

"Dog collar?"

"It was left in the driveway. It's supposed to be some kinda message." Isaiah froze. The fear was overwhelming. Skip was a hitman, cunning, brutal and erratic. They met on a case. At the time, Skip lived alone in the desert, murdering people for money and raising a pack of lethal canines. They were his family and the only source of love in his life. Isaiah sent Skip to jail and his loved ones were put down. Even five years later, Skip's hatred was palpable, a radiating heat, like standing in front of a blast furnace. "I'm on my way," Isaiah said.

Isaiah was on the road, the headlights carving a tunnel through the darkness. He was driving Grace's car. A 1968 Mustang GTI she'd lovingly restored in memory of her father. She'd given him the car before he went away. Isaiah could feel her presence, her small hands on his, turning the wheel, guiding him home. He'd pass through Lake Tahoe soon, take Highway 88 to Interstate 5 and an eighty-mile-an-hour sprint to Long Beach and home. A seven-hour drive. He'd do better than that.

There was a $25,000 bounty on Isaiah's head. A network of gangs across the breadth of SoCal were looking for him, along with drug dealers, junkies, thieves, hustlers, thugs and ex-cons of every sort. Manzo Gutierrez led the posse, the highly intelligent Khan of the Sureños Locos 13. Manzo and Isaiah weren't friends, but they respected each other's strengths, exchanged favors and stayed on their own sides of the street.

Isaiah had betrayed Manzo, not for his own gain, but to save an emotionally disabled young woman from murder charges. The reason was immaterial. Manzo was humiliated and the Locos lost out on a seven-figure arms deal. There was no forgiveness, only restitution and death. The bounty lured ordinary folks into the pursuit. That was a lot of coin for pointing a finger. Looking for Grace under those conditions was impossible, never knowing if the butcher, the baker, the crackheads in the parking lot or the checker at the supermarket would rat you out. Manzo would have to call them off and somehow rescind the reward. Convincing the shrewd gang leader would take ingenuity, conviction and a giant set of brass balls. Isaiah possessed all of the above but little hope he could pull it off. He was a fugitive from street justice.

With every mile, Isaiah felt IQ returning. Keen, relentless, senses wide open, his mind working smoothly, without doubts or indecision, measuring the meager data, considering options, making choices. He felt like a mother whose child is pinned under a car, that nexus of love, urgency and terror giving her the strength to lift the massive weight and save her baby. Maybe the PTSD would return after he found Grace, he thought. But it didn't matter. *Get her back, Isaiah.*

His phone buzzed. A number he didn't recognize.

"What's up, Q Fuck?" Skip said. Isaiah was stunned. His phone was new, a burner. Grace probably gave him the number.

"Skip," Isaiah said, hoping his voice didn't falter.

"Well, well, well, how things change," the killer said. Isaiah knew to avoid accusations and aggression. It gave Skip a reason to hurt Grace.

"Hey, Grace, I've got your boyfriend on the phone," he called out. She's not dead in a ditch, thought Isaiah. That means I can find her. "Funny thing," Skip went on. "We were just talking about you—weren't we, honey? By the way, she's not bad or anything but a guy like you could do way better than this." No, thought Isaiah. No one could do better than this. "She's not so great in the personality department either," Skip continued. "But we're getting along great. Oh, she got out of line a couple of times and I put her in her place. Holding a gun to her head took the starch right out of her, right, Grace?" Isaiah couldn't swallow, couldn't speak, he was trembling. "Are you there, asshole?" Skip said.

"Yes, I'm here." He let it hang. He wasn't going to say Please don't hurt her, or Is she okay? Or, especially, I'm going to kill you, motherfucker. Skip would taunt him all the more.

"Yeah, the strong, silent type," Skip said, contemptuous. "You always were. Do you want to talk to her?"

"You're in charge. I have no say in it," Isaiah said. Skip laughed.

"I like this, I like it when you're humble. Yeah, it suits you, and you know what? It's gonna get worse, Q Fuck. *It's gonna get much worse*. Hey, Grace, get over here!" There were rustling sounds. "Say the wrong thing and you're fucked," Skip said.

"Isaiah? Don't worry, I'm okay," she said. Her voice was soft and throaty, a lance through his soul. Just like her, he thought. Kidnapped and she's reassuring you.

"I'm glad. I'm glad you're okay," he said. *Stay steady, Isaiah.*

"I mean that, I'm really fine," she went on unconvincingly. "I'm not injured or anything and I'm all right. Skip's treating me fine." Isaiah opened his mouth but nothing came out. What could he say? Keep your chin up? You'll come home soon? I'll be there in a jiffy?

"That's good," he said. He didn't want her to talk anymore. He knew they were on speakerphone and he knew Skip was standing over her with a baseball bat. If she said the wrong thing she'd likely get her skull cracked open.

"Skip said he's going to let me go so don't worry," she said.

"You should get off, Grace," Isaiah said. There were more rustling sounds and Skip came on.

"All right, that's it." He was probably upset because Isaiah told her to get off and not him. "Go over there and sit down," Skip said. "Go on!" Skip threw something and Grace yelped.

"Okay! Okay!" she said distantly. Isaiah instigated the deaths of others, but he'd never killed anyone himself. *Oh, you will be punished, Skip*. For every mark that's on her, for every time she cried in pain, for every time you touched her, you will be punished and it won't stop until you're dead.

"You know what's gonna happen now, don't you?" Skip said. Isaiah did know. Skip would use Grace to torment him. "We're gonna play hide-and-seek," Skip said. "I hide Grace and you seek. Think you can do that, Q Fuck?"

"I, uh, I don't know," Isaiah said.

"I'm an impatient guy," said Skip. "If you don't find her and I get tired of waiting, I'll kill her and stuff her body in a dumpster. Better put a move on it, Q Fuck. Oh yeah, I left a message for you." Skip disconnected and Isaiah suddenly realized he was going nearly a hundred miles an hour. Skip said he left a message but didn't say where. It took him one second to figure it out. He called Dodson.

"It's Isaiah," he said.

"Where the hell are you?" Dodson said. "You couldn't send a text or something, let people know what's goin' on? You better be on your way back." Antagonism was Dodson's opening bid whatever the circumstances.

"Just leaving Fresno," Isaiah said. "What's happening?"

"Nothing here. Everybody's on the lookout. I told 'em Skip was long gone but they're still looking. I don't know why but lots of folks round here are fond of your ass."

"I talked to Skip."

"You *talked* to him?" Dodson said. "What's that crazy mutha-fucka got to say?"

"He has Grace. Wants to play hide-and-seek."

"Uh-huh," said Dodson like he knew it all along. "And you'll be runnin' around all crazy, following clues Skip made up, and you know what's gonna happen then? He'll lead you right into a trap."

"Seems like it," Isaiah said.

"I know what you gonna do too," Dodson replied.

"Oh really? What's that?"

"You'll see it coming like you usually do, then you'll walk right into it."

"Why would I do that?" Isaiah said.

"Because if you find Skip, you find Grace. That, and you think your freakishly large brain will get you out of anything even when it won't."

"I'll meet you at Blue Hill," Isaiah said.

Dodson's voice went falsetto. "Blue Hill? Ain't nothin' out there but—" Isaiah disconnected before Dodson could give him twelve reasons why that made no sense.

Dodson entered the kitchen. Cherise was sitting at the breakfast table with a stack of files and her laptop. She supervised a team of paralegals at a downtown law firm and brought work home all the time. Cherise was a fine-looking woman. She possessed a sweet, sexy side that still air-fried his hormones after six years of marriage. She was also churchgoing, frighteningly intelligent, so honest it was off-putting and a firm believer in earning your daily bread. On the whole, he was glad he married her. He'd still be a no-account, meandering low-life hustler if he'd continued his wayward ways. On the whole.

"I just got off the phone with Isaiah," he said.

"You did?" Cherise said.

"He's coming. Just leaving Fresno."

"That's fantastic news," Cherise said, pushing the laptop away. "I feel so sorry for Isaiah. He's such a good soul. He loves Grace and she loves him. I don't know what I'd do if—"

"What'd you do if—what?" Dodson said. "Somebody kidnapped me? Y'all should worry about the kidnapper."

"I didn't mean you, I meant our son, Micah. Remember him?" Their five-year-old boy, growing like a mushroom cloud.

"Isaiah wants me to meet him at Blue Hill," Dodson said.

"Good, I'm sure he'll need help," Cherise said. He turned away, relieved because they were supposed to have a "serious talk." Cherise said, "I haven't forgotten, Juanell. Sit down. This won't take long." Dodson closed his eyes. That meant it would take forever.

"Not now, baby, I'm upset."

"I'm upset too but that doesn't mean we have to put our life on hold." He sat. Cherise looked at him a moment. It wasn't a nice look. More like a linebacker on fourth and one.

"The last time we talked about your chronic unemployment, you said you were going to be a fixer," Cherise began. "I thought it was a shady idea but okay, I can see how it fits your personality. You said you wanted to help people with their problems, like you did with Deronda. I'm proud of you for that."

It happened months ago. A man named Bobby James tried to blackmail Deronda for half her business. Dodson stepped in. He made a shrewd calculation, squashed Bobby James and sent the asshole on his way. Deronda said he should be a fixer and regretfully, that was what he told Cherise.

"What I want to know is, why aren't you out there fixing things?" Cherise said.

"Because nobody knows about it," Dodson said. "It's hard to

flex that kind of thing. What do I say on social media? 'Hello, friends. I'm proud to announce my new career as a professional fixer. My qualifications? I was a street hustler, I sold drugs, I ran a Ponzi scheme and spent time in Vacaville.'" Cherise rolled her eyes. Dodson continued as if she wasn't there. "'It was there I got my degree in duplicity, deception, bribery, double-crossing, double-dealing, short cons, long cons, extortion and graft. Please have a look at my website. W W W dot sneaky muthafucka.'"

"You know how I feel about that language, Juanell, and as a matter of fact, I have a client for you." She looked at him, hesitant. She was never hesitant. He was getting a bad feeling.

"You gonna keep me guessing?" Dodson said.

"Reverend Arnall." Cherise said it like she was confessing something.

"Reverend Arnall? If he needs help, why don't he ask Jesus? Can't the Son of God help him out?"

"I'm angry with you already, Juanell," Cherise said, narrowing her eyes. "Profane Christ and you won't see me naked again until you're playing Chinese checkers at the senior center."

Dodson made a small groaning sound. "What does the Reverend want?"

"He can tell you himself," Cherise said. Dodson's relationship with the church was a puff of air.

"If this is about my chronic unemployment, is the Reverend gonna pay me?" Dodson said. Again, she hesitated.

"He'll pray for you and give you the Lord's blessing."

"Is that like Bitcoin?" Dodson said. "I need a new car."

"You'll be helping others, Juanell. Isn't that the point?" Cherise said.

"That's one of 'em. I believe the other was money."

"Never mind," Cherise said, waving like she was batting away a mosquito. "I've made an appointment for you with the Reverend on Thursday and don't you *dare* blow it off."

The sun was rising when Isaiah reached the desert, brown and barren, piles of gray boulders and low, dusky foothills. It was already in the eighties. The closest civilization to Skip's place was Fergus, a two-block truck stop that sold inedible donuts and bad coffee. Isaiah drove into the parking lot of the Dew Drop Inn and saw Dodson sitting in his car. A fifteen-year-old, gleaming white Lexus RS. Dodson was in the driver's seat, his arm straight out on the steering wheel, bobbing his head to Tupac's "How Do U Want It." Isaiah was glad with his whole heart. He pulled up, driver's side to driver's side. Dodson smiled his cocky, breezy, don't-you-ever-fuck-with-me smile.

"Whassup, Q?" Dodson said.

"Same old," Isaiah said.

"What happened to your hand?" Dodson asked. Isaiah's hand was bandaged. He burned it in the knife fight with William Crowe. Dodson added, "Did your brain get so big you had to punch yourself in the face?"

"Yeah, that's what happened," Isaiah said, smiling. "You ready?"

"Why you always ask me that?" Dodson complained. "When I fell out the womb I was ready."

"Whose car? Yours or mine."

"Mine," Dodson said decisively. "Goliath's kids might be up there and you drive too slow." Dodson had a pit bull phobia. It had worsened since Goliath nearly ate him for supper.

It was a short drive to the LANDFILL 6 MILES sign and the dirt road. Isaiah was elated to see Dodson again and he knew Dodson felt that way too. Showing it was uncool, embarrassing and confusing. Step outside their unspoken, long-established rules and who knows what would happen.

The road was full of potholes and stretches of washboard, Dodson wincing with every bump. "We shoulda called an Uber," he complained. "Biggie don't like this bullshit."

"Who's Biggie?" Isaiah said.

"My car—hey, man, look at all this goddamn dust! I can hardly see!"

"It washes off, you know."

"Hang on, Biggie," Dodson said, patting the dashboard. "I'll get you outta here soon enough." Dodson was into old-school rap, the nineties was his era. Biggie, Tupac, Nas, Lauryn Hill, Scarface and Jay-Z. He listened to contemporary rap but said it didn't move him. There were no memories attached to the songs.

The BLUE HILL PIT BULLS sign was where it had been before, grimy and faded and nailed into the same dead tree. They parked and walked across the rocky expanse of dirt that used to be the front yard. The small house was a wreck; broken windows, missing front door, crumbling stucco, a rain gutter hanging loose.

"I got a lotta bad memories about this place," Dodson said.

"Yeah, me too," Isaiah said.

"What are we doing here?"

"Skip said he left me a message, but he didn't say where."

"Then how do you know it's here?"

"Because I know," Isaiah said.

"You don't need to get snippy," Dodson said.

"I'm not snippy," Isaiah said. Another one of their perennial arguments.

"Normal people don't have your psychic powers," Dodson said. "Maybe while we're here you can talk to my dead grandmother and find out where she hid the silverware." It was comforting, Isaiah thought. The banter was something they did no matter what the situation. It kept the edge off the nervousness and covered over the fear.

They went in the house, ducking under the cobwebs, stepping over the broken glass, smashed furniture and assorted junk. Dodson glanced down at the floor. "See them footprints?"

"Yes, I see them," Isaiah said. "Work boots, size ten."

"There you go bein' snippy again," Dodson said.

"I'm not being—forget it."

They went down the hall and stopped at the bedroom. At one point in the Goliath case, Isaiah and Dodson tried to kidnap the dog as a means of coercing Skip into submission. All the dogs were kenneled in the barn—except Goliath. Skip left him loose as a kind of roving security guard. The dog chased Dodson into the house. He wanted to lock himself in the bedroom but there were no interior doors. Skip removed them so Goliath wouldn't have to slow down while he was chomping your ass to shreds. The dog cornered Dodson in the closet and was about to bite his face off when Isaiah shot the beast with a tranquilizer gun. He borrowed it from Harry Halderman.

"Could we move on, please?" Dodson said. "This place will give me nightmares." A rectangle of newspapers and flattened cardboard boxes was on the floor, fast-food debris scattered around.

"Skip spent the night," Isaiah said.

"Why?" Dodson said.

"The message. Whatever it is, it took some time."

The roof of the barn was caved in, grime, crud and cobwebs clinging to every surface, dust motes nearly stationary in the dim light. The kennels were in shambles. Frames broken, gates broken, ancient dog turds embedded in the cement.

"Goliath's kennel is at the end of the row," Isaiah said. It was intact, twice as big as the others, made of heavy chain link. The gate was new. Fresh-cut wood, pine smell, sawdust scattered. The floor was swept.

"Why'd Skip do all this?" Dodson said.

"He's telling me we're starting over," Isaiah said. "He's telling me it's a new day." A dog food can was set on the ground. It was shiny, no label, *Q FUCK* written on it with a red Sharpie. Isaiah did a quick scan for booby traps and stepped over the railing. He held his head back and nudged the can with his foot. No rattlesnake. Inside was a memory stick.

Isaiah and Dodson were in the car, the air conditioning up high. Isaiah inserted the memory stick into his laptop.

"What do you think is on there?" Dodson said.

"Photos."

"Take it slow, Q," Dodson said protectively.

Isaiah hesitated, gulped in a deep breath and brought up the first photo. At first, he couldn't focus, or maybe he didn't want to. He saw a young woman—but it wasn't Grace! He took in another breath and abruptly held it. No. It was Grace. She was sweaty and bedraggled, hair over her face, her wrists wrapped with duct tape, a strip over her mouth. Isaiah had been bound like that a number of times. It was terrifying. He stared at her, swallowing dry. Skip was standing next to her, a car behind them. The hitman was grinning triumphantly, his arm around her, hand gripping her shoulder. Rage exploded inside Isaiah's chest.

"He's touching her," he said. He growled through his teeth, shivered violently and snapped shut the laptop. He got out of the car and slammed the door.

Dodson watched his friend storm blindly into the brush. He stopped, stood there in the white-hot sun, quaking, veins bulging in his neck, breathing in short huffs, his whole body tight as a clenched fist. Then he lifted his head and screamed, loud and piercing, his voice an axe blade, leveling the tumbleweed and flattening the foothills, pausing only to suck in a breath before hurling more outrage at the sky. His throat was raw but he kept screaming until he choked up and stopped.

Dodson took a bottle of water, got out of the car and walked after him. He was surprised. Everything was the same, the rocks, the brush, the stunted trees and hazy sky. Like they didn't hear a thing. Like Isaiah was never there. Yeah, let that be a lesson to you, thought Dodson. Whatever your troubles, you on your own, son. The universe don't give a shit.

Isaiah was breathing hard, eyes closed, chin on his chest like God condemned him to misery ever after. Dodson handed him the bottle of water.

"Here. If you die of heatstroke I'm gonna leave you out here."

CHAPTER TWO
Suppertime! Yum! Yum!

They agreed to meet at TK's wrecking yard. Isaiah took the 210 to the 605 to the 710. He got off on PCH, crossed over the LA River into East Long Beach proper. He felt a rush of adrenaline. He was home, a feeling that dissipated as he drove past McClarin Park, a campground for the homeless and Tristar Liquor Mart, where the cash register was behind bulletproof glass and the clerk kept an assault rifle, and the street corner where Mrs. Crenshaw was dumped out of her wheelchair and robbed, and the apartment building where Nathan Chang threw his wife out of a fourteenth-story window, and the playground where a meth addict named Looney Hopkins bludgeoned his friend Teacup to death with a chunk of cement. Isaiah wanted to come home for months but now that he was here, the shine was off the memories. The hood was the hood wherever you went. This was probably how Robinson Crusoe felt. After he was rescued from the island, Crusoe returned to England, stayed briefly and went directly back to his sanctuary. If you didn't like your hometown before, there was no reason to like it now.

The police had to be informed about Skip, Blue Hill and the memory stick. They might be able to do more with the info. If

Isaiah went to the station in person he'd be stuck there half a day. He'd have to identify himself, wait for a detective to speak to him, get interviewed, make a formal statement, explain his relationship with Skip and Grace and how he got the information and on and on. Instead, he went to Printland and converted the digital photos to prints. He bought pen, paper and a manila envelope. He wrote a detailed explanatory note including the location of Blue Hill and Skip's real name. He also wrote down his phone number and the exact time Skip called. Maybe they could triangulate Skip's phone. He'd get another burner and throw the other away. He didn't want a dozen phone calls from a police detective.

Then he wiped his prints off the memory stick, the photos, the note and the manila envelope and dropped the envelope off at the Long Beach police station, holding the envelope with his fingernails as he handed it to the officer at the desk.

"It's about a missing persons case," he said. He left before questions were asked.

Isaiah crossed the river into Wilmington, made a left on Dockside, a narrow street with no road sign. The area was a no-man's-land of grimy oil rigs, old power lines, barrels of toxic waste, abandoned cars and appliances, stacks of rotten lumber and rolls of rusty chicken wire. He motored past the sign that said WRECKING YARD CAUTION and through the wide gate. If anything had changed it wasn't noticeable; stacks of flattened cars, the old warehouse, the looming crane, piles of auto parts, the smell of rust, oil and gasoline. Isaiah felt a rise in his throat. This was where he'd met Grace.

It was a happy sight, TK coming out of the warehouse. The shriveled old man, black as an eggplant, in oil-stained coveralls and a dingy STP cap, smiling broadly, his bloodhound face wrinkled as Jackie Robinson's baseball mitt. If Isaiah had a father, he'd want him to be like TK. Easygoing, funny and wise, decades of struggle on his knowing face and a backbone made of iron rebar. Isaiah stopped and got out of the car.

"How you doin', Isaiah?" TK said.

"I've been better," Isaiah said. They stood there, looking at each other. TK only hugged women. The old man frowned.

"You look terrible, boy. The hell happened to you?"

"I wish I had time to tell you," Isaiah said. A kid came ambling around the mountain of tires. He was white, scruffy, buzz cut, washed-out green polo shirt, frayed at the collar, baggy shorts, mismatched socks and battered All Stars. He held a radiator in both arms.

"This the one you wanted? I got it from that Civic like you said."

"Yeah, that's it," TK said. "Leave it over there. Customer's coming in the morning. You go on home now, everything's done. Isaiah, this is Andy Wright, he's been giving me a hand."

"Andy, it's good to meet you," Isaiah said.

"Hello," the kid mumbled as he hefted on his backpack and walked toward the gate. "Thanks for the food," he said as he walked out the gate.

"You did a good job today," TK called after him. "Yeah. I was a good friend of his dad, a welder, worked not far from here. I've known him and his family for damn near twenty years. Poor fella was barely making it and died of a stroke. Then his wife fell apart and started drinking. She beats the kid whenever she gets the chance. One morning, I found Andy sleeping in one of the cars. Didn't have a nickel to his name. I gave him a job and—forget all that. Come on in."

TK led Isaiah into the gloom of the warehouse. The sun shone through transoms high on the walls, and there, in a swath of golden light, were his friends. Deronda, Dodson, his wife, Cherise, their young son, Micah, and Cherise's mother, Gloria. There was old Harry Halderman from the animal shelter and Verna, a gnarly twig of a woman who owned the Coffee Cup. In unison, they grinned and shouted, "Welcome home, Isaiah!"

Isaiah was as averse to crying as any man alive but he bowed his head, put his hand over his eyes and let the tears roll down his face. The women gathered around, hugging him in turns, telling him how glad they were to see him, how much they loved him, that he was home now and everything would be all right. Hometown means nothing, Isaiah thought. Home is the people that love you.

Deronda smiled her brilliant, irresistible smile. "Come here, Isaiah. I'm so glad to see you I could bust." She threw her arms around him, warm and enveloping, her breath smelling like a strawberry sucker. "It's okay, baby," she said softly. "You with friends now." She held on for a few moments. He was embarrassed, but it was the best he'd felt in a long long time. He wiped his face with his forearm.

"You ever heard of my Happy As a Muthafucka Meal?" Deronda said.

"No, I haven't but I'd like to," he said. A lavish spread was laid out on the picnic table. Fried chicken, collard greens, mac and cheese, yams, ham hocks, black-eyed peas, sweet potato pie and corn on the cob. The women fussed over him, piling food on his plate, bringing him more napkins, filling his glass with Kool-Aid. He ate voraciously, despite the situation. He hadn't had good food since he left Long Beach.

Harry Halderman was supervisor at the animal shelter and Isaiah had worked for him as a teenager. Harry was built like an assemblage of pickup sticks, with a shock of white hair and thick bifocals. He was the only person Isaiah ever knew who seemed perpetually indignant, his grumping and grousing belying a lifelong dedication to animals. Isaiah saw the old man feed baby hummingbirds no bigger than bumblebees and build a chariot for a dog that lost its back legs and drive a wild raccoon all the way to the national forest to let it go and rescue baby ducks and raise them in a kiddie pool, replete with a handmade exit ramp.

"Guy comes in with a pit bull mix, a year old," Harry said. "Six months old, full of beans, couldn't sit still. Hell, it's a puppy. Man says the dog is untrainable, said he's been trying and trying and the dog just won't respond. 'There's something wrong with him,' the man said. 'I think the dog is retarded.' "

"Well, I told him he was the ignoramus and that no dog was untrainable. I told him every dog wasn't Rin Tin Tin but if it didn't respond, it was the owner's fault."

"What did he say?" TK asked.

"He said I should put my money where my mouth is, so I bet him a hundred bucks the dog would know basic obedience by the weekend." Harry went on, talking about gradients, keeping the dog's focus, building a relationship and breaking a command down into increments so the dog will understand.

"Did you win the hundred?" Dodson said.

"Of course I did," Harry said. "All it took was some treats, a kind word or two and a trainer who knew what he was doing. I kept the dog too. The man complained but I told him get lost."

TK had a sly smile on his face. Isaiah could tell a joke was soon to follow.

"I was over at my sister's day before yesterday," the old man said, wiping some corn kernels off his chin. "She got three kids. They was runnin' around, making a racket, so I had a cup of coffee and said I was leaving. Well I'm 'bout to walk out the door when her seven-year-old, Chester, stops me and says, 'Uncle? Where do babies come from?' Well, I didn't know what to say, I just wanna get out of there, so I says to him—the stork. And he says, 'Mom had sex with a stork?' " Dodson choked on a chicken bone.

Everyone laughed, including Isaiah. It was strange. He'd forgotten what it felt like.

Gloria, Cherise's mother, was vice-principal at Carver Middle School for twenty-five years. She was notoriously cranky, dismissive and demanding, wearing the same dark print dress and nurse's shoes she wore back then. But today, she was smiling and gracious, circling the table with potato salad and ladling it on plates. Dodson said she hooked up with TK and apparently, the union did her good. She had a long-standing feud with Dodson. She felt Cherise deserved better and she might have been right. When Gloria reached Dodson with the potato salad, he said, "I'd like some more of that please," and she said,

"You can have some when you get a job."

Then there was Deronda. Man, what a sight, thought Isaiah, the undisputed Queen of the Hood. "Try my hot sauce," she said, beaming. There were narrow cherry-red bottles on the table. The label said: DERONDA'S HEAT WAVE. THE BEST HOT SAUCE IN THE WORLD! Deronda was sporting tricolored leggings tight enough to suffocate her bountiful thighs, her hair a kind of auburn color with caramel highlights, jangling gold bracelets, gold hoop earrings, a gold nose ring, lavender flip-flops and the Fourth of July on her toenails. Some might mistake her for one more overdressed homegirl but Deronda wasn't one more of anything. She'd grown from, in her words, "Miss Ho of the Universe" to an entrepreneur, her business acumen sharp enough to slice warm cheese. She started with one broken-down food truck and built it into a string of eight. DERONDA'S DOWNHOME BUTTERMILK FRIED CHICKEN made ten-best lists all over LA. Deronda sold hats and T-shirts, gave lectures to aspiring food-truckers. And now the hot sauce.

"You amaze me, Deronda," said Isaiah. "This is truly impressive."

"So is the chicken," said TK, a connoisseur of all things fried. "How do you prepare it?"

"Prepare the chicken?" Deronda said. "I just tell him he's gonna die." Everybody burst out laughing. Dodson choked on some collard greens. Isaiah was having a good time and the moment he realized it, the feeling vanished. The voice in his head admonished him. *You should be looking for Grace.* He tried to keep smiling but couldn't. There was some more chatter and soon the group picked up on it and the mood turned somber.

"Have you heard anything about Grace?" Verna asked.

"Where will you start the investigation?" Cherise asked. "Not to be discouraging, but it seems to me you have very little to go on."

"I'm not sure yet," Isaiah said. "I've got to think on it for a while."

"Well, if anyone can find Grace, it's you," Verna said. Everybody nodded, agreed and offered their encouragement.

"Are the gangs looking for me?" he asked.

"It was intense for a while, but since you left it's cooled off," Dodson said. "Manzo ain't got his squads out trying to hunt your ass down."

"I told people you was dead," Deronda offered. "I said your right kidney went bust. The hospital didn't have but one left and they gave it to a white man."

"Sounds true to me," TK said.

Isaiah stood up. "Thank you, everybody," he said. "This is really..." He paused a moment, breathed a quavering sigh. "We all love Grace..." He faltered again, unable to finish the sentence. "I'm going to find her," he said. "I, um...I have work to do. If you'll excuse me."

TK's office was in the warehouse. Unlike the wrecking yard itself, the cramped space was immaculate. Repair manuals, parts catalogues in three-ring binders lined up neatly on the shelves. There were file cabinets and a large desk made from a door set on cinder blocks. Photos of loved ones on the walls. No rude calendars or posters of sports heroes and fancy cars. Isaiah sat down and Dodson pulled up a chair.

"What are we doing?" Dodson said.

"Looking at the photos."

Isaiah promised himself he would not lose control, no matter what he saw.

If he wanted to find Grace, he needed to be steady, take the emotion of it and see. Not look. *See.*

Grace was lying on the floor. Her eyes were closed. Her mind wasn't clear but it was clearing. Skip gave her a shot while she was tied up in the trunk. When he told her it was Rohypnol she screamed through the duct tape. After that, nothing. She half opened her eyes. She had a sideways view of a badly battered door. She sensed she was alone but wasn't sure. Skip could be sitting right behind her or watching her on video. She remembered him hauling her out of the trunk, limp, dehydrated and groggy. He took pictures, moving her around like a rag doll and cackling. Maybe she blacked out or he gave her something else but here she was, sprawled on the grimy linoleum.

She wasn't tied up. That was a relief. She put her ear to the floor. No sounds, no vibrations. Slowly, she sat up, one hand beneath her for support. She had a ripping headache. Her clothes were dirty and rumpled but intact. There was a jug of water on a folding table. She struggled to her feet, swayed a bit, then opened the jug and took a long drink. She wished she had a few Tylenol.

She was in a motel room. It was painted a bilious green, ragged holes in the wallboard, the ceiling water-stained and sagging in places, the spindly light fixture hanging by a naked wire, cobwebs in every angled corner. The windows were boarded up. It was hot, ovenlike, claustrophobic. I'm trapped, she thought. Then her breathing accelerated and fear took over. She went to the door. It wasn't original, this one made of solid wood. She didn't expect it to be open but she turned the knob back and forth and back and forth. "Shit," she said.

There were two new dead bolts. One at eye level, the other down by her knees. A peephole the size of a nickel was drilled through, something covering it on the other side. She went to the front window. It was boarded up from the outside. She shoved on a board hard, repeatedly with both hands. It didn't even creak, probably bolted in place. She peeked through the spaces between the boards. She couldn't see anything but desert. The fear became panic. She was caged in, helpless, at the mercy of a maniac. Skip would torture her, rape her, murder her.

"LET ME OUT! LET ME FUCKING OUT!" she screamed. She paced around the room, desperately searching for a way to escape. She ran her hands over the walls and checked every inch of the ceiling. The heating vent was no bigger than a hardback book but she tried to pry the cover off and broke her nails. She looked for a weapon but there were only a sofa, two white plastic chairs and a card table. She tried removing one of the legs but it was riveted in place. The windowless bathroom bore nothing. Grace was angry now, storming around the room, yelling and cursing, kicking over the table, vowing to kill Skip.

"YOU FUCKERRRR!" she roared. Exhausted, she sat down, breathing hard, glaring at the boarded-up window. "Great, Grace," she said wryly. "That was useful."

Anger had always been a problem for her. Her outbursts were as loud and heated as they were pointless. Small things would set her off. Small things rooted in big things, but self-destructive nonetheless. A very wise woman once told Grace that her tantrums weren't involuntary. They were decisions. A bad habit that she could break.

Rage obliterated thought, destroyed reason, the woman said. Bad things to lose especially in a crisis. Grace sat there in the soundless room, even the quiet seemed abandoned. She realized how alone she was, how there was no one to rely on but herself. “Get your shit together, Grace,” she said aloud. She wiped the sweat off with the back of her hand, her rational mind returning. Skip would show up sooner or later. In the meantime, she had to think her way out of this. She needed a strategy, she needed tactics.

When Grace was in middle school, she was captain of an all-girl paintball team called the Klein’s Killer Bees, their equipment donated by a car dealer named Sam Klein who sold Buicks to their parents. Grace and her father, Chuck, were sitting on the back porch, eating egg salad sandwiches, drinking Cokes and talking about the league tournament.

“The Young Guns are really aggressive, Dad,” Grace said. “They cover well and depend on their speed to get angles. They take a lot of chances but they win.”

“What are you going to do?” Chuck said.

“Our strategy is to be patient, play defense, lower their numbers, make a false charge and attack their flanks.”

“That’s not a strategy, those are tactics,” he said. “Strategy is your goals, objectives, best outcomes.”

“Isn’t that kind of obvious?” Grace said. “It’s to win.”

“Ultimately, but there are short-term objectives too,” her father said.

“Like what?”

Chuck set his Coke down, his face turning serious. “Okay, let’s say you’re on a battlefield, taking fire from multiple positions. Your ultimate objective is to exit the hot zone safely, but you’re pinned down by a sniper. He’s got the high ground and he’s shooting your squad to pieces. What’s your objective now?”

Grace shrugged. "Well, to take him out."

"Yes, exactly," Chuck said. "But how? How do you take the shooter out? Maybe you create a diversion or rush the shooter's position or call up an air strike. Those are your tactics, Grace, the means of achieving your objective. Then it's on to the next. Maybe it's skirting a minefield or avoiding artillery fire. You develop tactics for each obstacle until you reach your ultimate goal."

"I see," Grace said thoughtfully. "So, if the Young Guns get too far up the snake, the objective is pushing them back and the tactics are how you do it." Chuck smiled broadly.

"Exactly," he said, proud of his girl. "You reach your objective in increments. One after the other until you've won."

Grace heard a car arrive. The engine was shut off with a shudder, someone got out, crunching footsteps on the gravel. Her whole body tensed, stricken by fear. She'd been afraid before but not like this. Dodson had told her about Skip.

"The boy's a maniac," he said. "He kills people and don't give a shit. I know some other dudes like that but Skip's an expert and gets off on it, got a mean streak too." Maybe so, she thought. But you will not, under any circumstance, plead, snivel or beg for mercy. It would only make him feel more powerful.

"Get away from the door!" Skip barked. "Stand on the far wall where I can see. Show your hands." She obeyed. Silence for a few moments. He was looking at her through the peephole. "I'm coming in," he said. "Make a move and I'll smash your head in."

Grace kept her face expressionless, her eyes blank. An automaton. The locks were unlocked, the door swung open. Skip's stark silhouette was framed against the glaring white sunlight. His body was bunched and hostile, ready to fight, an axe handle in his hand. Grace shielded her eyes against the sun. The door closed.

She immediately looked down at the floor. She didn't want to challenge him in any way. She could feel his gaze crawling over her, a snake looking for a crack in the rocks.

"Sit down," he ordered. She sat at the card table. Skip's head was all angles, like an ancient tool chipped out of flint. His eyes were green but not like Grace's. Hers were pale and crystalline. Skip's were more like swamp water. He was rawboned, gaunt, his long arms hard-muscled, veins like night crawlers under a jumble of tattoos. He wore an Alpo T-shirt that was too big for him, indecipherable neck tats that covered his Adam's apple, his shaggy, dirty-blond hair falling over his forehead, covering a patch of red acne.

"Isaiah must have been hard up when he picked you," Skip said. "Christ. You look like shit. What's that smell?" He sat across from her, setting the axe handle between them as if to say, Yeah, try something and see what happens. He leaned back, chewing on a toothpick, his hands behind his head. He stared at her with intent, then snickered. "What do we have here?" He sounded like a redneck sheriff who'd caught the city girl shoplifting. He sneered. "What's up, Grace? Things are a little different this time. Remember this?" He pulled his T-shirt up, revealing three ugly scars, a lighter color than his skin. They looked like bad welds. At their last meeting, she hit him multiple times with a steel baton. She didn't reply. "I said, do you remember this?"

"Yes, I remember," she said. She tried to look remorseful though she felt no such thing. "I'm sorry. You were threatening me and I didn't know what to do."

He spat out the toothpick. "You're gonna pay for that. You're gonna pay."

"Yes, I know," she said in a grave whisper. He waited for her to say more. When she didn't, he glared. He was trying to terrify her and it was working. He teetered on the edge of control, as if a wrong word would send him into a fury. He got up abruptly and Grace started, her heart thumping against her rib cage. He meandered through the room, looking around like he might buy the place, turning his back, tempting her to grab the axe handle. Fat chance. There was a gun stuck in the back of his belt.

"Q Fuck thinks he's smart, but I'm way ahead of him," Skip said. The hell you are, thought Grace. Skip came back to the table and put his big, spidery hands on the back of the chair, skull tattoos on three of his hairy knuckles. "I'm gonna toy with him, mess with his head. I'll let him think he's getting closer and lead him right into a trap. I've got the whole thing planned—and when I've got him?" He made an imaginary gun with his hand and put his forefinger against his temple. "Pow! I'm gonna blow his brains out!" He reminded Grace of her little nephew describing the fort he built with pillows and a cardboard box. Grace knew Skip wasn't smart in the conventional sense but a professional hitman would be instinctively wary, cunning, able to anticipate what his prey might do.

"I'm gonna enjoy it," Skip went on. "Seeing Q Fuck beg for mercy. Maybe I'll get some dogs and make them eat that shithead alive." Skip nodded, smug. "I know where to get the dogs, mean fuckers too." He's trying to provoke you, thought Grace. She stayed still, impassive, like she was zoned out. He grinned at her expectantly, waiting for a reaction.

"Aren't you gonna plead for his life?" Skip said, disappointed. He was so transparent. It was pathetic, she thought.

She shook her head. "I'm not going to change your mind." Skip seemed confused by the answer. Now he was angry again, glowering, angrier than he was before, his face red and contorted into a snarl, his body so rigid he was trembling. "You're gonna play it like that? Huh? Be brave so Isaiah will be proud of you?" Grace realized she'd made a terrible mistake. By refusing to react she'd pissed him off. He wanted her pleading, sniveling and begging for mercy.

"No, I just—I'm not—" she sputtered. Skip flung the chair aside and slammed his palms down on the table. He leaned forward, swamp eyes blazing hatred, a rank heat coming off him. Grace recoiled, but Skip reached across the table, grabbed her shirt and yanked her close, his sour breath in her face, words sizzling through his crooked yellow teeth. "Okay, bitch. Let's see how brave you are."

Skip stormed out of the motel room, furious and sweating. He looked around, hoping no one heard the gunshots. Like he didn't have enough problems already. This "game" he was playing with Q Fuck. Make a mistake and he'd have your ass tied up, gagged and on your way to Folsom. That asshole was smart. The whole thing about the message and the photos and the dog food can took days to figure out. The kidnapping and securing the motel room took more time and a lot of sweaty manual labor. He worked at night because of the heat. He bragged to Grace about trapping Q Fuck but the truth was, he didn't know what he'd do next. There was another problem too. He was nearly broke. When he was released from prison he had a stash of seven grand, less the four hundred he spent on a preowned Silent Circle phone. It was untraceable, no way for the police to track it. A good thing to have but there were other expenses too, like feeding Grace, the bitch.

It was weird how the whole thing got started, almost like fate or something. He was at Raoul's apartment buying some weed. But it wasn't bagged up yet. Skip didn't want to sit down, the room was like the Hells Angels held a rodeo. He went to the kitchen to see if there was any beer. He was about to open the fridge when he saw Isaiah looking back at him. It was *a wanted poster*. Skip laughed. "Holy shit!" Somebody else was after that prick and the reward was twenty-five grand! One more reason to bag that son of a bitch. There was a phone number. Skip loaded it into his contact list under the caption REWARD. Which didn't solve his immediate problem. He only knew how to do one thing. Kill people.

In the old days, Jimmy Bonifant would call him with an assignment. Skip hoped the guy's number still worked. He hated to ask for things but he made the call and got voice mail. "Uh, Jimmy? It's me, Skip. Yeah, I'm out now, everything is, um, good, yeah, I'm doing okay. I'm back in business, if you know what I mean. Anyway, I just finished a job and I'm available. Okay then. Call me back." And he left the number.

Isaiah and Dodson were in TK's office, examining Skip's photos, particularly the one they'd seen before. Grace was squinting into the bright sun. Her wrists were bound with a zip tie. Skip's arm around her, a wide, smartass grin on his face. The car was parked on dirt, a shadow cutting across the hood, a light coating of dust on the dark blue paint, mud splatter on the passenger door. You could see brown foothills in the background.

"The car," Isaiah said. " It's a two-door, a coupe."

"How do you know? You can't see but one of the doors," Dodson said.

"Look how big it is. There wouldn't be room for another one—and the B pillar. See how far it's set back? If this was a sedan it'd be twenty feet long."

"You might be right," Dodson said, passing it off. "You ask me, they look to be in the desert somewhere. Maybe he took Grace to Blue Hill. Be smart. He knows we ain't goin' back there."

"No. He's someplace else," Isaiah said.

"How do you know?"

"See the shadow on the hood?"

"That's his house," Dodson said.

Isaiah shook his head. "Why would Skip Park nose in against the side of his house?"

"What about the barn?"

"You can't drive to the barn."

Here we go, thought Isaiah. Ever since they'd partnered on a case, it was the same contest, the same stakes. Who's on top here? Dodson was at a huge disadvantage but that didn't keep him from trying. He was the oink in pigheaded. He wouldn't stop until he was proven right, never mind if he was wrong.

"You ask me, Skip is in the desert somewhere," Dodson insisted. "That's his home turf and look at the dust on the car. Skip's been driving on a dirt road."

"If he was driving on a dirt road, the car would be covered with dust," Isaiah said. "Like yours when we went to Blue Hill. It was *coated* with dust. We couldn't see through the windshield. And see the mud splatter on the front door? How did that get there in the open desert? No, that's somebody leaving the hose on or dumping the water out of a cooler. And look at the ground. It's been graded and the gravel is more or less uniform. That's a parking lot," adding with a barb, "You don't usually find those in the desert."

"You telling me that's in a town somewhere?" Dodson replied, unfazed. "What kind of building has a dirt parking lot? McDonald's? Wells Fargo?"

"Could be a factory or a warehouse, something like that," Isaiah said. "Or maybe it's on the outskirts of a town."

"There's towns all over the goddamn desert," Dodson replied. A familiar move. When Dodson was pushed to the wall, he'd pivot to something that had no answer. "Must be a million of 'em just in California," he went on, "not to mention Arizona, Nevada, New Mexico and Texas."

"Yes, I know that, but you have to start with what you're given," Isaiah said. To himself, he stated, "The car is parked next to a building."

"What kind of building?" Dodson said.

Isaiah paused a moment. It was an impossible question to answer, there wasn't enough data. But the point of the exercise was to push him into the corner, however nonsensical. Isaiah realized, not for the first time, that in spite of his competitiveness, Dodson was trying to help. Isaiah didn't like conceding anything. Reluctantly, he said, "I don't know."

Dodson smiled. Victory.

Second photo. Grace was sitting on a sofa, her hands unbound. The sofa was a rough tweedy fabric, mustard-colored, dark stains, the trim a cheap wood veneer, scarred and scratched. Grace was expressionless, stoic, like she was waiting for something inevitable. But if you knew her, you'd see her lower jaw was extended a few millimeters, her pale green eyes were slightly narrowed, and wrinkles bunched between her eyebrows. Grace was angry and an angry Grace was something to stay away from, to escape from. She didn't seem threatening; small and slight, short blond hair and a long, graceful neck. An ordinary young woman, you'd think. But Grace's anger was forged long ago and never tempered. Skip sat next to her, his arm around her shoulder, pulling her into him so their cheeks were smashed together. The caption: HOME SWEET HOME!

"Easy, Q," Dodson cautioned.

Grace was a mess but she wasn't beat up and her clothes weren't torn. It didn't appear as if Skip had assaulted her, and he'd be better off not trying, thought Isaiah. Grace wouldn't let a man maul her if there was a knife to her throat and she was bleeding to death. Her will was equivalent to the Grand Canyon.

"Why'd Skip leave her hands free?" Dodson asked. "She could pick up somethin' and clock him one."

"It's a message to me and to her," Isaiah noted. "Skip's saying he's in complete control. She's secure. He owns her. He doesn't need to tie her up."

Dodson looked at him, a little awed. "It's like you plugged right into that crazy muthafucka's mind."

The third photo was a selfie, Skip greedily taking a bite out of a big cheeseburger, grease oozing from the sides of his mouth. The burger was wrapped in foil paper. The brand name was probably on there but only one letter was exposed. A C in blue. Grace was off to one side, sitting at a table, a Styrofoam cup and paper plate in front of her. Her meal consisted of a raw hot dog and an apple. The caption: SUPPERTIME! YUM YUM!

"He's fuckin' with you," Dodson said. "That's prison food." In the background, there were vertical lines of bright sunlight cutting through the darkness.

"He boarded up the windows," Isaiah said. "The boards look like one-by-twelves. There are four lines, that's four feet. There are probably more boards but we can't see them."

"A window more than four feet wide?" Dodson said. "That's a picture window, like Auntie May got in her living room. That's a house somewhere."

"I don't think so. Look at the sofa. That's the same kind you'd see at a Motel 6 or a Super 8. Nobody buys that kind of furniture for a house. And the paint color. It's like they bought the cheapest paint they could find. That's a motel. You can park nose in, right in front of your room. The roof over the walkway will put a shadow on your car."

"Uh-huh," Dodson said, nodding as if he'd come to the same conclusion.

"An abandoned motel wouldn't be in the center of things,"

Isaiah mused. "If it was valuable land, it would have been knocked down. Probably on the outskirts somewhere."

"The outskirts of where?" Dodson said.

Isaiah didn't answer. He paid the website fee and did a people search on Skip. His real name was Magnus Vestergard. He'd changed it to Skip Hanson, hoping he'd sound less foreign and more American. "Skip was born in San Bernardino," Isaiah said. "The outskirts are like that. Sad as hell."

"What are you looking at?" Dodson said.

"The wrapper on the burger," Isaiah said. "The last letter of the brand name is C. I don't eat fast food if I can help it."

"Sonic," Dodson said. "They're the only ones I know that use blue letters and shiny paper." He smiled, pleased with himself. Isaiah did another search.

"There's only one Sonic in San Bernardino," he said. "It's off the Ten, near the airport. Lots of places for an abandoned motel."

"Good thing I'm around," Dodson said. "You'd be nowhere without me."

"I want to check on something before we go," Isaiah said. He left the office and climbed the ladder to the loft. He'd stored his equipment there before he'd left town.

Shoved in a corner were two large plastic crates with lids. Inside were things he'd found handy on cases. Hand tools, a crowbar, a bolt cutter, a power drill, lockpicks, a grappling hook, a cordless saw, a sledgehammer and nonlethal weapons as well. Pellet gun, a Taser, Mace, a fighting stick and a sap cap. The cap looked ordinary, black with a small lightning bolt logo. But there was a hidden compartment just above the adjustable strap. It held a material that was 110 percent the density of lead. Smack somebody in the face and you'd shatter some bones. Isaiah took the crowbar and bolt cutter too, useful for breaking in doors, locked gates. The Taser and sap cap came along as well. He came down from the loft, stowed the stuff in Dodson's trunk.

"Let's go."

Grace was sitting in a corner, with her hands around her knees and her head down. She was trying to be small, trying to disappear. Her face hurt, her ears rang. Skip had slapped her a couple of times, knocking her out of the chair. Then he'd thrown the chair at her but it slammed into a wall. She curled up into a ball. Skip stood over her and fired the pistol into the floor, screaming and cursing, scaring the shit out of her and demolishing her eardrums. She thought she was hit, she thought she would die. She thought of revenge.

Grace met Isaiah out in the wrecking yard. She needed a wiring harness for her GTI. She found the one she wanted but getting it out of an old car was much harder than she imagined. There were dozens of nuts, bolts, screws, washers and fasteners to remove, some of them hidden, most hard to get to. A man appeared. He was trying to find a part for his car. He asked if he could help. He was soft-spoken, wasn't hitting on her and his vibe didn't set off any alarms. They worked side by side for a couple of hours. They spoke sparingly and only about what they were doing. He was skilled with tools and she thought he was nice-looking. His overall air was one of competence and self-sufficiency. More than that, she felt some connection with him. She hated people saying that but it was true. She couldn't identify the point of contact but later she realized it was sorrow. He'd suffered a lasting hurt and so had she.

Isaiah brought his dog with him. Ruffin, a misbehaving pit bull named after David Ruffin, lead singer for the original Temptations. Grace loved Motown too. The dog was untrained and unneutered, which put her off. She loved dogs and careless owners were anathema. She chastised Isaiah for that, then thanked him for his help and left. Afterward, she felt bad about it. She wanted to see what he was about but she was wary of men and did nothing.

Months later, she needed Isaiah's help. She'd caught a glimpse of her mother, who'd mysteriously disappeared ten years before. She wanted Isaiah to help find her. She had little money. She took him to her tiny studio and offered to pay him with a painting. He wasn't offended or dismissive and he didn't scoff. He carefully looked at her work, somehow choosing the painting most meaningful to her, the one she would never sell. He said he wanted that one or nothing. She was resentful but gave it to him. Later, she realized it was remarkable. That of all the scores of paintings, Isaiah picked the one that was closest to her heart. How did he know? He must have felt something, intimate without words, without awareness. She discovered that happened all the time.

During the case, she was hunted by a pack of brutal mercenaries. TK offered his loft as a place to stay. She climbed the ladder, anxious about what she'd find. Rust, cobwebs and auto parts. Instead, there was a space made scrupulously clean. A neatly made cot, food, drink, a mini-fridge, clothes in her size, a boom box with jazz and classical CDs, even a new area rug. It was cozy, like a nest. It moved her, Isaiah putting everything together. He didn't know how deeply she wanted a home and this was the closest thing to it she'd ever had.

The motel room was hotter than before. The gunsmoke smelled acrid and dense. Mixed with hamburger grease it was nauseating. It didn't seem to bother Skip. He was sitting in the plastic chair with his feet up on the rickety table, hands behind his head.

Her objective was obvious. Escape. But what were her tactics? The first thing was her relationship with Skip. She wanted him to let his guard down, work on him in baby steps. If he sensed he was getting played, he'd get violent. She tried to think of her approach. What should she say? It was Skip who broke the ice.

"Tell me something," he said. At first, Grace wasn't sure who he was talking to.

"Um, sure," she said meekly.

"What's so great about Isaiah? What's the big deal?"

She had to be cautious here. Play it down, she thought, no extolling virtues. Tell him something tepid and boring. In other words, lie.

"We grew up together," she said with a shrug. She was twenty-five when she met Isaiah. "Our parents were friends," she continued. "We were always at each other's houses. We went to the same schools, helped each other with homework, hung out, went places."

Skip seemed to be listening intently, pondering her words. "That doesn't explain anything."

"I guess I'm saying we spent a lot of time together," Grace replied. "I mean, people were calling us boyfriend and girlfriend since the eighth grade. We kind of—I don't know. Fell into it."

Skip seemed puzzled. "So it wasn't like—" His voice went up an octave. He clasped his hands together and gushed, "Oh, Isaiah! You're so smart and wonderful! You're like a superman!"

She frowned and shook her head. "No, nothing like that. He was always just—there." She realized Skip's curiosity wasn't about her relationship. He wanted to know what he was lacking; why he was isolated, why only dogs gave him love.

"If it's like that, why stay with him?" Skip said. He was staring off like he'd lost something, like he was trying to remember where he'd put it. A tactic was forming in Grace's mind. Make Skip feel like he's not alone. That she shares his alienation. That the world is as puzzling to her as it is to him. She sighed. "It's something,

I guess. Better than being by yourself." She shrugged. "I don't know. It's a mystery. Why you're with somebody. Why anybody is with anybody." She looked at him, seemingly embarrassed. "I don't know why I'm telling you this."

"Don't worry about it," Skip said.

Skip thought about being at Blue Hill with some chick in the house. She could have helped with the dogs, that was cool but it would also be creepy, someone always there, creeping around, spying on you. He wanted to talk more to Grace but didn't know what to say. He wondered what she did when she wasn't at the food truck. Where did she go at night? Did she watch movies? Did she like the ones he liked? He wondered what her bedroom looked like, and who was the Black girl she lived with. How did they know each other? Where did they meet? Did Grace like country music? What did she eat? Why was there a tattoo of a clock on her arm? Skip couldn't imagine anyone's life but his own. He was glad he didn't have to kill her yet.

It was sweltering in the room. Grace was a sweaty mess and so was Skip. "Come on," he said. He went out the door and she followed him. They were in a parking area behind the motel. "Stay there," he commanded. A hose was coiled on the ground. He turned on the faucet, dragged it over to Grace and held it over her head. She put her face up and closed her eyes, water splashing, sparkling, soaking her.

"Oh my God," she gasped. "This is lifesaving." He gave her the hose and she showered herself, breathing through her mouth, sometimes sputtering, sometimes groaning with pleasure. He turned off the hose. Her shirt was sticking to her skin. Her boobs were nothing to brag about. He'd been thinking about raping her, the ultimate insult, send naked pictures to Isaiah, make him lose his mind. But then she wouldn't talk to him and he had more questions. Was he intimidated? No. He just didn't want to. Even after the hose, Grace was filthy, her clothes too saturated with grime. Her greasy hair was plastered to her head, mud under her nails, no makeup, a ring of grime around her neck and she smelled terrible.

Anyway, he thought, there was no place to pin her down except the floor or the ground. Tying her spread-eagle was impossible. He'd have to knock her out or drug her again. Whoopee. She was also the kind that would fight and kick and scream, even if you held a gun to her temple. You could just tell. And what if he couldn't get it up? The badass hitman with a limp dick. Grace would laugh at him or feel sorry for him or think he was a homo. Skip never had a girlfriend, his sex life was restricted to hookers. In and out in ten minutes, maybe five if it was just a blowjob, but they didn't judge you, they just wanted you to hurry up, and they didn't make you feel bad except for being with them in the first place.

Grace made him self-conscious. He didn't want her to know he was living four doors away in a room as shitty as this one. He didn't want her to know he was running out of money. He was anxious too, waiting for Jimmy Bonifant to call. Hard to get a boner when you're jittery. No, he'd save sex for later when she was cleaned up and he had a better grip on things.

Half the motel rooms faced the desert. Nothing out there but a lot of scorched nothing, the only living things were insects with stingers, lizards, two different kinds of rattlesnakes and birds that ate dead things. Not a tree or green grass for a hundred miles, maybe two hundred. Jessica was crazy to let Ludvig build a motel, Skip thought for the thousandth time. What the fuck did he know about running a business? He was a moron.

* * *

Skip was twelve years old when Jessica hooked up with Ludvig. He remembered having breakfast, and there the big lug would be, sitting across from him eating a six-egg-white omelet and humming something that sounded like a polka. Ludvig was cocky and stupid. If the oaf went back to school, he'd start in the fifth grade. He wore muscle shirts, gold chains and his blond hair in a pompadour. Jessica was way different back then, forty pounds lighter, cheerful, hair dyed the same color as Ludvig's. She wore miniskirts and sported cleavage whenever it wasn't raining. She was goo-goo-eyed over that ox, making his favorite meals, doing his laundry, laughing over every dumbass thing he said. It was embarrassing.

One day, out of the blue, the idiot says in his stupid accent, "You know, Chessica? I sink we shut built a motel."

"Don't you have to own the motel before you shut it down?" Jessica said.

"Shut! Shut!" he said, annoyed.

"You mean should?" Magnus said.

Ludvig ignored him. "I can do all de wiring myself. Tink how much money we'll save!" Ludvig was an electrician and he did save money on the wiring. Unfortunately, the blundering imbecile wasn't a carpenter, plumber, roofer, painter or anything else useful. The construction went way over budget, and Ludvig made bad deals on TVs, beds, desks and chairs.

"We'll cut back, dat is all," he said, as if he'd planned it all along. He sent the desks and chairs back, saying, "Who neets dem? No one's going to study." One bed lamp instead of two. "If ta guests vant to read, they can take turns," he declared. Ludvig put down cheap linoleum instead of carpet and bought water-saving shower heads, the pressure so low you could only wash your body in sections. There were thirty rooms but only enough in the budget for six air conditioners. Ludvig said he'd install them in the best rooms and call them "premier suites." He grinned at his great idea. "Vee can charge dem more!"

"Won't it get hot in the other rooms?" Skip asked. Ludvig huffed and looked at the boy like he was a stinkbug.

"People come for ta outside, not ta inside," he said. "Look at all zee sunshine!" He made a sweeping gesture across the horizon, closing his eyes so the glare wouldn't strike him blind.

One night, young Magnus, Jessica and Ludvig were having dinner, eating something called sauerbraten. Magnus thought it tasted like a pickled meat loaf. Ludvig said he told the contractor to install windows that didn't open. They were cheaper, he said, adding, "Who neets dem? The guests vill be in nature." Only at night, thought young Magnus, because it was a hundred fucking degrees in the daytime.

Magnus couldn't restrain himself. "Why don't you finish some of the rooms? Like put in the chairs and carpet and all the other stuff, leave the others empty. You're not going to have a full house every night." Jessica frowned and asked if anybody wanted more red cabbage. Ludvig went still, brow knitted, confused. Then you could see it in his face, his brain slowly realizing the kid made sense. He drew himself up, indignant.

"You know nuttink, you little shit."

At the Desert Wonderland grand opening, there was one vehicle in the parking lot. A truck driver who got lost. He paid, went to his room and came back in two minutes demanding a refund, saying, "There's no place to sit down!" The bank foreclosed and Ludvig left. Jessica went back to her job, emptying bedpans at an old folks' home.

Skip's best years were at Blue Hill with the pit bulls. He kept fifteen dogs, all from fighting stock, trained with love and a cattle prod. On cool evenings, they'd roll through the parched hills, the dogs scaring up birds and critters, Skip blasting them with a riot gun or an assault rifle, the dogs fighting over the remains. He was General Patton and they were his troops. They worshipped him, jumping up and down just to be touched, to hear him say a kind word. They loved him and he loved them back. Isaiah took all that away.

The thought of killing him was there all the time. When Skip was driving, taking a shower, screwing a hooker. Sometimes he wished he could think of something else but the more he tried, the more it came back. He'd always been like that. Once he got something in his head, it repeated itself over and over again, getting stronger as time went on. It was like someone inside your head was shouting at you. Jimmy Bonifant told him he was obsessive. He said it was a good thing. "You won't quit until the job is done. You've got fortitude." Jimmy made it sound like he had something to do with it. Skip wished the shouting in his head would cut him some slack now and then. The dogs gave him peace but they were gone.

Grace sat in the open doorway hoping for a breeze. There was no difference in temperature between inside and outside the room. Skip was antsy, staring out at the desert, folding and unfolding his arms, pacing around and muttering to himself. She wondered what was up. Was he worried about Isaiah? He should be. She didn't know how he would find her but she knew he would. No, that wasn't true. She hoped he would. There was nothing to go on. If he didn't find her, she was dead. Skip would kill her. He didn't have a choice. If he left her alive, she'd go straight to the police.

Skip went to the car, got two beers out of the cooler and tossed her one. It was ice-cold. "Oh my God," she rasped. She popped it open and drank half the can in one draw.

"Good, huh?" Skip said, taking a gulp.

"Hell yeah, it's good." A shared experience, she thought. A little thing but it was a start. "How about leaving that cooler in the room?" she said. Skip huffed through his nose and smiled.

"Yeah, right." She held the can to her cheek and closed her eyes, thinking, There must be a way to advance the relationship. Here was an opportunity. How could she say something positive about him? If it was direct, he'd know it was a play. They were almost done with the beers. *Hurry, Grace. Think, goddammit!*

"Are you really a hitman?" she asked. She sounded like an awe-struck kid. Skip looked off and took a deep breath. He reminded her of her dad when he was asked about the war.

"Sure am."

"Are you—I don't know how to say this. Good at it?"

"I'm the best. I'm an ace."

Glamorize him, Grace. "I thought people like you were just in the movies."

"I'm as real as can be," he said.

"You must have stories." Skip gave a shake of his head and smiled.

"Do I ever."

"Tell me about one of your jobs," Grace said. "Please? You locked me up. The least you can do is tell me a story." She was treating a child like a child.

Skip thought a moment, rubbing his chin as if he was undecided. "*Please,* Skip?" she pleaded. "I've got nothing to do. Come on, brighten my day."

He shrugged. "Yeah, it's not like you can tell anybody," he said. He cleared his throat. "First of all I like to be creative, you know what I mean? Like do crazy shit, surprise the clients, get that *holy shit* reaction. I love it when they look at you like, You did *what*? Then they crack up and say something like, 'You're fucking insane, dude.'"

"You blow their minds?" Grace said, smiling, nodding.

"You're damn right I do!" he said gleefully. He told her how he put a titanium hunting bolt through a whistleblower's neck while he was washing his minivan. Another victim was an elderly Japanese woman. Her son was into the yakuza loan sharks and he needed his inheritance a little early. Skip backed her into her fish pond with a samurai sword and she drowned.

He set a bear trap for a gourmet-food-loving lawyer who liked to go mushroom hunting. Skip watched him from a hiding place while the poor schmuck got closer and closer to the camouflaged trap. "When the jaws snapped shut on the guy's leg he went into shock," Skip said. "I thought he'd bleed but he started screaming and yelling for help."

Grace was repulsed but didn't let on. "What'd you do?" she asked.

"I went over and talked to him," Skip said, pointedly nonchalant.

"You talked to a man who was bleeding to death?"

"Yeah, I figured why not, you know? I'd never done it before. Besides, I wanted him to shut up. So he's really fucked up, right? Like squirming around, blood all over, saying 'Help me, help me' like a bitch. That was the funny thing."

"What's that?" Grace said, dreading the answer.

Skip laughed. "The guy thought I was there to help him!"

Skip went on in graphic detail. It was revolting. Skip was more dangerous than she'd imagined. He was a sadist as well as a killer. He kept talking about one killing after another. She was about to throw up when his cell buzzed. He jumped, fumbling to get the phone out of his pocket. He shut his eyes and went still for a moment, breathing deeply like he was gathering himself. He let the phone ring twice more and answered. In a calm voice he said, "Jimmy?"

CHAPTER THREE
Mom Called

You were three times more likely to be a victim of violent crime in San Bernardino than you were in the rest of California. The city itself was a vast desert sprawl of strip malls, gas stations, used-car lots, outlet stores and near-identical housing developments. If you sold terra-cotta roofing tiles you were doing well. It took an hour and a half to get there on the freeway. Isaiah was spilling over with anxiety and adrenaline. He was on his way to save Grace. He would see her again. He would bring her home safe.

San Bernardino's one Sonic restaurant was their starting point. Dodson and Isaiah drove around for hours, making wider and wider concentric circles, asking people on the street if they knew of an abandoned motel. Nothing. Another internet search revealed there were Sonic restaurants spread out all over the area. Hemet, Hesperia, Rialto, Rancho Cucamonga, Corona, Apple Valley and others. All had desert at their edges. They could drive in circles forever. Isaiah's insides were churning; hoping, needing the motel to be right around the next corner. Every empty lot and blank stretch of desert felt more hopeless than the last.

There were government agencies that kept track of companies

that went under but their databases took too long to access. They sat in the car, not knowing what to do next. Isaiah was haggard, wilted, exhausted. He hadn't slept in more than twenty-four hours.

"You need to take a break," Dodson said. "If you don't lie down, you gonna fall over."

They argued. Dodson finally got Isaiah to check into a Travelers Inn. Dodson watched TV while Isaiah took a shower and slept a couple of hours. He had a terrible dream, thrashing and yelling. Dodson woke him up.

He went back to the people search report and studied the "Relatives" section. Skip's mother, Jessica Anne Vestergard, was listed. She was fifty-seven years old, divorced three times and presently employed at a home for senior citizens. She'd been arrested for petty theft, soliciting, running an unlicensed casino, bar fights and other offenses. She got pregnant with Magnus, the identity of the father was still in question.

"Anything?" Dodson said.

"Believe it or not, Skip has a mother," Isaiah said. "She lives here in San Bernardino. Fifty-nine twenty-one Tawny River Road."

There was no river on or near Tawny River Road and as far as Isaiah could tell, there'd never been one. The houses were old, small and dilapidated, peeling paint on wooden siding, stoops with missing boards, rust dripping from the burglar bars. No one watered their lawn. A few American flags jutted over porches. Jessica's house seemed more run-down than the others. Flowered sheets stood in for drapes, some of the roof worn down to the tar paper, a battered Ford pickup parked in the driveway. There was a bumper sticker displaying a hypodermic needle with a big red X through it. The caption: I WILL NOT COMPLY.

"A Black man on her doorstep is trouble," Dodson said. "Two and it's a home invasion."

"I think you're right. I'll go myself," Isaiah said. He got out of the car and opened the front gate. It scraped on the sidewalk. He thought about what he'd say to a blue-collar, down-and-out divorcee who raised a killer for a son. *Hi. I'm an attorney and my client has left a fortune to your Skip. Hi. I'm an old college friend of his. Is Skip around? Hi. I'm from the American Sweepstakes and we're holding a check for him.* There was nothing to do but go straight at her. If the door was slammed in his face he was no worse off than he was now.

He knocked. There was a pause, then footsteps. "Are you selling something?" Jessica said through the door. "There's a No Solicitors sign right in front of your goddamn face."

"I'm not a salesman," Isaiah said. "I want to talk about your son, Magnus."

"What do you want with him?"

"He kidnapped my girlfriend." Another pause, the chain was undone and the door swung open sharply. Jessica's bulk was wrapped in a muumuu decorated with garish daisies and food stains. Her round face was badly sunburned and she was barefoot, her arms pale and flabby, a cigarette dangling from her lips, eyes narrow and hostile, ready for a fight.

"Okay, what's this about?" she snapped.

"I'm sorry to bother you, but it's important and time is a factor," Isaiah said. "Skip—Magnus—kidnapped my friend Grace. I can't find them and neither can the police." Jessica's scowl was unwavering. "You probably don't believe me and I don't blame you but I'm telling the truth," Isaiah said. "I don't want to hurt him or have him arrested. I want Grace back. That's all." She stared at him a long moment.

"Come on in," she said.

The living room was crowded with cheap, mismatched furniture. There were knotty-pine wall paneling, brown shag carpeting, a dead fireplace. Beer bottles, a KFC bucket, balled-up napkins, copies of the *Star* and the *Enquirer* were scattered on the end tables.

"Wanna beer?" she said.

"No thank you."

"Make yourself at home."

She went to the kitchen and Isaiah took a look around. He admired a display of coffee cups. The Cowboy Wax Museum, Skimmers Water Park, Desert Wonderland, Back Nine Miniature Golf, Cavern of Reptiles and a few others he never heard of.

There were a few old photos on the mantel. Judging by the marks in the dust, most had been removed. The remaining pics were innocuous. One of Skip, eleven or twelve years old, at the helm of an earthmover, shooting a plastic AK at the camera. The rest were of Jessica and a Chihuahua. Hugging the dog, the dog sleeping in her lap, the dog with a toy in its mouth, the dog savaging a pillow.

One frame was facedown, a thick coating of dust. It hadn't been touched for years. Maybe Jessica tipped it over while she was removing the others. The photo was of a younger, voluptuous Jessica tongue-kissing a blond guy with big muscles and a muscle shirt that said: I DON'T GIVE A SCHNITZEL. One of her ex-husbands, thought Isaiah. He placed the photo facedown again. Jessica came back with her beer.

"Have a seat," she said. He took the sofa. She sat down on a beach chair and crossed her legs, blue-veined and white as Elmer's glue.

"What's your name?" she said.

"Isaiah Quintabe."

"Who are you?"

"I'm just a guy and Grace is my girlfriend."

"And you say Magnus kidnapped her?"

"That's right."

Jessica alternated glugs of beer with drags on her cigarette. "Why in the world would he do that," she said. "That's as dumb a thing as I've ever heard."

"Magnus has a grudge against me," Isaiah said. "I'm the one that sent him to prison. The kidnapping was retaliation."

"He hates you that much, huh?"

"Yes, he does. He called and told me. He put Grace on the line too. She's alive and he has her."

"How did you find me?" Jessica said.

"I did a people search on the internet."

"What was your name again?"

"Isaiah Quintabe," he said. Jessica found a tablet in the pocket of her muumuu. She did a search, scanned, pursing her lips. She looked at him frankly.

"I believe you," she said. He didn't see that coming. Jessica stubbed out her cigarette and lit another one. Isaiah could feel himself getting lung cancer. "Magnus was a hell-raiser since he was a kid," Jessica said. "Always in trouble, always fighting, always obsessed with guns." She huffed and shook her head. "And those goddamn dogs. He brought Goliath around here like he was some kinda show pony. It scared the living snot out of everybody, including me. Magnus thought it was funny, of course. He's about as funny as a chain saw."

"Do you know what he does for a living?" Isaiah asked.

"He's a criminal, I know that," she said. "And if you want to know the truth, I was glad when they locked him up. Kept him out of my hair and made the world safer at the same time."

"I think he's holding my friend in an abandoned motel," Isaiah said. Jessica's frown was immediate. It wasn't puzzlement. She's covering her surprise, he thought. *She knows something.*

"Is that so?" she said. She looked off, took another long drag and slowly exhaled. Then she sipped her beer and breathed a big sigh, taking her time, trying to figure out what to say. "I'm wracking my brains but I can't think of anything like that around here," she said. "It's too far from the freeway and nothing to see for tourists. You don't have to be Einstein to figure that out." There was a note of resentment in her voice. "I'm sorry I can't help you, Isaiah, but I don't know anything about Magnus. I haven't seen him in—my God, must be ten years by now."

"Okay, well, thank you for hearing me out," Isaiah said, rising. "I appreciate your time." He turned to leave.

"Oh, Isaiah?" she said. "If there's anything else I can do for you? Answer questions, anything at all?" She sounded sincere. "Call me anytime."

Isaiah left the house and hurried back to the car. "Anything?" Dodson said.

"For one, Jessica pretended to do a search on me."

"How do you know she was pretending?" Dodson said.

"She didn't ask how to spell my last name. She said she hadn't seen Skip in ten years but going to prison kept him out of her hair. That was five years ago. They were in contact then, maybe he was living here. And she was surprised I knew about the motel. She was resentful too. She said the motel was too far from the freeway and there was nothing for tourists to see."

"Sounds like an unhappy investor," Dodson said. "Maybe she got hustled into it."

"Maybe so," Isaiah said. "Something else, just as I was leaving. It was strange. She said to call if there was anything else she could do."

"What's strange about that?"

"It was the way she said it. Sincere. Like she was really hoping I'd call."

"She wants to keep track of you," Dodson said. Isaiah nodded again, thought a few moments. He cursed.

"I missed something."

Isaiah got out his laptop and went back to the people search website. There was a section titled "Businesses." Isaiah read it quickly. "Jessica and her third husband, Ludvig Vestergard, formed a corporation, Desert Wonderland, LLC," he said. "The name was on one of her coffee cups. They must have borrowed money to build the motel. According to this, the company went bankrupt." He looked at Dodson. "There's an address."

Dodson drove past the Desert Wonderland Motel and parked a little ways down the road. It looked very much abandoned. Trash in the dirt parking lot, broken windows, doors missing, no lights, no sounds, no movement. "The room might be on the back side," Isaiah said. "We've got to circle around." Isaiah took the bolt cutter, put the Taser in his back pocket and gave Dodson the crowbar.

The sun was dropping behind the hills. It was dim but they could still see. The back side of the motel was the same as the front. One of the rooms had its windows boarded up, light shining within. There was a hole drilled through the door about head height. There were beer cans on the walkway, a hose coiled on the ground and a plastic chair set near the door.

"Call the police?" Dodson said.

"No car. Skip's not here," Isaiah said. "If Grace is in there, I want to get her out now." They approached the room as quietly as they could. Isaiah put his ear to the door, heard nothing. Dodson was peeking through the slit between the boards.

"I don't see anything," he whispered. "That light is really bright." Isaiah picked up a slight scent of rotten eggs. Propane. The light was a Coleman lantern.

Isaiah said, "Grace? We're coming in." He kicked the door open and burst into the room. Empty. Nothing there but litter. There were footprints in the dust. "They were here," Isaiah said. "Look." He nodded at the Sonic wrapper balled up on the floor. He turned the lamp down. It was very bright. "With a full tank, these lamps can last for seven or eight hours. This is about half," he said. "They were here, couldn't be too long ago. We might have just missed them." He looked down, saw something.

"What?" Dodson said.

"Bullet holes." There were two of them in the floor. Isaiah got down on his hands and knees and sniffed. "Recent, maybe a day or two," he said.

"What was Skip shootin' at?" Dodson said. "Snakes?"

"Probably to scare, Grace," Isaiah said, fighting back the anger. "No blood, that's a relief."

"Look here," Dodson said. There was a note on the table, written on a white paper bag. Dodson picked it up and read it. "This is fucked up," he said. He held the bag up for Isaiah to see. In big block letters, Skip had scrawled, MOM CALLED! HA! HA! FUCK YOU ISAIAH. YOUR BITCH SAYS HELLO!

They went outside. Isaiah closed his eyes. "Another mistake," he said. "I should have known Jessica would call him."

"Why is that a mistake?" Dodson said.

"I should have looked at the people search thing more closely but I was too anxious. If I'd read the business section first, we could have avoided this and Grace would be free. *Fuck,* I'm stupid!"

"What you are is exhausted," Dodson said. "Hard to read the fine print when you 'bout to fall asleep."

One of the other rooms had its door ajar. Dodson went over and looked inside. "Do you believe this? Skip was staying there." Isaiah came in. The room smelled of mold and sewage. There were a cot and a sleeping bag, a microwave, food wrappers, a stack of toilet paper, a crate of water, a big bottle of tequila and Styrofoam cups.

"Nothing here," said Dodson. "Let's go home."

They drove. Traffic was bad, taillights clear to the horizon. Isaiah was tormented. He screwed up. They were only minutes behind Skip and he'd failed. How could he let that happen? How could he let that happen *now*? He imagined horrible scenarios, every one of them sickening. If Grace was killed, injured or assaulted he was at fault. He couldn't stand himself. He wanted to stomp on his celebrated brain and set it on fire. *Goddamn you, Isaiah. Goddamn your soul.*

TK was closing up the office when he heard a commotion outside. A second later, three young Latino men burst in, one of them holding his gun sideways, pointing at TK.

"You know you can't aim like that, don't you?" he said. "Pull the trigger and you're liable to hit one of your friends."

"Where is he, old man?" one of them demanded. Couldn't have been more than fifteen or sixteen. Manzo is scraping the bottom of the barrel, TK thought. The kid had more tattoos than skin, wearing a big white T-shirt and, of course, a gold chain. What were gangsters going to do when the world ran out of gold?

"Where's Isaiah?" the kid demanded.

"I don't know, but he ain't here," TK said. They hauled him out of the office. Must have been a dozen young guys, swarming around the warehouse, looking, knocking things over, shouting, making a helluva din. A couple of them ran up into the loft and started knocking things around. "Why you doin' all that?" TK said. "You could see he's not here."

"Shut up, ese," the kid said. "You lucky I don't cap you right now." Trying too hard, TK thought. Just the kind of punk that would kill you by accident. A Latino man entered the warehouse. The others stopped what they were doing. It was Manzo. He was obviously a leader; older, not a boy, a grown man, confident but no bravado, dressed nice too. Black pants, black guayabera shirt with a pattern down the middle.

"We're looking for Isaiah," Manzo said, his voice low and resonant.

"Like I told Junior here. I don't know where he is," TK said.

"Isaiah was here—don't lie, we know he was here," Manzo said.

"I'm not saying he wasn't here. I'm saying he ain't here now."

"Where did he go?" Manzo said. TK knew from long experience that "I don't know" was the wrong answer. The truth shall set you free.

"Somebody kidnapped his girlfriend," TK said. "Isaiah's out lookin' for 'em."

"Kidnapped his girlfriend?" the kid scoffed. "This is bullshit, Manzo."

"Shut the fuck up, Jorge," Manzo said. Jorge seemed to shrink a little.

"When did this happen?" Manzo asked.

"I guess it's been four or five days now," TK replied. "Snatched her right in front of her house. Police are lookin' for her too. You don't believe me, call 'em up and ask 'em."

"What's her name?"

"Grace."

"Who kidnapped her?" Manzo said.

"Somebody named Skip Hanson. The way I heard it, he's a hitman, just got out of the joint. Got a beef to settle with Isaiah."

"Him too, huh?" Manzo said. The gang leader seemed to consider that, like an idea was forming. The noise picked up again. The guys were yelling gleefully as they smashed, tipped over and stomped everything in sight.

"You guys don't need to do that," TK complained. "You come here yourself, you got that old Caprice. Parts for them things are hard to find. How'm I gonna help you if your boys mess everything up?"

Manzo considered and shouted:

"¡Oye! ¡Deja lo que estas haciendo!" Everything stopped. The fellas looked dazed, like they'd awoken from a trance. "Put everything back," Manzo ordered.

"What for, Manzo?" Jorge complained. "This old fuck helped Isaiah, man. He shouldn't get away with that."

Manzo gave Jorge a look so hard and cutting it could have sliced him in half. "You giving me advice, Jorge?" Manzo said. "Is that what you're doing, pendejo? Abre tu boca de nuevo y te mataré." Jorge looked at the floor and slunk off.

"What time is Isaiah getting back?" Manzo said.

"I don't know that he is," TK said.

"His Mustang is over there with the tarp over it. That thing's worth a fortune. He's coming back for it, he has to."

They cut the landline in TK's office, took his cell and locked him in. He could hear Manzo getting his boys organized. The front gate was to stay open, the spotlight covering the parking area left on, same for the lights inside the warehouse. It should look like TK was here and everything was okay. Manzo ordered his troops to take cover, making sure they weren't in each other's line of sight. "No friendly fire," the gang leader said. A couple of homies would man the gate and close it after Isaiah came in. "I want Isaiah alive; do you hear me?" Manzo said. "You shoot him, I shoot you. And be quiet. You spook him and I'll fuck you up."

There was a small, unwashed window in the office with a murky view of the yard. TK imagined what would happen; Isaiah and Dodson driving in unaware, the gate swinging closed behind them, the gangsters surrounding them with guns drawn. TK knew how vicious the Locos could be. After they slaughtered Isaiah and Dodson, they'd turn on him. He was a witness. They might let him go with a threat of retaliation or kill him and throw his body in the LA River. TK wondered how the Locos knew Isaiah was staying here and then immediately thought of young Andy. It saddened him. Father dead, mother a drunk, afraid to go home, penniless and hungry all the time. The kid wasn't making decisions about morals and ethics. He was thinking about survival. Poverty does that to you. People are shoved aside in favor of food, clothing and shelter. Twenty-five grand would last a long time.

TK had owned and operated the wrecking yard for decades. Big companies with lots of money came and went and here he was, an independent businessman, doing it by himself and still going strong. Along the way he was slapped down, jeered at, abused, cheated and defeated but he never, not even once, backed down from a fight. The hoodlums were many and well armed but he wouldn't back down this time either.

There was an old gym locker where he hung his jacket and extra coveralls. He opened the locker, reached through the clothes and found Mr. Brown standing at the back. TK's Browning twelve-gauge shotgun. It was for general protection and he shot skeet with it in the yard. He'd been doing it for years, hardly ever missed even at this age. Lately, the kick aggravated his arthritis. Never mind, he thought. Shotgun like this, all you do is aim in the general direction of the target. You might not hit the bull's-eye but you'll hit something. The idea these gangsters were going to kill his friends was infuriating. TK took the shells out of his desk drawer and loaded the gun.

Dodson and Isaiah drove back to Long Beach. There was no conversation, there was nothing to say. That damn note. MOM CALLED. Dodson knew it was driving Isaiah crazy. He was right about making a mistake. If he'd noted Jessica's business records, he could have skipped seeing her and she wouldn't have known to tip Skip off. Understandable, though, thought Dodson. Isaiah was on the brink, exhausted, sleep-deprived and in a constant state of terror. Cherise was kidnapped while she was pregnant and Dodson thought the top of his head would explode. He was so out of his mind he pulled a gun on Isaiah and in that moment, he would have used it. Dodson felt bad for his friend and felt bad for himself. Grace was his homegirl too. His anger at Skip was churning in his belly. When they caught that freak he was in for the beating of his life. And if he hurt Grace? They'd bury him at Blue Hill and cover him with dog shit.

They were nearly home. Dodson hoped they'd talk about a plan or a next move, but Isaiah was silent, staring, as removed as a foreign country. This usually meant he was thinking about the next move but you could never be sure.

Isaiah was angry and disappointed, but no less determined. He was frustrated. His next move was a blank space. He remembered a term Grace taught him, "breaking set." It meant challenging your assumptions and asking new questions. What was his main assumption? That he could find Skip by looking for him. That was proving futile. The new question: What was Skip's situation? He was living in that shitty motel a few rooms away from Grace. If he'd had somewhere better to go, he would have. Had he resumed his career as a hitman? Suppose he had. Even when Skip was working full-time, he made enough to get by and that was all. He needs money and a place to stay, Isaiah mused. A place that accommodated a kidnapper and his victim. Skip didn't have friends before he went to prison and there was no reason to think he had any now. He didn't have backup from a gang or a criminal network. Did he hole up at Jessica's? It was doubtful she'd have him. Her house was small and she had a criminal record. Harboring a kidnap victim was a dumb thing to do even for your son. Skip was broke. Interesting, thought Isaiah. Perhaps Grace didn't have to be found so much as paid for.

He remembered their case together, searching for Grace's long-lost mother. In the beginning, there was tension between investigator and client. She wanted him to hurry, but he was patient and methodical. As things progressed, they became closer but neither knew how to test the waters. TK described them as "a couple of lonely people who are too shy to say hello."

Grace thought her mom might be camping at party beach near Gaviota. Very unlikely but Isaiah went along. He'd be alone with her. He wondered if she was thinking the same thing. It was dark when they arrived. They parked under a stand of cypress trees. Grace opened the sunroof and they slid their seats back and watched the moon, veiled as the clouds drifted past. Isaiah woke at sunrise, the early light casting soft shadows on Grace's face. She looked beatific. She woke, yawned, stretched.

"Good morning," she said.

"Good morning," he said.

They snaked their way along a bluff to get to the sand. No one around, no sign of a campsite. The sea was steel blue and sparkled as if for the first time. A mist was rising, foam breakers like a frill around the bay. They sat together, enjoying the breeze, both aware they weren't here to find Grace's mom. They were here for the moment when he took her hand and she smiled and the world began anew.

Manzo Gutierrez, Khan of the Sureños Locos 13, stood on the roof of the warehouse with Guillermo, his longtime homeboy and brother-in-arms. G was a street veteran; fearless, violent and fiercely loyal to the Locos, the hood and Manzo. They were looking down Dockside, the street that led into the wrecking yard. It was almost completely dark. Oncoming headlights would be seen from blocks away. Manzo posted a lookout to give them a heads-up.

Isaiah's betrayal happened years ago but the anger and humiliation only grew larger with each new day. Manzo didn't just lose a deal, he lost everything. His rep, his money, his pride, his stature on the street and his relationship with the Sinaloa. He couldn't believe it even now. Manzo had brought the gang into the twenty-first century. He streamlined their drug operations, got the homies off the street, tightened security, mandated burners, and implemented counterintelligence, watching the police watching you. There were fewer arrests, fewer losses, no more surveillance video for prosecutors to show the jury. Manzo was the only shot caller in the city, the state, and maybe the whole of the US who invested the gang's profits. The gang owned a car wash, two apartment buildings, two coffee shops, a garage, a body shop, a bodega and a tire and rim store. Manzo made alliances with the other Latino gangs. No more turf wars, no more drive-bys. The Locos gave out turkeys at Christmas, left the local merchants alone and punished those who preyed on the neighborhood. Manzo was the Pablo Escobar of East Long Beach, walking with his head up, knowing every admiring eye was on him.

That was all gone now. Pockets empty, in debt, living in his mother's apartment, the gang whittled down to OGs and kids like that fucking Jorge. The $25,000 reward was forgotten. No one was looking, no one cared. Too much time had gone by. Manzo replayed the betrayal every time he shut his eyes.

* * *

Sinaloa was buying an M61 Vulcan Gatling-style machine gun from Angus Byrne, the foremost dealer in illegal weapons north of Tijuana. Sinaloa was in an endless war with Ochoa over status and territory and to avenge their fallen soldiers, more of them shot down every day. Thousands of combatants, police, soldiers and innocent civilians were killed. The Vulcan was equipped with six air-cooled rotating barrels that fired 20mm rounds at 6,000 rounds per minute. The military mounted the gun on helicopters and destroyed whole villages.

Manzo was acting as middleman, paying for the gun with a million dollars of the Sinaloa's money. The deal was in progress when another gang attacked, hoping to steal the Vulcan and the money. Manzo escaped with the gun. He was securing it in the gang's storage locker when Isaiah jumped him, shocked him with a Taser and drove away with the gun. Later, Manzo found out Isaiah had some bullshit white knight reasons for doing it, the gun ending up with the police. Bottom line, Manzo gave up a million dollars of the cartel's money with nothing to show for it.

Sinaloa held Manzo and the Locos responsible. They paid the vig with higher drug prices. They could refuse but it would end in a massacre. Many local gangs were affiliated with the cartel. They would turn on the Locos and the Sinaloa's sicarios would show up too. These were men who killed women and children. They cut off heads and body parts with chain saws, burned flesh with blowtorches and fed victims to their pet tigers.

Manzo forfeited his savings, his stock portfolio, his house, his mother's house, and all of the gang's businesses. He hid the Caprice so they wouldn't take it. The cartel sent Diego Ortega to sort it out. Diego was stringy and tall, his chest nearly concave, his arms long and loose like Nate Diaz, the UFC fighter. SINALOA was tattooed across his forehead. This motherfucker was committed.

They met in the parking lot at El Mejor. Diego's homies were there, smirking, enjoying Manzo's misery.

"You're taking *all* the businesses?" Manzo said. "They're worth a whole lot more than a million."

"It don't matter. Nobody gives a shit what you think," Diego said. "The only reason we don't kill you is because we need you to run things. Ain't that some shit? You used to be the boss and now you're nothing but a fucking employee." The fellas chuckled.

There was bad blood between Manzo and Diego. They were in high school and they fought over a girl. Diego came away with a broken cheekbone, a fractured arm and a damaged rep. He went back to Mexico and worked his way up the cartel's hierarchy.

"Don't even think about fighting back," Diego said. "We'll cut your mother's head off with a butcher knife and tie it to your car."

A breeze blew over the warehouse roof. Manzo could smell weed. The fellas were bored and lighting up. Isaiah would return sooner or later. A cherry '68 Mustang GTI was very rare, worth a lot of money, a collector's car. Manzo nodded to himself. He would be here when the fellas hauled that asshole out of the car, beat him and tied him down. He would do the work himself, he decided. Maybe with a baseball bat or a machete, he kept one of each in the Caprice.

Andy Wright was thirteen years old. When he told Jorge that Isaiah was staying at the wrecking yard, the newbie gangster went crazy. Laughing, high-fiving, jabbering about how this would give him cred.

"Manzo's gonna skin Isaiah alive and leave him in a ditch for the crows to eat," Jorge said, grinning. Andy and Jorge were on the school soccer team together. They knew each other to nod hello and that was all. Jorge called Manzo.

“The fuck do you want?” Manzo said. These days he was always pissed.

“I got somebody knows where Isaiah is.”

“Tell him to come see me. Like fucking now.”

McClarin Park and Manzo was standing near the dried-out fountain, a half circle of cement seating around it. They used to put on plays there. About twenty members of the Locos were there, Jorge among them, nervously rubbing his knees. Manzo stood tall, not in that gangsta slouch. He didn’t dress like a gangsta either, like real pants and a real shirt and shiny shoes, everything in black. Manzo was Mexican, but he looked more like the warrior on an Indian-head nickel. Proud and fearless, probably a chief, a shot caller. The Khan.

“What’s your name?” Manzo said.

“Andy,” Andy said, barely audible.

“Tell me what you saw,” the Khan said. Andy nervously took him through it. He was working at the wrecking yard for TK. He was just about to leave when two cars pulled in. One of them was a cherry Mustang. Isaiah got out and talked to TK like they were old friends.

“You sure it was Isaiah?” Manzo said.

“Um, yes, I, uh, I’m sure,” Andy mumbled. “I’ve seen him before.”

“Where?”

Andy shrugged. “Just around, you know. He’s sort of famous.” Manzo was staring at him. His voice was hard, his eyes like railroad spikes and so dark they looked endless. The gangsters watched, smiling, waiting for the white boy to fuck up.

“Is he staying there? At the wrecking yard?” Manzo asked.

“Yeah, I think so,” Andy replied. “When Isaiah got out of the car, he had his backpack, like he’d arrived from far away.”

“Do you know if Isaiah is there now?” Manzo said.

"Now? I don't know, but if he's staying around here it's probably there." Andy wanted to ask about the reward but he was too scared.

"We'll have to check it out," Manzo said. He gave a slight nod, like Andy should leave now. Andy didn't move, his lips were dry. He needed that money. He had to get away from home. Manzo looked at him, surprised he was still here.

"I, uh, I'm, uh, wondering—" Andy stammered.

"Do you get the reward? Yeah, you do," Manzo said. "But only if we get Isaiah. Now go, get out of here."

Andy turned and started walking, not believing he was dismissed. Some of the gangsters were laughing. He was so stupid. Manzo wouldn't pay him squat. He should have stayed out of the whole thing.

"Hey," Manzo said. Andy stopped and turned around. Manzo took out his wallet and withdrew two twenties. "Here. Thanks for the tip."

It was so dark Andy could barely see the ground. He was riding his bike down the alley, standing on the pedals, legs pumping, lungs scorched. Jorge told him about the Locos wanting to trap Isaiah in the yard. The more Andy thought about Isaiah getting killed, the worse he felt about ratting him out. He didn't know the guy but getting dumped in the dirt for the crows to eat? Having that on his head terrified him. Then there was TK. Breaking the trust of the only person who'd ever showed him kindness. Andy slowed as he approached the back side of the wrecking yard. A line of cars were parked there. Hot cars, tricked-out cars, fancy paint jobs, every one of them with shiny rims. Gangstas loved their rides.

There was a big split in the chain link fence. Andy took a deep breath and slipped through the opening, sidling and squeezing. He weaved through the stacks of wrecks. He was careful, keeping his hands out in front of him. He didn't want to use his phone for light. He ducked under a bumper, avoided a side mirror, stepped over a spare tire and skirted a jutting piece of chrome trim. As he approached the perimeter of the parking area, he slowed, creeping, quiet as possible. He stopped. The spotlight on the warehouse lit up the parking area. The ground was hard-packed dirt, oil-stained, bits of broken glass glittering. It looked like an arena, like gladiators would show up anytime now. Andy watched. He smelled weed. He saw movement on the roof, two men framed against the night sky. One of them was Manzo. He could tell by the upright stance and the shape of his head. "Oh man," Andy said. Isaiah wasn't there yet. Maybe he wouldn't come back to the wrecking yard at all. That would be the best thing.

Where was TK? Andy wondered. Did the Locos have him somewhere? Did they beat him up? Shoot him? The air was cool but Andy was sweating. He could smell himself, sour and damp. He called TK's cell, no answer. The landline was dead. Andy was panicking. He almost started to cry. He didn't want to watch a man get killed. He turned to go, but moved too quickly and caught his shoulder on something sharp. He cried out, grabbed his shoulder and dropped to his knees. *Fuck, it hurt,* and it was bleeding too. Then, a voice.

"Esteban? Is that you?" Andy froze. A Loco was somewhere very close. "Esteban? You okay, man?" Andy's mother was Mexican. He knew some Spanish. He lowered his voice and mumbled,

"Todo es bueno."

"Huh?" the voice said. "You don't sound right, man. Where are you?" There was a jumble of cars and a zigzag path between them. Andy went still. "Esteban? What's wrong with you, man? I'm coming over there."

"No, estoy meando," Andy said.

"It's not you, is it?" the Voice said, angry now. "Who the

fuck are you? Stay there, motherfucker." The Voice was weaving through the cars, using his phone's flashlight, slashes of light cutting through the crevices and shattered windows.

Andy stayed low and started moving. "I hear you, ese," the Voice said. "You ain't goin' nowhere." The pain in Andy's shoulder made his eyes water. He tripped and fell, then scrambled to his feet. The Voice was much closer, the flashlight getting brighter, quick shafts of light flashing in Andy's eyes.

"I'm coming for you, asshole," the Voice snarled. He sounded pissed, he sounded bloodthirsty. "Stay where you are or I'll fuck you up." Andy was frozen to the spot. He was surrounded by crushed cars. He could barely see. Andy snapped out of his terror, scrambling through the window of a wrecked car, cutting himself on the broken glass. He balled himself up on the floor below the backseat. The Voice approached, light footsteps, going slow.

"I know you're here," the Voice said. "I didn't hear you running away."

Andy stopped breathing, curling up tighter, trying to bury himself behind the front seat. He could hear the Voice breathing and smell the weed on his clothes. The gangster stopped, right outside the car. All he had to do was look inside. *Don't do it. Don't do it.* Seconds oozed by. Andy's mouth was so dry he couldn't swallow. He'd never felt so helpless, so afraid, even when his mother was beating him with a sawed-off broomstick.

"You in there, pendejo?" the Voice said. The flashlight beam burst through the broken window, bright as a prison searchlight and right over Andy's head. Andy could hear the man's feet scuffling in the dirt, the width of the door between them. The man put his hand on the door handle, he was pulling it open. "If you're in there, come out slow or I swear to God..."

Andy was crying, holding in the sobs, knowing he'd be beaten, or worse. His legs were numb. He couldn't run if he wanted to.

The rusty door hinges creaked—the Voice's phone buzzed. He hesitated a moment, apparently reading the message, and then he hurried off. Andy was trembling, his mouth open, he couldn't catch his breath. He waited until the footsteps faded and staggered out of the car. He used his phone to light the way and headed back to the alley, the guilt hitting him harder than ever. The Locos were going to kill Isaiah. *It's on your head, Andy. Do something!*

Manzo got a text from the lookout. *iq coming.* He immediately sent a group text to alert the others. He watched the street. He saw distant headlights. He drew his Glock and racked the slide. Guillermo did the same. Manzo's anger was radiating from his eyes and ears, his hands were sweaty, his heart was pounding. The motherfucker who ruined everything was going to pay. Pay with pain, pay with blood. The headlights were getting closer.

They were on Dockside, a few blocks away from the wrecking yard. Dodson driving, Isaiah was looking ahead, wary of trouble even when there wasn't any. Lights were on at the wrecking yard. He could see the front gate and part of the parking area. He thought a moment, something icy skittering up his spine. Something was wrong. *What is it, Isaiah?* They were two blocks away, Isaiah's anxiety burgeoning into panic. The gate loomed closer, they were nearly there. *What IS IT, Isaiah?* It came to him in a rush. TK left work at six and when he left, he turned everything off and locked the gate. They were going through the gate. "Wait, Dodson."

"What'd you say? Wait?"

Manzo saw a white car approaching the gate. He tensed. Guillermo put a hand on his arm. Revenge was moments away. And then, BOOM BOOM BOOM! Shotgun blasts. Instinctively, they ducked. "Who is that shooting?" Manzo said.

"I don't know," Guillermo said. "Everybody has pistols." BOOM BOOM BOOM! The blasts were coming from below.

"It's somebody in the warehouse," Manzo said.

"The old man," Guillermo said with disgust. Somebody returned fire. You could hear the rounds tearing holes in the warehouse walls. The homies surged out of the dark, screaming and waving their guns as a white car came through the gate, the driver slamming on the brakes. He put the car in reverse but it was too late. The Locos swarmed the car, banging on the hood, hollering in Spanish and aiming their weapons. They looked like hyenas savaging a carcass. The chain link gate swung closed. The driver couldn't back up, Locos were behind the car. Someone smashed the back window with a cinder block. Manzo couldn't see Isaiah through the crowd but he was there, scared out of his fucking mind. Ha! Manzo started to move but hesitated. For no reason he could see, the action was slowing down. Some of the guys were looking around, puzzled. Then Jorge shouted something that electrified the whole group. There was yelling back and forth and most of the group ran off, the others seemed stunned.

"The hell are you doing?" Manzo screamed. Then he heard what they heard. *Car alarms,* a lot of them, whooping, honking and wailing.

"That's coming from the alley," Guillermo said. "Somebody's fucking with our rides!" Guillermo hurried to the trapdoor and was gone. Manzo turned back to the yard. The white car wasn't surrounded anymore, only three guys were still there, not even paying attention to the car. Suddenly, the engine roared, the tires spun, the car lurched backward, busting through the gate and rocketing down the street. Manzo watched the headlights grow smaller. Then they were gone.

* * *

TK heard a car approaching. Must be Dodson and Isaiah, he thought. He raised Mr. Brown and blew the lock off the door. BOOM! He stepped from his office into the brightly lit warehouse. His eyes hadn't adjusted but he blasted away. BOOM BOOM BOOM! "Take that, goddammit!" he shouted. BOOM BOOM BOOM! Somebody shot back, bullet holes splintering the wood. TK cried out, spun around and fell to the floor. He was hit.

Manzo was having a latte at El Mejor, a coffee shop the gang used to own. He sat in his corner booth, his back to the wall, a view of the front door and the parking lot. The staff knew about the change of ownership but still treated him with respect. That wouldn't last long, he thought. He wondered who'd set off the car alarms. Probably a friend of Isaiah's or an ex-client. No, it couldn't be. The only ones who knew about the ambush were the Locos and they wouldn't've leaked it. "Jódete a tu madre!" he spat. It was that white boy, Andy. The kid changed his mind, couldn't take the heat. Probably pissed off too, knowing he wasn't going to collect.

Manzo knew he'd never find Isaiah. The wrecking yard was his best and last chance at getting him. Isaiah was on the alert now and smart as he was, he wouldn't leave a trail. No one said anything but the fellas were probably pissed, losing more confidence in their Khan. Waiting in that fucking junkyard for nothing. There would be defections, maybe a challenge to his leadership. He had to press on, he had to think. There was a link to Isaiah somewhere. All he had to do was find it.

Isaiah was sleeping in the Dodsons' den. Dodson was out on the balcony smoking a J. That was some serious shit at the wrecking yard. It rattled him, nearly being beaten to death by the Locos. Those savage muthafuckas banging on the car, aiming their guns and swearing in Spanish. He didn't understand why they ran off but he was glad they did. The weed was settling him down. Last night was scary as a muthafucka but he'd be fine. He didn't have nightmares or get paranoid or depressed or anything else. It was one more crazy-ass life-threatening situation to add to his long list of others. Dodson was sensitive to danger but he also knew when the danger was over.

It was the fixer thing that worried him. Cherise was adamant. He said he wanted to be a fixer so he would be a fixer and if he failed he'd be cleaning Deronda's food trucks for minimum wage. "Reverend Arnall is not only my pastor, he's a friend to the whole neighborhood," Cherise said. "But if you can help him, you'll have accomplished something meaningful. I'm serious, Juanell. Do not play this off."

He wouldn't, either. He was sensitive to danger.

Dodson had seen Reverend Arnall a number of times but never on purpose. It was mostly when he was courting Cherise. He went to service so he could see her afterward. As it turned out, an excellent strategy. The church had lost some of its glory since its glory days, when the chapel was standing room only, the choir had a waiting list and the collection plates overflowed. These days young people worshipped money, cars and rappers. It was more fun bobbing your head to Roddy Ricch and Young Thug than it was looking up at the ceiling, waving your hands in the air and singing "Steal Away to Jesus." Dodson's relationship with God was sketchy. The whole thing confused him, and raised too many questions. For a long time, he thought self-examination was the province of white people but it was happening to him more and more.

The church itself was in fine shape: the white paint unblemished, the stained-glass windows sparkling, the lawn as green as green onions. There wasn't enough money for a grounds keeper anymore, Reverend Arnall did all the maintenance himself. The neon cross atop the steeple never worked but it was working now. The Reverend was a steadfast man. Cherise said the congregation was half what it used to be, but those that remained were resolute in their beliefs. "That goes for me too," she added.

The chapel was as he remembered it. Gleaming, dark wooden pews, tinted sunlight shooting through. Old oak crossbeams supported the cathedral ceiling. The smells were familiar. Well-worn hymnals, choir robes, old ladies' perfume and lemon Pledge. There was a quiet in the room Dodson never encountered anywhere else. It was a place that demanded soul-searching even if locating your soul might take a while. Behind the elevated pulpit, a crucifix was haloed in mournful blue light. It represented sacrifice and you didn't have to be devout to feel that.

"Hello, Juanell," boomed a rich, resonant voice. The Reverend came striding in, handsome and vigorous, glowing with warmth and inclusion, wearing a light gray suit and a white shirt with the collar open. He was well into his sixties. His hair was nearly white but the spirit still moved him. "Thank you for coming by," the Reverend said. "I'd like your advice about something."

"*My* advice?" Dodson said. That puzzled him. Did the Reverend want to know how to steal a car?

"Yes. I've encountered a problem of my own making," the Reverend went on, "and there seems no conventional means of resolving it. Cherise suggested I speak with you. She said you were creative and because of your, what shall we call it? Background, you frequently develop unusual solutions for unusual problems. Is that true?"

"Yes, I believe it is," Dodson said. There was no point lying in church.

"She also said you were good at finding common ground and mitigating conflict."

"Also true," Dodson said. Finding common ground with your gangsta cellmates at Vacaville state prison was essential and mitigating conflict between yourself and the bruthas who wanted to abuse you was fundamental to your overall health. The skills were also useful to a professional hustler and occasional drug dealer; placating an angry mark, calming a crazed dope fiend or preventing your fellow conspirators from shooting one another.

"This is wonderful news, Juanell," the Reverend said. "The Lord blesses you and so do I." Cherise was right, thought Dodson. This feels pretty good. His pleasure vanished as he realized he'd just been hustled by a man of God.

They sat in the Reverend's office. A tiny space filled with books, notebooks, a desk with a laptop, aging Bibles and an overflowing inbox. "It begins with two longtime members of my congregation," the Reverend said. "Elvira Atkins and her next-door neighbor, Mrs. Yakashima. They've been feuding for a long time. Years, in fact. They never liked each other. Mrs. Yakashima tells her friends Elvira is a bossy know-it-all, and Elvira says the same thing about her. They're both right but that's another matter. They're very competitive. Their gardens, their houses, their cooking and so on." This was a hundred and five miles out of Dodson's comfort zone. What was he doing here?

"The two women are members of the charity committee," the Reverend continued. "This year, they decided to make quilts for a homeless shelter in El Segundo. That would have been all right if I hadn't suggested a prize be given for the quilt best representing the spirit of the church. I should have asked the Lord for guidance before I made that decision. The prize was a cordless vacuum cleaner donated by one of the local appliance stores. Unwittingly, I turned a charity event into a competition."

Elvira and Mrs. Yakashima were both excellent quilt makers, the Reverend said. Elvira stitched a spectacular quilt depicting the Star of Bethlehem, proclaiming the birth of the Christ. Mrs. Yakashima created a spectacular quilt depicting a Communion chalice, commemorating the Lord's Supper.

"After a brief deliberation, too brief according to some, I chose Mrs. Yakashima's quilt," the Reverend said. "Frankly, I didn't give much thought to it. I had no idea I fanned the flames of the feud." Unfortunately, the Reverend went on, gloating was one of Mrs. Yakashima's hobbies. She put the vacuum cleaner in the box in her front window so Elvira would see it every day. She vacuumed her porch, she vacuumed her front lawn and the sidewalk in front of Elvira's house. Dodson wondered if there was an end to the story. The Reverend opened a bottle of water and sipped, clearing his throat.

"Would you like one, Juanell?" he said.

"No, thanks."

"The more serious problem began when we needed a new choir director," the Reverend continued. "I make the selection, which I have to do soon. There are a number of possibles, but Elvira and Mrs. Yakashima are the obvious choices. Mrs. Yakashima can read music and has a better voice but Elvira has been a choir member longer and knows all the hymns by heart." There was a lot of lobbying for both candidates, the Reverend said, their friends and supporters dropping hints whenever they were offered the chance.

"Frankly, it's driving me crazy," the Reverend said. "I lose no matter who I choose. For some reason unknown to me, most folks believe Elvira is the clear winner. Ridiculous since I don't know myself, and of course I hear Elvira is delighted with the news, despite its dubious nature."

The Reverend said Elvira, in a very un-Christian-like way, sought to avenge her loss in the quilt-making competition. Elvira left her windows open and played hymns on her tuneless piano, loudly saying things like, "I sure wish I could read music," and "I sure wish I could sing better." Unfortunately, Mrs. Yakashima seemed to have skipped the passage in Romans 12 about vengeance being the Lord's prerogative.

Mrs. Yakashima kept rabbits. Late one evening, she let them out of their pen and took a board out of the fence. Overnight, the rabbits feasted on Elvira's flower garden, doing more damage than the plague of locusts in Exodus 10, verses twelve through fifteen. "I'm so sorry," Mrs. Yakashima said to an apoplectic Elvira. "I'll go to the nursery tomorrow and buy you some new seeds." In retaliation, Elvira scooped a koi out of Mrs. Yakashima's pond and put it on the grill.

"It was Mrs. Yakashima's favorite," the Reverend said. "She named it Ramón after her dead husband. Dodson, are you awake?"

"Oh yes," Dodson said, snapping his eyes open. "It helps me concentrate."

"It came to blows," the Reverend said gravely. "Elvira's daughter, Sidney, told me the whole story."

Elvira sat on her porch, eating the fish on a paper plate. It was a bony thing but it tasted okay. She fed bits of it to her cat, Johnny Mathis, named for Elvira's favorite singer. Mrs. Yakashima was in front of her house, getting the mail. Elvira waved and said, "I like the orange part best." Mrs. Yakashima didn't have any idea what she was talking about until she went out to feed the koi.

"Ramón?" she said.

Livid, Mrs. Yakashima charged over to Elvira's and rang the bell ten times. When Elvira finally answered the door, Mrs. Yakashima growled,

"Did you cook Ramón?"

"I'm sorry, dear," Elvira said. "It was an accident. I'll go to the market right now and buy you a trout." Johnny Mathis meandered by. Mrs. Yakashima snatched the cat up by its tail and slung it into the bushes.

"Why, you old nag!" Elvira shouted. She came out and shoved Mrs. Yakashima over the porch railing. Fortunately, the drop was short and her fall was broken by the azalea bushes. Elvira came down the steps intending to finish her off. Mrs. Yakashima got up, grabbed Elvira by the hair and yanked out her weave. They tussled. An apron was torn, bifocals were broken, a pierced earring was jerked out of its lobe.

"Neighbors came out to watch and urge on their favorites," the Reverend said woefully. "Fortunately, Sidney was there. She broke up the fight." Dodson was watching a daddy longlegs creep across the ceiling fan.

"What happened to Johnny Mathis?" he said with a yawn.

"Yes, I realize this may seem inconsequential," the Reverend replied. "But I am responsible for the spiritual health of my congregation and the whole sad affair is snowballing. I can't have the house of worship become a place of squabbles, vanity and misconduct. I need to straighten this out, Juanell, but no matter who I choose there'll be backlash and a backlash after that. Members of the congregation might flee to quieter pastures and we're struggling as it is." The Reverend leaned forward, intense and urgent. "The life of the church is at stake here, Juanell, and my life is the church. Can you help me?"

Dodson was about to say no but a vision of Cherise's face appeared like the Burning Bush. There were flames in her eyes. "I'll do my best," Dodson said.

"That's all I can ask," the Reverend breathed.

CHAPTER FOUR
Dealer to the Stars

Dodson got back from his meeting with the Reverend. He was in the kitchen, making breakfast. He was a good cook. When he was a teenager, he wanted to be an Iron Chef. Isaiah sat on a stool and watched his friend at work. Dodson was mixing things together in a bowl. "The flour is crucial," he said. "Too much and the pancakes are too thick, too little and they come out flat. Two and a half cups is perfect. Then you need a leavener. You can use baking powder or baking soda but baking powder alone tastes kinda soapy. Baking soda alone tastes like aluminum foil. I use both. The taste is right and they come out fluffier... add a little sugar, a little salt, and melted butter."

"That's a lot of butter," Isaiah said.

"Do you want them to taste good or don't you?" Dodson said, getting testy. "This here's important too. Separate the yolk from the whites and add the yolk first. If you add them together—"

"Wait a second," Isaiah said. "You are making pancakes, aren't you? Not rocket fuel or a cancer medicine?"

"Yes, I am making pancakes," Dodson declared. "And they'll be the best pancakes you ever ate."

"I've had some pretty good pancakes at IHOP," Isaiah said. Dodson stopped what he was doing and looked at him.

"Son, you don't know nothin' about it, okay?" Dodson said. "Your taste buds are like ants."

"Ants?"

"They work hard but they don't know what they doin'."

"Ants know what they're—"

"Could you please let me do this?" Dodson said, raising his voice. "Why don't you get a cup of coffee and stick the cup down your throat."

Dodson served the pancakes with Irish butter, real maple syrup and crispy bacon he somehow made in the microwave. They ate in silence, except for their forks clinking against the plates.

"You're right," Isaiah said as he poured more syrup. "These are the best."

"You going back to IHOP?"

"Never in my life."

"Do you know what we're doing next?" Dodson asked.

Isaiah wiped his chin with a napkin and put down his fork. "There's no direction, no leads to follow."

"What then?"

"I'll have to manufacture something."

Isaiah was making a call, Dodson standing by, wondering what "manufacture" meant. Skip answered the phone.

"What's up, Q Fuck?" he said cheerily. Strange, Isaiah thought. What's he so happy about?

"Sorry I missed you at the motel," Isaiah said.

"Accept it, dude. I'll always be one step ahead of you."

"I guess so," Isaiah said glumly. "Any chance I could talk to Grace?"

"'Fraid not, pal. You'll have to make an appointment. My assistant will get back to you. Gotta go."

"Please, Skip, just a half a minute," Isaiah pleaded.

"Sorry, buddy boy, I'm on a job," Skip said, sounding cocky. "Big money too. A lotta big companies are gonna be happy when they hear the news. In a way, it's too bad. I love it when they get nailed. It's like, hey Exxon, you remember that beach you fucked up? You're gonna pay."

"I never thought of you as a public servant," Isaiah said. He's keeping Skip on the line, thought Dodson. He's waiting for a slipup, a clue.

"Look, I know you want to kill me and if I was in your position, I'd be the same. But Grace didn't have anything to do with all that. I didn't even know her then. If you're as confident about getting me as you say you are, let her go, and you and I can go head-to-head."

"Nice try, but no dice."

"Why no dice?" Isaiah said. "Don't you want to get back at me? I wiped out your dogs, remember?" There was no come-back. Several long seconds went by. Isaiah exchanged a look with Dodson. Skip spoke, his voice was deep, guttural and so full of hate it felt like a thing, a physical presence.

"You fucked up my whole life, my whole fucking life," he said. His voice broke. "You... killed... my... dogs. YOU KILLED MY GOLIATH!" he screamed. He was breathing in short, harsh breaths, words sizzling through his teeth. "I'm gonna shit on your grave, Isaiah, and then I'm gonna kill Grace." Abruptly, the call ended.

"Damn, man. That's a frightening muthafucka," Dodson said. "Did you get something out of that? I didn't hear anything useful."

"Skip said he's on a job. He's working again."

"I don't see how that helps us."

"Remember Jimmy Bonifant, dealer to the stars?" Isaiah said. "Bonifant was a player in the Goliath case."

"Yeah, I remember him," said Dodson. "He was Skip's middleman. You wanted to hire Skip, you went through Jimmy."

Isaiah didn't reply, staring off like he was seeing something far away. He's cogitating, cooking up something, Dodson thought.

"We need Bonifant to tell us about the job," Isaiah said. "If we know that, we'll know where Skip will be."

"And you think Bonifant's gonna volunteer that information?" Dodson said. A sudden fear gave his pulse a bump. "Wait a second. Is that what you thinking? You gonna strong-arm Jimmy Bonifant?"

"I'm not sure yet."

"Well, *be* sure and take that option off the table," Dodson said. "You ain't strappin' and neither am I and even if we was both carryin' bazookas it's a bad idea. Drug dealers have guns all over the house, they don't like strangers and everybody on they contact list is on parole."

Isaiah was still in the zone. Then, a glimmer of a smile.

"Out with it," Dodson said. "What are you gonna do?"

"I'm gonna talk to Bonifant, have a conversation."

"Talk? That's your plan? That makes no sense," Dodson said. "Why would he talk to you?"

"Curiosity," Isaiah replied. "He'll want to know what I'm up to."

Jimmy Bonifant finally called him back. Skip was thrilled but kept his cool, stayed businesslike. The job was dangerous, bordering on idiocy, but it was fifty K. Jessica's house was just as he remembered it. Nothing was changed except the TV was bigger and she had another chin. Jess was wearing a sack dress, no bra and bare feet. Skip hated her feet. They were stumpy with big square nails. They'd fit better on a hippo or a rhinoceros.

"Magnus, are you insane?" Jessica said. "That girl cannot stay here."

"I've got no place else." He went to the fridge, got a beer and popped the cap.

"I don't care," she said. "You got yourself into this, you can get yourself out of it."

"I'm trying." He guzzled the beer.

"Well, try somewhere else," Jessica said. "She's a kidnap victim, for Christ's sake! I don't want any part of this! She could start screaming any minute."

"Nobody will hear and I told her not to," Skip said.

"Oh great. That makes me feel sooo much better."

"Mom, if you could just hear me out."

"What am I supposed to do? Guard her night and day?"

"It's one day, that's all."

"That's all, huh? I could still go to jail no matter how many days it is."

"You're not going to jail. Could you just—"

"Isaiah found me. Why not the police?" she argued. "I can just hear myself. What's that, Officer? Who's that tied up in the basement? That's my son's girlfriend. They're into S&M and he forgot his whip. He should be home anytime now."

"Mom, could you just listen?" Skip shouted. Jessica huffed, sat down on the beach chair and lit a cigarette. Skip grimaced and batted the smoke away.

"Jesus. Could we open a window?"

"No. The girl might crawl out and tell the neighbors," Jessica replied.

"Do you remember Jimmy Bonifant?" Skip said.

"The drug dealer? Is he in on this too? That's all I need. A possession charge on top of harboring a fugitive."

"Mom, *shut up*!" Jessica shrugged and blew a smoke ring at his face. "Jimmy's got a job for me and get this," Skip said. "It pays fifty thousand dollars!"

Jess was unimpressed. "Great. Then you can afford to keep the girl at the Holiday Inn and get the fuck out of my house."

"I'll give you a split," he said. Jessica pursed her lips, her brow knitted. A sign she was thinking, or more likely, conniving.

"How much?" she said.

"Ten grand."

"No. Twenty."

"Twenty? I'm doing all the work!" Skip complained. It was a mistake, telling her what he was making.

"It's off-season. I'll bet you can get a great deal on Orbitz."

"Okay, okay, twenty," Skip said, pissed. Jessica grinned. She'll never collect it, he thought.

The basement was dank, dimly lit, crowded with junk. Cement floor, cement walls. There were transoms but she'd have trouble getting her hand through them. Skip brought her here in the trunk of his car, though she begged him not to. He drove around to the back of the house, took her inside and shoved her through a door and down some wooden stairs. He closed the door and locked it. He came back two minutes later and set a water jug inside and another fucking Snickers bar.

This is classic, Grace thought. Locked in a basement. It was like a horror movie, Leatherface lurking somewhere in the shadows. When Skip hauled her into the house she'd caught a glimpse of a disheveled woman who looked astonished. Grace could hear them arguing upstairs. Who was that? His mother? Sounded like it.

She thought about Isaiah. Whatever their issues, he loved her. She was sure of it. But she'd rejected him. Would that put him off? No. Isaiah will come back for you, she thought. If he were half dead and buried under the snow he would come. It made her cry. This beautiful man. As decent, courageous and loyal a person as you'd ever find anywhere. She was going to stay alive. To love him and be loved in return.

Isaiah owned a house before he sold it to Tudor. Grace stayed with him for a time. One afternoon, a girl named BB came to the door. She was distraught. Patches, her cat, ran away. She'd adopted it eight days ago. Grace expected Isaiah to say something mollifying and close the door, there were cases he was working on, but he responded to BB courteously, respectfully, asking her questions like he would with any other client.

"When's the last time you saw Patches?" he said.

"Two days ago."

"Where?"

"In my room. She was sleeping on the windowsill."

"What does Patches look like?"

"She's black and white and she has green eyes that glow in the dark."

"Is she an indoor or an outdoor cat?"

"Indoor."

"Shy?"

"Yes, very. She was just getting used to me."

"Did she leave food in her bowl?"

BB thought a moment. "Yes, she did. She usually eats everything. She's kind of fat."

"Let's take a look," Isaiah said.

They went to BB's house. It wasn't far but Grace was still surprised, Isaiah taking all this trouble to find a cat. She wondered if there were any other unlicensed, underground private investigators who found lost pets.

"If Patches has only been here eight days, something unusual might have scared her," Isaiah said. "A vacuum cleaner, loud music, strangers dropping in. A lot of times, they hide in the house."

They set about searching. Grace struck out. She found Isaiah in the kitchen, looking under the breakfast table. "Look. Against the baseboard," he said. A mousetrap. The trap had gone off, a crumble of Velveeta clung to the tripping mechanism. Isaiah retrieved the trap, examining it closely. "See?" he said. There was a near-microscopic smear of blood on the hammer bar. "If a mouse set this off, its dead body would be somewhere close."

"You think the cat did it?" Grace said.

Isaiah nodded. "Cats love cheese. Lots of protein, lots of fat."

"Have you ever owned a cat?" she asked.

"No. But I've found more than a few. Along with a couple of dozen dogs, a boa constrictor, an iguana and a box turtle." Somehow, this impressed Grace more than getting murderers off the street. "So let's say Patches is hurt," Isaiah continued. "The environment is new and she hasn't quite adapted yet. She might have gone outside." Isaiah nodded at the kitchen window. It was open slightly. "Cats can squeeze through anything that's the height of their head. Their collarbones and spine are flexible." Grace was incredulous. If Isaiah encountered a problem, he studied up on it. He probably had a graduate degree in wayward felines.

They went out to the backyard. "The cat probably came this way. Too much noise and traffic on the street side."

"Where do we start?" Grace said.

"An indoor cat will usually hide within a forty-yard radius but that's still a lot of ground to cover. Look for small spaces. Somewhere the cat could curl up and not be seen." They began the search and fifteen minutes later, BB found Patches under a tipped-over wheelbarrow, frightened, dried blood on its paw. The girl was overjoyed, cradling the cat in her arms and rocking it back and forth.

"Thank you, Isaiah!" she said. "Say thank you, Patches."

Grace and Isaiah walked home. She hooked her arm through his, proud to be with him. Proud to know him. Proud to be his woman.

The only light in the basement came from one forty-watt bulb. It threw off a weak glow that didn't go very far. Grace went up the steps, got the water jug and Snickers bar and came back down. She took a long drink and ate the Snickers bar, hard to do with your wrists bound together. She struggled not to panic, not to fall apart. *Don't cry, you stupid cow. Think.*

Strategy. To get out, of course. Her first objective? Cut the zip tie around her wrists. She listened, the argument was still going on. Skip and his mom were toward the front of the house, the basement door was toward the back. It was awkward but she began to explore. She needed some sort of blade. There were boxes of clothes, magazines and shoes. There were a bicycle with a bent frame, broken lamps, a dented microwave, a washing machine and dryer that weren't hooked up to anything, folding chairs, a plastic container of flatware but you can't stab with a butter knife, then another box full of dead batteries, fishing equipment, an awful painting of a sunset, auto parts, and on and on and on. But no blade.

It was close and warm. The gas heater and water heater were down here, hot-water pipes on the ceiling. Everything was covered with dust and she was draped with cobwebs. She was sweating. She stank, her clothes were filthy, a grit seemed to cover her whole body. If she screamed no one would hear her. When she was brought from the car to the house, she saw the roof of a neighboring house. A cinder block fence and runaway bougainvillea between the two properties. That, and she was half underground. They were still arguing upstairs.

Grace continued her search, sidling around, over and between the piles of junk. She stopped. “Huh,” she said. A stack of left-over plumbing pipes was piled on the floor. They were different lengths, threads rusty and heavily oxidized. She picked up one about the length of a baseball bat. “Yeah, this’ll do.”

She heard footsteps. Skip was moving toward the basement side of the house. She had to get back to the stairs. If he caught her nosing around he’d chain her to the water heater. She hurried, everything in the way, everything an obstacle, clumsy with the pipe and her hands tied up. She banged her body against things, fell twice and circled around immovable objects. Skip’s footsteps were getting closer. She kept going, gasping, desperate. *Christ, he’s in the hallway!* She pushed aside some boxes and went around the heating unit. She heard the lock snap open, the doorknob creaking. She dropped the pipe and stumbled into the clearing at the bottom of the stairs. The door opened. Skip came halfway down the stairs. “Back up.”

“Back up?” Grace said, trying not to breathe hard. “What am I going to do, bite you to death?”

“Just do it.” Grace obeyed, stepping away. He came down the stairs, carrying a cafeteria tray. He set it down on the washing machine. There were a bowl of chili, a few pieces of white bread and a wooden spoon. She was starving.

“Skip? It’s going to be hard to eat like this.” She held up her hands. Skip came over, took a folding knife out of his pocket and cut the tape. She rubbed her wrists to get the circulation going and chowed down. She hadn’t eaten white bread and canned chili since she was a kid but *Oh my God,* it was ambrosia. When she finished, she wiped her mouth with her forearm and wished there were more.

“By the way, is there a bathroom down here?” she asked.

"Jessica doesn't want to come down here for any reason," Skip said. "Helping you eat chili and piss is not on the program. I tried to argue but it's her house." He came closer and gave her a warning look. "Don't fuck with her, Grace. She's armed, twice your size and tough as a feral hog. If she hit you she'd break your spine. Christ, you stink."

"Who's Jessica?"

"None of your business."

"She's your mom, isn't she? What's wrong with that?"

"Wait'll you get to know her better."

"Are you going someplace?" Grace asked.

"Yeah, I am," Skip said. He smiled. He's got a contract, she thought. She widened her eyes with fake excitement.

"You're going on a job, aren't you?" she gushed. "Who is it? What are you going to do?" Skip shrugged, like he wasn't going to tell you but you knew that he would.

"It's not a big deal."

"But it's dangerous, right?" she said.

"It's always dangerous. But that's the job, you know?"

"God, I don't know how you do it. Who's your target?" Skip thought a moment.

"I'm not going to tell you his name," he said, "but he's a big-time guy and I'm getting *paid*, you know what I mean?"

"What does he do? Drug dealer? Mafia?"

"He's an attorney and very hard to get to. His house is secure, his limo is bulletproof and he works in a Century City high-rise. He also has a bodyguard, a former marine. I'm really gonna have to watch myself."

"Do you know how you're going to do it?" she said with the same enthusiasm.

"You're a freak, you know that?" He grinned.

"Ski-ip. Come onnn, I'm bored."

“I don’t know yet,” the hitman said grimly. “I’ve got to do my surveillance, assess the situation, figure out my options.”

“Are you going to use the bear trap?” she said, smiling.

“I don’t think so,” he said, smiling back.

“How long will you be gone?” She tried to sound sad.

“Overnight.” He started up the stairs. He was leaving. She needed time to work on him. She blurted out,

“I’ll help you catch Isaiah if you let me go.” Skip stopped and turned around.

“How would you do that?”

She ad-libbed. “I’ll get a message to him, like I had to do something sneaky, you know? I won’t say exactly where I am, I’ll give him clues, make it hard for him. Otherwise, he won’t believe it.”

Skip huffed. “Let me get this straight. You’re gonna lure your boyfriend into a trap and then I kill him? What would you be doing, watching? Tell me another one.” She wished she’d thought this through. Time to get desperate.

“Come on, Skip!” she pleaded. “When this is over you’ll have to kill me!” She worked up some tears, most of them hateful. “I didn’t do anything to you, Isaiah did and that’s not my fault.” She had to put a crack in Skip’s indifference. She crumpled to her knees. “Please, Skip, *please*! I don’t want to die. I’ll do anything you say!” She wept, as pitifully as she could. Skip hesitated, apparently dismayed. He opened his mouth to speak, but then he turned, went up the stairs and left. The moment the door closed, Grace stopped crying. She hated crying, she hated begging but there was no choice. She thought she was making progress but he was so erratic, so suspicious. She needed another angle.

Skip told Jessica he was leaving. There was a lot to do before tonight. Grace’s offer stayed with him. He really didn’t want to kill her. If he let her go, maybe she'd let him fuck her. Maybe they could keep it going, you know, be like running buddies, Bonnie and Clyde, something like that. The idea made him feel good for a heartbeat or two. More likely, Grace was lying her ass off, but then he remembered what she said before, how she just "fell into it" with Isaiah and being with him was better than being alone. She was probably bored with him. Who wouldn't be, with a do-gooder boyfriend and a job at a stupid food truck. Maybe she really likes you, Skip thought. You're not bad-looking, you've got swagger and you don't take shit from anybody. You're a "bad boy" and that's what all chicks want, isn't it?

Skip got in the car and backed out of Jessica's yard.

Yeah, he thought. It's definitely something to think about.

As soon as she heard Skip drive away, Grace went back and picked up the pipe. She placed it on the ground, at the side of the stairs. You wouldn't see it unless you were looking for it. When and how she would use it wasn't clear. She sat down with her back against the washing machine. Despair seeped into her veins, but with it now was a practical hope: how to use the pipe; how to manipulate Skip; how to get free.

Jessica's coarse, gravelly voice came through the door. "If you're anywhere near the stairs, back up or I'll clock you one."

"I'm not. I'm by the washing machine." Grace stood up and thought about the pipe. The door opened a crack. Jessica peered in, then opened the door. She had a gun.

"Okay, come on up. Slowly." The pipe was useless. Grace plodded up the steps to the top. "Turn around and back out," Jessica said. Grace did, Jessica behind her now. Grace felt the gun barrel between her shoulder blades. "Bathroom, first door on your left—Jesus Christ, you smell like a sewer." They went into the bathroom. "Take all your clothes off, do what you've gotta do and take a shower," Jessica said. "There's nothing in here you can use to hurt me. Not even a cuticle scissor so don't even try."

The shower was amazing. Grace soaped herself thoroughly and washed her hair, the hot water sluicing off streams of dirt. She rinsed her mouth out three times and brushed her teeth with her finger. Jessica was milling around the bathroom door.

"Hurry up, will you? I'm going to miss my show."

Grace came out of the shower and Jessica threw her a towel. "There's some clothes on the hook, your shoes are there too. Put 'em on." A few minutes later, Grace emerged from the bathroom wearing a man's jeans with paint stains on them and a huge T-shirt. The jeans were probably a foot too long but Jessica had raggedly cut them down. The T-shirt said I'M ON MY WURST BEHAVIOR over a picture of a sausage.

"My ex-husband," Jessica said. "I should have burned all his crap a long time ago." They went down the hall, Jessica muttering about the hassle and inconvenience, Grace holding the pants up so they wouldn't slide off. It occurred to her that Jessica wasn't doing this out of motherly love, the risk was too great. She must be getting paid, Grace thought.

"I hope Skip comes through for you," she said.

"What are you talking about?" Jessica said.

"Skip mentioned he was going on a job and a lot of money was involved. I hope you're getting your share, it's a lot of risk."

"The last thing you need to be doing is worrying about me," Jessica said. "I'd be thinking about my own ass if I were you."

"Uh, I don't know if I should say this," Grace said tentatively. "Well, never mind. I don't want to start anything."

"Say it or I'll bust you one," Jessica said.

"Don't be mad at me, okay? But Skip was talking to somebody on the phone. He said when he finished the job, he'd pick me up and go."

"Yeah, what about it?"

"I'm just guessing, okay?" Grace said. "But he sounded like… like he was keeping all the money." They reached the basement door, Jessica angry now.

"Shut your goddamn face and get in there," she said. Grace started down the stairs, saying over her shoulder,

"Why don't you keep it?"

"What? What did you say?" Jessica said. Grace turned around.

"Why don't you keep all the money?" Grace said, adding, "I could help you." Jessica looked at her a moment—and shut the door.

CHAPTER FIVE
RIP

Jimmy Bonifant was a small-time dealer from Sacramento. Once in LA, he went to parties and clubs, met people, sold coke and weed and used the profits to buy the best product he could find. He was surprisingly successful. He was charming and attractive, people said he reminded them of Paul Newman. He looked trustworthy, a nice guy, someone you'd like to know.

One night he was at the Nightingale Plaza, a hip nightclub on La Cienega, $600 for a bottle of booze. He was at the bar, nursing a beer, and he met a man named Bug. Bug was big, Black, decked out in hip-hop's finest. He threw back a drink, said he was in a hurry and asked if Jimmy knew where he could get some blow. Jimmy instinctively knew this was a guy to get next to. He sold him a few grams of his best stuff at a good price.

Jimmy found out later that Bug was a member of Black the Knife's entourage. At the time BTK was at the top of the rap world. He had the requisite mansion, a car collection, his own brand of tequila and a battalion of groupies. Jimmy met Bug again at the club and Bug asked him if he wanted to go to a party at BTK's house. Jimmy sold more blow to the partygoers and became a regular at the rapper's festive occasions, of which there were many. Gregarious and friendly, Jimmy sold to lots of people, including BTK himself. Word got around. Soon, he was selling to other recording artists, actors, agents and studio execs. Jimmy became successful. He was Dealer to the Stars. He drove a Maserati and lived in the Hollywood Hills and his girlfriend was second runner-up for Miss San Diego. Isaiah hoped he was still in business.

The Hollywood Hills was an exclusive neighborhood above Hollywood Boulevard, not far from the Hollywood Bowl and the Chateau Marmont. Dodson said a lot of celebs had houses in the area. DiCaprio, Halle Berry, Lady Gaga and a bunch of other people Isaiah knew nothing about. The chic homes were built wherever there was room, some of them clinging to hillsides, others cheek by jowl, or directly abutting the street. Bonifant's house was an asymmetrical stack of white blocks and big windows, surrounded by a thick hedge and a wrought-iron fence.

"Want me to come with you?" Dodson said.

"Thanks, I'll look like less of a threat if I'm alone."

"That's my point. Bonifant is a drug dealer. You *need* to look like a threat."

They got out of the car, went up to the gate and rang the call box. Above it was a sign: YOU ARE BEING VIDEOTAPED. A woman's voice, flinty and belligerent.

"Yeah?"

"My name's Isaiah Quintabe. I'd like to talk to Jimmy Bonifant."

"No one by that name here. You've got the wrong address."

"Jimmy knows me."

"Like I said—"

"Tell him my name, that's all. Isaiah Quintabe. He'll see me." Isaiah didn't know if that was true but the longer the exchange went on, the more combative she'd get. They waited. Finally, a buzz and the gate clicked open. Isaiah and Dodson moved through slowly, their palms out. The front door opened and a young woman appeared behind the security screen. She looked suspicious, hostile, her hand behind her, no doubt holding a gun.

"Are you armed?" she said.

"No, we're not," Isaiah said.

"I'm gonna frisk you." The woman was weary and wiry, no makeup, an old dress, hair in a messy bun; a schoolmarm teaching shoeless children their sums. She opened the screen and they stepped into the house. "Against the wall," she said.

"Just like old times," Dodson said. She adeptly patted them down. There was another woman standing a little ways off. You could see the similarity. Same scowl, gray eyes and long chin. The second woman wore tight skinny jeans, stylishly ripped, a red tank top, bare midriff and shoulders, brassy yellow hair, and tiger-striped fingernails. She looked hungover. The living room was unexpected. No black leather sofa or TV the size of a delivery van. No bong, beer bottles, takeout cartons or PlayStation controllers on the coffee table. The furnishings were staid, muted, bought from department stores, more suited to a middle-aged couple from Ohio.

"You stay here," the second woman said to Dodson. "Tell Dad, Ironside is on track."

Jimmy Bonifant was in the kitchen, sitting at the center island eating a bowl of cereal, the sports page spread out in front of him. "I bet this game, Dolphins and Jets. I put five hundred on the Jets at plus six. The goddamn Dolphins won by fourteen. Sit down, Isaiah. Or should I call you IQ?"

"Isaiah is good."

"I remember you," Jimmy said, closing the newspaper. "Yeah,

it was years ago, right? Skip was after that rapper. What was his name?"

"Black the Knife."

"If there was ever a guy who needed to be shot—" Jimmy shook his head. "Only Skip would try to off a guy with his dog. He's a maniac but he always gets the job done." Bonifant was in good shape, still handsome, athletic build, salt-and-pepper hair, wearing a white shirt with the sleeves tightly rolled.

"How can I help you, Isaiah?"

"I sent Skip Hanson to prison and he wants revenge," Isaiah said. "He couldn't get to me so he kidnapped my girlfriend, Grace."

"Yeah, that sounds about right," Jimmy said. "Did you meet my daughter Giselle?" Giselle was leaning against the counter. She took a gun from the back of her pants and set it down.

"Where's Janet?" Jimmy said.

"Isaiah brought a guest. They're in the living room."

"Everything okay?" he asked.

She nodded. "On track."

"I'm sorry about your girlfriend, Isaiah," Jimmy said, "but what do you want from me?"

"Skip's on a job, he told me so. I'd like to know when and where. I need him to tell me where he's hiding Grace." Bonifant looked at him a moment, like he couldn't believe the proposal.

"Pour him a cup of coffee, Giselle."

Dodson sat in the easy chair, the second woman slouched on the sofa, a gun beside her. She eyed him skeptically, bored with the whole thing.

"I'm Juanell Dodson," Dodson said with his most charming smile. The woman sighed, as if answering would require too much effort.

"Janet," she said.

"You're Jimmy's girlfriend?"

"Daughter."

"No shit? And that other woman is—"

"My sister, Giselle," she said sullenly.

"Y'all are *sisters*?" Dodson said. "Damn. She needs to see your stylist. Who does her hair? Wait, lemme guess, the housekeeper, but she died before she combed it out."

Giselle smiled. "You're funny."

"I'm a lot more than funny," he said slyly.

"Oh really?" They were flirting now. Dodson glanced at his watch. "Got a date?" she said.

"No, but right about now I'd like to smoke. Got any tree?"

She smirked. "Tree? I've got the Amazon rain forest in my handbag."

A resentful Giselle poured Isaiah coffee. "Cream? Sugar? Almond milk?"

"That's enough, Giselle," Jimmy said.

"Jimmy. I need to find Skip," Isaiah said.

"I can't help you."

"He's retired," Giselle said. Jimmy shot her an annoyed glance.

"For the sake of argument, say you found Skip," Jimmy went on. "You know what he's like. He wouldn't talk if you stuck a gun in his ear but let's say, hypothetically, that I am in a position to help you."

"Da-ad," Giselle complained.

"Why would I?" Jimmy said.

"Because it's in your best interests," Isaiah said. "It's a win-win, Jimmy."

Giselle snorted. "You've gotta be kidding."

Jimmy turned dark, offended by the presumption. "You have

no idea what my interests are, Isaiah, and I don't see anybody winning anything."

"I'll take Skip down *after* he does the job," Isaiah said.

"So?" Gisele said. Bonifant thought a moment—and brightened. A revelation. He nodded like he was working it out in his head.

"Hypothetically then, the middleman wouldn't have to pay Skip's fee but he would still collect from his client."

"That's right," Isaiah said.

"Very clever," Bonifant said appreciatively. "But there's a flaw in your plan."

"What's that?"

"If Skip doesn't succeed, he'll go after the middleman," Bonifant said. "No one else can rat him out."

"But isn't Skip always successful?" said Isaiah. "That's his rep."

"But what if the job is really tough? Logistics, location, not enough time. Maybe the target's got his own security, who knows?" Jimmy said. Giselle stirred uncomfortably.

"You've got that phone call, Dad," she said pointedly. Jimmy glanced at her, nodded. He got up and brushed off his lap.

"Giselle keeps me on the straight and narrow," he said.

"Jimmy, please—" Isaiah began.

"Sorry I couldn't help." Jimmy left. Giselle picked up the gun and toyed with it.

"Don't fuck with my dad. The Bonifants don't play."

Dodson and Janet were on the veranda, sharing a blunt and laughing.

Isaiah appeared. "We have to go."

"Aww, really?" Janet complained. "Can't you stay a little while?"

"'Fraid not, baby," Dodson said. He kissed her on the cheek and they hugged. "I'll see you on the upside."

"Come back anytime."

* * *

They got in the car. Isaiah was upset.

"I don't think this is a good time to be high."

"I know you stressin', but could you try not to be so condescending?" Dodson said. "Giselle was supposed to tell Jimmy, 'Ironside is on track.'"

"Ironside," Isaiah said. "A code word?"

"I think so. Jimmy's up to something," Dodson said.

"Yeah, Jimmy used the present tense," Isaiah said. "He said Skip gets the job done."

"I asked Janet if she ever met Skip and she said she heard Jimmy talking to him a couple of days ago."

Isaiah thought a moment. "Remember that morning you were making pancakes? I called Skip, trying to stir something up. He said something about big companies being happy when he finished the job and—what else did he say? He said it was too bad because he loved it when the companies like Exxon got busted."

"What about it?" Dodson said.

"Skip was saying that the guy he was going to kill was in the business of nailing big companies. The target could be law enforcement."

"That shit never works," Dodson said. "Kill a DA or a judge and they come back extra hard."

"Okay, suppose it's not law enforcement," Isaiah said. "Who else?" Dodson's prodding made him sharper. "Ironsides... Ironsides," Isaiah said, thinking aloud. "There was the USS *Constitution,* a sailing ship they called *Old Ironsides,* but I wouldn't think Jimmy was a history buff."

"There's *Ironside,* the TV show," Dodson said. "My dad watched them reruns all the time. The character was an attorney in a wheelchair."

"When did it run?"

"The show? In the sixties, I think."

"The time frame fits. Jimmy could have watched it," Isaiah said. "Did Ironside bust big companies?"

"I don't think so," Dodson said. "Mostly, it was a wife poisoning her husband, or somebody getting blackmailed, stealing from the company, that kind of thing."

"Ironside," Isaiah said again. He was good at times like these. Taking long shots with tenuous connections to the question. He got out his phone and did a search. "The actor that played Ironside was Raymond Burr." He quickly did another search. He smiled. "The present-day Raymond Burr is a class-action attorney. He sues companies like Exxon!" They pounded fists.

"Did Janet say anything about timing?" Isaiah said.

"Yeah," Dodson said. "She said her dad was uptight because the shit was going down tonight."

Jimmy Bonifant had hired another hitter to take out Raymond Burr. The guy put together a file but quit, saying the job was too hard, too risky. Skip read the file. Burr lived in Hancock Park, a wealthy neighborhood between Highland Avenue and Rossmore just off Wilshire Boulevard. The houses were more like old-school mansions, big lawns, brick chimneys and willow trees. If you saw a Bentley in the driveway you wouldn't be surprised. It looked like rich old people lived there. Burr's place had a lawn and garden in front, then a twelve-foot cement wall with an arched doorway, wrought-iron spikes running along the top, everything covered with ivy so it didn't look like a fort or a prison. Burr had a routine, the report said, but there were no obvious weaknesses. Burr went to his office in Century City, his bodyguard driving. There were photos of the guy. He was big, muscled up, intimidating. A former marine according to the file.

Burr occasionally walked to a nearby restaurant for lunch but it was sporadic and the bodyguard always went with him. His car was parked in the underground garage. Not a good place to shoot somebody. The bodyguard drove him home. Maybe get Burr long-range, Skip thought. When he was in the joint, a prison guard beat him up. When Skip was released, he lay in wait and shot the asshole with a Barrett M95 from a thousand yards away. Skip drove Burr's route to and from work. There was no place to get an angle. Getting on the roof of a high-rise wasn't like the movies. You have to get permission from the manager and even if you did, he'd come with you.

Skip smoked a blunt. It helped his creativity, different scenarios going through his mind, what would work and what wouldn't. It felt right to be on the job. Doing what he was good at. He studied the photos in Burr's file. Pics of his crib were detailed, from different sides and vantage points. The hitter who worked the case before was solid. Skip nodded. An idea came to him. He had to hurry. He looked at his crappy watch. When he finished the job he'd replace his plastic Timex with something cool, eat at the Outback, order a sixteen-ounce rib eye, hire a hooker or two and get rid of that goddamn junker and buy a nice car.

He would never give Jessica forty percent of his money. If she believed that, she was dumber than Ludvig. She'd treated Skip like crap his whole life. Ludvig beat him all the time and she never said a thing. His clothes were in rags and his sneakers worn smooth and a size and a half too small. The school counselor said her son needed to see a psychiatrist. He was suffering from a severe personality disorder. Jessica said, "Oh yeah? Who doesn't?" No, thought Skip. Jessica wasn't getting a baloney sandwich.

Skip drove to the Desert Wonderland. His guns were in two plastic crates hidden in the crawl space under the office. He liked looking at them. The grips and stocks and hammers, the smoothness of the barrels. He liked the way the magazines clicked into place and the pressure of the trigger pull and the sound of a round sliding into the chamber. There were handguns, different makes and different calibers, a sawed-off shotgun, a Chiappa triple-barrel shotgun, a Winchester 30 06 deer rifle, the Barrett M95, a Kel-Tec P3AT micropistol with a three-inch barrel and a six-shot capacity. Skip already owned enough weapons to arm the Proud Boys for another insurrection but he always wanted more. He was like that as a kid. If he stole a Snickers bar, he'd go back for another one, and another one and another one until he got caught. It was like he was making up for something, like he'd been gypped. Even if he got everything he wanted, there was always a hunger for something just out of reach.

He chose a gun for the Burr job. A Benelli MP 90 .22-caliber pistol, known for its accuracy, and a Dead Air Mask 22 silencer, and a box of RIP ammo. When he was nineteen he worked in his uncle's gun store. Hugo Vestergard's Guns America store in San Bernardino was the third-largest gun dealer in California. It was the "Supermarket of Firearms," a pretty accurate description, thought Skip. Uncle Hugo was a big man who wore leather vests, big belt buckles and a medallion of turquoise on a leather thong. He spoke like a cowboy but that was bullshit. He was born in New Jersey. Uncle Hugo believed the Second Amendment was the most important. "Without guns, there wouldn't be any other amendments," he liked to say. "If you want to keep your freedom, you have to shoot the people who want to take it away."

Uncle Hugo lectured Skip on specialized ammo. "You've got your dumdums, of course," he said. "See the X cut into the nose? When it hits, it expands, causing a lot of damage, but they're kind of passé now. Hell. Your everyday jacketed hollow-point is more lethal."

"Why are they hollow?" Skip asked.

"When the round hits, it blossoms, like a flower," Uncle Hugo said. "The bullet gets a lot bigger. You should see the hole they make." Uncle Hugo opened another box of ammo and spilled out some rounds. They looked like regular bullets, a little blunter with thin grooves on either side. "Multiple-impact round. Ever heard of 'em?" Uncle Hugo said.

"Never have," Skip said. He was smiling, eager to learn.

"Get this. When you fire the round, the bullet fragments into three parts and they're held together with strings of Kevlar."

"No shit?"

"No shit. It comes at you spinning, like a South American bolo. And this is the beauty part. It's got a fourteen-inch spread."

"You mean—"

"That's right. I can miss by thirteen inches and still blow your head off."

"Amazing!"

"In my opinion, the most lethal round of all is this one here," Uncle Hugo said. He opened another box of bullets. The label said G2 RIP. "RIP means 'radically invasive projectile,'" Hugo explained. The tip of the bullet was like a round mouth with six copper fangs. "This thing is a doozy," Buck said. "Yeah, whoever came up with this puppy had some evil in him. When it hits you, it flies apart, like shrapnel from an explosion. It doesn't go through you, it—let me show you."

Uncle Hugo had a roast chicken he bought at the supermarket. He was going to eat it for lunch. He took the thing outside to the range. He removed the wrapping and set the chicken on top of a post. He loaded a 9mm with RIP rounds and handed the gun to Skip. "Go on, have a go at it."

The chicken was thirty feet away. Skip was an excellent marksman. He aimed and fired. The chicken wasn't knocked off the post. It exploded into strings of fat, flesh and sinew. If you didn't see it before you wouldn't know it was a chicken. "Now imagine that's your insides," Uncle Hugo said, with a chuckle. "If there was an autopsy, they'd have to pick your organs out with a tweezer and a soup ladle."

Skip wondered why anyone would need a bullet like that. To make sure your opponent was dead? A couple of bullets in the head would do it. This ammo wasn't about efficiency, it was about the shooter, Skip thought. His pleasure, his satisfaction, knowing he not only killed his man, but destroyed him. He went shopping. The Buy Buy Baby store, the Footlocker, Walmart and Ace Hardware. He took the stuff back to Jessica's and prepped. He studied the photos one more time, set his alarm and dozed off. Everything was set.

Jessica sat at the top of the basement stairs, holding the gun. Grace was at the bottom, looking up, hand on the rail. She'd found a bungee cord to hold up her pants.

"What you were saying before, about the money," Jessica said. "What did you mean?"

"I mean, Skip's only giving you forty percent," Grace said. "Why not take the whole thing? That's what I would do."

Jessica huffed. "Jesus, you're a piece of work."

"When this is over, Skip's going to kill me, you know that, right? I'll do anything to get out of this mess and you would too, and if you don't mind me saying, you're being a little naive."

"Me? Naive?" Jessica scoffed. "You're barking up the wrong bitch."

"You know Skip better than I do. He's not going to pay you diddly. You *have* to take it all and you'll need help."

Jessica thought a beat. "Help doing what?" she said.

"What if Skip hides the money before he gets here? That would be the smart thing to do. You'll have to make him talk. Are you going to do that by yourself? Incapacitate him, tie him to a chair, knock him around and hold a gun on him at the same time? I don't see it."

"Now you're being stupid," Jessica said. "If I take Skip's money, he'll take revenge. He'll hunt me down for the rest of his life."

"Yes, I know," Grace said. She let the implication hang in the air.

"Well, I'm not going to kill him," Jessica said, suddenly indignant. "He's my son."

"You don't have to," Grace said. "After we take the money, we call the police. Skip is a kidnapper, there's probably an arrest warrant out for him right now. All we have to do is hold him while we find the money."

"Well, let's say I go along with this," Jessica said, warming up to the idea. "I turn my head for a second and the next thing I know, you're in the wind, and what do you do then? You go straight to the police."

"No, I wouldn't."

"Why?"

"Because I want a cut of the money," Grace said. Jessica grinned and shook her head. This was something she could believe.

"Like I said, you're a piece of work. How much?"

"Seven thousand for me, forty-three thousand for you," Grace said. "That's more than twice what Skip was offering."

"Seven grand, huh?" Jessica said.

"I need twelve more credits to get my RN. I need tuition, books, to pay my bills until I finish," Grace said. She gave Jessica a finite answer, a specific reason why she needed the money, and seven grand sounded better than ten. The amount also implied that Grace didn't need anything past the seven. She'd learned that from Dodson.

"Nurses make good money," Jessica mused.

"There's a shortage. I could make seventy-five K plus benefits," Grace said, making that up. "I've always wanted to be a nurse."

Jessica considered, eyeing Grace suspiciously.

"We're doing it, then?" Grace said.

"Let me tell you something, sweetheart," replied Jessica. "You might be young but you've got nothing on me. I've dealt drugs, worked in bars, pool halls, whorehouses, gambling dens, and the list of my boyfriends could fill up cellblock D at San Quentin. That's where my first husband is right now. He's got a hole in his shoulder where I stabbed him with an ice pick. I've seen more double-dealing and sneaky underhanded bullshit than you'll ever see if you live to be a hundred and one. What I'm trying to tell you is, don't fuck with me."

"I don't have the balls for it," Grace said with a sigh. We'll see, she thought.

They were at the breakfast table eating Marie Callender's chicken pot pies. Jessica was sitting between Grace and the back door. The gun was in the pocket of Jessica's muumuu.

"You're right about Magnus," Jessica said. "He'll come waltzing in here with some story about how he didn't get the guy and then it's 'Toodle-oo! I'll be going now!'"

"What if Skip screws up and doesn't kill the guy?" Grace said.

"Honey, Skip never screws up."

"What's he going to do when he comes back?"

Jessica explained that Skip always parked behind the house and entered through the back door. "After a job he's hyped up, talking about how he did this, how he did that. He doesn't even look at you. Then he gets a beer and drinks it in three gulps."

"That's when we'll get him," said Grace. "He won't be expecting it, won't have his gun at the ready. How will we get him to talk?"

Jessica came up with a number of creative alternatives. Twisting his nipples with a needle-nose pliers. Stamping on his toes. Putting a block of dry ice in his boxers or splashing barbecue sauce in his eyes or tapping him on the head with a metal spoon a thousand times. "Like that water torture thing," Jessica said. "Drives you crazy." Grace's favorite: sealing a centipede in Skip's ear with candle wax.

"It might get more extreme," Grace said. "We might have to get nasty. You up for that?"

"Honey," Jessica said. "I've got 'nasty' tattooed on my left tit."

"The rest is pretty simple," Grace said. "You give me my split, we call the police and Skip is carted away."

"What if he tells them about the money?" Jessica said.

"He won't," Grace said.

"Why?"

"Because he got it for killing somebody. I'm telling you, Jess. This is a cakewalk."

Jessica looked off, as if she was seeing it unfold. She smiled. "I think you're right." Even jaded characters like Jessica believed what suited their needs, Grace thought. And nothing was ever a cakewalk. The best you could do was set the scene. Life taught her that.

CHAPTER SIX
Don't Say Money

It was just after dark. McCadden Place in Hancock Park was quiet and serene, no cars parked on the street. Skip circled Burr's block a couple of times. If he parked nearby, the car would be conspicuous, especially this piece of shit. He found what he wanted three blocks away, farther than he wanted but the conditions were right. It was in front of a construction site; dark, no house lights, no cameras, inconspicuous. It might be a worker's car with a dead battery. He got the baby stroller out of the trunk. It was a trike, three rubber wheels, made for daddies who liked to run. He tucked a blanket around a high-tech doll named Melissa. The only thing she didn't do was fart. Skip zipped his Adidas tracksuit all the way up to hide the neck tats and made sure his new sneakers were tied tight. Wear all black and you were either a ninja or a burglar. He looked like a resident, getting his exercise and taking the baby out for a little night air.

He went along McCadden, pushing the stroller ahead of him. Latex gloves might be noticeable so he'd wrapped the stroller's handle in an ultrathin polymer film tape that didn't take fingerprints. It was seven-thirty. If he'd come any later, it'd be weird, a guy taking his baby out when it should be asleep. A man was coming toward him, jogging, a dog on a leash. You could tell he was rich just by looking at him. Maybe it was the haircut or the confident way he moved. The dog was a pit bull. It made Skip flinch, but he stayed calm. The man nodded as he went by, another rich people thing. They acknowledge each other for no reason.

A neighborhood security car drove past him, the guy not even looking over. Skip smiled. He loved it when his plans worked. He felt smart, in control. He felt cool. He went past Burr's place, glanced across the lawn to the twelve-foot wall. He continued to the end of the block, turned right and turned again into the cleanest alley he'd ever seen. Skip had burgled a lot of houses. You couldn't have a twelve-foot wall around the perimeter of your house. It was against the building code. That was why Burr's wall was set back from the street. It also meant the wall was lower along the sides and rear of the property. Max was eight feet.

The next-door neighbor had a wooden fence, a narrow space between it and Burr's wall. It was just wide enough to park your baby stroller out of view. Earlier that day, Skip had gutted the stroller, removing all the lining and padding. Underneath Melissa were a folding footstool, a ski mask, disposable gloves, a small backpack, the gun and the silencer. The silencer added five inches to the length of the gun but it improved accuracy. There was less recoil, less sound, so you weren't as likely to react before you pulled the trigger. Skip took latex gloves out of his pocket and put them on. He screwed the silencer into the gun and put it in the backpack. He slipped on the backpack and set the footstool next to the wall. It was a little more than a foot tall and he was just under six feet. The spikes on top of the wall were in easy reach. Getting over them was another thing. Skip did a lot of weight lifting in the joint. He grabbed a spike in each hand and swung a leg up to the ledge of the wall. The ledge was three inches wide, maybe less. Skip struggled lifting his body weight but got the other knee up too. Now he was holding the spikes and sitting on his knees in a very narrow space. With several grunts, he got one foot on the other side of the spikes. He pushed himself upright and got his other foot under him. He was standing, his crotch directly over the spikes. *Whatever you do, don't sit down.*

He lost his balance, swaying and windmilling his arms, nothing to do but jump down. He landed hard, knees bent and falling forward on his hands. He waited a moment to see if he'd hurt himself and got up. "You idiot," he whispered. He'd made a mistake. How would he get back without the stepladder? Fuck it. *It's fifty grand, asshole. Improvise.* Skip was facing Burr's yard. There were a lawn, pool off to one side, then a brick courtyard, then the house. He saw fancy lawn furniture in the courtyard, a bottle of wine and glasses on the table. Did Burr have a girlfriend? Didn't see her car. Maybe she left. *Too bad if she's still there.*

Skip muttered a curse. There were French doors on the back of the house but the glass was electronic. At night, they turned into mirrors but the people inside could still see through them. Skip was hoping to shoot Burr through a window or a sliding door. Couldn't anything be easy? he thought. He had to get inside. Risky but Burr wasn't expecting trouble. He wouldn't be on guard, he wouldn't be carrying a gun. Once you got in there, the rest was easy.

Raymond Burr's office was in a high-rise in Century City, a business and shopping enclave adjacent to Beverly Hills.

"The easiest thing is to shoot Burr long-range," Isaiah said as they drove slowly past Burr's building, looking up and around.

"No place to get a shot," Isaiah said.

"What about a drive-by? When Burr comes out of the garage," Dodson said.

"Mm, I don't like it. There's a million cameras around here. Rich people are safer than the rest of us. Call his office."

Dodson called. "May I speak to Mr. Burr, please? It's a matter of some urgency." Dodson listened a moment and ended the call. "He's left the office."

"Early for an attorney," Isaiah said. The plan was to follow Burr's car and warn him if they saw trouble.

"He's gone home," Dodson said.

"It's getting dark, dammit, Skip could strike at any time." There was traffic, impossible to go fast. They waited at stoplights, the *60 Minutes* stopwatch ticking in their ears.

"Hurry," Isaiah said.

The French doors were open. Not a surprise really. If you're sharing wine with your woman, you don't immediately lock the door. Skip quietly turned the handle. He opened the door a couple of inches, waited, then stuck his head inside. He was in the great room. It was big, forty feet from here to the fireplace and almost as wide. The sleek furniture looked uncomfortable, big thick area rug with designs on it, expensive stuff on the shelves, ceiling lights turned down low. Skip listened. He could hear the TV coming from another room. The news by the sound of it. Good, Burr was occupied.

Skip crossed the great room and entered the hall. He crept forward. The TV was coming from the next doorway. Skip got low and peeked around the corner. Burr was on the sofa, facing the other way, his head just visible over the top, the TV beyond him on the wall. No girl. A .22 might not kill the guy if the bullet went through the sofa, even an RIP round. It might hit the wooden structure and fragment. He needed to get closer. He went forward, one slow step at a time. He could see more of Burr's head and his feet resting on the ottoman. He raised the gun, aiming at the back of Burr's head just as the bodyguard came in. No shirt and boxer shorts. Burr said, "Darling, do you have the—" Skip was so startled, he swung his arm around too far, fired and missed. The guard dropped to his knee, grabbed his gun off the end table.

"Get down, Ray!" he shouted. He fired. BLAM! BLAM! Skip was already around the corner and sprinting down the hall. A shoot-out would bring the cops. He started toward the French doors but hesitated. He'd never get over the wall in time. He ran for the front door. There were another two shots in his wake, the guard coming out of the hall, screaming, furious, some asshole trying to kill his baby daddy. Skip cut hard into the foyer, opened the front door and raced off down the street, tossing his gun into the shrubbery. If he was arrested, he didn't want a weapon on him.

Dodson turned off Wilshire onto McCadden Place.

"I hope we in time," Dodson said.

They hadn't gone a block when Isaiah said, "Stop. There's Skip's car." He'd recognized it from the rear. A ten-year-old two-door Altima. "Park a little ways behind it," Isaiah said. "Turn off the lights and leave the engine running." Dodson did so. They heard distant gunshots. *Oh shit. Was Burr dead?* Moments later, they saw him, Skip, a block away and running hard.

"There's that muthafucka," Dodson said. "Better get down." They slid low in their seats, eyes just above the dashboard.

"I brought the Taser," Isaiah said. "When Skip gets in his car, I'll come from behind and shock him, we'll drag him, put him in the trunk."

"Make your move when I turn my wipers on," Dodson said.

Isaiah slipped out of the car. He got behind Skip's Altima and hunched down beside the trunk. He waited, trying to slow his breathing, his heart like a tom-tom in his throat, clutching the Taser tightly. This was it. Skip was either going to talk or get his gonads fried. *I'm coming, Grace. Hang on*. Isaiah heard Skip approach, harsh breathing, sneakers slapping the asphalt, slowing as he neared the car.

Dodson flashed the wipers, and Isaiah started to move—"Excuse me," a man said. "But can I help you?"

He looked like a resident and here were two Black guys lurking around, one of them crouched behind a car. The man had a pit bull on a leash, probably why he was so confident. "Do I need to call the police?" he said. Isaiah stood up just in time to see Skip get in his car, start the engine and drive away. He stuck his arm out of the window and gave Isaiah the finger.

"We were just leaving," Isaiah said. The impact of failure nearly buckled his knees. Of all the times to come up empty, it had to be now, this case, the most important of his life. He felt the PTSD descending like a shroud, the depression and self-loathing enclosing him, oozing over him like warm mud. He'd forgotten its power. He wanted to give up. He wanted to get away. His hands were shaking, a chill ran through him and he shuddered. His face crinkled, he grimaced, tears held on the brims of his eyes.

"What's wrong with you?" Dodson said, glaring at him.

"Nothing, I'm just...disappointed," Isaiah said. He could barely speak.

"That don't look like disappointment to me. Looks like you fallin' apart."

"I'm not."

"Yes, you are," Dodson said. He was angry. "I know you, son. You can't hide nothin' from me, and I'm tellin' you right now. If Grace dies, it's on you. That's right, muthafucka. *You*. Fuck your PTSD."

"It's not like that. I can't just shrug it off."

"Save it for Grace's funeral. Nothin's gonna get you off the hook. I don't care if you can't walk and your right eye is missing.

You the only one that can save her and if you cry like a pussy and let that happen, you'll hate yourself and so will I. Now straighten your spine, Q. Gather up your manhood and come up with a goddamn plan!"

Skip drove, in a rage, hardly able to see. Where did Isaiah come from? How did he know where to find him? There was only one person who knew about the job. "Jimmy Bonifant," Skip said aloud. Another score to settle. And that asshole only advanced him five grand. It was usually half the fee. Jimmy said the job was tricky, that Skip would probably strike out.

"I get half the fee because just trying is dangerous," Skip had complained.

"You're making too much of it," Bonifant said. "If you can't do it, you leave." Ordinarily, Skip would hold out but he really needed the money. If he didn't get paid he was at the mercy of Jessica. A disgusting thought, but there were no other options. Jessica was going to be pissed when he came home with a measly five grand. She'd think he was holding back. No, she wouldn't think it, she'd be convinced. *Prepare for the worst, Skip. That mean bitch is going to throw you out.*

Isaiah called him.

"Close call, right?" Skip gloated. "I timed it so I'd get there with the man with the dog. Faked you out, huh?" A complete lie but Isaiah let it go.

"I'll pay you to release Grace," he said.

"I don't think so," Skip said. "Too dicey and you've always got some bullshit up your sleeve."

"Thirteen thousand seven hundred and forty dollars in cash," Isaiah said. "No traps, no bullshit. I get Grace, you get the money."

"Thirteen seven? That's all, huh?" Skip said.

"It was all I could scrape together," Isaiah said.

"It's not worth it," Skip said. "I'm not taking a chance for chickenshit money like that."

"Think about it, Skip. I don't care about catching you. I hope you live happily ever after. I want Grace, and that's all. What good is she, anyway? You get busted with her and you're done."

Skip paused for a bit, letting Isaiah dangle. "Yeah, well, I'd have to get more than that. Let's say twenty thousand."

"Best I can do," Isaiah said. "It really is, Skip. I borrowed the money. I can't squeeze any more out of my friends. They're not rich." Dodson told Isaiah to offer an uneven amount. That was what would happen if he really borrowed the money. He told Isaiah to stick to his price or Skip would keep upping the ante. Now it was twenty thousand. When he went to make the exchange, it would be thirty. Skip needed to be convinced that $13,740 was all he had. Dodson advised him to say he borrowed the money. It sounded more desperate.

"Come on, Skip," Isaiah said. "I've got the money in cash. I'm looking at it right now." Another of Dodson's tips: Don't say "money," say "cash." You can visualize it. Skip took his time and said,

"Well, okay."

"You have to give me a time and place," Isaiah said.

"Let me think about it. I'll get back to you." The call ended.

CHAPTER SEVEN
Winnie the Hand

Winnie Hando was a detective with the Long Beach Police Department. She was with the department for eleven years, working Major Crimes the last three. Winnie's father was Japanese, her mother was Korean. Her last name was pronounced HAWN-DOE but her male colleagues nicknamed her Handcuffs, Handout, Handgun, Handful, Handyman, Hand Job and, when they were really annoyed with her, the Hand. *The Hand is really full of herself. The Hand is bitching at the lieutenant again. The Hand said she'd report me.*

Sworn female officers in the LAPD hovered around twenty percent, the number of Asians was about eight percent, the number of female Asians was significantly less than that. Many people who met her were surprised she was a police officer and still more surprised that she was Asian, an aphrodisiac for a lot of men. Winnie was witness to the "yellow fever" phenomenon quite often in college. Buff white guy with his delicate Asian girlfriend. There was the long-standing, seemingly unshakable belief that Asian women were docile and submissive. Patently untrue and getting more so every day. The idea that "yellow fever" was an honest inclination toward long black hair and almond eyes was sketchy at best, thought Winnie. The idea also implied that women of other races were too independent and demanding, ruling out the possibility that women of any ethnicity were individuals.

Yesterday she was assigned to a kidnapping case. The victim, Grace Monarova, was white, female, age thirty-one. She was allegedly abducted by Magnus Vestergard, aka Skip Hanson, a known felon and a suspected hitman. Grace was taken from her housemate's driveway in the late afternoon. There were no witnesses and no physical evidence except a dog collar that bore no fingerprints or DNA. Grace's housemate, Deronda Simmons, explained the animosity between Vestergard and Grace's boyfriend, Isaiah Quintabe. Revenge was the likely motive.

Quintabe was most certainly the man who left the envelope of information in the lobby. He owned quite a reputation as an unofficial PI with a remarkable ability to resolve cases but his activities weren't confined to investigation. He was more like the ombudsman for East Long Beach, Winnie thought. Helping his neighbors with problems the police could not or would not get involved in. Quintabe reportedly accepted payment in the form of tuna casseroles, blueberry muffins, lawn care and oil changes. Hard to believe, thought Winnie. Quintabe had first-hand knowledge of both Grace and Vestergard. They needed to talk.

Winnie met her CO as he was coming out of his office. Lieutenant Aaron McKee didn't seem glad to see her. He stopped, tried not to frown and ran his hand through his silvery brush cut.

"We have a meeting, sir," Winnie said.

"Do we?" McKee said.

"I made a request for a new partner."

"You don't need a new partner. Duvall is good police." The lieutenant reminded Winnie of Alan Alda, from *M*A*S*H.* A kindly English professor with sparkling eyes and a bright, sad smile.

He was a veteran detective and a competent administrator and he knew how the bureaucracy worked.

"Duvall is a slob who doesn't use deodorant," Winnie said.

"That's true," the lieutenant said.

"And he's always eating. You should see the squad car, sir. It's like a crumb factory. I go home smelling like Flamin' Hot Doritos and flatulence."

"Give him a break. Duvall has irritable bowel syndrome."

"He's distracting, and it interferes with my job performance," Winnie complained. "He called me a rich bitch right to my face!"

"Do you want to lodge a complaint?"

"No, I don't want to besmirch the man's record but I don't want to die of asphyxiation either."

"Besmirch?" the lieutenant said. Using an unusual word around here was like speaking Korean. "You know, it's a funny thing," he added. "Duvall's put in for a new partner too."

"What? Why?"

"He says you're an annoying prig that thinks she knows more than everybody else and you're always stopping at Starbucks because you want a mocha latte with soy milk every twenty minutes."

"It's more like twenty-five," Winnie said wanly.

"The captain complained about your clothes again," the lieutenant said.

"What does that have to do with being a police officer?" Winnie replied. She was wearing Ferragamo Chelsea boots with a thick tread, AG jeans, a fitted cashmere sweater and a black blazer she had custom-made. She'd been criticized for her wardrobe since the academy. The silliness might have passed but a vice detective named Mahalia Lipscomb told Winnie she didn't look like a cop. Unfortunately, Winnie replied, "Why? Because I'm not wearing a pants suit from 1975?" Which did nothing to lessen her rich bitch image.

"If Quintabe doesn't want to be found, you won't catch up with him," the lieutenant said. "They call him IQ, you know."

"I don't care if they call him Salman Rushdie," Winnie said.

"We're talking about fish now?"

"Why wouldn't I catch him, sir?"

"Because he's smarter than you," the lieutenant replied, hitching up his pants. He gave her a fatherly smile, sidled past her and was gone.

Winnie stood there a moment. Plenty of officers, male and female, were more experienced than her, knew more about the job. She relied on them every day. But smarter than her outside of work? Hardly. The lieutenant's most demanding intellectual activity was not hitting his golf ball into the trees. Duvall was finishing his degree in slow-pitch softball and the captain studiously made foam grasshoppers for fly-fishing.

They called him IQ, Winnie thought. This was someone you had to meet.

Jessica's life was hardscrabble all the way. Her father was a salesman who sold parts for boat engines made in China. Sometimes he'd take his daughter outside, point up in the sky and say, "See that, Jess? That's the poverty line." Her mother was a housewife when she wasn't dropping pills and boning high school students.

Jessica had to work. She got a job at Wendy's but was fired for stealing change. She worked at a Black Angus Steakhouse but was fired for stealing tips. The day she left, there were four pounds of top sirloin in her backpack. She was also a cocktail waitress who went home with the customers as well as an excellent pool hustler, rattling the other players with her knockers spilling out of their D cups. She was a dealer in Reno, an escort in Reno, had married an Israeli gangster, divorced him, married a bowling champion and divorced him too. He was probably Magnus's father but it was hard to be sure. There were a lot of members on the team.

As if her life wasn't shitty enough, little Magnus made it worse. Every day, she regretted not posting a sign over her bed that said NO CONDOM NO NOOKIE. Christ, you had to lug the kid around everywhere. If you left him by himself for five minutes, he'd burn himself on the floor heater, burn himself on the waffle iron, pull down the drapes or eat a piece of memory foam. He left the freezer open, unlocked all the windows and turned the oven on. When she came back late, the porch lights were off so she couldn't find her keys. If she brought one of her "drinking buddies" home, he'd wait until they were having sex, then bang on the door and call out, "Is my wife in there?" or "Mom? The doctor said it's syphilis."

When he was older, his pranks and antics became crimes and arrests. He shot a pigeon out of a potato gun and hit Mrs. Delgado in the face. He took a dump on the hood of a police car. He barbecued the North Carson Rams mascot, Tilly. Jessica threw him out of the house on his sixteenth birthday. She would have let him stay but she caught him throwing darts at her cat. A year or two would go by and he'd show up at the house. Just show up. He walked in like he never left. He'd bring a bottle of Jose Cuervo, make a baloney sandwich and plunk himself in front of the TV. If she asked, "What are you doing here?" he answered, "I came to see my mom. Is that okay with you?" She let him stay. She didn't know why. Maybe because she was alone with no connections to anybody. At least Skip was family.

Then he'd be completely weird. He was home every night, bought groceries, washed the dishes, they'd watch TV together and he drove her to work. She found herself cooking, making his bed, tidying things around the house and waiting for him to come home. Then he'd leave. Just leave. He never said anything or left a note. One day, she woke up and he was gone. She was part relieved, part not. For however many days Magnus stayed, he was almost like a son and she was almost like a parent.

Grace and Jessica were in the kitchen, waiting for Skip to get back from the job. Jessica was worried, anxious. She'd made half a package of bacon in a cast-iron frying pan and ate the whole thing, her lips shiny with grease. Now she was sweating, restless, twiddling with the gun.

"I don't know about this," she said. "Maybe I'll have a drink."

"Later, Jess. You've got to stay sharp," Grace said.

"You don't know Skip like I do. He's paranoid, quick on his feet. It's like sneaking up on a rattlesnake." Jessica was really afraid of him, Grace thought. Yelling at her son was one thing. Holding him at gunpoint was another. You wondered what she'd seen over the years, how much savagery. You wondered how many tales she'd heard about titanium hunting bolts, samurai swords, bear traps and talking to victims while they lay bleeding to death.

"The plan is foolproof," said Grace. "Skip comes in the back door, he's all excited, he doesn't expect trouble. He goes to the fridge to get a beer and you show the gun. You make him sit down in the chair, then I come out of the pantry and tie him up." Somewhere during the scrum, Grace would make a break. The back door was only twenty feet away but it was close quarters and there'd be two people with guns. Instead, she'd run for the hallway. It was nearly the length of the house. There was no cover but if she could get to the front door she could escape.

"What if I have to shoot him?" Jessica said.

"Then shoot him."

"What if he doesn't go down? When he was thirteen years old, some kid dropped a brick on his head from a second-story window. Skip got up, found the kid and beat the snot out of him. We found out later Skip had a skull fracture."

"Jess, it's *fifty thousand dollars,*" Grace said.

Jessica nodded to reassure herself. "Right, right," she said.

They heard Skip's car swing around the house and park in the backyard. Jessica panicked. "Where do I hide the gun?"

"Step behind the island and put it in the drawer," Grace said calmly though she wasn't calm at all. "He won't see it until the last moment. Remember, everything is normal, everything is fine." Grace hated clichés but she said it anyway. "You've got this, Jess."

Grace stepped into the pantry, the door open just enough for her to see out. A moment later, Skip barged in, frustrated and furious. "Well, that was fucked! Everything went wrong! That goddamn Q Fuck nearly got me!" Skip put his gun down and yanked open the fridge. "Can't something go right once? One time, that's all I ask!" He turned around and looked at Jessica expectantly. She stood there, mute, a sickly smile on her face. Grace watched, horrified. *Say something, Jess. Engage him!*

"What's wrong with you?" Skip said.

"Uh, I think I've got food poisoning," she said. She opened the drawer partway and closed it again.

"What's in the drawer?" Skip said.

"Uh—spoons. I'm supposed to eat yogurt." Grace closed her eyes. *Oh my God. Stupid stupid stupid!*

"The spoons are in the other drawer and we don't have any yogurt," Skip said. He knew something was up, his eyes were darting around the room. Grace was apoplectic. *Open the drawer, Jess! Pull the gun!* "Where's Grace?" Skip said.

"In the basement, where else?" The trash can was full to overflowing, the two empty Marie Callender boxes on top.

"You ate two pot pies?" Skip said.

"Yeah, no wonder I've got food poisoning, huh?" Jessica said with a fake laugh. Skip looked at her, scratching his cheek. He glared at her, his jaw tightened.

"Something's wrong," he said. *Pull the gun, Jess. Pull the fucking gun!*

"No, everything's fine! Really fine!"

"Why haven't you asked about the money?" Skip said.

"I, um, figured you'd tell me about it sooner or later." Jessica chuckled lamely.

"Tell me, Jess. I'm not shittin' you, what's going on!" Skip demanded.

"Nothing! Nothing!" Jessica cried in a strangled voice. She had the drawer open and was pawing around, trying to find the gun.

"What's in the drawer?" Skip said.

"Nothing!"

"Get out of my way!" Skip bulled her aside to get to the drawer. She snatched the cast-iron frying pan off the stove, swung it like a club and clobbered Skip on the head with a resounding *clonk*! Skip howled like a coyote, grabbed his head and dropped to his knees. Grace almost made her break but Jess and Skip were in the space between the pantry and the hallway. *Damn damn damn get out of my way!* Something snapped inside Jessica. She pulled up and swung again, and again, screaming the whole time.

"You ruined my life, you prick! You asshole! I would've been okay but you came along!" Skip was trying to defend himself, holding his forearms up, but Jessica pounded those too.

"Cut it out, Ma! Cut it out!" Skip shouted. He tried to get up but she cracked him on the head again. He fell flat and she started kicking him. "Ma, please stop!" he pleaded. *Now or never, Grace! Go!* Grace made her break, slipping around the preoccupied Jess and into the hall.

"Hey!" Jess said. Grace sprinted, reaching the living room and the front door. There were two locks and a chain.

"Dammit!" she said. She fumbled with them, her hands suddenly fingerless. She was almost free! ZIP ZIP ZIP! Bullets punched holes in the door. Grace ducked and turned around. ZIP! ZIP! ZIP! Jessica coming toward her, snarling, aiming Skip's gun.

"Hold it right there, you little weasel!"

The basement was as cold as before. Skip sat on the floor, his back against a support post. He was beat to shit. Dried blood everywhere and a huge bump on his head, dark hematomas on his arms. Grace leaning against the washing machine, morose and brooding. She got the water jug and took a drink.

"Could I get some of that?" Skip said. She looked at him in disbelief.

"You were going to kill me and now you're asking for water?" Grace said. "What are you going to do with it, drown me?"

"I wasn't going to kill you. Honest, I wasn't. I never said that, did I? I knew all along I'd let you go."

"I see. The man who kills people with bear traps was going to let me slide? Let me go to the police? Sure you were. You want water, come and get it."

They could hear Jessica stomping around and swearing. Her footsteps got louder, the basement door was unlocked. The door swung open. Jessica's silhouette framed in the door, light from the hall behind her. Her silhouette was horrifying, like Annie Wilkes in *Misery* except with a gun.

"Where's the money, Skip?"

"I fucked up the job," he replied, his voice crusty. "I don't have it."

"Liar."

"I don't have it, I swear."

"I have proof," Jessica said. She held up a wad of bills. "Five grand. I found it in the car. Where's the rest?"

"That's all Bonifant gave me."

"Stop bullshitting. He always gives you half."

"I'm telling you, that's all he gave me! He said the job was tough and—"

"You think you can fool me?" Jessica said. "You always kill the mark. You hid the rest because you weren't gonna give me my cut."

"Think what you want," Skip said, giving up.

"And you, you cunt," Jessica said, casting a dirty look at Grace. Jess came down a couple of steps. Her bland face was contorted with anger, pig eyes flashing. "Thought you could double-cross me? What'd I tell you about that?"

"You weren't gonna give me my cut either," Grace said. Jessica hesitated. "That's what I thought," Grace added.

"Skip, if you don't tell me where the money is, I'll leave you here to starve," Jessica said. She turned, went up the steps, closed the door and locked it.

"She wants the money," Skip said. "She'll be back in ten minutes."

"You really don't have it?" Grace said.

"I really don't have it."

"We have nothing to bargain with."

"If I tell her to go someplace and the money's not there she really will starve us. Her mean streak is wider than she is." Skip got up, slowly, groaning and holding his head. He got the water jug and drank, most of the water dripping down his chin. Suddenly, he stopped, his forehead wrinkled, squinting like he saw something dangerous in the dark.

"Skip?" Grace said.

"We have to take her out."

* * *

Jessica fumed, cursed, took the cast-iron frying pan and slung it into the wall. She was better off before this mess. Suppose Skip wasn't bullshitting and he didn't have the money? What then? Shoot them and leave them in the basement like a serial killer? They'd rot and turn black. She'd have to take the bodies somewhere and bury them, except they were too heavy to lift. There was no chance she was digging a hole big enough for one of them, let alone two. She found the tequila, poured herself three fingers and threw it back. She shivered. Fuck, that's good. She huffed through her nose and shook her head. If the best thing in your day was a shot of booze you were living a fucked-up life.

She was absolutely fed up with her small, suffocating world, with no comfort, no luxuries and nothing to be proud of. *Fifty grand!* A tic pulsed under her eye. The things she could do, the things she could buy. The money wouldn't last forever but at least she could look back and say, "Honey, I had me a time." She had to make Skip talk. She knew threatening and pleading would have no effect on him. What did Grace say? It might get nasty? Jessica snorted. Are you kidding? Nasty was for kids.

The doorbell rang. She jumped. Nobody ever dropped by except the UPS guy with something from Amazon. She peeked through the blinds. A man and a woman. The man was dumpy and wore a cheap sport coat and a crooked tie. Cops, Jessica thought. The woman was probably in her late twenties or early thirties. Hard to tell with Asians. If it wasn't for the badge on her belt you wouldn't make her as a cop. Her hair and makeup were perfect. She rang the fucking bell again. Jess thought a moment and then turned on the stereo.

* * *

Winnie removed her finger from the doorbell. "Mrs. Vestergard? I'm Detective Hando from the Long Beach Police. You are not in any trouble, but we do need information from you." Duvall stood behind her. His paunch spilled over his belt, the short end of his tie two inches longer than the fat end. He'd eaten a cheese and bean burrito from Taco Bell and was wiping pico de gallo off his chin.

A woman opened the door just enough for them to see her doughy face. She could pass for Duvall's sister.

"Yeah?" The woman was already belligerent. Something was up.

"We're looking for your son, Magnus," Winnie said. "We have some questions we'd like to ask him."

"Who's we?" Jessica said, looking around.

"Police," Duvall said. He belched and waved the effluent away.

"Have you seen my sheet?" Mrs. Vestergard said.

"You mean your arrest record? Yes, we have," Winnie said.

"Then you can understand why I don't like cops, I don't speak to cops and I don't cooperate unless I have to, which means arrest me or take a hike." It was important at these times to remain businesslike, although Winnie wouldn't mind cuffing this harridan and leaving her in the sun. The music was loud. Willie Nelson playing a guitar solo so rudimentary you'd think he'd lost his thumbs.

"Would you mind turning down the music, ma'am? It's hard to have a conversation," Winnie said.

"I don't want a conversation," the woman retorted. "I want you to get off my porch."

"Mrs. Vestergard, it's only a few questions," Duvall said. He drew himself up and looked her in the eye. "We'd appreciate your cooperation in this matter."

"I don't care if you appreciate it or not," Jessica said, returning the look.

"Is your son here, Mrs. Vestergard?" Winnie said.

"I haven't seen that weasel in a long time."

"Do you remember when?"

"No, I don't."

"Why would you call your son a weasel?"

"Because he's not a beaver or a bobcat," Jessica shot back. "I'd like you to go now."

Winnie had a feeling about something.

"Mrs. Vestergard, has anyone else been inquiring about your son?"

"Yeah, as a matter of fact. Isaiah something," Jessica said. "He told me Magnus kidnapped his girlfriend."

"And what did you say?"

"I said what I'm saying to you. I don't know where he is or what he's doing. Okay, we're done." She closed the door a little harder than necessary.

"She's hiding something," Winnie said as they walked away.

"Very observant, grasshopper," Duvall said.

"Grasshopper?"

"You never saw *Kung Fu*? David Carradine? The seventies?"

"I wasn't even an idea in the seventies."

"What do you think she was hiding?" Duvall said.

"I'm thinking a kidnapping victim calling for help," Winnie said.

"Possibly. Maybe we should hang around. If Vestergard is in there, maybe he'll make a run for it." The thought of spending more time with Duvall was repugnant but he was right. She got a text from Lieutenant McKee.

"We have to go," she said. "Double murder. The lieutenant wants us there now."

CHAPTER EIGHT
Chances Are

The cruiser was noisy, the suspension shot, the smell of Duvall's junk food and Duvall himself was ingrained in the upholstery. He was eating a sandwich the size of a sofa cushion while he sang a country and western song, something about a woman driving away with your heart in a pickup truck with deer antlers on the hood. Winnie wished she was in her Lexus but you weren't allowed to drive your personal car on the job.

Years ago, Winnie was questioned by Internal Affairs about her predilection for nice things. She explained that her father was the "Almond King," the biggest almond grower and distributor in the state of California with vast acreage in the San Joaquin Valley. He sold untold tons of almonds under a variety of brand names. She saw them in Whole Foods, Gelson's, Bristol Farms and other places she shopped.

Winnie's youth was decidedly privileged. A BMW at sixteen, designer clothes, a membership at the El Miguel Country Club, a ten-thousand-square-foot house and a full-time chef. She rode dressage. Her horse was a Dutch warmblood, imported from the Netherlands. Her father wouldn't talk about the cost. She named the horse Tomoe, after Tomoe Gozin, an infamous female fighter born in the twelfth century. It was said Tomoe Gozin was quite beautiful, her skin pale as a white rose and with long hair that hung below her waist. Her skill as an archer was unsurpassed, she was a superb rider and she fought with a sword as well as any man. She was first captain in the Genpei War, leading three hundred samurai against two thousand warriors from another clan. She was one of five fighters left standing.

Winnie wasn't affected negatively by her background, at least she didn't think so though her colleagues and friends might've argued the point. Generally, she was happy with herself. Her work ethic was sound, she was good at her job and she treated people fairly. She was opinionated to be sure, but most of her less positive assessments were discreet, unless it was Duvall.

Winnie's parents were stern, traditional and adamant about three things. That Winnie pursue her education and perform well. That she marry someone with a similar economic status and that she work for a company with a solid reputation. One out of three ain't bad, she told her father. She'd split with her fiancé a year earlier, Ben calling off the wedding three days before the ceremony, beating her to the punch by fifteen minutes.

Ben didn't have any idea how to conduct a relationship and neither did she. They both wanted intimacy without change, without adjusting their routines and acceding to the other's needs. Since then, Winnie dated infrequently, assiduously avoiding her colleagues. Cops frequently developed a number of unpleasant personality traits. Aloofness, cynicism, alienation, suspicion. Not something to come home to.

Winnie looked for possibilities on a dating website. Her profile said, *I want to be with someone who is literate, educated and financially stable. Someone who doesn't watch movies based on Marvel Comics, who eschews McDonald's and has never been to a car show.*

He must be articulate, an engaging conversationalist, well-traveled with a polished appearance and a tendency to listen more than talk. He must have integrity. He must be patient and kind. He must be—

There were more criteria along the same lines. In eight months she received two messages. One from a man who thought she was "smokin' hot" and another who said she was a stuck-up bitch. She went on one date. The man said he was a surgeon, which was minimally true. He was a podiatrist who sawed off bunions and removed ingrown toenails all day, which he told her about in great detail.

Winnie and Duvall drove back to Long Beach. She thought about Quintabe. He got to Jessica's ahead of her, suggesting he knew more than he was telling. He was withholding information germane to the case. A violation punishable by six months in the county jail. She needed to contact him but his friends said they didn't have his new number.

No two murders were the same but the circumstances were often familiar. An attempted robbery. A known gang member tried to strong-arm a drug dealer named Archie "the Arch" Lamont. A gunfight ensued, both were killed. By the time Winnie and Duvall arrived, the forensics team was already at work.

"It's simple enough," Duvall said, surveying the carnage. "Idiot number one kicked down the door. He killed idiot number two and idiot number two killed him."

"Did you know Archie?" Winnie said.

"Ran into him once or twice. Small-time guy. Occasionally, he pushed a kilo or two but mostly it was kibbles and bits. He's no loss to the world, believe me."

It was the standard drug dealer's abode. Piles of dirty clothes, dirty dishes, dirty sofa scarred with rips and burn marks, a blackened bong, a lot of empty liquor bottles and pizza boxes. The smell was damp and garbagy with undertones of weed and alcohol and unwashed socks.

Winnie took a look around and saw nothing of note. No evidence of other players, or people who'd left the scene. The bedroom was in the same shape. There was an Adidas bag half under the bed, bundles of used bills in there. With a quick glance Winnie counted seven bundles. "We've got cash in the bedroom," she called out. "Can I get someone to bag it up?" She left, passing Duvall in the hallway.

"I heard Archie has a machine gun," he said as he lumbered past. She went outside, talked to the ME and returned twenty minutes later to the bedroom. A CSI was bagging the cash.

"Wait a second," she said. "How many bundles are there?"

"Six," he said.

"Are you sure?"

"Yes, Detective. I'm pretty sure I can count to six."

She went home, thinking about what happened. Did she really see seven bundles? She was tired. Maybe there were six. They were in an overlapping pile. But her recall was excellent. She counted on it. She took the same memory tests administered by intelligence agencies and aced them. No, there were seven bundles. She was sure of it. If anything, she would have undercounted. She remembered Duvall passing her in the hallway. He wasn't allowed to use the bathroom, it was part of a crime scene. He was headed to the bedroom, there was no place else to go and no place else to look for a machine gun. Duvall was a lot of things but was he a thief? "Oh God," Winnie murmured.

It was a dilemma. Tell the lieutenant and let the bureaucracy take its course? Duvall was fifty-five, he'd been an officer for nineteen years. One more year and he could collect his pension. He received a number of commendations and a distinguished service medal. He had a family. His son was a firefighter. His daughter, Greta, was in grad school. Winnie had met his wife. A lovely woman and a schoolteacher. Winnie never saw any indication that Duvall was corrupt. Police work was hard enough without this crap, she thought. Tomorrow is tomorrow. She skipped dinner, had a glass of Zinfandel and went to bed.

"Yes?" Elvira Atkins said through the screen door.

"Elvira? I'm Juanell Dodson, Cherise's husband."

She looked him up and down. "You are?" she said.

"Yes, ma'am, I am," Dodson said. "I'm actually here on behalf of Reverend Arnall."

"You are?" she said, squinting at him. Elvira was a foul-tempered prune of a woman of indeterminate shape wearing a sweater that went down to her thighs. "There's something familiar about you," she said. "Well, come on in." The living room was just like Dodson's auntie May's house. Dark furniture, plastic covers on the lamps, lots of knickknacks and framed photographs. There was a crucifix on the wall bigger than Dodson's five-year-old son. "Please, take a seat," Elvira said. "May I get you something to drink?"

"No, thank you."

"You say you're here on behalf of the Reverend?"

"Yes, I am. He's very concerned about your feud with—"

"The heifer?" Elvira interjected.

"Mrs. Yakashima, yes, her," Dodson said.

Elvira eyed him carefully. "I know you from someplace."

"Well, I've been to church a few times."

"What does the good Reverend want me to do?" Elvira said.

"He wants you to reconcile with—"

"The heifer," Elvira said. She sucked her teeth. "Come with me, there's something I have to show you."

Walking behind a shuffling senior citizen took patience. They went through the kitchen door and into the backyard. There was a small green lawn but something had dug holes in it. Gophers maybe? thought Dodson. Off to the right was an oblong patch of dirt about thirty feet long. All the plants were decimated, nothing there now but stems, leaves, dried-up flower petals and more holes.

"The heifer keeps rabbits," Elvira said disgustedly. "Look what they did. I wish't I'd been here but it was the middle of the night. I still have Earl's deer rifle in the hallway closet. I would have mowed 'em down and put 'em in a rabbit casserole." Elvira harrumphed. "How can the Reverend possibly expect me to reconcile with that, that—"

"Heifer?" Dodson said.

"You said it, not me." A black-and-white cat sauntered by, a mouse clutched in its jaws. "Don't bring that filthy thing inside," Elvira said.

"Is that Johnny Mathis?" Dodson said.

"Yes. He's my favorite singer. I listen to 'Chances Are' every night before I go to sleep." Elvira giggled. "I've been training Johnny to do his business at the heifer's house."

"You see, Elvira, this is the kind of thing that makes the situation worse, and that's what the Reverend doesn't want," Dodson said. Elvira was staring at him with a mixture of shock and recognition.

"Ma'am?" Dodson said.

"It's you! You the one sold me shares in that Ponzi scheme!"

"Uh, well, you might be wrong about that," Dodson mumbled. "I don't remember participating in a—what'd you call it?"

"Where the hell's my deer rifle?" she cried. She turned and charged inside. Dodson almost followed her in but the thought of an angry old lady with a thirty-ought-six made him change his mind. He ran around the house to his car. Just as he keyed the ignition, BOOM! A blast from somewhere inside.

"Lord have mercy," Dodson said as he hit the gas.

"So you go over there to make peace and Elvira fires a rifle into her ceiling?" Cherise said.

"That's what happened," Dodson said.

"How is that a reconciliation?"

"It's not." He didn't want to tell Cherise that Elvira was a victim of his Ponzi scheme. That was over ten years ago. No need to dig that up.

"Is it true Elvira was a victim of your Ponzi scheme?" Cherise said. Word about the incident got home before you did, thought Dodson.

"Afraid she was—but this is what I was trying to tell you," he said, exasperated. "I'm not the one who should be doing this."

"You told Reverend Arnall you would try."

"I *did* try!"

"And the net result is three hundred dollars' worth of damage to Elvira's ceiling, which we have to pay for," Cherise said.

"So what am I supposed to do?"

"Fix it!"

Dodson sat down at the breakfast table and sighed. "Is there any coffee?" he said. Cherise looked at him, seeming to soften. She sat next to him and kissed his cheek.

"I know I'm hard on you and I'm sorry about that," Cherise said. "It's just that I worry about you. I want you to succeed, I want you to have purpose. I love you, my husband. I want to be proud of you." That hurt, thought Dodson, and he realized that for all his swagger, all his charm, all his animal intelligence, he wasn't good for anything except cleaning Deronda's food trucks at minimum wage.

* * *

The cement floor was making Grace's tailbone ache. "Jessica really likes Willie Nelson," she said, listening to the awful guitar solo.

"She doesn't," Skip said. "Somebody must be up there. Didn't you hear the bell?"

Somebody like who? Grace thought. The cops? Isaiah? She felt a badly needed spark of hope. Skip was holding his head, the giant bump had become two, the rest of him a mass of bruises and abrasions. A cast-iron frying pan is a lethal weapon. Grace sat opposite him cross-legged. She felt no pity, no sympathy, only anger and hate.

"Would you really have killed me?" she said.

"Oh Jesus, are we back to that again? How 'bout leaving me alone? I'm really fucked up here, okay?"

"I'm curious," Grace went on. "Do you feel bad about the people you've murdered?" Skip groaned, maybe in pain, maybe in irritation.

"Not really."

"So the man you killed with a bear trap. That was nothing to you?"

"It wasn't nothing. It was a job."

"A job like what? Fixing the lawn mower? Selling refrigerators?"

"Yeah, like that, okay? Will you shut up now? I got other things on my mind, like a bullet hole in my leg."

"What about the victims' families?" Grace said. "Wives and kids, mothers and fathers. Do you feel anything about them?"

"I don't even know them, okay? Why would I feel anything?" Grace knew she should stop. They needed each other to get out of this mess. But this sociopathic asshole slaughtered people without guilt or remorse or anything. To him, it was a job. A fucking job.

"Tell me something, Skippy," she went on. "How were you gonna do it? Stab me? Hit me with a rock? Throw me off a cliff?"

"I'm warning you, bitch," Skip said. "Keep it up and see what happens."

Grace huffed. "What are you gonna do? Kill me?"

"If I wasn't hurt—"

"You'd kill me!" Grace laughed. "That's your answer for everything, Skip. You live in a bubble. The only people you know are other shit-scum like you. They never tell you what a sick fuck you are. That's why you'll always be alone and unless you get another dog, no one will ever love you."

"Oh man," Skip said, glaring through bloodshot eyes, drool and blood dripping out of his mouth. "Are you ever gonna be sorry."

"Mission accomplished, asshole. I've never been sorrier than I am right now." Grace shook her head. "It's bizarre. You can't kill me but your crazy mother will." She was angry at Isaiah too. This was what she was afraid of. His world swallowing her up and cutting her to pieces. To have never loved at all would be better than this, she mused. Locked in a basement with a man who wanted to exterminate you while his lunatic mother plotted to get money the asshole didn't have. She'd been drugged, bound, thrown in a trunk, held captive in a suffocating motel, ate Snickers bars for dinner and was terrified every single moment. No. No more. She loved Isaiah, but if she ever got out of this alive, she'd leave him flat.

Willie Nelson finally stopped singing and they heard clomping footsteps. Jessica was at the basement door. "If you're anywhere near the stairs I'll shoot you." She peeked in, the silencer protruding. She opened the door, stood on the landing and shouted.

"That was the police, Magnus, the goddamn *police*! I told you this would happen, you dumb shit! I should have turned you in!" Skip said nothing and neither did Grace. "I must have brain damage," Jessica went on. "This is what happens when I listen to you. You were always a lying little weasel and you're a lying little weasel now." The words were getting to Skip. Head bowed, face blank, staring at the floor, a penitent listening to his sins. Jessica heaped it on. "You know I almost got an abortion but I didn't. Worst mistake I ever made. You wrecked my marriage, you wrecked any chance I had to live a decent life. I should have given you away or thrown you off a bridge. I should have—"

"Jessica, I don't think this is helping," Grace said. "Wasn't there something else you wanted to say?" Jessica calmed herself and sucked in a deep breath.

"I want to make a deal, Magnus," she said. That didn't sound right, thought Grace. What kind of deal was there to make? "Are you gonna tell me where the rest of the money is? Yes or no," Jessica said.

"I don't have it," Skip said. Jessica came down the stairs about halfway. She's really wound up, Grace thought; eyes wide open, sweat on her forehead. She was holding the gun down and tight against her side, almost like she was hiding it. She's not angry, Grace thought, she's scared. Why would Jessica be scared? Why did she come down the stairs? They could hear her just fine.

"So what's this deal?" Skip said.

"Stand up and get into the light where I can see you," Jessica said.

"I can't. I'm beat to fuck."

Grace gasped. She knew what was happening.

"Jess, don't—"

Jessica raised the gun and shot Skip in the leg. He screamed and fell to the floor. He held his calf, writhing, bleeding, grunting with pain. The gun with the silencer made no more noise than clapping your hands.

"I can't believe you did that," Grace said.

"You're lucky I don't shoot you," Jessica retorted. "Magnus, you have from now until you bleed to death to tell me where that goddamn money is." She went back up the stairs and slammed the door behind her.

"Help me," Skip moaned. Grace looked at him a moment. Why not let him die? she thought. She'd be saving lives, including her own. She watched him a few more moments and knew she couldn't let him bleed to death. She found some old sheets and tore them into rags.

"Lie still. We've gotta get your pants off."

"I don't want to," Skip said.

"I have to put a tourniquet on or you'll bleed out." He lay flat on his back and she pulled his jeans off. Skip was hairier than a fox terrier. The wound was small, surprising for the amount of blood. The bullet had gone straight through his calf. She wrapped the tourniquet around his leg just below his knee.

Skip hollered. "Ohhhh SHIT it hurts!"

"Skip, I can't stop the bleeding. You've got to get Jessica down here, or you're going to die."

"Okay, okay," he said. "I know what to do, but we need something."

"Tell me."

CHAPTER NINE
No Nookie for You

Grace was hiding. She couldn't believe she was cooperating with her executioner. Her view was narrow, she could barely see him. He was sitting against the washing machine, blood pooling around his leg.

"Jessica! Jessica!" Skip hollered. "Okay, you win! I'll tell you! Just call a fucking ambulance!"

The basement door opened. Jessica must have been waiting right outside. Grace heard her coming down a few steps, her weight making the boards creak.

"Where's Grace?" she said.

"I... don't know. She's... afraid... you'll shoot her," Skip said, each word an effort.

"Yeah, I just might. Now where's the fucking money and don't give me the runaround."

"The money is..." Skip's voice trailed off into a groan, he dropped his chin to his chest.

"What'd you say? I didn't hear you," Jessica said impatiently. Grace was tensed, knees bent, ready to move. *Come down, Jessica, come down the stairs.* Skip groaned and mumbled something inaudible.

"What? Goddammit, Skip, speak up!" Jessica said. She came down a few steps. *Not enough, keep coming.*

"I'm bleeding, I'm blacking out," Skip said, rocking back and forth.

"If you black out, I'll kick you to death," Jessica said. "Where's the damn money?"

Skip said something low and garbled. Jessica cursed and began to come down. Grace stepped out from under the stairs and jammed the pipe between Jessica's ankles. She yelped and pitched forward, the heavy mass of her tumbling down and landing on the cement right in front of Skip. She grunted and lay still, blood leaking from her ear.

"Oh God. Did I kill her?" Grace said. She looked at Skip. He was grinning through his pain. He had the gun now.

"Ironic, isn't it?" he said. "This?"

A few minutes later, Skip was sitting on the toilet lid, stretched back, grimacing, his leg out, the pistol with the silencer held against his chest. He was groaning and sweating, his face distorted. Grace washed the wound with hydrogen peroxide, put a QuikClot gauze pad on the entry wound and wrapped a self-adhesive bandage around it, all at his direction. Skip had been shot before. He bought the first aid supplies and left them here. He kept his escape kit in the hallway closet. Fake ID, stolen credit cards, a real passport, some cash, and a couple of guns.

The bathroom door was closed. Skip told Grace to put the hamper in front of it. By the time she pushed it aside and opened the door she'd be shot in the back.

"Glad it was a twenty-two," Skip said. "Anything else would have cut my leg in half. Check the medicine cabinet, see if Jessica's got any painkillers." Grace opened the cabinet.

"Well, you've got a choice. Tylenol or OxyContin."

"What...do...you think?" Skip replied, squeezing out the words between his teeth.

She gave him the pill container. He looked at the label. "Fifteen milligrams every twelve hours. Not to be broken, chewed or crushed."

"Do you think fifteen is enough?" Grace said.

"No, but if I take two I'll go to sleep," he said accusingly. "Give me water." She brought him water in Jessica's toothbrush cup. Their heavy breathing and the closed window made the atmosphere warm and humid. "Get in the bathtub and sit down," Skip said. Grace obeyed. She put her arms around her knees and her forehead against them.

"Is this ever going to end?"

Skip felt the same way. He was never this low. He hurt everywhere, he was shot and bleeding, the cops were after him and the FBI might be looking for him too. He'd have to leave the state, find a place to stay, get healthy again. He looked at Grace, hunched in the bathtub. The things she said pissed him off, enraged him. He was reluctant to shoot her but there were no qualms now. Fire through the shower curtain and you'd only see the blood splatter. Skip suppressed the urge. He needed her.

"Shit," he said to no one. He'd done a lot of stupid things but never this stupid. Why did he go to all this trouble to get back at Isaiah? he thought. The asshole made you feel bad and sent you to the joint but the past was the past. Why didn't you go about your business? Why didn't you use your stash money to rehab Blue Hill instead of fucking around with this? He was stupid to send those photos to Isaiah. Some police detective was looking them over right now.

Skip always realized his mistakes after he'd made them, the consequences piling up like the bills Jessica didn't pay. Jimmy Bonifant told him, "Everything you do, you have to think about the unintended consequences. Say you rob somebody and you've got a lot of cash. You think, Okay, I'll buy my girlfriend a new car. So, fine. You buy it, she's happy, you think that was a good thing to do, right? But then your next robbery goes bad and you're broke. Well, now it's her birthday—"

"Jimmy, could you hurry this up?" Skip had said.

"Like I said, now it's her birthday. You have to get her something. Do you think she's gonna be happy with a new doormat or a pair of thong panties with your name on 'em? No, she's not. She's pissed off, and you know what happens next?"

"Jimmy, I get it."

"No nookie for you," Jimmy continued. "She closes up shop, so what do you do? You get a little something on the side and you think, Okay, this will hold me over. But then what happens? Your girlfriend catches you in bed with the little something, shoots you and now you're dead."

It was kind of funny then, but not anymore. If Skip was arrested for kidnapping he'd get twenty-five to life, locked in a cage with a bunch of animals who either wanted to fuck you or kill you. You have to keep fighting, he told himself. Back down and you'll never get up again. What he needed now was money. If he was going on the run, his five plus Isaiah's thirteen wouldn't last long.

"What are we doing, Skip?" Grace said, lifting her head off her knees.

"One more time," Skip growled. "Shut up!" He tried to sit up, grunting, the pain piercing and terrible. He leaned back, put his wounded leg on the edge of the tub and rested. He got out his phone.

CHAPTER TEN
Infinite Sadness

Skip hasn't called back," Isaiah said to Dodson. "He might have already killed Grace."

They were on the back patio of the animal shelter, Isaiah pacing back and forth.

"I don't think so," Dodson said. "He gets nothing out of it. He ain't gonna turn down cash."

"No, no, you're right," Isaiah said, hoping that was true.

"I have something for you." Dodson brought an actual picnic basket. He put it on the table and opened it. There were plastic containers of different sizes. He opened them, revealing barbecued ribs, corn bread, coleslaw, peach cobbler and a large Mason jar of lemonade.

"Oh man," Isaiah said, eating with his eyes. Food was the only thing that muzzled the anxiety.

"TK did the ribs," Dodson said. "Gloria and Cherise did the rest. Check this out." There were also a tablecloth, silverware, cloth napkins and wineglasses. "This was my touch," Dodson said. "I find they make a meal much more pleasant, don't you think?"

Dodson made a big deal of setting the table, spreading out the cloth, carefully placing the silverware, plates and glasses in what Isaiah assumed were their proper places. "Don't forget, Your Highness," Dodson said with a bow. "We out huntin' foxes today." Dodson gestured at the plastic chair with a flourish. Isaiah sat, smiling, shaking his head. Dodson stayed standing and served the food. "I hope everything is to your liking, sire. If it ain't, I'll go in the kitchen and torture the cook." He glanced at a parrot.

"Don't say anything," Isaiah warned him. "Sit down, will you?" Dodson poured lemonade and they raised their glasses for a toast.

"To your health," he said.

"To my health," Isaiah said.

They ate without talking, only the satisfying sounds of two men eating delicious home cooking, ice tinkling in the lemonade glasses. Isaiah glanced at Dodson. He was a short man, belying a large stature, as lean and cut as he was in high school. His white T-shirt never had a stain on it. His hair was slicked back, the same hairstyle he'd worn all his life. Some people walk into a room and convey interest or fear or nothing at all. Juanell Dodson, ex-con, ex-criminal, ex-hustler, emanated confidence in that old-school way. Like, you better stand up to scrutiny, son. Mr. Dodson is in the house. He was featherweight champ at Vacaville correctional facility for men, he loved his family and was as loyal as a lion to its cubs. Remarkable to have a friend like that, Isaiah thought. You're lucky. You really are. Isaiah's phone buzzed. He looked at the number and nodded at Dodson. He put it on speakerphone. "Hello?"

"It's me, Q Fuck," Skip said. He sounded stressed, like he was breathing through his teeth, like he was in pain. "Thirteen won't do it. I need fifty."

"Skip, I don't have it," Isaiah said. "I told you, I had to borrow—"

There were scuffling sounds and then BLAM BLAM BLAM! Gunshots, bullets whanging into metal, the sound echoing, Grace screaming.

"Stop, Skip! Stop!" Isaiah shouted.

"When you've got the fifty call me," Skip said. "You have forty-eight hours. After that—" The call ended. Isaiah was stunned, horrified. The screaming. Grace was *screaming*. Dodson was in the same state.

"I don't have fifty," Isaiah said. "I can't get fifty."

Dodson threw his napkin on the table. "Don't even worry about it, Q. I'll see you later." He left and Isaiah was alone, Grace's voice still oscillating the air; a single keening note, high, piercing and unbearable. He put his hands over his ears but it didn't stop.

Skip's wound bled through the bandage. He needed antibiotics. He needed a tetanus shot. He locked Grace in the basement with Jessica and drove to an urgent care facility. The nurse took a look at his leg and he was taken right in. A Pakistani doctor did an X-ray, cleaned the wound, dressed it and gave him a shot. He said Skip was fortunate. "You barely avoided major surgery," he said. The doctor doled out some pain pills, only a few. Skip said nothing about the Oxy.

"You have no ID and this is a gunshot wound," said the doctor. "I suppose you are aware I have to call the police."

"Uh-huh," Skip said. Then he got up, hobbled past the doctor and was gone.

Grace sat on the basement floor, looking at Jessica. The woman was lying facedown, cheek smushed into the cement, an ugly bump on her head. She probably has a concussion, thought Grace.

Grace took a Red Cross first aid class at the community center. Many people believe you should keep a concussion patient from sleeping for twenty-four hours. Wrong, said the nurse. The best thing a patient can do is rest. Grace checked Jessica over. She was breathing okay, she wasn't bleeding anymore, her heartbeat was slow but not too slow. Occasionally, she sighed or groaned. Best to leave her be.

Grace thought things couldn't get worse but here she was, locked in a basement again with a woman who wanted her dead and might be dying, waiting for Skip to come back and kill her. What if Skip didn't return? Unless Grace turned to cannibalism, she really would starve to death. Jessica moaned. She opened her eyes.

"Water," she rasped.

"We're out," Grace said. "We'll have to wait for Skip."

"I'm going to shoot that son of a bitch."

"I'll load the gun."

"And then I'm going to shoot you," Jessica said. She started moving, getting her arms underneath her, trying to sit up. "Aren't you gonna help me?"

"Didn't you just say you're going to shoot me?" Grace said. "Get up yourself." Groaning and grumbling, Jessica sat up in herks and jerks. It took her a while. Dirt was embedded in her cheek, her hair matted with blood.

"Oh God, my head hurts. You could have killed me, you know." The comment didn't warrant a response. They sat in silence for a while.

"You knew Skip was a hired killer, didn't you?" Grace said.

"Not exactly," Jessica muttered.

"Stop bullshitting. You knew." Grace despised this woman, who would have killed her son and Grace as well.

"So what? So what if I knew?" Jessica said.

"You knew Skip was murdering people and didn't say anything? Pretty coldhearted, Jess."

Jessica seemed to rise off the floor. "You think I'm like this *on purpose*?" she said angrily. "You don't know what I've been through! You don't know my life. You think there was a fork in the road and a sign that said turn left and be a good person, turn right and be an asshole? It doesn't happen that way, you pampered little shit!" Jess was sobbing now. "I was born into a shitty life with shitty parents and shitty friends and that was all I knew. You grow up like that and you don't make things happen, things happen to you!"

"There were choices," Grace said.

"Choices?" Jessica scoffed. "Yeah, sure there were. Like, do this or go hungry. Do that or get your ass beat. Do this or go to jail! Have you ever felt that way, princess? Like anytime you did something your goddamn *life* was at stake? Shit, I'm thirsty." Jessica used her sleeve to wipe the snot and sweat off her face.

No, Grace thought. She struggled, but nothing like that. Drowning in your own life and all you could do was hope and even that was evaporating. In another circumstance, Grace might have felt sorry for her.

"You want to know my biggest ambition?" Jessica continued. "One more day. That's all. Please God, let me sit here and watch TV and drink tequila until I'm blotto. It's my dream come true!" Jessica groaned and held her head. "Oh shit that hurts! I'm getting dizzy."

The lock rattled, the basement door opened. Skip appeared. He looked worse than before, the swelling and bruising on his face were blooming. His pant leg was cut off, his calf heavily bandaged.

"Are you gonna leave me down here?" Jess shouted. "I'm gonna die!"

"She really might, Skip," Grace said.

"Yeah, yeah, I know. Let's go," he said. Grace went up the stairs. Mother and son exchanged a look Grace never saw before. Hate, heartbreak and infinite sadness all in one.

"Get out of here, you fuck," Jessica said.

CHAPTER ELEVEN
I'd Rather Share My Left Lung

They left. Jessica was alone, her head hurt worse than before. She tried to stand but she was overwhelmed with vertigo and puked in the corner. Skip left the basement door open. If she could only get up the stairs. She struggled to her feet, rested and staggered forward, using the washing machine, the wall, a stack of boxes and a water heater for support. By the time she reached the stairs, the basement was whirling around her and the pain was worse. She hung on to the railing so she wouldn't fall down.

She looked up at the basement door. It was so far away, like the fucking moon or Australia. "You're a tough old bitch, Jess," she said to herself. "You can do it." She put her foot on the first step, began putting her weight down but her vision wobbled and her knees buckled and she clung to the railing. She let herself down as easily as she could and sat. Her breathing was gritty and slow, her head was an exploding minefield. She wanted to sleep. She glanced up the stairs again, the open door calling to her. *I'll never make it,* she thought.

It was the morning after Skip demanded a $50,000 ransom. Dodson made calls and the group met at his apartment. TK, Gloria,

Harry Halderman and Verna. Cherise with a pad and pen. Gloria was going through her contact list. "I'll take Addison Wong, Mr. Moreno, Laurie Blake and Reverend Arnall," she said.

"I got Bart Dillard, Donald Erwin and Charles Ford," TK said. "Bart might be dead, I'll have to check that out."

"I'll start with Mrs. Abbas, Gemi Lantos and Celia my sister," Verna said. "I have regulars at the coffee shop. I'm sure they'll donate."

"I'll talk to Carter Simpson, the cop," Dodson said. "If it wasn't for Isaiah he'd be homeless and beggin' for spare change. I'll hit him up good. And Tudor, the mortgage broker."

"He's rich but he's a penny-pincher," said Gloria.

"I'll talk to him," Dodson said, as if that explained everything.

"I'm adding Willie Chiles, Mary Reynolds, Ira Smith and Don Kim to the list," Cherise said.

"That's not very many people," Gloria said.

"We just getting started," Dodson said.

The group fanned out over the neighborhood, knocking on doors and collecting donations from a growing list of people who knew and admired Isaiah. Practically everyone had heard about the kidnapping and some knew Grace from the food truck. Most folks went directly into their handbags, wallets and cookie jars, giving whatever they could. There were larger donations but mostly it was small bills and paper bags full of change. At the Coffee Cup, Verna solicited her customers. She went from one to the other, saying, "Your coffee will taste better if you give." Her tone suggesting it might taste worse if you didn't do so.

Bart Dillard wasn't dead. He was still top chef at Meaty Meat Burger. He gave Dodson everything in the cash register, $176. Carter Simpson, the cop, gave $1,500. He took money from his daughter's college fund. Isaiah saved him from a family catastrophe. People who weren't Isaiah's clients donated because they knew he served the community. Reverend Arnall's congregation pooled their money and gave $900. Craig Sanchez sold preowned luxury cars. Isaiah had recovered a vintage Corvette worth six figures. Sanchez chipped in two grand. Mo the wino was going to buy a bottle of Mogen David Concord but sacrificed the $3 for Isaiah. TK called Dodson.

"We'll never get to fifty thousand," TK said. "If things keep going like this the most we can do is around twenty."

Gloria was fearful of getting robbed. Many of her former students were grown now. Some held grudges, remembering the long hours in detention and notes home to their parents. Cherise volunteered Dodson as Gloria's bodyguard. "For lack of better alternatives," Gloria said. They called on her friends. Louise Sadiwhite, Denise Walker and Barnell Green, none could give more than a few dollars.

"I hear the Reverend sent you to settle the dispute between Elvira and Mrs. Yakashima," Gloria said. She chuckled. "Leave it to you to do something that ends in a fistfight and gunshots."

"I was trying to make them—" Dodson began.

"All you do is try, Juanell," Gloria interjected. "Doesn't that tell you something about yourself?"

"Like what?"

"Like maybe you should stop embarrassing Cherise and make some other woman unhappy."

"You goin' too far, Gloria. Me and Cherise—"

"It's Cherise *and I,*" Gloria retorted. "How are you ever going to get someplace if you can't speak proper English?"

"It *is* proper, depending on where you at," Dodson replied.

"May I give you some advice?" Gloria said.

"No you may not."

"You should start at the beginning. They have remedial classes for adults with learning disabilities."

"I don't have a disability," Dodson said.

"What would you call your personality? If that's not a disability my name is Martin Luther King."

"He would have liked you," Dodson said. "You could have marched with him and scared away the rednecks."

Otis J. Tudor's office was on Atlantic Boulevard. Nice place on the second floor of the Bank of America building. Dodson and Gloria waited ten minutes in the reception area. The receptionist was a bright young woman named Regina. "He'll be right with you, Mr. Dodson," she said with a prim smile. "He's on a conference call."

"Is he? Or is he making us wait just to make us wait?" Dodson said. Regina lowered her eyes.

"It will only be a few minutes."

When Dodson and Gloria were finally admitted, they found Tudor sitting behind a glass desk the size of a Ping-Pong table, leaning back in a throne chair covered in leopard skin. Tudor wore a shiny blue suit, a big gold chain, tinted aviators and tan alligator loafers.

"Hello, Juanell, hello, Gloria," he said, sounding a little like James Earl Jones. "It's a pleasure to see you again. How is the lovely Cherise?"

"She could be better," Gloria said with a glance at Dodson.

"You heard about Grace?" Dodson interjected.

"Yes I have. How unfortunate," Tudor said. "It's a damn shame is what it is. Isaiah must be devastated. I've known him for years. A fine young man. He's helped hundreds of people."

"Including you," Dodson said. Tudor cleared his throat, suggesting he'd like to change the subject. "Isaiah's in trouble and he needs money," Dodson said.

"May I ask for what?" Tudor said.

"To pay a ransom for Grace."

"I see. I didn't have any idea things were this serious," Tudor said, frowning and rubbing his chin. He told Regina to bring in a checkbook and he wrote out a check. He folded it in half and handed it to Dodson. "I hope that helps."

Dodson unfolded the check and looked at it. "A hundred dollars?" he said, incredulous.

"Yes. What's wrong?"

"That pen in your pocket is worth more than a hundred," Gloria said.

"Considerably more than that but I don't know what that has to do with it," Tudor said indignantly. "Try to understand, I am not prepared to give money to everyone who asks for it. Now, I'm sorry but that's the best I can do. If you'll excuse me, I have a meeting."

They left the office.

"Well, that was fruitless," Gloria said. "I told you he was a penny-pincher."

Dodson took Gloria to Tudor's house, an authentic Mediterranean villa except for the aluminum windows, the Astroturf lawn and a statue of Tudor's half-naked wife, Anita. She was a tall, statuesque woman who carried herself like Cleopatra, if Cleopatra wore a full-length silk dashiki, hair in elaborate blond curls, jewelry that jangled and aquamarine daggers instead of fingernails.

"Isaiah's in serious trouble," Dodson said. "He needs money." He explained the situation about Grace and the ransom, Anita listening carefully, a growing dismay on her face.

"Oh my God, I didn't know things were that bad. Have you asked Tudor?"

"Yeah, we did. He gave us a hundred dollars."

Anita was appalled. "I don't believe you." Years ago, Isaiah saved

Anita's teenage daughter from running off with a drug dealer. Now she called Tudor, yelled at him for ten minutes and wrote out a check for $5,000. Instead of acknowledging Dodson's success, Gloria grumbled,

"Leave it to the women. They have all the power."

They went to see Mark Hebner, CEO of Assured Insurance Services. They rode up in the elevator. "This is an important man," Gloria said. "Let me speak to him. You'll be offensive."

"Sometimes you need to be offensive," Dodson said.

"All the time?" she replied. Hebner's office was lavish, befitting a CEO.

"I'm sorry about Grace but Isaiah did us a service and he was paid accordingly," Hebner said. He brushed some imaginary lint off his expensive lapel.

"We're not here to argue the payment. We're asking for a donation," Gloria said.

"No, we're here to renegotiate," Dodson said.

"Renegotiate the fee? I'm afraid we can't do that," Hebner said.

"He recovered two hundred thousand dollars' worth of bling and you paid him fifteen hundred dollars," Dodson said.

"That was the deal."

"Isaiah ain't no businessman and he doesn't care about money. He took your first offer, didn't he?"

"That's not Mr. Hebner's fault," said Gloria. "Let's talk about a donation."

"Lou Raines is your client, isn't he?" Dodson said, ignoring her. "Has that big company, armored cars for banks and such? Bet he's got a lot of insurance."

"Yes, he does," Hebner said. "Lou is one of our premier clients."

"He's one of Isaiah's clients too. Isaiah saved his father from going to jail. I talked to him this morning," Dodson said. "Too bad if he canceled his policies." Dodson and the CEO locked eyes.

"Will five thousand do it?" Hebner said.

"Make it twenty."

Dodson and Gloria rode down in the elevator.

"How do you know Lou Raines?" Gloria asked.

"I never met him but I knew he was Isaiah's client."

"Did Isaiah save his father?"

"No. Lou's father is dead," Dodson said.

"Does everything you do involve coercion?"

"No, sometimes I cheat at cards."

Winnie received an email from Isaiah. He reported finding an abandoned motel where Grace was held captive. Skip was alerted and escaped. Grace's condition was unknown. Winnie and Duvall drove back to San Bernardino. They examined the motel room as well as the room where Skip had stayed. They found nothing useful but she was obliged to call in a forensics team. They took pictures and gathered fibers, fingerprints and DNA samples, useful if the case went to trial but nothing to help them now. Isaiah's lack of cooperation peeved her.

"If Isaiah had involved the department, we could have cordoned off the area and Grace would be safe by now," Winnie said. "I don't understand. If Isaiah is so smart, why doesn't he realize this?"

"Hero complex," Duvall said. "He's gonna get his girlfriend killed." There was burrito debris on Duvall's shirt but he didn't seem to notice. They drove back to Long Beach, Winnie full of worry and dread. Should she confront him about the missing bundle of cash? Maybe let it go and hope it doesn't happen again. Maybe not.

Juanell Dodson had a record of youthful offenses under the general heading of street hustling. He'd been clean for years but his employment record was a blank page. Winnie and Duvall knocked on the door. To their surprise, Dodson welcomed them in, saying his wife was at work and they should be quiet. Their son, Micah, was asleep in the other room. The apartment was modest but well-kept and furnished with care. Dodson was unfazed by the appearance of two detectives. He was calm—no, that's not the word, Winnie thought. Cool was more accurate. Confident, laid-back, even a little amused. They sat at the breakfast table. He said it was easier to talk there than in the living room. He was right. The kitchen was a friendly place, associated with family, food and warm conversation. Duvall took the lead.

"We're trying to locate your friend Isaiah Quintabe," he said. "He has firsthand knowledge about the abduction and we'd like to talk to him."

"He'll talk to you when he thinks it's right," Dodson said.

"The police can help him," Duvall said. "We deal with kidnapping all the time. We've got a lot of experience locating suspects and we know how to deal with violent offenders."

"So does Isaiah."

"Can you tell me where he is?"

"Yes, but I'm not going to," Dodson replied. "Isaiah is my friend, my homeboy. We've been through a lot of shit together and there's no chance I'll give him up." Dodson wasn't hostile or belligerent. He was stating the facts.

"Will he talk to us on the phone?" Winnie asked.

"If he wants to talk, he'll call you," Dodson said.

"You could be endangering Grace's life," Duvall said.

"Naw, you can't pin that on me," Dodson said with a wave of his hand. "If anybody's endangering anybody it's Skip. Do you know Isaiah's rep?"

"I know what I've read in the media," Winnie said.

"Isaiah is not a vigilante out there with his ego calling the shots. He cogitates, sees all the angles and figures out new ones. He is so outside the box he doesn't know there is one and his mind is quicker than a Sugar Ray jab. He'll find Grace before you do."

"I doubt that," Winnie said.

"Do you? Let's make a bet."

"You know I can't do that."

"Let's make it hypothetical. If you win, I'll give you a nickel. If I win, you give me a nickel."

"Hypothetically," she said.

"My money's on Quintabe," Duvall said.

"My mother-in-law is the Wicked Witch of East Long Beach but she's a mean cook," Dodson said. "May I interest you in the best cookies you've ever had in your life?"

"No, I'm afraid we can't," Winnie said.

"Sure we can. I could use a little pick-me-up," Duvall said. "And you happen to be wrong, Hand Job. Accepting cookies is fine if it promotes good relations with the community. Would you happen to have any milk, Mr. Dodson?"

They sat in the kitchen, eating soft, chewy molasses cookies with glasses of cold milk. Winnie couldn't resist. Dodson regaled them with stories about Isaiah. His many rescues, escapes, chases, puzzles solved, the numerous criminals he'd brought to justice and the lives he'd saved. Isaiah caught his brother's murderer, busted two serial killers, outwitted mercenaries, brought down the biggest illegal gun-smuggling ring on the West Coast, sent the leader of a Chinese triad to prison for forty years and broke up a white nationalist gang.

"Thank you, Mr. Dodson. It's been enlightening," Winnie said.

"I've never had a pleasant conversation with a police officer before," Dodson said. "Cherise should have been here to see this. Drop by anytime."

Winnie was impressed by Isaiah's exploits but there were still questions. How could any private citizen be that good? And if he was that good, why wasn't he a cop or an FBI agent or working for a big security firm? What was he doing running around freelancing and getting paid with tuna casseroles?

Winnie and Duvall went back to the car. She got behind the wheel and sat there.

"What?" Duvall said.

"I'm not looking forward to this conversation," she said, looking him in the eye.

"Whatever it is, I'm not either."

"Archie, the drug dealer? I saw seven bundles of cash in the bedroom," Winnie said. "I called for a CSI to bag it up. I left and passed you in the hallway. You said Archie might have a machine gun, remember?"

"Yeah, I remember."

"When I went back to the bedroom, there were only six bundles. No one mentioned a machine gun to me and there's nothing in Archie's record to suggest he was into illegal arms. Do you know anything about the missing money?"

Duvall looked at her sharply. "You think I stole it?"

"I'm asking if you know anything about it."

Duvall was instantaneously angry, almost like he was waiting for it. "Here's my answer," he said. "No, I don't know anything about it and if you tell anyone that I do? Your name will be shit anywhere you go."

"It's very close to that now," Winnie said. "Look, Duvall, I'm talking to you, not the lieutenant. Doesn't that tell you something? I know we don't get along but if it's nothing, it's nothing."

"Piss off, Winnie. I know what you think of me but that doesn't mean you know me. If I go down the toilet so do you."

She was truly taken aback. "Is that a threat?"

"Fuck yeah, it's a threat. Except for my wife and kids, the job is everything to me. Take that away and—" He finished the sentence with a look so heated it was a wonder she didn't melt. "I'll get back myself." He got out of the car, slammed the door and walked away.

Winnie started the engine and stared through the windshield. Well done, Winnifred. You made a dubious accusation with nothing to back it up. What did she make of Duvall's reaction? Lots of people believed anger implied guilt, but that wasn't necessarily true. If you're wrongly accused, *of course* you get angry because it's unjust and it could pose a threat to your person and livelihood. There was also the belief that a calm response was more indicative of innocence but that too was misleading. The tobacco CEOs testifying before Congress declared nicotine didn't cause cancer and the Exxon execs denied climate change, each and every one of them lying through their stock options with a straight face. Winnie needed more information.

CHAPTER TWELVE
Calmate, Mamá

Isaiah's friends met again that evening. They'd collected nearly $30,000, plus Isaiah's $13,000 made it $43,000 and the group made up the rest. Dodson called Isaiah and told him to come over.

"What's it about?" he said.

"Don't argue, just come over, aight?"

Isaiah arrived, tentative, wary. He didn't like the secrecy. His friends were gathered around the dining table. "Hello," he said. "Do you need me for something?" It took him a moment to realize what he was looking at. Stacks of cash, bound with rubber bands.

"Each one of those is a thousand dollars," Gloria said proudly. "It's easier to count them that way." An ache settled in Isaiah's chest, an empty well of needs now filling to the brim; all the years he spent alone and lonely, a recluse who left the house only to serve his clients, now reckoning with a love he never imagined. He felt unworthy.

"Where did it come from?" he said.

"It's from the people who love and appreciate you," Cherise said. "Who are grateful for the things you've done and your devotion to the neighborhood." You could see Isaiah shrinking into himself, as if the limelight might hurt or open a trapdoor.

Almost inaudibly, he said, "It's not that big a deal."

"Not a big deal?" Cherise retorted. "I don't know if you realize how you've affected folks around here. The hood is not an easy place to live. Most people have to struggle every day. To have someone who offers a hand when no one else will, that's something precious. To be admired and celebrated." The others smiled and mumbled their agreement. Isaiah always questioned whether he'd chosen the right path. Maybe he should have found a more conventional career. Maybe his capabilities were destined for higher ground. But as he looked around at his friends' beaming faces, he knew there was no higher ground. He was right where he should be.

"Thank you," he said. He bit his lip, his eyes glassy.

"We have to go," Dodson said. The money was quickly gathered and put in a backpack before any more could be said. Isaiah and Dodson rode down in the elevator, Isaiah grateful without the words to express it. If they'd stayed two more seconds, he would have broken down in tears. Something he hated doing. Yes, he thought, having a friend like Dodson was lucky indeed.

Winnie and Duvall canvassed Isaiah's friends again. Deronda Simmons, Verna Little who ran the Coffee Cup, Thomas Kahill, otherwise known as TK, owner-operator of a wrecking yard, TK's unpleasant lady love Gloria Johnson, and Gloria's daughter, Cherise, Juanell Dodson's wife. All claimed to be ignorant of Isaiah's whereabouts and all were believable. Winnie and Duvall called on Harry Halderman, supervisor at the animal shelter, reportedly Isaiah's longtime friend.

Halderman was a recalcitrant hard-ass. He insisted on talking while he fed the dogs, which was something like conversing with a fan during a FIFA playoff game.

"I don't know where Isaiah is and if I did, I wouldn't tell you," said Halderman.

"Why?" Duvall shouted over the barking. "He knows more about Grace's disappearance than anyone. We want to talk to him, not arrest him."

"The police can lie all they want and nobody can do diddly about it," Harry retorted.

"Mr. Halderman. Believe me, we're not lying," Duvall replied.

"Could you not eat that in here?" Harry said. "It makes the dogs crazy." Harry kneeled beside a kennel, a terrier mix in there yapping wildly. "Want to adopt a dog?"

"Mr. Halderman," Winnie said, "surely skepticism is not your only reason for obstructing the investigation," the word "obstructing" an implied threat. "We'll catch up with him sooner or later."

"I don't think so," Harry retorted. "Isaiah's smarter than you."

Duvall smiled.

"You hear that, Detective?"

They went back to the car. Duvall couldn't hide his glee.

"Lots of people are smarter than I am," Winnie said defensively. "It's not important."

"It is to you," he said. His smirk turned hostile and angry.

"What's the matter?" Winnie said.

"Don't fuck with me, Winnie."

"Don't fu—what are you saying, Duvall?"

"I'm saying don't fuck with me."

"We had a conversation, okay?" Winnie said. "It's over and done. Get over it, will you, please?"

"Oh, I'm over it," Duvall replied. "But you aren't. I know you.

You have to know everything and you won't quit until you do." She looked at him, his bloodshot eyes, his jowly face, worry and alarm coming out of every pore.

"I can't deal with this," she said. "I'll get back myself." She got out of the car, slammed the door and walked away. Duvall was right. She really did have to know everything and she wouldn't give up until she did.

Harry Halderman held out his forearm and the parrot hopped on. Isaiah followed him into the office. Harry set the bird on its perch and said, "Leave him outside and the raccoons might get him. That detective got nothing from me. College girl, snooty too. You could just tell."

"Thanks, Harry."

"I'm sorry you have to stay here. I'd have you over to my place but my wife's sister, Lulu, is staying with us. Her screws aren't loose. There never were any in the first place. Lulu's the only person I've ever met who never shuts her mouth. My God, you wish she'd inhale a dragonfly or choke on her tonsils but yap-yap-yap, on and on she goes, and it's all nonsense, crazy talk. Did I know Ronald and Nancy Reagan weren't really married? Did I know Vienna sausage and peanut butter made a great sandwich? Did I know she used to be a stripper and called herself the One and Only Miss Bustier? You know what she wanted me to do? Look at the rash in her armpit. I told her I'd only do that if she were a fruit bat or an orangutan."

"Something I've always wanted to ask you, Harry," Isaiah said.

"What's that?"

"Why are you such a grouch? It's like you're annoyed with the whole human race."

"I am and that's a good way to put it," Harry declared. "I don't have to tell you how perfidious, stupid and deceitful people are, and how they want to settle everything with a gun or a grenade or a heat-seeking missile."

"No, I guess you don't," Isaiah said.

"Give me a life among animals anytime," Harry said. "Animals are honest. Lions and tigers and bears don't lie to you, steal your wallet or drive while they're drunk or tell you a worthless stock will make you a fortune. You know what they are and what they do and all you have to do is leave 'em alone. Animals are smarter too. Did you know an iguana can detect the temperature of the sand within two degrees? And listen to this. There's a kind of frog that only lives in the north of Alaska. It survives the winter by freezing. Its heart stops beating, respiration ceases. When the weather gets better, the frog thaws out and a day later, it's normal. You know anybody that can do that?"

"No, I don't," Isaiah said. They went past the kennels, the dogs like prisoners, barking, howling, snarling, through the chain link, or withdrawn into a corner, too frightened or depressed to participate. Many were pit bulls. Some of the dogs attacked humans but it wasn't their fault, Harry said. They were left alone and tied to a tree all day or starved or beaten. "Do that to a human and he'll be one mean son of a bitch."

They stopped at a kennel. Staring at them intently was a large German shepherd. His coat was shiny black, his ears up, he was obviously well cared for. He wasn't making a sound, his gaze unrelenting, like he was waiting for a wrong move.

"What's up with him?" Isaiah said.

"A beauty, isn't he?" Harry said. "The Secret Service uses them to patrol the White House. See how he's not barking? These dogs are trained to watch, assess and attack when there's a threat. Raise a gun and he'll tear your goddamn arm off."

"What's he doing here?"

"The dog was part of a commando unit. His handler died and

for some reason, no one wants to adopt a military-grade, highly trained attack animal."

They reached the birdcages. A parakeet, baby crows, a hummingbird nest, the hatchlings no bigger than bumblebees. Harry fed them sugar water with an eyedropper. "I had a reindeer in here once, a refugee from a petting zoo," Harry went on. "When food gets scarce a reindeer can stretch its vision into ultraviolet so the lichen they eat glows purple. I've got a boa constrictor over there. Lady said she bought it for her son as a pet. She turned it in when she saw it swallowing a puppy. The snake's got a forked tongue. Each tip swirls, creates a funnel of air. The ends of the tips are collecting smells. Snake pulls its tongue in, touches a sensory organ on its soft palate and tastes the air. It's better than a second pair of eyes. Hell, I don't prefer animals. I'd like to *be* an animal." Isaiah had never seen Harry smile. It wasn't pretty, more like a very wrinkled baby eating a lime.

The police kept their mounted unit here. Four brown horses with black manes. "Originally, they used draft horses for this kind of work. They're steady and reliable but too big for long city rides," explained Harry. "They were crossed with a smaller horse and now they're ideal." Harry fed them oats and stroked their necks.

"They're trained to ignore every natural instinct. Not to run, jump or kick or react to loud noises; they'll walk through water without knowing the depth, and they'll step over logs, garbage and parking cones without knowing what they are. Would you do that? And have you seen them do a moving wall? Sidestepping against a crowd of morons and nutjobs, waving signs and hollering slogans? I wish I had half their patience."

"You'd need more than that," Isaiah said.

"That's what my wife says."

While Harry stood by, Isaiah used a pitchfork to pry apart a bale of alfalfa. He put armfuls in the horses' stalls and changed out their water buckets.

"You haven't mentioned Grace," Harry said. "I take it things aren't going well."

"No, they're not," Isaiah said. "I don't know, Harry. I've been making mistakes, bad mistakes. Grace would be home by now if I hadn't screwed up." Isaiah stopped and leaned on the pitchfork. "I have to push harder, I have to be smarter. I keep thinking, what's happening to Grace? What if I don't get her back. What if she's—"

"Okay, okay, I get the picture," Harry said impatiently. "First of all, you've already made the mistakes, so why are you going on about that now? What's happening to Grace? What kind of question is that? Hell's bells, Isaiah, you can do that from here till Christmas and you'll be wrong every time. Nobody can say what's going to happen or what's happening now. Let me ask you a question."

"Okay."

"Did you ever have a case where you were backed into a corner, attacked from all sides and the only way out was another corner?"

"That's happened, yeah," Isaiah said.

"Did you get out of the corner? Did you solve the case?"

"Yes, I did."

"Have you done that more than once?"

"Many times."

"Between then and now, have you somehow lost your instincts?" Harry said. "Your street smarts, your abilities?"

"No, I'm the same."

"Don't you see?" Harry said irritably. "You don't have to push harder and you don't need to be smarter. You're telling yourself you can't do it unless you're more than you are right now. Believe me, Isaiah. Everything you need you already have. Just do what you do and get all that other nonsense out of your head. Do you understand?"

"Yes, Harry, I do."

Isaiah was lying on a cot in the storeroom, pondering Harry's words not long after he'd left. The old man was right. His skills and the acumen were intact. He was still IQ. He lay there thinking about Grace. How she saved his life. A white nationalist gang, the Starks, were holding him in their clubhouse. There was zero chance Grace could free him. The house was well guarded, armed men and women inside and out. But Grace reasoned that if she couldn't get in, she'd get them to leave.

The gang's boss was Angus Byrne, a major West Coast arms dealer robbed of a Gatling gun worth seven figures. Grace talked to Angus, convincing him the weapon was stolen by a rival gang, and she gave him the location. Angus's goons rushed off en masse, leaving a skeleton crew behind. Grace conned them into believing she was Angus's daughter. They let her inside their clubhouse but she was found out and beaten, distracting them long enough for Isaiah to escape. Grace hadn't mentioned it since then, like it was assumed she'd risk her life for him. If it were Dodson, he'd hold it over Isaiah's head and extract favors until the end of time.

It was late. Isaiah was trying to sleep. Everything quiet, save for the occasional bark, meow and peep. Intermittently, the parrot would screech "NEVERMORE!" Loud, even though the bird was in Harry's office. Isaiah hated the parrot and he hated Edgar Allan Poe. Harry said the African gray was caged by itself for a long time. The bird came to him weak, feathers missing, tucked into itself, watery green droppings. He kept it in the office to maintain a constant temperature. He gave it antiviral medication and made its food. Pellets ground up fine and mixed with mashed ripe bananas, sweet potatoes and boiled carrots. He fed the bird with a syringe. When it was healthy again, Harry kept it on a perch on the patio. Isaiah asked why it didn't escape. Harry said the bird was lonely and he'd become the bird's flock. He said it expressed its affection by regurgitating food.

"I wish it'd send me a card," Harry said.

"Will it ever fly away?" Isaiah asked.

"Maybe. And if it does, I wish it well." Freedom versus safety, everybody's choice, thought Isaiah. The bird screamed "NEVER-MORE!" again. There was zero chance Isaiah could sleep. He got up, went down the hall and turned the corner into reception. The bird was on its perch, pacing nervously back and forth, moving its head in a figure eight.

"Could you please shut up?" Isaiah said in a reasonable tone of voice. And the bird screeched back, "SHUT UP! SHUT UP! SHUT UP!" Isaiah returned to the storeroom and lay down on the cot. He gave up on sleeping.

He wondered why Skip didn't get back to him. The thought made his pulse speed up. It shouldn't be taking this long. Maybe he should call Skip and make a suggestion. No, Skip would think he was setting up a trap. Maybe Skip couldn't make the exchange because Grace was dead. Isaiah's heart accelerated, thumped against his chest, the acid heat of bile rising in his throat. *Don't go there, Isaiah.* But he couldn't help it. Loving someone was terrifying. Loving someone was like basking in the sun with a cold beer while an enormous killer tornado bore down on you, blowing your house away, sending shrapnel screaming past your head. Isaiah had experienced emotional pain before but the thought of Grace's death was near death itself. He knew it was the wrong thing to do but he grabbed his phone and called Skip. It rang and rang. *Where the hell are you, Skip?* Voice mail. Isaiah froze a moment, not knowing what to say.

"Um, let's get this done, Skip." And he ended the call. He kicked himself. He sounded scared, like he was losing it, and in fact he was.

Early morning. Dodson went to meet Reverend Arnall. He wondered if Grace and Isaiah would finally get together and be like normal people, like him and Cherise. The idea bothered him. Was that what they were? Normal people? Cherise maybe. She was normal in a good way. Dodson was trying to be, but the thought chafed his ego. It was like throwing in the towel, like saying your days of independence and free choice were over. You were officially fenced in by convention and adulthood. Yes, you made your own decisions but they weren't on your own behalf. You made them to benefit others, to make things go smoothly, to avoid trouble, to meet responsibilities and a list of other boring-ass things.

That was why he resented his mission to end the granny feud. It was imposed on him. He liked helping people, he truly did, but this was Cherise's idea, not his. Now he was compelled to speak to the Reverend, a hard man to talk to because he knew his place in the world; where he stood and what his mission was. That kind of clarity was intimidating. Here you were, your situation tenuous at best, talking to a man who knew the path of righteousness and had an absolute lock on what was good and what was bad. If you weren't in his camp you weren't necessarily bad but a watery form of good, and even then, it wasn't all the time. Supposedly, God would forgive you for doing things like letting Elvira and Mrs. Yakashima fight, but Cherise wouldn't. When she chastised him for the third time, he came back with "The Bible says blessed are the merciful, for they shall receive mercy." And she replied,

"What does it say about the stupid?" Harsh, but she was angry and embarrassed. The church was important to her and here was her husband, the alleged fixer, sticking his hand in the nest and stirring up the hornets. Cherise might have been kinder but his sloth had been going on for years. She wanted him to make her proud and that hadn't happened in a long time. He was afraid of losing her. Why be with a man who refused to get a job?

The Reverend's greeting wasn't quite as warm as their previous meeting. He'd no doubt heard about Dodson's failure and what form it took.

"Well, I can't say I'm not disappointed, although I don't know what I expected you to do," the Reverend said.

"Some things can't be fixed," Dodson said.

"Perhaps. But at this point I'm more worried about myself than I am the two ladies. I'm Solomon about to cut that baby in half with a hacksaw. Maybe I should abolish the choir."

"I asked Mrs. Yakashima if she'd share the position," Dodson said. "She sent me an email just this morning. It said, 'I'd rather share my left lung.'"

"I suppose you want to lay this burden down," the Reverend said.

"I'm afraid I do."

"That's fine. It was Mission Impossible in the first place."

"It wasn't Cherise's fault. She wants me to be—"

"A grown-up?" the Reverend said. "A productive member of the community and so forth."

"Yeah. Something like that."

"I'm curious, Juanell," the Reverend said. "You are intelligent, able and ambitious, I would think, but you haven't made any progress or none that I can see."

"I haven't found my place," Dodson said.

The Reverend smiled and put his warm hand on Dodson's shoulder. "You haven't asked for help." Dodson left. He'd done what he could but felt bad anyway. More than anything, he wished he'd come through for Cherise.

Manzo was in the Caprice having his usual morning latte. In the coffee shop, he felt like people were watching him, looking at him with pity. He couldn't believe everything was turning to shit. He'd struggled so hard to have power, to be leader, to see his ideas become real. Now he was afraid of having a cup of coffee in public.

Manzo grew up with his family in Mexico City. His father was an administrator at the Tecnologico de Tijuana. He took occasional bribes from the cartels like everybody else, granting admission to undeserving sons, daughters and nephews and handing out undeserved academic achievement awards. Manzo's family wasn't wealthy but they lived comfortably. When his father, a heavy smoker, died of COPD, he left his widow and two kids with almost nothing. The rest of the family was in Culiacán and they had their own problems.

When Manzo was a freshman in high school, his cousin Julio got him a job packaging cocaine for shipment across the border. A kilo of coke was vacuum-packed in plastic. A crisscross of tape around it to hold the shape. The package was wrapped with four layers of plastic wrap, then painted with diesel fuel, then wrapped three more times in plastic, seven wraps the minimum. Then another coating of diesel fuel. The boss said the fuel molecules kept the drug dogs from detecting the cocaine. Manzo would discover that was hit-or-miss. The boy recruited his mother as a drug mule. She was afraid but there was hardly enough money to buy food.

Sixty kilos were packed in the false floor of a car. The license number was on record as having crossed the border a number of times without a stop. Manzo took care of everything. He made sure they all had ID and the trunk held suitcases, enough clothes and things for a week. He wore new jeans and sneakers from Walmart and so did his little brother, Duarte. His mother was dressed nice and wore perfume. There was a three-hour wait at the Tijuana border crossing. A dozen lines of cars backed up for a mile. As their line got shorter, Manzo could feel himself tensing up, his mouth was dry. He was in the backseat. His little brother, Duarte, was sleeping. His mother was rigid, squeezing the steering wheel, knuckles white, neck muscles tight, breathing in short huffs. Manzo leaned forward, put his hand on her shoulder and said, "Calmate, Mamá."

"¡No puedo, no puedo!" she said. She was doing just what border agents look for. He thought a moment and told her what to do. As they approached the booth, Manzo jabbed the sleeping Duarte in the ribs. The kid woke up and started crying but Manzo kept poking him. His mother caught on instantly. She reached back and slapped at them, yelling at them in Spanish, telling them to stop or they would go back home. When she pulled up beside the agent, Manzo could see her face in the mirror. She looked pissed off and frustrated but not fearful. The agent asked her where they were going. She said San Diego while she continued slapping at the kids. The agent glanced in the car, glanced at Manzo, still teasing his brother, and let them pass. When they were on the freeway, his mother smiled at him in the mirror and said, "Eres un chico muy listo, Manzo."

They dropped the drugs off at an address in Pacoima. His mother was paid $5,000. The man said he would stay in touch, there were more jobs for her. Then they drove to East Long Beach, where his mother's sister lived. She never went back to Mexico and never carried drugs again.

Manzo hung out with Julio. He was a Loco and Manzo became a Loco too. His initiation was a beatdown in McClarin Park, a cluster of homies punching and kicking him until they fractured a rib and dislocated his jaw.

Manzo was a foot soldier, rising quickly in the gang's hierarchy. He had good ideas, they said. He was smart. A cool dude, even for a youngsta, they said. Manzo was quiet, no braggadocio, spoke when there was something to say. He thought things through, pictured things before they happened, but he wasn't a bookworm or a pussy. He was down for his brothers, his barrio. He went on drive-bys, beatdowns, robberies. He shot Armando Torres for cheating him on a drug deal. He fought in backyard fight clubs and knocked some chollos out.

Manzo had good relations with gun dealers, Sinaloa liked him and he was one of the first to deal fentanyl. He went to San Quentin for involuntary manslaughter. He was sentenced to forty-eight months and served thirty-two. The Locos were a La Eme affiliate. The higher-ups ordered him to kill a dropout, not allowed under the gang's rules. Manzo stabbed the man three times with a shank made from a mop handle, split in half, cut into six-inch pieces and sharpened on the cement. The guy didn't die but was never seen on the yard again. La Eme got on Manzo's case for not finishing the job but he wasn't punished.

When he got out, he returned to the Locos. It was around then that Frankie "the Stone" Montez stepped down from his leadership role, and Manzo was the natural choice. There was no discussion. He was Khan and that was it.

Manzo finished his latte and threw the cup out of the window. He was pathetic and it scared him. More than being shot or stabbed or going to prison. You were alone, no one there to reflect back who you were or where you belonged. Lose your cred and it was almost impossible to get it back. He knew he had to fight for it, do something people noticed, something that shocked them, something to remind them he was still Manzo Maximo Gutierrez, fearless leader of the Locos. He had to do something violent.

Manzo started the car and let it idle. He sat there for a long time, the big V8 burbling low. He'd installed a Magnaflow performance exhaust. He loved the way it sounded when he stomped on the gas, hearing the revs, throaty as they sang higher with every shift. You could tell he was coming without even seeing the car. An idea was forming. Manzo nodded to himself. He drew in a long breath and let it out slow. Maybe he couldn't find Isaiah—but he could find Dodson.

CHAPTER THIRTEEN
Aren't You Happy?

Isaiah waited all day on the patio. There was nothing to do but sit around and wait for Skip's call. He couldn't unclench his jaw or his fists. He couldn't take a long breath. He couldn't stop the horrifying images in his head or quell his roiling insides. The tension was stultifying. He wondered if he would react differently without the PTSD.

It was always there, lurking just around the corner, ready to attack if Isaiah let down his guard. The parrot seemed to sense the mood; no shrieks, no pacing, squatting on its perch and picking at its feathers. Dodson joined Isaiah in the evening. He brought two beers and drank one.

"I don't understand why Skip hasn't called unless he's—" Isaiah began.

"Isaiah, I said it five times already," Dodson said, cutting him off. "Change the channel, will you please? You making us both crazy."

Isaiah's phone buzzed, and he jumped. "Skip?" he said. He listened for a moment and disconnected. He picked up the backpack, the fifty thousand in there.

"I have to do this by myself."

"That makes no sense," Dodson replied. "Skip's got a gun and you've got nothing but your personality and that's always been a handicap. I'll hide in the backseat."

"No. At some point, Skip's going to make me switch cars," Isaiah said. "A taxi, an Uber, a bicycle, whatever."

"What if I'm way behind you, like a mile or so?" Dodson argued. "Wherever you are, I can be there in a minute."

"It's too risky. Skip will be watching for trail cars," Isaiah said.

"I'll only come if you call."

"I don't want to argue about it." Isaiah left the office and hurried to the parking lot, Dodson behind him, doing something with his phone. Isaiah got in and started the engine. Dodson knocked on the passenger window and Isaiah rolled it down.

"What if you get hurt? What if Grace gets hurt?" Dodson said. "Maybe something will happen your freakishly large brain can't predict."

"I'm not letting you get involved," Isaiah insisted. "You have a family, Dodson. I have to go."

"Isaiah, come on, man," Dodson said. For some reason he thought of Reverend Arnall gripping his shoulder. "You need somebody to watch your back."

Dodson's head and shoulders were in the car. He was groping around, trying to find the door lock. Isaiah rolled up the window and Dodson retreated a step. Isaiah put the car in gear and drove away, Dodson in the rearview mirror, hands on his hips, looking at the ground.

Skip and Grace left Jessica in the basement and went out to Skip's car. An old Nissan something, a two-door.

"Get in the back, sit on the passenger side," he said. She opened the door, folded the front seat forward and got in. She wondered why he didn't seat her in the front. He made her zip-tie her left wrist to a headrest support, her hand nearly behind her head, elbow pointed at the ceiling.

"This hurts, Skip."

"Hurry up, I'm in no mood to fuck around!" Skip shouted. "Pull it tighter—no, tighter!"

"It *hurts,* Skip!"

"Yeah? Well. I really don't give a shit."

He opened the trunk. A big plastic storage box held a hunting knife, a folding knife, an ice pick, brass knuckles, throwing stars, a collapsible fighting stick, duct tape and a large binocular case. He grabbed the binoculars and got in the driver's seat. He'd thought a lot about how to make the exchange. He'd studied Google Maps and Google Earth. He'd driven to the locations he'd been thinking about. He'd left a shopping bag under a bus bench.

"What's that all about?" Grace asked. He didn't answer. He needed a vantage point. A place to watch Isaiah approach long before he arrived. He was raised in San Bernardino. He knew the area well. Nogales Hill. Just like all the other hills except it overlooked the highway. From there, you could see the oncoming traffic, the Alton Road off-ramp, and the intersection where Alton met Dunhill. There was a 360-degree view of the sky. Better to see choppers. He called Isaiah. "Where are you?"

"On the Ten, just passing Whitmore."

"What are you driving?"

"It's a Kia, an old one. Small, silver, four doors, front right fender is bashed in."

"Anybody in the car with you?" Skip asked.

"No, no one. You can have the money, Skip. I have it, fifty thousand dollars in used bills. All I want is a clean deal. I give you the money, you give me Grace. No cops, no other players, no trail cars, nothing."

"Stay on the line." Skip set up the tripod. The binocs were Nikon 12x50s, good enough to see a deer across the Grand Canyon. There was almost no traffic, only the occasional car or truck. "Good," he murmured. He carefully scanned for helicopters. They were equipped with navigation lights, red on the right, green on the left. That way you could tell if it was flying at you or away. He left Grace in the car. It was parked off the road in a gulley. She couldn't see anyone and no one could see her.

Skip's leg throbbed, the OxyContin wearing off. The sweat stung his eyes. He was a tough son of a bitch and he'd never met a situation he couldn't handle. Even in the joint, he fought off guys with forty pounds on him. The fights got so bloody there was no point going on. He drew in a quick breath—there was the car! Small, silver, with a bashed-in fender. He watched, his phone held to his mouth. "Get in the left lane," he said. Isaiah swerved from the middle to the left lane. Skip waited until the car was approaching the Alton exit. "Take the Alton exit. *Right now!*" he barked. Isaiah turned sharply, tires screeching, the back end of the car swinging out, swerving over three lanes to the exit.

"Turn right at the light," Skip said. "Stop and get out of the car." Isaiah obeyed. "Take your keys and throw them in the bushes. Okay, now take off your shirt and your cap. Okay, put your hands up and turn in a circle. Pull your cuffs up over your ankles." Isaiah did as he was told. He was wearing earbuds with a mike. "Where's the money?" Skip said.

"In a backpack. It's on the passenger seat."

"Put your shirt on, the backpack too. Walk north on Dunhill to the Shell station. Keep the line open." Isaiah put on his gear and walked off. Skip stayed, waited, binoculars scanning the highway and the sky. He would have stayed longer but his leg was killing him. He got in the car, looked at Grace.

"Well, that was your boyfriend," he said. "Aren't you happy?"

"I'll be happy when I get the fuck away from you."

Isaiah headed toward the Shell station, nothing around him but darkness. Skip had seen him coming, he thought, maybe from that hill overlooking the Alton Road off-ramp. That was well behind him now. If Skip wanted to track him, he'd have to move fast, on foot and through the brush. Unlikely. The killer probably jumped ahead, circling around to the gas station. Skip would pick him up or provide some other kind of transportation. He wouldn't risk an Uber. The driver might see something. Out here, it was probably the bus.

He kept going but his train of thought was drifting. It puzzled him, nothing would come, and he realized his pace was slowing, his legs heavy and tired. He was sweating, the night breeze felt arctic, the dark an endless hallway. The pressure was too much. The PTSD was returning and the thought made him panic. He stopped and closed his eyes. The crickets were shrill and too loud. He stood there for a long minute, trying to breathe, his heart pounding a hole in his chest. He heard Dodson so clearly it was like they were side by side. *You the only one that can save her and if you cry like a pussy and let that happen, you'll hate yourself and so will I.*

"The fuck are you doing?" Isaiah said aloud. He broke into a run.

Skip drove to his next vantage point, a rise overlooking the Shell station. He scanned the area and the sky with the Nikons. Isaiah should arrive in about fifteen minutes. He was early, of course. From this distance he was only a small, dark figure with the gas station behind him.

"Isaiah," Grace whispered. There was a bus stop in front of the station.

"See the bus stop?" Skip said into his phone. "Sit down on the bench." Isaiah did so.

"I'm sitting down," he said. Skip knew there might be a GPS device hidden in the backpack. It wouldn't be attached to the money itself. It might fall off or be noticed.

"Underneath the bench. There's a shopping bag," Skip said. "Take the money out of the backpack and put it in the bag. Do it fast. I'm watching. You screw around and Grace will pay." Isaiah quickly transferred the money. According to the bus schedule, the bus should arrive in less than five minutes. "Take the next bus," Skip said. Isaiah boarded and the bus left. Skip waited, no one tailed the bus. There was nothing in the sky. He raced ahead of the bus to the next location.

The location was a soccer field on Twenty-Second Street; unlit, skirted by eucalyptus trees, the surrounding streets lined with low-rise buildings and warehouses. They were closed at this hour, no one around. Skip circled the field to the opposite side of Twenty-Third Street and parked. You couldn't see the car from the field. It was eerily quiet, the only light from the surrounding buildings. Grace understood why Skip put her in the backseat. When he left the car, she couldn't turn on the headlights or the radio or beep the horn. Skip adjusted the mirror so he could see her at a glance.

"Please, Skip. Do the deal straight, okay?" she pleaded. "If Isaiah said he has the money, he has the money. He won't try anything."

"Wait, wait. What's that you said?" Skip said, putting a hand to his ear. "'Do the deal straight'? I can't believe it. You mean a shit-scum like me? I don't know, Grace. I'm a sick fuck, just like you said. No telling what I'll do."

"I'm sorry I said that, but I—"

"Shut up, okay? Just shut the fuck up!" he roared, nearly lifting out of his seat.

He raised his hand to hit her but she was too far away. She shouldn't have said anything. She provoked him, a stupid, stupid thing to do. Skip was breathing hard, beads of sweat winking in the minimal light, his mouth was parched, he kept smacking his lips. He glanced at her in the mirror. His eyes looked blacked out as if they'd been torn from their sockets. He bared his teeth. You could feel the heat of his hatred. That was when she knew. *He'll kill Isaiah, and then he'll kill you.* She started to say something but held back. Begging for Isaiah's life would do no good, she realized. It would only serve to egg Skip on, increase his pleasure and sense of power.

"You're going to kill Isaiah anyway, aren't you? Even if he has the money," she said. "And then you're going to kill me too."

"Yeah, I am," Skip said. He sounded sad, regretful. Not about the killings, she thought. About his life. How he lived and what it had come to.

"Skip, that's a double murder," Grace said. "A million cops will be looking for you."

"They're looking for me already but I've got a plan. First I'm gonna burn through the money and then I'm gonna kill myself." He said it matter-of-factly, like the decision was final. "Might as well, right? I mean, why should I stay around? The world will do fine without me." Right, Grace thought.

Isaiah would be here soon. Grace's only opportunity to save him was the time between Skip leaving the car and reaching the killing ground. Somewhere during that interval, she was going to escape. The zip tie was cutting off her circulation, her hand was tingling, her shoulder sore from the awkward sitting position. The area was deserted. Isaiah wouldn't hear her scream from inside the car and the engine would be off. She couldn't roll down the window.

"Should be here about now," Skip said, glancing at his watch. He texted something. They waited. Through the trees, they could see across the dark field to Twenty-Second Street and the bus stop. *Think, Grace. Be Isaiah. How would he get out of here?* The bus arrived, air brakes wheezing, the doors unbuckling. The bus drove on and there was Isaiah. From this distance, he looked pixelated. Grace leaned forward. There was her savior, her affliction. Skip turned in his seat and took a picture of her with his phone, the flash making her blink.

"What's that for?" she said.

Isaiah stood at the edge of the soccer field. Skip can watch you, see that you're alone, he thought. Skip spoke through the earbuds. "Walk down the middle of the field." Isaiah walked, dry grass crunching under his feet, a vague breeze cooling the sweat on his face. There was nothing ahead of him but a long stretch of darkness, the silhouettes of shaggy trees on the far side. That's where he is, Isaiah thought. His car is somewhere close. Grace is somewhere close.

Isaiah knew there was a good chance Skip would kill them both. He held on to a tiny hope that the killer's common sense would kick in. A kidnapping charge was one thing. First-degree double murder was another. His other option was slim to not possible. Disarming Skip and taking him down. Dodson was right. He knew it was a trap and he was walking right into it. There were no other pedestrians around the park, only the occasional car passing on Twenty-Second.

Isaiah's heart pulsed blood in surges, its beat a gong in his ears. He smeared the sweat out of his eyes. *Keep it together or Grace will die.* He was halfway across the field. He stopped.

"What are you doing?" Skip said. "Keep walking."

"I need to see Grace," Isaiah said. "Proof of life." A few seconds later, his phone pinged. A text with a photo of Grace. She was in the backseat of a car, her wrist behind her head. She was haggard and drawn and frightened. The photo was time-stamped seven minutes ago. Skip was cunning and he knew his business. Isaiah kept walking.

Skip was gone. Grace's left wrist was zip-tied around one of the headrest supports. She swiveled to her left and tucked her knee under, turning until she faced the headrest, her left arm crossed in front of her. The zip tie was unbreakable. Then it struck her. She almost laughed. She could take the headrest off!

"Grace, you're a genius," she said. Her left hand was useless, the zip tie held it too close to the support. Everything had to be done with her right hand. She gripped the headrest, pressing the release button and lifting with all her strength. She barely moved it, if it moved at all. There was no leverage. It was like lifting a ten-pound beer mug with your arm straight out. She shook the headrest hard and tried again. It moved half an inch and no more. It was an old car, there was probably rust and corrosion in there. It was hot and close, the windows were shut. Grace was soaked with sweat. She hurried. She shook the headrest violently and lifted, straining, grunting at the effort, the muscles in her arm and shoulder burning. She did it again. She was frantic. She had to warn Isaiah. She did it again.

Skip was kneeling half hidden behind the tree, watching Isaiah coming across the dark field, his silhouette backlit by the light at the bus stop. Sometimes Skip memorized lines of dialogue from movies and said them in the mirror. Like Sonny Corleone saying, "What do you think this is, the army? Where you shoot 'em from a mile away? You've gotta get up close like this and—bada BING! You blow their brains out!" Joe Pesci saying, "You said I'm funny. How the fuck am I funny? What the fuck is so funny about me?

Tell me, tell me what's funny!" And Ray Liotta shitting bricks. He remembered Isaiah ridiculing him, his lies, his loneliness.

Do all the members of your gun club sit in that one chair? Do they all drink Red Bull? Do all their burgers fit on that one hibachi? Where do they eat them? On the picnic table you don't have? It's just you, Skip. Lying on that couch at night reading to the puppies. The last part really got to him, because that was what he did at Blue Hill night after night. He read articles from dog magazines to the sleeping puppies. Because there was no one else to read to. Because there was no one else for anything.

People were always talking about love. It seemed like everybody was either in love, wanted love, lost their love or would never love again. Sometimes it bothered him, all this bullshit about something no one could put their finger on. He liked Grace but did he love her? She was so prickly and weird. Maybe that was it. When you loved somebody you put up with that shit. Nah, that couldn't be right. If he lived with Grace one of them would be dead by now. Jessica loved that ox, Ludvig. Jesus. If making a complete idiot of yourself was love he'd pass. Maybe other people didn't know either. Maybe they just did what they did and called it love.

Suddenly, Skip was very tired. He wanted to lie down and sleep. He wanted to light up. He wanted to leave. Like, really leave. He was an adrenaline junkie, maybe jump off a cliff. You could watch the ground rushing up at you and feel the wind roaring in your face and listen to yourself screaming and hear your own bones breaking. Isaiah was thirty yards away. Skip perked up. He breathed slow and deep. He was calm. Killing people was his profession.

Grace's shoulder and arm muscles were in cinders, she tore something in her elbow. She kept it up. Shake the headrest, lift it. Shake the headrest. Lift it. How deep was the support embedded, she wondered. Four inches? Five? She rested a few moments, shook the headrest and—it wobbled! She was almost there. The adrenaline gave her strength. She lifted and wobbled again and again—and the whole headrest came off! She slid the zip tie off the support rod. She was free. *Hurry, Grace, hurry!* She was clambering into the front seat when someone broke the window, shattered glass flying at her. Grace fell back into the seat.

Leaves shushed in the night breeze. Isaiah neared the end of the field. He saw something shift between two trees. "Keep coming," Skip said. "That's far enough. Turn off your phone and toss it. Now take off the backpack and drop it on the ground."

Isaiah obeyed.

Skip didn't appear, he materialized; Colonel Kurtz rising in the shadows of the dark hut. Skip's head was misshapen, his features distorted. He was grimacing, his voice tight, breathing quick. He'd been injured. He had a limp. He was holding a gun with a silencer, aiming at the ground in between them.

"Hello, Q Fuck," he said, enough contempt, hatred and violence in those three words to poison everyone in the neighborhood. In that moment, Isaiah knew. He wasn't leaving here alive and neither was Grace. There was a card to play but everything had to unfold just right. Skip used the dim glow of his phone to look him over. "Open the backpack and let me see the money," he said. Isaiah leaned over and opened the bag, angling it toward Skip so he could see inside. "Okay, close it up and toss it over here—slowly." Isaiah stood up and tossed the bag. *Get him closer, Isaiah. You have to get him closer.* There was silence, as if Skip was loading up the words to say. When they came, they were from somewhere bottomless, putrid and lethal.

"You fucked up my life, you fucked up everything!" Skip shouted. "You killed my dogs, you killed my Goliath!" He was crying, pinpoints of light reflecting off his tears. "I've got nothing! NOTHING!" He aimed the gun at Isaiah. "Got anything else to say before you die? Huh? Anything about the hibachi? About the picnic table? Anything more about the *puppies*?" Isaiah said nothing. Skip advanced a step. *Come on, Skip, get closer.*

"Get down on your knees," Skip said. Isaiah didn't move. "I said, get down on your fucking knees!" *Hold your ground, Isaiah.* Skip came closer, snarling from deep in his throat, the gun straight out in front of him. "I SAID GET ON YOUR FUCKING KNEES!" *Hold your ground, Isaiah.* Skip kept coming, his body shaking, he was an arm's length away. You could see his finger about to squeeze.

"Okay! Okay!" Isaiah said, holding up his hands. He bent his knees and started to lower himself. *Now, Isaiah. Do it now!* He grabbed the brim of the sap cap and brought it down on Skip's gun hand with an audible *thwack*! Skip howled but didn't drop the gun. Isaiah turned to run but his foot slipped on the damp grass. He went down.

Skip stood over him, a looming shadow against the dark sky. He aimed the gun.

"That's it, Q Fuck. You're done."

They heard a car bumping over a curb, scraping the undercarriage, horn honking, headlights bouncing wildly. Skip turned to look. The car was on the field roaring straight toward them. Isaiah rolled, got up and darted off. Skip fired in his direction, swiveled and fired at the car. The headlights blinded him, the engine loud as a hurricane. He ran. The car sped past him, skidded, made a crazy U-turn that churned up earth. Skip disappeared into the darkness.

"Grace!" Isaiah shouted. He ran through the trees and saw Skip's car parked a half block away. He raced toward it, arms pumping, nearly skimming over the blacktop. The passenger-side window was smashed. He skittered to a stop beside the car and looked in. It was empty. "Grace?" he said, as if the word might make her appear. He popped the trunk. No Grace.

"What—" he began. He turned in a circle, no one was around. The street was deserted. In the quiet, he heard a car, the exhaust note loud, the engine revving higher as it shifted gears, the sound fading as it got farther away. He'd heard that car before. The Caprice . . . Manzo . . .

Dodson drove Isaiah back to his car. The backpack was in the trunk.

"How'd you find me?" Isaiah said.

"At the animal shelter, when I was leanin' in your car? I dropped my phone in there. It's got a tracking app. I followed you on my laptop."

"Thanks," Isaiah said. "How did Manzo get onto us?"

"I think he tailed me," Dodson said regretfully. "He saw some action on the field, circled the block and found Grace. I'm sorry, Isaiah, I truly fucked up."

"Better Manzo than Skip," Isaiah said. "At least Manzo isn't crazy."

Winnie finally got the call from Isaiah.

"Ten minutes ago, Skip Hanson was in San Bernardino, on a soccer field," he said. "It's on Crescent between Twenty-Second and Twenty-Third Street. He's on foot, injured and he's armed." He told her what happened and how Manzo Gutierrez had taken Grace.

"This is what happens when you meddle, Mr. Quintabe," Winnie said angrily. "If the police were there, Skip Hanson would be in custody by now."

"No, Skip took precautions," Isaiah said. "He would have made you and gotten away. Either that, or he'd have shot Grace. You don't know him like I do—no, don't say anything. You haven't seen him in action. You don't know about all the unreported murders he's committed, or understand the lengths he'll go to get what he wants."

"Yes, but—" Winnie began.

"We're at cross purposes," Isaiah said. "You want to catch Skip but all I care about is finding Grace."

"I don't understand your point. Aren't they one and the same?"

"No, they're not," Isaiah replied. "Suppose you do catch Skip. Do you think he's going to tell you where he's hidden Grace? He'll never do that—and what if Grace is alone and locked up somewhere? She'll starve to death or die of exposure. I'll let Skip go free to get her back. You'll arrest him and he'll go to prison for a hundred years rather than let me off the hook. Are you going to call San Bernardino PD or will I?"

"I'll call them now," Winnie said, "but we have to talk."

"I don't have time to talk," Isaiah said. "You'll haul me down to the station, interview me, have me write out a statement, make me wait a couple of hours and take me into custody for interfering with an investigation." True enough, thought Winnie. It was a legal method of getting him out of the way.

"First of all, the police aren't as incpt as you seem to think they are," she said. "And you might have heard we have experience with kidnappings. Quite a lot, actually. We also have helicopters equipped with surveillance cameras, infrared cameras, night vision, tear gas dispensers and searchlights."

"Skip was looking for helicopters. That's the main thing he was afraid of," Isaiah said.

"How do you know?" Winnie said.

"If you were hovering over that soccer field, the first thing he'd do is shoot me and then Grace. Your cameras and searchlights wouldn't find anything but two dead bodies. I know this, Detective, *because I know Skip*!" Isaiah was furious, abject, desperate. His voice trembled. For the first time in recent memory, Winnie had nothing to say. "I'll keep you informed," Isaiah added, and ended the call.

CHAPTER FOURTEEN
SL13 LBC

Manzo followed Dodson from his apartment to the animal shelter. He parked across the street and waited. After a while, Isaiah came out with Dodson. They were arguing. Isaiah got in the car. Dodson stuck his head in the window and they argued some more. Isaiah drove off. Manzo was tempted to go after him but Isaiah was hella smart. He'd spot a tail with one eye closed and he knew Manzo's car. No, follow Dodson, he thought. They'd hook up sooner or later.

As soon as Isaiah left, Dodson got in his car and drove off, Manzo a few cars behind him. It was weird. Dodson kept stopping. He'd pull over and look at his laptop, you could tell by the glow on his face. Dodson got off the freeway in San Bernardino and took the streets to a soccer field. Dodson pulled over, watching, something happening out there but it was too dark to see.

Suddenly, Dodson gunned it, drove up over the curb and onto the field. There were flashes of gunfire. In the car's headlights, Manzo saw a white dude running away, Isaiah was on the ground. Manzo drove around the block and saw a car, a girl in there, climbing over the seat to get into the front. It was her, *it was*

Grace! He always kept an aluminum baseball bat in the backseat. He grabbed the bat, jumped out and smashed the car window. Opening the door, he grabbed Grace by the back of the neck and dragged her to the Caprice. She was screaming and fighting the whole way. She only shut up when he threatened to bust her head open.

Manzo was exhausted. He was tired of chasing Isaiah, tired of thinking about Isaiah. He was tired of the risk and the danger of arrest. He'd captured the girl but what was he going to do with her? ¡Ay chingao! He was so pissed off, so desperate to be who he used to be, he didn't do what he was known for. Thinking things through. It was like he ran off the end of the Long Beach Pier and his legs were still pumping in the air, nowhere to go except the cold, merciless ocean. He had to find someplace to put the bitch until he could figure this out. He called his girlfriend Lupe.

"Just temporarily," Manzo said.

"Hold up, cabron," Lupe said. "¿Acer con ella, encerrarla en el baño? ¿Qué le digo a mi hija cuando me pregunta quién es la niña? Manzo la secuestró. Mamá la tiene aquí hasta que lo arresten—" He ended the call. He was staying at his mother's house. He couldn't take her there.

"Uh, excuse me," Grace said. "But you're going really fast." The speedometer said 91 mph. Manzo slowed, lucky he wasn't pulled over. He cursed himself for not thinking of it first. He'd go see his homeboy, Guillermo.

Winnie notified San Bernardino PD and told Lieutenant McKee about the night's activities. "If Skip Hanson is on foot and injured, somebody must have seen him," McKee said. "San Bernardino PD has probably set up a perimeter and has people canvassing the area. They'll bust him and you won't have to do another thing. You should be happy."

"I'm *not* happy," Winnie said. "Isaiah is a material witness and he's simply not allowed to evade the police."

"Is that what this is about? A matter of principle?" the lieutenant said. "Because it sounds to me like you're being competitive."

"Competitive? How so?"

"Isaiah ignores you, doesn't ask you for advice and you want to impose your will. You want to come out on top for once. It's personal."

"That's not true. I simply want Isaiah to obey the law," Winnie said, more forcefully than she intended. The lieutenant looked at her hard for a moment.

"Go home, Winnie."

The apartment was a mess. A few weeks ago, Winnie let the housekeeper go. She preferred to do the chores herself, except there was never time. She made supper. A small piece of Wagyu, grilled medium rare, and a simple salad. She made a vinaigrette from Meyer lemons and safflower oil. Olive oil was a little heavy. She ate sitting at the center island with a glass of Zinfandel and the news on her tablet. She washed the dishes and left them on the rack to dry.

Winnie thought about what the lieutenant said about being competitive. She wasn't embarrassed by it. Competition was good. It kept you alert, increased your productivity and helped you assess your strengths and weaknesses. The competitive aspect was one of the things that drew her to dressage. The sport was a test of your skills, wits and reflexes; combined with her innate love of horses it became something of an obsession, even at age eight when she began to take lessons. She thrived. The sport demanded precision, discipline and control, although she discovered very quickly that control was an illusion. She didn't control Tomoe. She asked her to do things and the horse obliged because she trusted Winnie. In large part, that relationship determined your success or failure.

Winnie loved the precision. You held the reins between your pinkie and ring finger, neither too high nor too low, the reins in a straight line to the horse's mouth. Your head, knees and feet in perfect alignment, keeping the correct posture, even at a full gallop. You had to communicate with the horse without seeming to. A squeeze of the thighs, a near-imperceptible movement of the reins or slight shift in your seat. It was thrilling, working in unison with an animal that stood sixteen hands high and weighed over half a ton of pure muscle and grace.

Winnie grew up with Tomoe and sometimes slept in her stall. She spent hours preparing her for an event. It was like giving a friend a makeover. While her classmates were playing video games, Winnie was busy with a currycomb, gently removing dirt and dead hair, cleaning and polishing Tomoe's hooves, trimming her muzzle, wrapping her legs. The horse was brilliant on the course, a hard worker and as disciplined as any of her competitors. If Tomoe stumbled on a pirouette or flying change, it was Winnie's fault, for losing her concentration at a crucial moment. Tomoe taught Winnie patience, focus and determination; in some ways the horse played a larger role in her maturation than her parents.

Horse and rider won the Desert Dressage, the Greenville Equestrian and the Dressage at Spirit events. They nearly won the LA National. Winnie saw her friend whenever possible but the time between visits was getting longer.

Since their conversation about Archie's money, Winnie and Duvall spoke in monosyllables and avoided eye contact. Difficult, when you're working together. The tension was wearing, knowing her partner was bitter and resentful, waiting for a chance to disparage her. She had to finish this. Either find out for sure whether Duvall was corrupt or let it go. If he did steal the seventh bundle, it wasn't the first time, she thought. Most people who steal money have an ongoing need. Was Duvall a gambler? Did he suffer some great financial loss? She needed to prove he was a thief but catching him in the act wasn't possible. Maybe there was something in their previous cases. She'd have to look into that.

Grace presumed the man who'd taken her from the field was Manzo. She suggested he slow down. He did. He was obviously scared and anxious, his right hand on the steering wheel, left hand holding a gun across his lap, the barrel aimed at her.

"Don't try no shit with me." He gave her a hard glance. "I got no problems shooting you. Keep your hands where I can see them."

"Okay."

She saw no point in asking him what he wanted or where they were going. It was clear he didn't know either. They drove for a while, the engine droning. Jesus, it was so loud you couldn't talk, you yelled. Manzo was staring straight ahead. She could see the outline of his jaw. His teeth were clenched. A good moment to keep quiet but that never stopped her.

"Why do you want to hurt Isaiah?" she asked.

Manzo thought a moment and said, "He didn't tell you about the Gatling gun?"

"That was a long time ago. Why are you still after him?"

"Suppose he burned down my house?" Manzo said. "Don't matter if he did it a long time ago. I still don't have no house." He has a point, she thought.

"Is it worth it?" Grace countered. "I mean, you go to all this trouble to kill somebody but how is that a positive thing? All you end up with is a dead body and me to get rid of."

Manzo looked uncomfortable. He took a few moments before answering, "You won't understand."

"Why? Because I'm not a gangster?" Grace argued. "Come on, tell me. What are you getting out of this besides trouble?"

"My pride! My identity," Manzo replied fiercely. She thought he was going to hit her. "When you grow up with nothing that's all you have. Let somebody take it from you and who are you? A piece of shit."

"How does killing Isaiah remedy that?" Grace said.

"It doesn't remedy nothing. It's like saying to the world, nobody disrespects me like that. I don't roll over for nobody and I don't turn my fucking cheek."

"Yes, but—"

"It's not about Isaiah. It's about me," Manzo declared. "What's my rep in the barrio? Am I some kinda pussy who lets people rob them and destroy their whole life? You let that pass and you're not a shot caller, you're a victim, and if you're a victim, you might as well move to the sticks because you won't survive out here."

"You won't *survive*?" Grace said, disbelief in your voice. "You have a whole community that's doing just fine and they're not victims."

"I'm talking about the street. I'm talking about the drug business," Manzo said. "If you want power, you do violence. If you want to make money, you do violence. If you want to be somebody, you do violence! Violence works for us, okay? Now shut up and don't say nothing else!"

She was in the exact same position she was with Skip, thought Grace. Kidnapped by someone who would, in the end, have to kill her. Her anger, desperation and helplessness flamed, a bonfire roaring up to the sky. No more passiveness, she thought. No more talking, no waiting for something to happen. She'd been thinking about escape—instead of violence. Better to be killed escaping than lying prostrate and getting shot in the head. Strategy: Hurt

Manzo. Hurt him bad. Tactics: Find a weapon, use it—and fuck what happens next.

Skip hobbled away from the soccer field. He had to get to his car. He doubled back, approached it from an alley. A strange sight. Isaiah was already there, looking around, confused. The side window smashed, broken glass on the ground. Skip realized, *Somebody took Grace!* Who the hell could that be? Skip heard sirens. He hurried down a side street, then another. He went on until he couldn't hear the sirens anymore. His body was beat to shit, his hand broken, his head pounded. His leg throbbed. His calf was bleeding.

He found a passageway between two apartment buildings. It was dark, unpaved, little used. He stopped to rest, sitting down on the gravel, broken glass and the smell of dog shit. He leaned back against the stucco and took another Oxy. He couldn't believe it. Of all the shootings, chases, narrow escapes, accidents and disasters he'd been through, this was the absolute worst. Not only did he lose the ransom money, Grace was kidnapped by somebody else!

A hooker had told Skip about karma. They were lying in bed smoking a blunt. She didn't have anything else to do and neither did he. She said when you died, you came back in a different life. The kind of life depended upon the number of bad things you'd done. "I figure I'll be all right," she said. "Fuckin' don't hurt nobody."

"So if you did a lot of bad things you come back as like a crackhead?" Skip said.

"Could be. Could be worse than that," she said knowingly. "You could come back as a dog or a goat." If that was the case, Skip thought, he'd come back as a dung beetle. Or maybe he *was* a dung beetle and he came back as a hitman with the police on his trail, a shot leg, and nowhere to go. The only thing Skip knew for certain: these were his last days.

In the morning, Skip took the bus from San Bernardino to LA and from there to East Long Beach. It was a crappy area. Isaiah and his friends lived around here. Skip stopped at one of those Mexican stores that sold everything. He bought some cheap clothes, a hat and sunglasses. He went to the liquor store and bought a bottle of tequila. He got a room at the shittiest motel in the world, the Crest on Long Beach Boulevard. He showed his ID to the Korean guy. He gave it a glance but didn't scan it. He asked for a credit card. "I don't have one," Skip said. "I'll give you a damage deposit. A hundred bucks, that okay? I'm just gonna sleep."

It hurt parting with the money but he needed to rest. He got a room, took a shower, changed into the new clothes. He poured himself a drink. He should have bought a coffee mug or something. Styrofoam soaked up the taste. He slept a few hours, had another drink and turned on the TV. Not to watch, just for company. He'd never thought of it before, but he needed help.

He thought about the soccer field; what he saw when he circled around. Isaiah at the car, confused, the door open, Grace gone. Was it happenstance? Somebody else came along and *also* thought it was a good idea to kidnap her? Fuck that. That made no sense. Somebody else has a beef with Isaiah, Skip thought, and he must have followed him to the soccer field. Whoever the mystery man was, he was motivated. What now? Would he ransom Grace or maybe use her as bait? Then what? Skip wondered. When it was over, he'd have to kill Grace or she'd go to the police. The mystery man was willing to risk a murder charge. *He's out for blood just like you.*

Skip remembered something. The wanted poster on Raoul's fridge. The guy who created that poster was motivated too.

Twenty-five grand is a lot of money to spend on settling a score. Is the guy who made the poster the same one who kidnapped Grace? The more Skip thought about it, the more it seemed possible. What didn't seem possible was that there were *three* people who wanted Isaiah dead and they happened to bump into each other on the soccer field. No. The guy who created the poster and the guy who took Grace were one and the same. Maybe the mystery man is the help you're looking for, Skip thought. Could be. Or maybe the mystery man is a trapdoor with sharks at the bottom.

Skip found REWARD in his contact list. He called and got voice mail. "Um, I was there that night," he said. "At the soccer field. I don't know if you saw, but I was trying to kill Isaiah, until the car ran me off the field. My name is, um, Skip." It was an alias so why not? he thought. "I'm a contractor and I don't mean building houses," he went on. "I think we've got something in common. We both want Q Fuck dead. But he's a smart son of a bitch and I guess you know that. I'm thinking maybe we could join up. Two heads are better than one, right?" Skip paused. He realized the guy wouldn't call back unless somebody vouched for him. He remembered the wanted poster. It was signed LS13 LBC. He didn't know what LS stood for but 13 meant you were hooked up with La Eme. So the guy is Mexican. LBC meant Long Beach Crew. "I'm trying to think of somebody who could vouch for me," Skip continued, "somebody we both know. What about Angus Byrne, they call him Top Gun? Sold guns to everybody. Wait, he's dead now." This is taking too long, Skip thought. He talked faster.

"Uh, who else? Do you know a guy named Chuckles? Black guy from El Segundo. A dealer, pushes weight, works out of an apartment on Benoit? He knows me...and there was somebody else...hold on, let me think." Skip was flustered, struggling to come up with a name. "Oh wait, I've got it! Maybe you know Vincent Ortiz. He was a banger from Long Beach, he was hooked up with La Eme. I met him at Vacaville. We worked in the laundry together. Ask him if he knows Skip Hanson." Skip thought he didn't say enough but he was out of words.

"Okay, uh, anyway, I'll wrap this up," Skip said. "I'm not bullshitting, okay? I mean, I'm serious. This is no joke. Really. Um, call me." He left his number and ended the call. He felt like an idiot. Phoning up a stranger and asking if he'd like to be partners to kill somebody. For all he knew, he was talking to the cops. That's the trouble with speaking out loud. You can hear what a moron you are. He felt stupid. He always worked alone, why fuck with success?

He took a couple of days just to rest, ice down his bumps and bruises, take the occasional Oxy, watch TV and sit on a chaise next to the empty pool, catch some sun, drink beer and watch the dragonflies flit around the rotting leaves. He wondered if Jessica was dead. He hadn't heard from her. Maybe she was still in the basement, a hundred and seventy-five pounds of rat food. She shot him and would probably have killed him once she got the money. No wonder he was the way he was. How else could he be with a mother like that?

He was going to kill Isaiah. He didn't have or need reasons anymore. That asshole was gonna die. Period. Knowing that made everything simpler; not second-guessing yourself and thinking about all the pros and cons and driving yourself insane. *Relax with it, Skip. You're a professional killer. You know what to do.*

They locked Grace in the laundry room. Tiny but at least it was clean. They gave her some water, a few energy bars and a blanket. She couldn't take any more of this. She could feel herself coming apart, a searing panic coursing through her.

"Oh God, oh God..." she whispered, again and again. She heard footsteps and voices.

"You're gonna leave her in there until tomorrow?" a woman said. "What's wrong with you, Manzo? What? What did you say? That's fucking stupid and you know it."

A man spoke, someone she didn't recognize. "Cut him some slack, Maria. Manzo's in a tough spot."

"Why are you worried about him, G? *I'm* in a tough spot," she said heatedly. "I don't want some girl you kidnapped in my house. I'm trying to get my kids back, remember?"

"It's too late to do anything now, Maria. She'll be gone by tomorrow."

"She better be or I'll throw her out myself," Maria said. "And cut the fucking tape off her wrists. How she gonna do anything? You gonna help her to the bathroom?" The voices faded and were gone. Grace cried in great, heaving sobs.

"Let me outta here!" she wailed. "Let me fucking out! You have no right to do this! Let me out!" Footsteps came back, someone pounding on the door.

"Hey, hold it down," Manzo said.

"Fuck you hold it down!" she screamed. She started kicking the door. WHAM! WHAM! WHAM! Manzo burst in, furious.

"Shut up, you hear me, bitch? I'll kill you right now!" She got in his face.

"Do it! Do it, you fuck!" she yelled. Manzo raised a fist to hit her but a big hand landed on his shoulder.

"Stop, Manzo," G said. "I'm in enough trouble as it is." G was a big teddy bear with a Pancho Villa moustache and gangsta flannel. "Come on, bro, you brought this shit on yourself." Manzo glared at Grace and walked out.

"If I wasn't here, he would have killed you," G said. He cut the tape off her wrists with a kitchen knife and left.

* * *

Guillermo and Manzo were in the backyard, sharing a joint. "You've done some crazy shit, my brother, but this time you went too far," G said.

"I know that, I fucked up big-time."

"Use the girl to bait Isaiah? That's loco, Manzo. I mean like, how was that supposed to work? Tie her to a tree in McClarin Park and wait for Isaiah to show up?"

"It was stupid, okay? I know that!" Manzo said, defensive. "I don't need you to rub it in."

"You gonna off her?" Guillermo said.

"I could but I don't want to. What if that shit comes back on me? Kill a white girl and every cop in LA will come after me." Manzo took a hit off the joint, looked up at the sky and blew out the smoke. They were quiet a moment. "So there's nothing I can do? I'm fucked and that's it?" he said.

Guillermo considered. "You could..."

"Could what?"

"Get rid of her but not kill her."

"How?" Manzo said.

"You could sell her."

CHAPTER FIFTEEN
El Paso

It was all arranged. Isaiah was staying at Verna's tonight. Her coffee and croissants were the only thing he willingly stood in line for. Verna was probably in her seventies though she looked the same as she did twenty years ago. Wizened, her body like a bundle of dark twigs in a prim sky-blue uniform with a white apron and a white spread collar and a smile as welcoming as a homecoming.

"I don't want to stay at Verna's," Isaiah said. "I'll go back to TK's or get a room somewhere."

"Your friends want to help you," Dodson said. "Let 'em help. That's why you have friends."

"Really, Dodson. I don't want to impose."

"You're not. Verna's all happy about it. Said she spent the whole day cooking and getting a room ready."

"But I—"

"Don't be such a hardhead," Dodson said, annoyed now. "If you don't let her do this, you'll hurt her feelings. She'll be deprived."

"Deprived of what?"

"The pleasure of helping you."

* * *

Isaiah rode up in the elevator, dreading what was to come. He was down on himself and vulnerable, fighting the PTSD every second. He didn't want to answer questions and he didn't want to be polite. He didn't like the whole idea of it. He was carrying the load. Why was this about Verna?

"Hello, Isaiah!" Verna said, delighted. "Please come in!" She was wearing her sky-blue uniform. He wondered if she slept in it. "Sit down, anywhere you like, poor dear. You must be exhausted." She took his backpack and guided him toward the BarcaLounger. "Now you just relax, doctor's orders. Here, put your feet up," she said. He didn't want to but Verna pushed a lever on the chair and a footrest sprang up under his feet. "The den is all ready for you, you'll be perfectly comfortable," she went on. "Would you like something to eat?"

"No, thank you. I'm fine."

"I made the best beef stroganoff you'll ever have in your life. Are you sure?"

"Yes, I'm sure."

"You're just being polite." She went into the kitchen and brought him back a beer. "Would you like to watch TV? I know how you men are."

"No, I'm—" She turned on the TV and handed him the remote.

"There. Why don't you watch sports or something. I want you to do whatever you'd do at home." She went back in the kitchen. Isaiah remembered this was for Verna's benefit, not his. He didn't know how to work the remote. He never had cable or a satellite dish and he didn't own a TV. The news was full of mayhem and suffering and Isaiah's life was already full of mayhem and suffering. Why voluntarily absorb more? It was like signing up to lose faith. There were a hundred buttons on the remote, the labels so small only insects could read them. He tried to change the channel and got a menu. He tried again and got another menu. He put the remote down.

"Would you like to wash your hands?" Verna called from the kitchen.

"Yes, thank you."

"Down the hall on your left."

Isaiah washed his hands. A basket on the counter held colorful little bottles of hotel shampoo and moisturizer. There was a mirror over the sink. He looked gaunt. He was unshaven, bloodshot eyes, mouth downturned, face about to melt off his skull. He looked old. He looked whipped. He wished he wasn't at Verna's. She wanted to feed him, have a conversation, comfort him. He couldn't deal. People should ask first. He'd make his excuses and leave.

When he returned to the living room, Verna called out, "Come and get it!" An elaborate meal was laid out on the dining table. There were a lacy white tablecloth and intricately woven place mats. The dishware and glasses were too delicate for humans and she'd prepared enough food to feed a family of twelve. It was too much. He was about to make his excuses when she said,

"Let us pray." She folded her hands and closed her eyes. "Dearest Lord. You know this is a terrible time for us, especially our friend, Isaiah. He is one of your best children, God. You may not know it, but he's been doing your work for a long time. We beseech you, O Lord. Isaiah's burden is too great for one man to bear. He cannot do this alone. He needs your help." Isaiah never heard anyone say a prayer with such conviction. Verna was really trying to convince the Lord to intervene. "Please give Isaiah the strength, wisdom and courage to find our beloved Grace," Verna said. "She is in your care, God. We ask that you keep her well and safe from harm. We ask that you protect her from evil and evil men. We thank you, O Lord, for all that you've given us. Our faith in you is everlasting. Amen."

Isaiah stared at his plate the whole time. He wasn't religious but he was moved. It was easy to be skeptical about religion; to dismiss it as a presumptuous set of moral guidelines based on a book full of fearmongering, fallacies and Draconian punishments. But what would you call Verna's prayer? he thought. It was religion in its granular form; expressing a deeply held faith and through it, love for the people you cared about.

"Let me serve you some of this, Isaiah," Verna said. "Give me your plate."

"Yes, thank you," Isaiah said, spreading the cloth napkin on his lap. "Everything looks delicious."

Grace spent the night in the laundry room. Maria brought her some warmed-up stew, flour tortillas and a box of orange juice. She was fuming, though it didn't seem aimed at Grace, more toward the situation. The stew was good. Later, the woman came back and escorted her to a bedroom, a strong hand clamped on her neck. "You try something and I'll fuck you up." She didn't have a weapon. Apparently, she didn't need one.

Aside from the bed, there were a sofa and an easy chair, both in front of the TV. Everything in the room was tidy, folded and put away. Grace thought about escaping through a window but there were burglar bars.

"Sit down," Maria said. Grace sat down on one end of the sofa. Maria was on the other end, a few feet away. She curled her knees up under her, used the remote and turned on the TV. A Mexican sitcom was playing, one of those shows where everyone is yelling no matter what's happening.

Maria was probably midthirties, maybe older. She was wearing a white T-shirt and a blue headscarf. Her plum lipstick was outlined in black. Her coal-black eyebrows drawn in and shaped like sickles, the black eyeliner in an upward tail at the corners of her eyes. There was a maelstrom of tats on her arms. The one Grace could make out clearly was a girl's face, a young teen, a cholla, beautiful smile, hands folded in prayer, outspread wings like an eagle. REST IN PEACE JUANA 2001–2015 *Mi Angel Caida*. Was that a friend? A sister? There was part of a tat above Maria's collar. A beast with horns and red eyes. We all have an inner beast, Grace thought.

She once heard a TV commentator say, "If these girls took off the costume, ditched the tats and wore regular makeup they'd be attractive." In whose eyes? Grace thought. If the commentator wore her business suit and low heels around here, she wouldn't be attractive. She'd be ridiculous. The sitcom was giving her a headache. She asked meekly, "Can I have some water, please?" Maria gave a slight nod.

"Right there." A half bottle of water stood on the coffee table. Grace took it, sat down again and drank.

"Thank you," she said. Judging by Maria's expression, the sitcom wasn't funny. It was the saddest thing in the world.

"If you gotta piss, the bathroom's right there." Maria pointed with her chin.

"Yeah, I think I will."

"Remember what I told you," Maria said.

Grace went into the bathroom. It was small and cramped. She did her business, washed her hands, eyes darting around frantically. *You need a weapon.* She left the water running and searched. There was a stockpile of makeup and hair products; squeeze bottles, jars, spray cans, tubes, a dozen eyebrow pencils in a coffee cup, a million lipsticks in a plastic box. There were hand soap, body wash, several shampoos and conditioners but no scissors, metal nail files or anything else. Grace was anxious, this was taking too long. She wasn't finished searching but Maria was probably suspicious. Grace turned off the water, dried her hands with a towel and started to leave. Impulsively slid open a drawer.

Hiding there amid the hairbrushes, bobby pins and barrettes was a rattail comb.

Grace returned to the sofa. Maria clearly impatient, restless, glaring at the TV. She tilted her head back and shouted, "Guillermo! How long do I have to stay in here? I got things to do."

"Gimme a few minutes, Maria," he replied. "We're working something out." Maria groaned and stared at the TV again.

"You're Isaiah's girlfriend?" Maria said, her eyes never leaving the screen.

"Yes," Grace said.

"He's a cool guy, helps people, even some friends of mine. Too bad he fucked up. Manzo took a big hit behind that shit. He lost his house and everything."

"I didn't know that," Grace said. "Can I ask you something?"

"What?"

"Do they have to *kill* Isaiah? Isn't there something else? Some other way to resolve this? If Manzo kills him, that doesn't get him anything."

Maria shrugged. "It never gets them nothing but they do it anyway. They say it's for cred, you know? Like being established. Being for real. Then they go to jail. I used to visit Guillermo in County. He played it off, like it wasn't nothing, but I could tell. He was sorry he did that shit. When he gets out, he does it all over again."

"If you don't mind me asking, why doesn't he do something else?"

"He doesn't know anything else," Maria said, annoyed but not at Grace. "Telling him to go straight is like asking him to go to Siberia. He doesn't know shit about Siberia. It's not even a choice. I mean, someday he might quit, but he'll do what all the burned-out gangsters do. Work in a body shop, or construction, or lie around and do fuck-all. He'll drink a lot, smoke crank and die before he's sixty—Guillermo! Hurry up! I can't do this shit forever!"

Maria entered the kitchen. Guillermo was standing at the sink washing the dishes. "Hey, did you hear me? I'm not gonna babysit her, okay?"

"Just leave her there," Guillermo replied. "She can't go no place. The back door is right here. Manzo's in the living room. She can't go out the front. Can you make me something to eat?"

"No, I can't," Maria said. Guillermo stopped what he was doing.

"What's your problem?" he said. A sure way to start a fight.

"You really need to ask me that?" she said sharply. Manzo came in.

"Chico said he'll come by and take a look. He's not gonna pay a lot, you know. Even for a white girl."

"Where will he take her?" Guillermo said.

"He said El Paso. They got a big operation there."

"Wait, are you talking about that girl in there?" Maria said.

"Yeah," Manzo answered like it wasn't nothing. Maria possessed different degrees of anger. Regular anger. Anger at Guillermo for being stupid. And outrage anger, violent anger, I-can't-fucking-believe-this-shit anger.

"You're gonna *traffic* her?" Maria said, her voice going high. She felt the blood rushing to her face, she tightened her fists. "What's wrong with you pendejos? Do you know what's going to happen to her? Chico is Sinaloa and they don't care about shit. They'll lock her in a room and she'll be fucking campesinos forty times a day!"

Guillermo shrugged. "It's not that bad." Maria stared at him with her mouth open.

"Not that bad?" she said. "What do you know about it, G? Hey,

I got raped, remember? Do you think it wasn't that bad? Do you think I didn't have nightmares for fucking years?"

G put his palms up. "Okay, okay, but it's not my problem!"

"You're setting this up, G! What do you mean it's not your problem?"

"Hey, come on, Maria, I got a situation—" Manzo said as he came in.

"Fuck you, Manzo!" she shouted. "Bringing your bullshit *situation* into my house? If you weren't G's homie I'd fucking shoot you."

"Hey, go to your mother's or something," G said, losing patience. "Don't worry about it."

"I'm gonna worry about it for a long time, you heartless motherfucker," she replied. "And Manzo? Don't ever come back here. You hear me? You come back and I'll fucking cut your throat!"

As soon as Maria left, Grace got off the sofa, went to the door and listened. She turned back to the room, scanned for another weapon, something heavier. She was trying to remember the layout of the house. Manzo perp-walked her through the kitchen down the hall and threw her in here. She'd have to go left to get to the door. She could hear Maria and Guillermo arguing. Did that mean Manzo was in another room or was he standing there watching? She hesitated, her hand on the doorknob. She heard footsteps coming down the hall and quickly returned to the couch. Manzo burst in. He was pissed, breathing through his nose, hard eyes, nearly vibrating with anger. He shot her an ugly look, plunked down on the couch and stared blankly at the screen.

After watching a few moments of the sitcom he said, "What is this shit?" He changed the channel to a boxing match. It was quiet except for the commentator and the crowd noise going up and down. "Alvarez and his combinations," Manzo muttered appreciatively. "He's too much for this guy—oh shit, that uppercut." Manzo was really watching now, sometimes shaking his head or saying *Oh shit,* an admiring grin on his face. Grace felt the rattail comb in her back pocket. There was no place to stab him with the plastic tip except his throat. She was afraid. Maybe wait and see what happens, she thought. No, she was being timid again. Stick this asshole and go.

"Guillermo!" Manzo shouted. "You gotta see this."

"Can I go to the bathroom, please?" Grace said.

Manzo nodded, his eyes still on the TV. "Don't take too long." She got up. She wanted to walk around the sofa, behind him, but he might call her on it. *Do it or don't do it, Grace.* She got up and as nonchalantly as she could, she started to go behind him.

"Not that way," he said.

"I didn't want to block your view." She continued around him, drawing the comb from her pocket. Maria came in, furious, nearly hysterical. Guillermo right behind her. They were yelling at each other. Grace pushed the comb back in her pocket and continued to the bathroom. She went in and closed the door. Maria was screaming in Spanish, Guillermo muttering defensively.

"You're not doing this, G!" she yelled. "Call that fucking Chico and tell him it's off!"

"Chico's already on his way," Manzo said. "You know who he is, right?"

"Yeah, I don't give a shit! You're not doing it!" Marisa yelled.

Guillermo was exasperated. He said, "Calm down, Maria," a phrase that never worked. But what was Maria talking about? Grace thought. What was Guillermo not supposed to do?

"That girl's not going nowhere!" Maria said. Going? Going where? Grace thought. The doorbell rang.

"Shit, that's Chico," Guillermo said. "Let him in, Manzo." Manzo moved off. Maria was still yelling at him. "You're not doing it, G! No! I won't let you! I swear to God, if you let this happen I'll fucking leave you!"

"You ain't leaving nobody," he said. Grace opened the bathroom door partway. Maria looked into the hallway, flinched at what she saw.

"Don't come in here, Chico!" she screamed. "Get outta my house!" Guillermo grabbed her and held her back.

"Stop, goddammit!" He was angry now. Maria twisted around, trying to get away from him, screaming. "No, G, let me go, you fuck!" Guillermo hit her with a closed fist. She fell to the floor, holding herself up on all fours. She was quiet, not even crying, breathing hard, blood dripping from her nose.

"I told you to stop, didn't I?" Guillermo said, as if that justified hitting her. Without a word, she got up and left. Grace caught something on Maria's face. She'd made a decision. Manzo and two other men came in.

"Sorry about that, Chico," Guillermo said. "You know how it is."

"Shit, man. You married a wild one."

"Tell me about it," Guillermo replied. Chico was fortyish, gray pants that puddled around his cheap sneakers, blue polo shirt, a paunch and a Raiders cap. His companion was a smaller version of Chico. "That's her?" he said, looking at Grace. He sounded disappointed.

"Yeah," Manzo said. He wouldn't look at her and neither would Guillermo.

"Let's go, chica," Chico said. "Don't gimme no trouble, okay?" Grace thought a moment. If she struggled, he'd get violent and there were three other men in the room. This was a fight she couldn't win. She came forward. She'd have to wait for an opportunity. *You should have stabbed Manzo sooner*. "You don't have to force me," Grace said. "I'll walk."

"Let's get this over with," G said, fed up. He led the way down the hall. Beyond him were the kitchen and the back door. Maria stepped out in front of them, she was aiming a gun sideways.

"The hell are you doing, Maria? Put that down," Guillermo said.

"You're not taking her! You're not making her into no slave!" Maria shouted. "I'm not shitting you, G. Let her go." Grace was horrified. Did she say *slave*?

Guillermo came toward her. "Give me the goddamn gun."

Maria fired, BLAM! BLAM!, the bullets going high. Chico let go of Grace, everybody diving to the floor. The men started to get up, but Maria fired again. BLAM! BLAM! Chico, his confederate and Manzo turned and scrambled the other way toward the living room. Guillermo got to his feet. Maria stood her ground, her aim steady. Guillermo was rabid. He walked toward her.

"What are you gonna do, bitch? Huh? You gonna shoot me? You show me up in front of my homies? I'm gonna kick your ass, Maria." He kept coming. She didn't budge. "Put it down, Maria," he snarled. "You know you're not gonna shoot me." He reached for the gun. BLAM! She shot him. Grace raced past them, down the hall to the back door. The fresh air filled her lungs, she felt crazed and disoriented. *I'm free, motherfuckers!* But Manzo was there. He'd circled around the house. She tried to run by him, he grabbed for her and she swung and stabbed him in the neck with the comb, getting her weight behind it, the cheap black plastic snapping in half. Manzo screamed, grabbed his neck and let her go. She broke free, but Chico was there aiming a gun at her head.

"Where're you going, chica?"

Isaiah was in Verna's second bedroom. He couldn't sleep. He'd called his contacts but none knew where Manzo was staying. Finally, he contacted a Latina woman he knew from a previous case. She said Manzo was at his mother's place. Isaiah was about to head over there when his phone buzzed. The caller ID said LA COUNTY. A recorded voice said there was a collect call from an inmate. Isaiah accepted.

"Hello?" he said.

"Your girlfriend, it's Grace, right?" a woman said. She was hurried, her voice tense and quick. There was background noise, a buzz of people talking in a big room.

"Who's this?" Isaiah said.

"It don't matter, let me talk, okay? Manzo don't have Grace no more. Sinaloa took her. They're gonna traffic her in El Paso."

"What?"

"Listen, will you? I been arrested. This is my last call." If you were arrested in California you were allowed three phone calls, not one. "The cartel has a stash house," she went on. "But I don't know if she's there for sure, okay? I can't promise you nothing."

"Where's the house?"

"Shit, man, I don't really know. I mean, like, it's in Pacoima but I don't remember nothing else."

"Did you get there by freeway?" Isaiah said.

"Yeah, G drove me out there a couple of times to make a drop."

"If you're going to Pacoima on the freeway you take the 210. Where did you get off?" The background voices were getting louder.

"Fuck, man, I don't know," the woman said. To someone else she snapped, "I'm almost done, okay? Will you give it a fucking rest?" Isaiah saw the scene. The woman in an orange jumpsuit at a pay phone, a line of other inmates behind her, impatient, talking shit.

"Were there any landmarks?" Isaiah said. "Like a billboard or an office building or—"

"Wait, yeah, there was like a fork, okay? Like another freeway split off."

"Did you take it?"

"No, we stayed straight, yeah, and we got off like, right after that. I remember because I asked G if he knew where he was going because he don't look at his GPS even though he has it." The voices were louder. "We gotta hurry, Isaiah. These bitches are like gangsta."

He talked faster. "Okay, you go down the off-ramp and you reach an intersection. Did you turn left or right?"

"Um, right, I think, but I'm not sure."

"Let's say you turned right. Did you drive for a short time or a long time? I mean, was it five minutes or a half an hour?" He could hear individual voices, one louder than the rest.

"More like five minutes, maybe ten," the woman said. Isaiah struggled to keep his voice even and focus so he could ask the right questions.

"You said you and G went there twice," he said. "Did you ever stop for food? Gas?"

"Yeah, we stopped for gas! At Costco. It's the cheapest."

"Okay, you stop for gas and you get back on the road. Ahead of you, what do you see?"

"I don't know, I don't remember, it's just a street—hey, come on! I get a fucking phone call just like you!"

"Yes, most of it's a blur but did anything stand out?" Isaiah said. His throat was dry. "A restaurant, school, club—"

"Yes! Yes! There was a strip club!" the woman said. "But I don't know the name of it." Again, to someone else, she said, "What'd you say? Oh. I'm supposed to be afraid of you? We can throw down anytime, okay? Wait'll we get on the block."

"You said there was a strip club," Isaiah said insistently.

"I only remember it because G said I would make a good stripper and he wanted to take me in there. He said they make good money."

"All right, you go past the strip club and you keep going. Anything else stand out?"

"I said one fucking minute, okay?" she shouted. "Yeah? Fuck you, bitch. I can talk about anything I want!" Then, to Isaiah, "Oh yeah, I remember! Railroad tracks! There was a train going by and we stopped, G said we went too far. So we made a crazy U-turn, people honking at us and shit."

"So you're going back in the direction of the strip club. Somewhere between there and the railroad tracks you must have turned." A shrill voice was louder than the rest, angry and threatening.

"Yeah, but I don't remember where," the woman said. "There's a bunch of streets—hey, step back, okay? I'll be finished when I'm fucking finished."

"When you turned, were you closer to the railroad tracks or the strip club?" Isaiah said.

"I think the strip club—yeah, because G asked me if I changed my mind."

The shrill voice hollered, "I gotta talk to my baby before she goes to sleep! Now get off the muthafuckin' phone!"

"Back up, or I'll put you on the ground," the woman said.

"Okay, you get to the street that leads to the stash house," Isaiah said. "Did you turn left or right?"

"Fuck, I don't know!" Other voices joined the shrill one, the volume building. Isaiah could hardly hear her. He was forced to yell.

"The house, the stash house! Anything you remember about it?"

"It was just a house, like stucco, it was like beige with a chain link fence," she said. That was useless. Every house in the hood was stucco with a chain link fence. "It was on a dead end, I remember that," she added.

"Okay, you're driving toward the stash house, three, four, five blocks. There were street signs. Do you remember anything about them? A letter? A number?"

The woman's voice was more distant. "Look, bitch. I told you to get off my case. Shit, you wanna throw down?" The voices became a din, like everybody in the room was yelling.

"The street signs!" Isaiah shouted. "Do you remember anything about them?"

"I remember it was a weird name," she said. "Like it didn't—hey, get your fucking hands off me!"

"I'm gonna beat your ass!" the shrill voice cried. There were scuffling, screams, hooting laughter and the call ended.

"Dammit!" Isaiah said.

CHAPTER SIXTEEN
At Last We Meet

Grace was in the back of a van. The ride was rough and noisy. She was sitting on the floor with a teenage girl and a woman around forty, their wrists bound with duct tape. Chico took their shoes. The teenager was holding her knees, staring blankly, makeup mixed with tears smeared all over her face. The other was a woman in a torn business suit, a bruise on her face. She looked like she worked at a bank. The woman was crying softly, running her prayer beads between her fingers. Chico was driving, his confederate in the passenger seat.

Grace was in a stupor, burned out on fear and anguish. Maria's voice was on a loop in her head. *You're not making her into no slave!* Until now, Grace had held a glimmer of hope that somehow she would escape. Not anymore. She was in the hands of a cartel. There was no escape. Isaiah would never find her. No one would ever find her. She'd made a vow that she wouldn't fall into despair. But here she was, in the thick of it, dying inside her mind. *If only you didn't... if only you had... why didn't you think of...* She thought of Isaiah and her heart turned black with rage. He got her into this. Because of him, her life was over. Because of him she'd be a slave. Because of him she'd be tortured and assaulted over and over again until she perished. She hated Isaiah and if she ever saw him again, she'd kill him.

Isaiah and Dodson were on the 210 Freeway, heading toward Pacoima. They reached the split, stayed the course and took the first exit, Decker Avenue. They drove a distance, past the Costco station and, a little farther on, saw a red neon sign, CLUB SPICE.

"The street is between the club and the railroad tracks," Isaiah said.

"She didn't know the name of the street?" Dodson said.

"She said it was a weird name, and that it didn't—and that was all. It didn't. It didn't."

"Didn't what?" Dodson said. Isaiah pulled over and got out his phone. He brought up Google Maps, found Pacoima and Decker Avenue. He located the stretch between the club and the railroad tracks. Dodson did the same on his phone.

"The street didn't... the street didn't," Isaiah muttered. There were ten streets between the club and the tracks. Dodson read the names aloud.

"Claymore Street, Clark Street, Lincoln Avenue, Detroit Street, Grant Street, Baltimore Boulevard, Wright Avenue, Arizona Street and Versailles Street."

Isaiah stared at the names, mumbling, his brain working at high speed. If the street didn't..., the woman was probably comparing it to something. It was discrepant. "The street name didn't belong," Isaiah said.

"How can a street name not belong?" Dodson said.

"It's different from the rest," Isaiah said. He looked at the names again. "They're all American names except—"

"Versailles," Dodson said. "That don't belong in a neighborhood like this." They drove into traffic, approached Versailles. "Right or left?" Dodson said.

"She said it dead-ended. It's to the right."

"Why right?"

"The street runs into the freeway."

They made the turn, Isaiah hoping his logic was sound. "Slow down." They went past small, seedy apartment buildings. Farther ahead, there was a NO EXIT sign. "Pull over and turn the lights off," Isaiah said. They were a block away from the end of the street.

"A stash house probably has cameras," Isaiah said. "Even if we drive up there and turn around, it'll look suspicious."

"Uh-huh," Dodson said. "But how you gonna tell if you got the right house?"

"I'll have to check."

Before Dodson could reply, Isaiah got out of the car and walked. He tried to seem casual, phone to his ear, moving his lips. Talking on your cell made you look legit, like you knew where you were going and didn't need to look. The woman on the phone said the stash house was "on a dead end." Did that mean at the very end or along the way? The houses Isaiah passed were very close together. At the end of the dead end, the houses were farther apart. Probably there, he thought. He stopped, feigning an argument while he took in the scene. "Aww man, why didn't you tell me?" he said, raising his voice. "I been walkin' around everywhere and now I'm lost."

There were two houses on each side of the street, all of them dilapidated, all with chain link fences. There were a swing set and toys in one of the yards. Unlikely Sinaloa would keep their dope in a house with kids. Three others to choose from. One of the front doors wore a cheap wood veneer, the kind you find in an old office building. It was too easily kicked in, Isaiah thought. It was one of the other two.

"So what the fuck do I do now?" Isaiah said into the phone. "That's bullshit, nigga. You ain't got a brain in your head." He could hear a TV from the house on the left, a pickup in the driveway. There was rap music from the house on the right, but no car. Isaiah turned and headed back the way he came. You can't transport your sex slaves in a pickup, but you need some kind of transportation, he thought. A van, say, but if you parked it in the driveway you couldn't move your dope, guns and kidnap victims in and out of the house without being seen. It was probably parked in the garage, if it was there at all.

Isaiah got back into the driver's seat and described what he saw. Dodson said, "If Grace is in there, hallelujah. If she's not there, there's nothing we can do."

"Let's assume she is," Isaiah said. "If that's the case we can't get her out ourselves."

"The police?" Dodson said. Isaiah was already dialing.

"Detective Hando," she said. He told her what had happened so far.

"Who was the woman that called you?" the detective asked.

"Doesn't matter. Grace might be in that house."

"And that's all the information you have?"

"Yes, that's it. Could you please put a move on it?"

"Give me your location."

Isaiah gave her the address and sent her a photo of the street.

"I can't send in tactical without intel," Winnie said. "I'll get a surveillance team to replace you and get a chopper in the air. You stay put and stay on the line. If something happens say so immediately. Once our operation begins, you stay clear of it, or I'll arrest you for obstruction."

Isaiah and Dodson waited, slumped down in their seats, the engine off. Someone might see the exhaust. Two unidentified bruthas waiting on a dark street was trouble.

"Detective? How long before your people get set up?" Isaiah said. "Grace could be hurt, she might be getting raped."

"We're expediting, moving as fast as we can," Winnie said.

"Which isn't fast enough. How long before that chopper gets here?"

"Soon," she said. "LAPD has sixteen, seventeen of them. This is where police resources come in handy."

"All the choppers aren't in the air at the same time," Isaiah responded sharply, "and they're covering a huge area, four hundred square miles, something like that. If a chopper is on the ground, it takes at least twenty minutes before it can take off. As for your surveillance team, it'll take longer than that to organize." Winnie said nothing. Time passed like you were waiting for your turn at the DMV. "Where's that goddamn chopper?" Isaiah said.

"We've got an officer down," Winnie said. "The closest unit is looking for the suspects, two of them on foot. The pilot will have to wrap it up there first. I've got another one coming but his ETA is twenty-two minutes."

"*Twenty-two minutes?* So much for damn resources!"

"Isaiah?" Dodson said. A car appeared from the dead end, the headlights were blinding. They slumped down farther in their seats. The car wasn't a car, it was a delivery van. As it drove by, Isaiah saw a Latino man at the wheel. The man on the passenger side was half out of his seat, talking to someone in the cargo bay. The van went by them, heading toward Decker. Isaiah whipped around in his seat to see the license plates but there wasn't enough light.

"A van," he said to Winnie. "White Ford Econoline, no windows, Latino driver, Raiders cap, another man with him. Grace is in there."

"How do you know?" Winnie said.

"The guy in the passenger seat was talking to somebody in the back. Delivery vans don't have any seats. Whoever he was talking to was on the floor. We're going after them." Dodson tromped on the accelerator but by the time they got to Decker, the van had disappeared.

"Which way?" Dodson said.

"Left."

"Do you have eyes on the van?" Winnie said.

"Not anymore."

"How do you know it went left?"

"If they're going to El Paso, they're headed to the 101."

"I'm giving you to dispatch," Winnie said.

Isaiah learned to drive when he worked at the wrecking yard. In his youth, TK piloted a highly modified Honda CRX in SCCA races and won a lot of trophies. He said if Isaiah kept at it, he could go pro.

Isaiah got on the 101, keeping his speed to seventy-five miles an hour, any more would invite an accident or the highway patrol. The van had a two-minute lead and was going at or near the sixty-five-mile-an-hour speed limit to avoid getting pulled over. Isaiah calculated they'd catch up in twelve minutes give or take. Cars were like rainwater streaming off to the sides of the windshield as Isaiah cut through traffic. The clock on the dash counted down the minutes. Eleven... ten... nine. Isaiah was plagued with doubts. Did he calculate correctly? Was the van on the same freeway? Six... five... four minutes. What if the van was going someplace else? What if the driver and his friend pulled over for a cheeseburger? Three... two... one. No van. Isaiah's doubts went viral.

"Shit!" he said.

"I don't see it yet," Dodson said. Another agonizing thirty seconds went by. "There it is!" Dodson shouted. They nearly overshot it. The van was over one lane. Isaiah slowed more quickly than he wanted to. He wondered if the driver saw him. If you're transporting human cargo for Sinaloa, you're on your toes. Isaiah dropped back three cars, swung in behind the van.

"I've got eyes on the van," Isaiah said to the dispatcher. "Part of the license plate is obscured but the first three digits are seven, one, five—that's seven, one, five—we're on the 101 heading south, van's in the middle lane, we're passing the Entrada exit."

"Roger that," the dispatcher said. "Command is sending units ahead of the van. They need time to assemble and set up. Keep the van in sight, but do not interfere with its progress."

Grace huddled with the other two women. Chico was looking in the rearview mirror, seemingly alarmed.

"We've got a tail," he said.

"You sure?" the second man said.

"Sí. Three, maybe four cars back, two guys in a black car. They almost passed us, then they slowed down and now they're behind us."

"Cops?"

"I don't think so."

"Maybe they're from another gang."

The second man turned his head and glared at the women. "We're gonna move fast now. Keep your heads down and shut up!"

"Next exit," Chico said. "Me voy de allí."

Hope split Grace wide open, like an axe blade had descended, letting in the sunshine. If it wasn't the police following them, it was Isaiah. *Oh my God,* how could she ever have doubted him? The second man produced an Uzi. He snapped in a magazine and slid a round into the chamber. He climbed over the seat into the cargo bay, scuttling past the women to the rear doors. He cradled the gun in one hand, his other on the door handle.

"Wait, wait, too soon," Chico said. "Maybe I can lose him."

The van was still three cars ahead, slowing some, edging toward the right lane. "I think he's getting off the freeway," Isaiah said to the dispatcher. "We're approaching Alta."

"Roger that," the dispatcher said. "The units are almost in position."

The van slid over in the right lane, moderate speed, nothing wild. Isaiah stayed back, four cars separating him from the van. They were approaching the Lennox exit.

"Coming up on the Lennox exit," Isaiah said. "He's in the right lane." But the van passed the exit, pulled sharply into the emergency lane and made a hard stop.

"He made us," Dodson said.

There was no option but to drive past the van. "Dammit," Isaiah said as he pulled over into the emergency lane.

"The van's backing up," Dodson said. The van was in reverse, speeding backward. It reached the Lennox exit, stopped and zoomed down the off-ramp. Isaiah put the car in reverse and stomped on it, the car running straight back without a waver, the transmission winding up like it was going to explode. By the time they reached the Lennox off-ramp, the van was gone.

Isaiah roared down the off-ramp to the intersection, screeching to a halt at the stop sign. A two-lane residential street, Orchard Avenue. It went in both directions, eucalyptus trees lined up on one side, their branches hanging over the road like dead arms.

"Which way?" Dodson said.

The leaves on the left weren't moving. The ones on the right were. Isaiah made the turn and floored it.

"I lost the visual," Isaiah said to the dispatcher. "The van got off at Lennox and went left on Orchard."

"Copy that," she said. Isaiah sped down Orchard. Ahead were a barrier and an arrow indicating you could only go left. Isaiah was going fast, the barrier filling the windshield.

"Watch it!" Dodson said. Isaiah lifted his foot off the gas, cranked the wheel, the rear wheels sliding, the car turning sideways, pointing left. Isaiah was about to accelerate but there was the van, going slowly, waiting in ambush. The door swung open, revealing a man with an Uzi.

"Incoming!" Dodson yelled. The man opened fire. Bullets spiderwebbed the windshield. Isaiah swerved off the road and into a ditch.

Grace watched the second man hold open the door with one hand and shoot with the other. She duck-walked past the other women, let out a war cry and shoved the man in the back. He screamed and went tumbling onto the street, the Uzi clattering after him. Chico glanced in the mirror but didn't stop. He accelerated, cursing in Spanish.

"Get him!" Grace shouted. But the two women were already attacking him. The teenager was behind Chico, clubbing him with her bound hands, the woman in the suit had clambered over into the front. She was screaming, grabbing at his face, trying to rip out the man's eyes. Chico steered with one hand and fended her off with the other. The van was zigzagging, Grace was thrown to one side, hard. She grunted, the wind knocked out of her.

Chico found his gun but the teenager looped her arms around his neck, choking him. The older woman was grappling with his gun hand. He couldn't get an angle and fired into the ceiling—BLAM! BLAM!—the gunshots incredibly loud, like a grenade going off in a closet, flattening Grace's eardrums and filling the van with smoke. The gunshots made the women fall away but the van was out of control, wildly wagging back and forth, Chico yelling, his face bleeding. Grace saw the drop-off coming. "We're going over!"

The van bucked and bounded down the incline, smashing its way through the brush. The women were thrown around, their bodies banging into the sides and ceiling, the van hitting something solid, everyone thrown forward into a heap behind the front seats. Abruptly, it went quiet, save for creaking metal and something hissing. The other women were groaning, Grace was immobile, pain all over, hardly able to breathe. She smelled gasoline. She smelled smoke.

Dodson and Isaiah ran down the incline to the crashed van, smoke and flames coming from under the hood. They dragged Grace and two other women to safety. Grace was conscious but dazed and in pain. Isaiah carried her to an open spot and gently set her down. She was bleeding from a cut on her head, the blood dripping down her face. Her eyes were closed and she was babbling in a hoarse voice, the words unintelligible. Isaiah was helpless, tormented, he couldn't stand to see her like this.

"Help!" he cried. "SOMEBODY HELP HER!"

There was the deafening *whap-whap* of the chopper, the blinding searchlight, dust, leaves, branches blown helter-skelter, then a dozen sirens and shouting voices, firefighters in yellow hard hats yelling and dragging equipment. They strapped Grace onto a stretcher, carried her up the hill and loaded her into an ambulance. The siren wailed, the lights whirled and she was gone.

Isaiah wanted to follow the ambulance to the hospital. He ran up the incline and was stopped by a trim Asian woman in a tailored gray suit. She held out her badge.

"At last we meet. I'm Detective Hando, Mr. Quintabe."

"And you're right on time," he said angrily.

Isaiah was taken into custody and put in an interview room. Winnie and Duvall watched him through the two-way glass. The tension between them was bristling and obvious.

"So that's IQ, huh?" Duvall said skeptically. Isaiah was good-looking in a modest way, dressed in jeans and a hoodless sweat shirt, intelligence in his eyes despite their weariness. Isaiah's hands were folded on the table, he didn't seem stressed or nervous, he wasn't fidgeting and he didn't look confused. He was preternaturally still, his breathing even, his gaze faraway. He looked defeated but his dignity was intact. You could see it on his face plain as day.

Prior to meeting Ben, Winnie had an African American boyfriend, or "partner," a term she rarely used. It sounded like they were associates at a law firm. The boyfriend did his graduate work at Louisiana State University. His thesis was about Reconstruction and how it failed because of political pressure, mob rule and white terrorism. The university library possessed an extensive photo collection of Black slaves taken around the time of the Civil War. Her boyfriend had made a copy of a striking portrait of a boy who was probably ten or eleven. He was emaciated, his clothes so tattered and torn they hardly held together, his expression sad and expectant, like he was waiting for something he knew would never come. The photo was titled "Three Hundred Miles Through Swamp and Cane Brake to Fight for Freedom." Every mile, lash of the whip, insult and long day in the broiling sun was etched on the boy's face. But his dignity was intact. You could see it plain as day.

"You talk to him," Duvall said. "Maybe you can have a spelling bee."

* * *

Winnie entered the interview room. Isaiah glanced at her but otherwise didn't move. He gave off an air of acceptance and an odd kind of confidence. He'd get through this, his demeanor said, there was an end in sight. She gave him a bottle of water. He opened it and drank.

"Thank you," he said. Manners too, she thought.

"I want you to take me through this from beginning to end," she said.

"I can't."

"Why not?"

"It's too long of a story. The events took place over a week's time and if you want the history, it's even longer."

She pushed a notepad and pen at him. "Then write it out." He pushed them back.

"And you think that will take less time? Detective, I'm happy to answer your questions but look at me. I'm worn through."

"You know, I can detain you for forty-eight hours," Winnie said.

"That's fine. I'll lawyer up, which only complicates things. Let me sleep and you can question me all you want. I'm not hiding anything. I was looking for Grace and doing it better than you, by the way."

"Is that so?" she said, the best answer she could muster.

"If it wasn't for me your chopper would still be flying around looking at nothing and Grace would be a sex slave in El Paso." Winnie didn't have a comeback. She knew Duvall was enjoying this.

"All right, Mr. Quintabe," she said, as if she was tired of the whole thing. "Because you have no record and your intentions were to help law enforcement—" He halted her with a look.

"Not intentions," he said heatedly. "I didn't *intend* to help law enforcement. I *did* help and you know it." He looked at Winnie, accusing, angry and contemptuous. She didn't like it. Scrutinizing someone was her job.

"Is there anything else?" Winnie said.

"Yeah, there is," Isaiah said as he rose. "Loosen up, Detective. It's fluid out there." Winnie escorted him to reception. She gave him a nickel.

"What's this for?" Isaiah said.

"I lost a bet to your friend Mr. Dodson." She watched Isaiah go, stung by the back-and-forth. Yes, he's smart, she decided. He's also a brave and relentless seeker of justice just like you, but "loosen up"? What does that mean?

Grace was in a state of suspended animation, conscious but unfeeling, there but not. The nurse awakened her several times from nightmares she couldn't remember, thank God. She appreciated the bland, sterile hospital room. Nothing there to stir up emotion or create an image. She asked the nurse to leave the door open. It was comforting, people in their green scrubs walking by, serious and intentional. The doctor said she suffered primarily from exhaustion, dehydration and psychological trauma. She would be released the following day.

Isaiah was sitting beside the bed, miserable and sad. She knew he was waiting for an acknowledgment, for some sign that they were still connected, but she said nothing. Not out of meanness, but because she felt nothing. He stirred nothing inside her. Not even anger. Nothing like modern medicine to separate you from your feelings.

Maybe when she was over the ordeal, she mused. Her love would come back and she could have everything she wanted. Isaiah, a home, a sense of security, pursuing her art, domestic life. No more guns and blood and evil men. But what happened after that? she wondered. What happens when everything turns out fine? When you're suddenly living the life you dreamed about? She supposed a new life meant becoming a new person. That's the way of things. You grow, evolve, your world changes, you change. But what happens to the old you? The one who's obsolete? Grace would miss her. She would miss the yearning, the passion. She'd become accustomed to waiting for Isaiah, hoping desperately to see him and wondering if she ever would. The thoughts consumed her. The feelings were painfully delicious and she realized she reveled in them. They stirred her. The anticipation. The tantalizing fantasy that she could have her heart's desire and the constant machinations to make that happen. Maybe that was all she wanted. The struggle. Maybe what she wanted was what she'd always known.

Isaiah remained at Grace's bedside. She slept. There were stitches on her forehead. She was hooked up to an IV and a monitor with numbers and oscillating lines.

The doctor said the head wound was superficial and the rest was cuts and bruises. Otherwise she was okay, he said, but Isaiah knew she wasn't. Trauma left the deepest scar. He'd ruined her like he ruined himself. Nightmares, flashbacks, fear, isolation—kidnapped from her life and held hostage in another one. "Making it up to her" was a cliché. There was no way to make her whole again. No way to make her feel better or help her through the crisis.

Grace was so pale she seemed permeable, as if words would slip through her untouched. A nurse came in, gently woke her and helped her sit up. Grace took her meds, thanked the nurse but otherwise didn't speak. She lay down again and closed her eyes. Isaiah thought she saw him but couldn't be sure. He wondered if he should speak. Nothing but clichés came to mind. Saying "How are you feeling?" or "You're gonna be okay" seemed grotesque. The media got hold of the story. The kidnapping, the chase, the rescue.

They made the ordeal into something romantic. They made it into a movie.

Isaiah had no idea what Grace was thinking or whether she was thinking at all. He knew what happened was everything she'd feared. He was woefully sorry. He was afraid she'd end the relationship. She had every right. His life had infected hers. His monsters jumped the moat. That was why they broke up before he went away, so this very thing wouldn't happen. He wanted to tell her he was giving the whole thing up. That no matter what happened, no matter who came to him with what kind of problem, he'd say no. He wanted to tell her he'd dedicate his life to keeping her safe. If she'd only give him a chance.

Grace didn't stir. When someone is sleeping their eyes are lightly closed. Grace's eyelids were fluttering slightly. She wasn't asleep. She was pretending while she thought of something to say, or maybe the suspense was his punishment. She breathed a long sigh and sat up, stretched her arms and blinked the sleep away.

"Hi," Isaiah said softly. Grace didn't react, said nothing, eyes empty but somehow dire. Hoping to forestall what was coming, he said, "I'm sorry, Grace. For everything." She remained mute, nearly still. A lifetime passed. It was so quiet. Someone walking in the hall seemed shockingly loud. Her small hands rested in her lap.

"It's over," she told him.

CHAPTER SEVENTEEN
The IRS Hates Camilla Lightfoot

He didn't know why he was surprised. In his heart, he knew Grace would break up with him, should break up with him. He'd anticipated the pain. The reality was much worse, like a long fall down a mine shaft, flailing through the blackness, crash-landing, rubble and coal dust piling over you, the weight of it crushing your lungs. He'd lost Grace. This time for good. He thought about their past, the ecstatic highs and catastrophic lows. Together, they endured violence, terror and hairbreadth escapes. He saved her life and she saved his. He witnessed her bravery, resourcefulness and devotion. He admired her.

He remembered sitting together on an empty beach, the sea sparkling like heaven's bling, her face to the sunshine. She was some other category of beautiful. He remembered seeing her paintings for the first time and her unintentional portrait that stunned him. He remembered their midnight ride, speeding along the highway with the windows open, her hair like a golden flag, singing Motown to the moon. He knew there was, and always would be, one Grace. People said heartbreak was inescapable. They said loss helps you grow, that you come away from these experiences stronger than you were before. Such bullshit, he thought.

The only thing he'd come away with was a heightened sense of mistrust. He could never trust someone with his love.

Isaiah waited for the hospital elevator. A second-floor walkway connected the hospital and the parking garage. He hesitated and stepped back. He saw himself crossing the walkway and pushing open the double glass doors into the garage. He saw his enemies appear, shooting him until they emptied their guns. This was a good place to do it. Skip and Manzo knew Grace was here, it was publicized, and it followed that Isaiah would come to visit. He imagined their plan. Covid masks were a great disguise. Everyone but stupid people was wearing them. Isaiah's assassins would take up positions near the car or maybe at the exit kiosk. There was only one way in or out.

He took the elevator down to the ground level. He exited the hospital and went on foot to the garage. He went up the stairs to the second floor. He peeked out.

A few cars passing. A smattering of people exiting the walkway. He waited a few moments, looking for a shadow or sudden movement. He dashed to the first row of cars. He slid and wriggled through the space between the front bumpers and the abutment, pausing to look underneath the cars. Maybe Skip was crouched and waiting, ready to blast his legs apart.

It took a long time to make his way down the row, bobbing up and down. He was sweating by the time he got to his car. He thought about the exit kiosk. There was no cover there. When he inserted his ticket into the machine, he'd be stationary and in plain view. Skip could shoot him with his sniper rifle or Manzo could do a walk-up, blast him at close range. Should he leave his car and come back later to get it? He was overcome with weariness and loss. "Fuck it," he muttered. If they shot him they shot him. He drove down the ramp and waited in line.

* * *

Skip was idling in the red zone, across the street from the parking garage. Grace was in the hospital and you didn't have to be a genius to know Isaiah would visit. Skip moved a couple of times, parking enforcement waving him on. He drove around the block and came back. He saw Isaiah's car emerge from the garage, stop at the kiosk while he paid for his ticket. An easy shot, Skip thought, but there were too many people and he was still limping, still taking Oxy.

Isaiah drove off. Skip waited a bit and went after him, keeping well back. It was weird, Q Fuck wasn't even checking his mirrors. Once, he pulled over. There was no reason to. What was he doing? Skip thought. Calling someone? Maybe he was upset after seeing Grace. Maybe he was crying like a bitch. Skip followed Isaiah to a street lined with warehouses. He stopped and watched Q Fuck approach the animal shelter and turn into the parking lot. He thought a moment, smiled and drove off.

Grace and Deronda lived together. They were close. They were easy. They could be quiet together. Grace paid no rent. "It's kind of a rule in my family," Deronda told her at the start, "whoever has the money, spends the money." That was a total lie. No one in her family would say anything like that. When Grace left a check on the dining table, Deronda immediately tore it up. "What am I gonna do with this?" she'd say. "Buy a pair of sneakers?"

Grace was an ideal roomie. She was an excellent confidante, played her white people's music at a reasonable volume and adored Deronda's son. She painted in the backyard when "the light was right," whatever that meant. Deronda didn't understand Grace's art but she appreciated her friend's dedication. She hung Grace's work all over the house, even the paintings that looked like a carnival blew up or the second ice age killed all the people and only amoebas remained.

Her feelings were mixed feelings when Isaiah came to the door. He sat on the sofa, hunched over, staring at the floor. He looked beaten and used up. "I have to get her back," he said. He was so pitiful and his self-pity pissed Deronda off. But Isaiah was a dear, loyal and longtime friend. She wanted to gather him up, hug him and rock him to sleep. "I have to get her back," he said.

There was no point giving him hope, Deronda thought. The truth might set you free but it'll tear your guts out along the way. "I'm sorry, Isaiah, but there's no way to get her back or make it up," she said. "I know you never intended anything like this but your intentions don't mean jack. Your intentions are just words in the air."

"Maybe I'll stop by later," he said.

"If you show up, I won't open the door," Deronda said. "You and Grace are done. Your situation nearly killed her and if she doesn't protect herself, I will." She took him by the elbow and walked him to the door. "You need to take care of yourself before your self takes care of you." She opened the door and hugged him. "You know I love you, Isaiah. If I can do something else for you, just call."

Isaiah got in the car and started the engine. He closed his eyes and rested his forehead on the steering wheel. His brain was under siege, bombarded by remorse, self-loathing and fury. He couldn't stand it anymore; the terrible loss, the constant stress, the awful feeling of fragmentation, like he was breaking into pieces that could never be rejoined.

He drove away watching Deronda's house fade in the distance. Watching Grace fade in the distance. He'd never see her again. Suddenly, something bored up inside him; a pulverizing drill, grinding a tunnel through his insides, white sparks flying hot, bloodlust in his bloodshot eyes, his rational mind a pinball, ricocheting through his skull. Two depraved sons of bitches robbed him of everything he valued. It was time to attack, to put those two assholes on defense. Make them wary of every shadow. Make them fear for their lives. He wanted them to know. *IQ is on your case and he won't stop until you're dead.*

Dodson worried about Isaiah. He didn't answer his calls and texts. Dodson was going to drive over to the animal shelter when Deronda called. "Michael Stokeley wants to meet you," she said.

"Meet me? He already knows me," Dodson said.

"No, I mean meet *with* you. He didn't tell me why."

"Did he seem upset?"

"Hard to tell. He seemed like Stokeley."

"What'd you tell him?"

"I told him you'd meet him," Deronda said.

"What? Why?"

"The man asked for you. Are you seriously thinking about *not* meeting him?" Deronda was right, Dodson thought. There was no way out of it unless he buried himself under his apartment building. "When and where?"

"McClarin Park in twenty minutes," Deronda said.

"Twenty minutes? What if I was busy?"

"That's what I told Stokeley."

"And what did he say?"

"Nineteen minutes."

Dodson hustled over to the park. Stokeley and his crew were hangin' in the children's playground area. They looked like bears who'd just eaten some schoolkids. Stokeley was sitting on the hobbyhorse, smoking some tree. A disturbing sight. You could hardly see the horse. Mako was standing on the merry-go-round, the whole thing tilted to the side. Do-Right was on top of the slide, seemingly stuck.

"I can't get down, I'm too wide."

"Then stay up there till you lose weight," Mako said.

Dodson approached. Stokeley got up. The horse creaked with relief. It was nearly compressed flat. "I heard you wanted to meet up, Stoke," Dodson said.

"Yeah. I called Isaiah but he's got troubles," Stokeley said. "He said to call you. Said you was a fixer now." Stokeley looked at Dodson like he wasn't the best or even second-best option. He offered the joint.

"No thanks," Dodson said. "That weed y'all smoke would get Jamaica high." Stokeley was six-five, two-fifty, his shoulders like wrecking balls, a scarred-over bullet hole near his clavicle, skin nearly black with tats, his hair in a Mohawk of copper-colored dreds. There were lots of scary bruthas around. What made Stokeley stand out was his disposition, his readiness, like a wolf waiting in the weeds, every taut muscle of its body poised to attack. Stokeley was like that all the damn time.

"Here's the thing," Stokeley said. "My PO, cat named Flyn. He's fuckin' with me. I don't do what he says he'll revoke my parole." Dodson was surprised Stokeley hadn't already stomped this guy to death. "Couple of weeks ago, we had a meeting," he said. "This muthafucka be lookin' at my file, talkin' 'bout everything I done and I better keep my nose clean." Stokeley huffed, dropped the roach and crushed it with a foot the size of a battleship. "Check dis," he continued. "Flyn gave me fourteen thousand dollars in cash and tells me to buy a kilo of coke."

"Oh shit," Dodson said, seeing the scam in his mind. "Then you supposed to sell it retail and give Flyn the proceeds?"

"That's right," Stokeley said.

"Ain't dis a bitch. Flyn don't touch the dope and you take all the risk."

"If I get busted I'm on my own," Stokeley said. "What am I gonna tell the police? My PO gave me fourteen thousand dollars? Who gonna believe me? I get tagged I'm goin' back to Folsom."

"Where'd the money change hands?" Dodson asked.

"In his office. He always take my phone before we talk. Buyin' and sellin' the coke wasn't no problem. I know every dealer in Long Beach. I left Flyn's cut at a dead drop."

"When's your next run?" Dodson said.

"It's already happening. Flyn gave me another fourteen K." Stokeley slowly shook his head and looked down at the ground. "I can't be doin' this shit, Dodson. I'm too goddamn old to be slingin' dope. I'm gettin' off the street."

"You don't mind my sayin', the street is happy to see you go," Dodson replied.

"My cousin, Randal, you know him?" Stokeley went on. "He's got some tow trucks and a contract with the city. He needed another driver on the midnight shift. I mean like, the work ain't exactly on the high side but it's okay. We goin' in together on another truck. I'll have my own rig if I'm not in lockup."

"Let me look into it. I need some time," Dodson said.

"How much time? I'm sweatin' it, man," Stokeley said, his voice rising.

"I hear you. I'm on it," Dodson said.

"Can you ask Isaiah to help you out?"

"Like you said, he's got troubles," Dodson replied. He carefully avoided saying no. Deronda told him the word irritated Stokeley. Maybe because he'd heard it so few times.

"I'm on it, Stoke. I'm on it right now," Dodson declared. He sounded more confident than he was. He left the playground. Stokeley sounded tired and vulnerable, he thought. Even hard-core gangstas get weary of the life. Even gangstas long for safety and peace. Dodson remembered his days of running the streets. He was afraid all the time, though he'd never admit it. Stokeley was fearful too. Imagine that, thought Dodson. All this time, baddest muthafucka in the hood was walking around scared like everybody else. Scared because he was getting older, scared because all he'd done was terrorize people and poison them with drugs. Grow up in the hood, live a violent life with nothing but bad choices, and all you can do is more of what you've been doing. If you stop, what are you?

Dodson did a search on Flyn and got some basic information. Forty-one years old, a face like a bearded sweet potato, a PO for six years, worked out of the Long Beach office. Flyn used Facebook and there were the usual photos. Some were probably family, they looked like spuds too. The latest pics saw Flyn in a shiny candy-apple-red bass boat, sitting in the pilot's chair grinning proudly, holding up a big fish he'd caught. There were others with his buddies, in matching shirts on a softball field and tailgating at a ballpark. Flyn was leaning against a glistening white Subaru with no rear license plate while he ate something that looked like a dinosaur rib.

Dodson went to Flyn's place, a small, bleak house in El Segundo. It was in bad shape, peeling paint, trash on the lawn. Dodson checked out the garage, locked with a big chain and brass padlock. He peeked through the crack between the doors. The candy-apple-red bass boat was there, set on its trailer. Dodson had a ring of bump keys left over from his hustling days. He went in the side door and looked around. Mismatched furniture, a huge TV, unmade bed and dirty dishes in the sink, thick smells of booze and mildewed laundry.

Dodson drove to a strip mall on Atlantic Boulevard. Camilla's office was between a dry cleaner's and a Dunkin'. The sign on the window glass said CAMILLA LIGHTFOOT, LICENSED TAX PREPARER AND CPA. During Dodson's hustling days, Camilla helped him with his Ponzi scheme, drawing up phony contracts, sales forms and other legal documents that were complete bullshit. She did her own infomercials and advertised on bus benches. *THE IRS HATES CAMILLA LIGHTFOOT!* the ads proclaimed. LIGHTFOOT WAS AN IRS AGENT FOR 15 YEARS. IF SHE MISSES A DEDUCTION *SHE'LL PAY YOUR TAXES.* There was a picture of her, a serious woman in horn-rimmed glasses and a bulldog expression. Very few people noticed the microscopic asterisk in the right corner of the ad. *Taxes calculated by Camilla Lightfoot at her sole discretion.* As far as Dodson knew, Camilla didn't pay anybody enough to catch the bus.

They had coffee and maple bars at Dunkin'. "The research is easy enough but the rest is illegal," Camilla said.

"Since when do you have a problem with illegal?" Dodson said.

"I don't."

"You worried about gettin' paid?"

Camilla looked just like her picture. Serious, studious, a severe haircut, horn-rimmed glasses and a gray business suit. "I'm always worried about getting paid and the extracurricular stuff will cost you more."

"That's cool but I have a better idea," Dodson said.

"A better idea than getting paid?" She chuckled. "I'm not into drugs or stolen merchandise."

"I didn't say you were. Let me ask you something."

"Okay."

"How long have you owned your car?"

Flyn had been a parole officer for four years. The scam he created worked like a charm. He wasn't rich but he was living better than he ever did before. A house with a garage instead of a shitty apartment, a new Subaru Outback, the Onyx edition, bleacher seats at Dodger Stadium, weekends fishing at Castaic, the 150 Merc went like hell. The parolees were dumb as hockey pucks. Pick one with the right background, work him for a while, promise him no urine tests and no surprise visits and he was happy to sign on.

Flyn contacted them on a burner and only saw them at their scheduled appointments. He left the dope money at a dead drop and picked up his profits at another, always careful to surveil the area beforehand. His present pigeon was Michael Stokeley. He was perfect. In and out of prison on drug and assault charges, DUI and grand theft. If his parole was revoked, he'd do twenty years. Stokeley was supposed to deliver the proceeds tomorrow.

Flyn was in his office. His first appointment was with a crackhead who smelled like garbage. Flyn listened for thirty seconds and kicked him out. He rejected I-131, some asshole applying for emergency travel to see his three-month-old daughter supposedly diagnosed with lymphoma. The guy was Mexican. He'd skedaddle in a heartbeat and open a hot dog cart in Alhambra. A big no on that one.

Flyn made a surprise visit on a woman who was supposed to be at work, an industrial laundry six blocks from the office. What happens? She's not there. You ask her supervisor, he says she's at lunch and disappears into his office. He's Black, she's Black, it's bullshit. Then the woman comes sauntering in telling you she was just getting back. More bullshit called. She screamed like a kid when he revoked her parole. The cops picked her up.

Flyn drove home. The Subaru still smelled new and he wondered how long that would last. He heard you can buy the smell in a spray can. He parked in the driveway, front bumper nearly touching the garage. He slipped the car cover on. He entered the living room, dropped his keys in the candy dish and turned on the lights. He smelled coffee. Strange, did he forget to turn the Mr. Coffee off? He went into the kitchen to check. Startled, he jumped, shouting, "HEY!" Two people were sitting at the breakfast table. They were calm, no guns, sipping coffee like they lived there.

"Who the hell are you and what are you doing in my house?" Flyn said angrily.

"Just a conversation and we be on our way," said one of them. He was a short guy, Black, dressed in a white T-shirt and jeans.

Flyn backed away, fumbling around, trying to reach his gun in the back holster. "I'm calling the cops."

"I'd advise against it and I'll tell you why," said the woman. She looked like Miss Hathaway in *The Beverly Hillbillies.*

"You'd advise against it?" Flyn scoffed. "I advise you to get out of my house." He finally had his gun out.

"You shouldn't draw your weapon unless you plan to shoot somebody," the Black guy said coolly. "Is that what you're gonna do? Kill a Black man and a white woman in your kitchen?" That gave Flyn pause.

"My researches indicate you recently bought a new Subaru Outback for approximately thirty-eight thousand dollars," Miss Hathaway said, "and a fully equipped Ranger bass boat for twenty-six thousand dollars. Do I have that right?" A sick feeling was creeping into Flyn's stomach.

"So what?" he said. "Lots of people buy boats and cars."

"Lots of people who make more than fifty-nine thousand dollars a year less taxes. You also paid cash. The car plus the boat is approximately sixty-four thousand dollars. A considerable sum."

The bad feeling turned to alarm. "I, um, bought them with my savings," Flyn sputtered.

The Black guy seemed to think that was funny. "If your supervisor wants to know where you got the money, is that what you'd say? I saved sixty-four thousand dollars from my previous job as a security guard, making sixteen dollars an hour?"

Flyn thought bugs were landing on his forehead but they were beads of sweat. "Listen, this is none of your fucking business. Now get up and get out or I will call the cops."

It was like the Black guy didn't hear him. "What's the rent on this place?" he asked.

"Seventeen-fifty a month, or twenty-one thousand dollars a year," Miss Hathaway said.

"Fifty-nine thousand less twenty-one thousand leaves thirty-eight thousand dollars to live on," the Black guy added.

"No, you've forgotten taxes," she said. "A single adult with no dependents would pay a nominal rate of twenty-two percent. That's about six thousand dollars, leaving you a net of—"

"I can do the math, okay?" Flyn said. "This is a shakedown!"

"In a way," the Black guy said.

"How can you shake down somebody *in a way*?"

"Lay off Michael Stokeley."

"Stokeley? Is he behind this?" Flyn said.

"Don't matter who's behind what. All you have to do is let him alone. No more selling dope and no reprisals. Let him finish out his parole and that's it."

"I don't know, let me think about it," Flyn said. He saw his scam going up in smoke.

The Black guy huffed. "Do I sound like I'm asking you?"

"Failure to comply will result in severe consequences," Miss Hathaway said. "Your supervisor, a Mrs. Damon I believe, will receive a lengthy report detailing your extortion scheme and accompanied by the relevant documents. A copy will go to the police." Flyn was stuck. He didn't know who they were but they had the goods.

"So all I have to do is lay off Stokeley?" Flyn said.

"That's right," the Black guy said. "Don't mess up. We pull the trigger on this and you'll be in Quentin with a bunch of muthafuckas you sent there." Flyn was stunned, there with his mouth open, his gun hand slack and by his side. As the two rose to leave, Miss Hathaway said to the short guy,

"Haven't you forgotten something?"

"Oh yeah, you're right," he said. "Flyn, can I borrow a pen? I'm gonna need your signature."

"My signature? For what?"

"Your pink slip."

The hobbyhorse would never gallop again. Stokeley gave Dodson the handshake and a hug. The hug nearly collapsed his lungs.

"Hey, man, I talked to Flyn," Stokeley said. "You saved my shit, Dodson."

"My pleasure, Stoke."

"Flyn say I don't have to come in no more. I can go on my merry fucking way."

"I'm happy for you, Stoke. If y'all decide to gangsta up again, put an ad in the paper so I can avoid your ass." The fellas chuckled.

"I'm keeping Flyn's money," Stokeley said. "How much do I owe you?"

"On the house," Dodson said.

"I'm gonna buy that tow truck," Stokeley said, smiling. Dodson was still feeling the effects of the hug. This nigga don't need a truck to tow cars. He could pick them up and drag 'em down the street. "This ain't no joke, man, I'm serious," Stokeley continued. "Y'all ever need something, gimme a call."

"I appreciate that, Stoke, I really do," said Dodson. "Y'all take care now." Dodson went home, feeling good about himself. He didn't tell Cherise. She'd say he helped a known thug but couldn't help the Reverend. Cherise had never mentioned the fiasco again but there was a coldness in her manner. He tried, didn't he? Elvira and Mrs. Yakashima had irreconcilable differences. But dammit, he hated disappointing Cherise. He drove home, brooding. He parked the car and sat there a moment. He smiled. His brain wasn't freakishly large but it did the job. He got out his phone and dialed the Reverend.

Winnie met Isaiah at the Coffee Cup. The owner, a twiglike Black woman who might have been around since the Truman administration, treated Isaiah like a hero. He was embarrassed but thanked her. She kissed him on top of his head.

"Don't you worry now," she said. "Our Lord and Savior has Grace in his loving arms. You'll get her back." The woman returned to work. Isaiah didn't touch his espresso, staring into his cup. Winnie sipped her mocha latte with soy milk. It was awful. It wasn't on the menu but the old woman made it special for her. Duvall was supposed to be here but he didn't show up.

"Thank you for meeting me," Winnie said. She opened her Montblanc notepad and took a pencil out of her bag. "Talk to me about the kidnapping," she said.

Isaiah was despondent and exhausted, head held low, a deep anger simmering in his watery eyes. A warning sign, she thought. She'd seen this in men she'd arrested and in court when the judge sent the prisoner away for thirty years. People did extreme things in this state. "Mr. Quintabe?" Winnie said. "I can't imagine how you must feel but I think it would be better for both of us if we get this out of the way. The basics will be fine."

He didn't move or look at her. She felt unnecessary. He cleared his throat.

"I was up north in the hospital," he said. "I got a call from Deronda. She said Grace was..." He sat there, his shoulders slumped, the bubbling anger churning. He sighed deeply but didn't speak.

"Mr. Quintabe. I hope you don't do anything extreme," Winnie said gently. He looked at her as if the words were laughable.

"There isn't anything to do," he said.

"Yes," she said. She put down the pencil and closed the notebook. "I saw Grace in the hospital." He looked at her. Plaintively.

"Is she okay? I'm off the visitors' list."

"No serious injuries but she's traumatized. And she's pretty beat up. She's been through a lot."

"Those motherfuckers," he hissed. He looked off for a moment and nodded once. He's made a decision, thought Winnie. She was alarmed. He stood up and said, "They're going to pay."

"Mr. Quintabe—" Winnie began. Isaiah walked out. She shut her eyes, her chin dropping to her chest. She shouldn't have told him. She thought it would ease his mind, knowing Grace wasn't grievously injured. What now, Winnifred? She wished Duvall was here. He was immune to compassion. His presence would have stopped her.

CHAPTER EIGHTEEN
Bone Chips and Blood

Raoul was a small-time neighborhood dealer. He sold weed and prescription pills. He wasn't greedy and he didn't overcharge. All he wanted was enough money to eat what he wanted, pay his bills, pay his child support and hire the occasional prostitute. He was surprised when Isaiah came to the door. He asked for Adderall, twenty-milligram tabs.

"These for real?" Isaiah said. He held the vial up to the light.

"Name brand, no fillers," Raoul said. He was well aware Isaiah could put him out of business, send him to the joint or have his ex-clients beat him to shit.

"How much?" Isaiah said.

"Fifteen bucks apiece, that's a discount price." Raoul had never seen Isaiah like this. Like he'd been run over by a bus and was lying on the pavement. "Are you . . . all right?" he said. Isaiah paid and left.

Isaiah sat in the car and dry-swallowed two tabs. Half an hour later, he was still exhausted but now he was wired, his brain abuzz and blank, save for a single blue laser beam of revenge and retribution. Doubt left him and his conscience went with it.

* * *

Isaiah had studied guns for years. It was an essential part of knowing thine enemy. Contrary to popular belief, only a small percentage of illegal guns are stolen. The same goes for those acquired on the dark net. A common source is straw buyers who purchase them at gun shows. But the bulk of illegal firearms come from a legal source. FFLs. A licensed federal firearms dealer. To get an FFL in California, you need to be a US citizen over the age of twenty-one who can legally own a gun. The approval process and paperwork are a bitch. You need a lot of patience. Nevertheless, the FFL might be your local gun store, an arms ring or some guy working out of his garage. Isaiah called Eddie Hunter.

When he looked in the mirror Eddie saw a middle-aged white guy, sallow and unhealthy, baggy suit, hair the color of a dust bunny. His ex-wife said he looked like a novelty salesman with a catalogue of rubber chickens and whoopee cushions. Eddie met Isaiah at the Holiday Inn in downtown Long Beach, a nice room, no place for illegal transactions.

Over the years, Isaiah had consulted Eddie about various guns, learning how they worked and what they could do. A couple of times, Eddie took Isaiah to his place in Palmdale and let him shoot a few of the guns, just to get the feel. Isaiah was an incredible shot, firing tight clusters no matter what type or caliber of gun. Eddie kept his goods in three large suitcases. They were old, mismatched and beat up. Carrying Halliburtons was an invitation to get robbed. The suitcases were open, laid out on the two queen-size beds. There were handguns in popular calibers, some in their original cases, some not. There was a sawed-off shotgun broken down into parts. There were an assault rifle and two Uzis, nicely folded and wrapped in plastic.

"Why do you need a gun?" Eddie said.

"Self-defense," Isaiah said. He gave Eddie a look.

"Uh, okay, sure. Didn't mean to offend," Eddie said, scratching the back of his neck. Isaiah looked like shit. His clothes were rumpled, lint in his hair, his eyes squinting and red... He looks my age, thought Eddie. "Do you know what you want?" he asked. "I've got a Glock seventeen but it's used."

"I want a new gun," Isaiah said.

"I've got a Sig Sauer P320M, the compact model. Shoots great." Eddie paused a moment, not sure he should speak. "Um, if you don't mind me saying, Isaiah, you don't look so good."

"Neither do you," came the reply, Isaiah's voice suggesting Eddie could look a lot worse.

"Right. Down to business."

The Sig came in its own hard plastic case. There were labels on the side. Serial number, gun model, date it was made. Isaiah checked them and opened the case. A Sig sticker was on top, along with various brochures, where they should be. There were a travel-size tube of gun oil, two fifteen-round magazines and a trigger guard, all in their foam inserts. You have to buy a trigger guard to buy a gun. The matte-black Sig was wrapped in plastic. An orange chamber flag kept the chamber open. Isaiah removed the flag and closely examined the gun. He slid the ejector up and back, sniffed the barrel, turned the gun this way and that, probably looking for scratches.

"Do you think I'd sell you a used gun?" Eddie said, a little offended.

"No. But whoever sold it to you might have," Isaiah replied. Eddie and Isaiah's relationship was strained, but mutually beneficial. Isaiah didn't bust Eddie and in return, Eddie passed on the scuttlebutt about arms dealers, arms shipments, contract killings, homegrown terrorists, suspected mass shooters and other violent crimes. Isaiah said more guns were taken off the streets and more lives were saved by "letting you exist" than an arrest and prison time. Eddie knew about Isaiah's exploits, helping people with their problems big and small. In a way, Eddie was helping Isaiah help the community. I'm saving lives, Eddie thought. He felt good about that.

"Have you got an extended mag?" Isaiah said.

"I've got a ProMag, thirty-two rounds. Jesus, Isaiah, who're you going to war with?"

Isaiah ignored the question. "What about a textured grip?"

"I have them but you'll have to put it on yourself," Eddie said. "It's easy enough. They're stick-on." Eddie wasn't allowed to work in Long Beach. A tacit understanding. He thought it was unfair, restricting access to customers, and yet, here's Isaiah buying an illegal gun in a hotel room a few blocks away from the police station.

"A suppressor," Isaiah said.

"I've got an MODX, the segmented model. A new one will run you eight hundred bucks. I have one at half price. It's used, but nothing to worry about. The thing's got no moving parts."

"Ammo?" Isaiah said.

"I've got Elite Crowns, hollow-points."

"A box."

"You need a holster," Eddie added. A statement. "Sticking the gun in your pants isn't secure and you might blow your dick off."

"It needs to be inconspicuous," Isaiah said.

"Try this. It's called a Sneaky Pete." It looked like a larger-than-normal phone case. You clipped it to your belt. Isaiah shook his head. To get your hand on the gun you had to lift the flap. Too clumsy, too noticeable.

"Let me see something else."

"I've got a paddle holster," Eddie said. "People call it the quick-draw holster." Eddie explained it was worn inside your pants. A concave piece of plastic held the holster against your body and more of the gun's grip was exposed. "It won't come off when you draw," Eddie said. He found one in his luggage and gave it to Isaiah for inspection. "Easier to take on and off than a clip-on," Eddie continued. "You don't have to take your belt off. That one's made for the Three-Twenty Compact. Fits exactly. It's popular with police detectives. I wear one myself."

"How much?" Isaiah said.

"For everything?" Eddie said. "Buy the Sig in a store and it'll run around seven hundred bucks. Let's say a thousand for the gun and retail for everything else. Thirty bucks for the ProMag, the ammo's sixty, same for the holster, the grip is twenty and what did I say? Four hundred for the suppressor. That's what? Fifteen seventy? Call it an even sixteen hundred."

Eddie had bought the gun from an FFL for six hundred and the rest at a steep discount. He knew Isaiah knew but he didn't try to negotiate. Isaiah peeled off the amount from a stack of used bills, bound with a rubber band. Eddie wondered where that came from. Was Isaiah robbing banks? Eddie put the goods into a Whole Foods shopping bag. "There you go," he said brightly. He wanted this to end well. "For all anybody knows, it's a bunch of organic bananas." Isaiah took the bag and left.

Eddie was worried. Something was really wrong. Was Isaiah going to shoot somebody? *Kill* somebody? Buying the gun was premeditation. Murder One.

Isaiah went to the wrecking yard. He wanted to ditch the junker he was driving and get another.

"Why?" TK said. "Yours is running fine."

Isaiah closed his eyes. The conversation just started and he was exasperated, about ready to bust. The Adderall does nothing for your patience. "You're high," TK said. "What are you on?"

"Could I get the keys? I need to go."

"Why don't you stay here awhile?" TK said. "Go on up in the loft and get some rest."

"I said I need to go!" Isaiah shouted. He snatched the keys out of TK's hand and drove off, tossing some bills out of the window.

Isaiah was back at the animal shelter. He was sitting at Harry's desk, loading Elite Crown rounds into the ProMag. He was starting to feel ridiculous. He didn't need all this firepower or the holster or anything else. Pull the gun, shoot the gun. Two shots, max. He was so tired and engrossed, he didn't hear Dodson's car arriving.

"What are you doing here?" Isaiah said. "How'd you get in?"

"You left the front door open," Dodson said.

"TK called you?" Isaiah said.

"Uh-huh. So did Raoul and Eddie Hunter. They'd never seen you like that before. If a drug dealer and a gun dealer are worried about you, you know you in trouble."

"I can't keep looking over my shoulder," Isaiah said. He was furious, hands shaking. "Even if I quit being IQ, Skip and Manzo might take me out while I'm bagging groceries or washing dishes or whatever I end up doing. Maybe I'll take Grace's old job at the food truck."

"So you're gonna shoot Skip and Manzo before they shoot you? Is that the plan?" Dodson said. Isaiah didn't answer. "As somebody who's shot a few people, it ain't no fun," Dodson said. "The bullet makes a big-ass hole and blood comes out, more blood than you've ever seen—"

"I know that!" Isaiah barked. He fumbled with the magazine and spilled the shells all over the floor. "Fuck!"

"A gun is messy," Dodson continued unfazed, "blood and bone chips all over the place. A knife will work but you might have to stab 'em more than once. It's harder than it looks. Most people don't stay still and let you." Isaiah stood. He was seething, sweat running down his temples, feverish eyes, the veins in his arms popping. He looked unhinged.

"Leave me alone," he said, and he walked out of the office.

"You my homeboy, Q," Dodson said, trailing behind. "I can't let you do something you'll be sorry for forever. What if the police get on it?"

"They won't," Isaiah said. They walked across the patio to the kennels and the dogs started barking. Dodson yelled over the noise.

"Why? Because you're too smart? Is that what you think? Your ego has kicked your brain right outta your head." Isaiah stopped and looked directly at him.

"In the first place, you don't *let* me do anything, and what am I supposed to do? Let them kill me? Let them kill Grace? Are we supposed to stay hiding for the rest of our lives?" The dogs keyed in on the emotion and barked louder, some were howling.

"Grace has friends! We'll keep her safe!" Dodson shouted.

"What about me? What about *me*?" Isaiah cried. "I'm wrecked! I'm destroyed! Everything's been taken from me. I'm not living like that. Those two assholes are finished!"

"You won't do it," Dodson said. Isaiah leaned in close.

"I've never come as close to kicking your ass as right now!"

"You won't off them because I'll tell Grace," Dodson said. He'd been punched by people a lot bigger and stronger than Isaiah. "She'll hate you forever," he said.

"Let her hate me!" Isaiah said. "What difference does it make?

She hates me already. So go ahead, call her! I really don't give a shit! Now back off, Dodson, or I'll make you sorry." He shoved Dodson away with both hands. Dodson staggered back a few paces but didn't fall. Isaiah screamed at the dogs.

"Shut the fuck up, do you hear me? SHUT THE FUCK UP OR I'LL KILL EVERY ONE OF YOU!" He stopped and stood there, shaking, tears falling on the ground. Dodson considered a man hug but Isaiah was too defiant, too belligerent, being comforting was a reason to push you away.

"Okay, nigga, I'll help you then," Dodson said.

"Fuck off."

"I'm not kidding." And he wasn't either. "But do we have to kill 'em? Can't we take a pound or two of flesh?"

"*We* aren't doing anything," Isaiah said. Dodson followed him back to Harry's office. Isaiah plunked down in the office chair, eyes glazed and hateful. Dodson considered saying more, but not now. It was enough to sow some doubt, let him catch his breath. Dodson knew Isaiah didn't really want to do this. Slaughtering somebody was extreme and disgusting. Nobody is happy killing, even if they say they are, even if it's war, even if you're saving your own life. The justification might be righteous as hell, but the act itself and the impact on you are always fucked up. If Isaiah wasn't so stressed out, pissed off and fatigued, he'd remember that.

"I've gotta go. Cherise wants me home," Dodson said. "Get some sleep, Q. Talk to me before you do anything." Isaiah didn't answer. "Did you hear me?"

"Yeah, I heard you, I'll call, okay?" Isaiah said. Dodson almost asked if he could keep the gun but thought better of it.

"Go easy, Q," Dodson said. He moved for the door, expecting an answer, but Isaiah turned away.

* * *

The next day, Isaiah was standing at a bus stop, behind the bench, his hands on it for support. He couldn't sit down because of the paddle holster. He was across the street from the coffee shop. Manzo habitually went there for his morning latte. Isaiah's cap was pulled low, he was wearing a Covid mask and some anonymous clothes from a Goodwill store. His escape plan. After shooting Manzo, he'd run around the corner to where the new junker was parked. No registration and the license plate obscured. It was clean of fingerprints. Isaiah was wearing latex gloves, not unusual during the pandemic. He'd drive somewhere, ditch the car and catch the bus back to the animal shelter.

It was warm. The mask itched. Isaiah was sweating and unsteady, the Adderall accelerating his already thudding heart. He'd taken the max dose all at once. He waited, seemingly a long time, but when he glanced at his watch ten minutes had passed. Manzo's Caprice went by right in front of him and turned into the coffee shop parking lot. Isaiah took some deep breaths and wiped his sweaty face. The Adderall was keeping him awake but it added no clarity or restraint. He felt numb and robotic. He was aware of nothing but his hammering heart and the roar of adrenaline in his ears. He crossed the street and approached the lot. Manzo got out of his car. The Khan looked anxious and he'd lost weight. He kept rubbing something on his face. He had the look. High on meth, Isaiah thought, too invincible to worry about arrest. Manzo went toward the coffee shop.

Isaiah jogged across the street and followed him, his hand stuck under his shirt. He gripped the gun. He couldn't stop himself. He didn't want to stop himself. He was walking through an image, a scene, something made up by a screenwriter. Manzo wasn't a person anymore. He was a thing, a square of gangsta flannel getting bigger and closer. *Shoot him, Isaiah*. It was inevitable. He was ten feet away. *Shoot him, Isaiah. Shoot the bastard!* He drew the weapon—as Dodson came out of the coffee shop. He walked toward Manzo, smiling his hustler's smile.

"What's up, Manzo? How you doin', son?"

"Fuck off, cabron. I'll get you too," Manzo said. He shouldered Dodson out of the way and went inside. Dodson took the gun away from Isaiah and hurriedly tucked it under his hoodie.

"Gimme that goddamn thing," Dodson muttered. "I should shoot your ass for bein' so stupid."

They drove away in Dodson's car. "How'd you know I'd be here?" Isaiah said.

"I been in this neighborhood as long as you have. I know who hangs where." Isaiah almost said thank you but it wasn't necessary. Dodson knew how he felt. They said nothing on the drive. Reality slapped Isaiah out of his trance, waking him up, his near disaster so close he could have shaved with it. He couldn't believe himself. He'd nearly shot a man in the back. You don't realize what bad shape you're in until you do, he thought. More than anything, he needed rest. There were no bad guys to chase, no cases to solve, no way to find Skip. The thought of his friends warmed him. He remembered gathering around Cherise's dining table, beaming over the money they'd raised for him. He wondered how they did it. There were other good things. Verna's earnest prayer, and Harry telling him everything he needed he already had, and TK's jokes, and Dodson saving his life more than once.

He remembered when he started his career as IQ; living alone, eating soup standing at the counter, watching documentaries on his laptop and spending his weekends reading and listening to music. He remembered the villains he'd faced. His brother's murderer, Seb Habimana, and Walczak, the monster of Abu Ghraib, and Tommy Lau, the treacherous leader of a Chinese triad, and Angus Byrne, the West Coast's premier dealer of illegal arms, and William Crowe, the serial killer, and the Starks, a white nationalist gang, and many others. They all tried to kill him but he'd never thought of his mortality until now. Maybe it was losing Grace. Maybe it was dying and never seeing her again.

The rattail comb had punctured Manzo's skin. The neck wound bled like he was shot. It was bandaged now, a black-and-green bruise around the edges. The word was out. Isaiah's girl stuck the Khan in the neck with a goddamn comb. He was humiliated. He was ashamed. He actually tried to sell the girl into *slavery.* Hard-core even for a gangster. That would get around too. The neighborhood women, young and old, would hate him forever.

Manzo was lying on the couch in his mother's living room holding a bag of ice to his temple. Until recently, he never got headaches. The doorbell rang. "Mamita, I got it," he called out. She wasn't speaking to him. She cooked his dinner and left it out to get cold. He got up, crossed to the front window and looked through the blinds. Diego and his two homies were on the porch, grinning and chuckling, eager to humble him even more. He opened the door.

"What's up, ese?" Diego said with that fucking smirk. "I heard some white girl put it to you. What was it? She stabbed you with a bobby pin?" The homies laughed. Manzo didn't answer. He came out and closed the door behind him. "The bosses are taking over your territory," Diego said. "They don't want a pussy representing the brand. I'm shot caller now." Manzo said nothing. Diego stepped closer, nearly face to face. "Your time is over, chief," Diego said. "You're officially a nobody. You're still on the hook for the money too. You better figure out how to pay or move to Alaska." Diego grinned like a kid with a dirty secret. "Did you know Isaiah was gonna shoot you in the back?"

"What?" Manzo said.

"At El Mejor. People saw him walking you down. His homie stopped him or you'd be in the fucking ground already. It's fucking pitiful. All that big talk about offing Isaiah and he's the one stalking you! That's some funny shit, man." Manzo had no recollection of that day. He was high.

"You should give up," one of the homies said. "You're giving up everything else."

"I'll never give up," Manzo mumbled.

"I'll believe it when I read Isaiah's obituary," Diego said. "Until then? You ain't shit."

They left. Manzo felt hollowed out, an outline around nothing. He was always somebody, at least in his own eyes. People would pity him. He was more fearful now than he'd ever been in a gunfight or prison or getting beaten by the police. He always saw his future as a steady expansion of power, wealth and reach. Now it was a long line of zeros. What would he do without the gang? What would he do for money? How would he live? He'd be sleeping on the couch until he was an old man if Isaiah didn't kill him first.

His mother didn't like him smoking in the house. She thought weed was like heroin or something. He went in the backyard and sparked a blunt. The only light came from the neighbor's house. Manzo could see a patch of lawn, the dead barbecue and the silhouette of the rusty swing set he'd played on as a boy. His life was in the past now. His life was a memory, that was all. Now there were two reasons to kill Isaiah. His hatred. And survival. Manzo went back inside and turned on the TV. Seven million movies on Netflix and nothing to watch. He'd never felt this paralyzed, this powerless. Maybe he'd go back to Mexico and live with his relatives.

His burners were on the bed table, charging. There was one

for Sinaloa exclusively and another for Locos business, the messages in coded text. He looked at it, thinking it was the last time he'd need it. The messages were days old. There was one voice mail from a number he didn't recognize. Maybe one of the outliers talking shit. He listened to it and couldn't believe what he was hearing. He sat down on the bed and wondered what to do.

Dodson went shopping and came back with two bags of groceries. Cherise was in the living room with Regina Freeman, Tudor's receptionist. They were sitting on the sofa. Regina was tearful, Cherise's hand on top of hers.

"Oh, there you are," Cherise said. "You remember Regina, don't you?"

"Sho do. How you doin', Regina?" Dodson said.

"Not very well." She was a trim young woman, prim and earnest, hands holding her skirt over her knees. Cherise gave Dodson a look and exited. Dodson sat down.

Regina took a moment and said, "Tudor is harassing me."

"Harassing you how?" Dodson said.

"He's always putting his hand on my shoulder and looking down my front and he's always talking about my body and brushing up against me." Her voice cracked. Tudor had demeaned her. She was hurt and humiliated. Poor girl, just trying to make her way, thought Dodson. "It's a two-person office," she said. "There's no one to report him to and it gets worse." She lowered her head and folded her arms. "He gave me a raise." She said it like she'd done something wrong. "He tells me everything could go away. He says it all the time."

"If Anita knew, she'd string him up by his nuts," Dodson said.

"I'll get fired anyway," Regina said. "Anita won't want me around her husband." There was a box of tissues on the coffee table. She took one and dabbed at her eyes. "I need that raise, Mr. Dodson," Regina said. "I've got school to pay for and I'm supporting my mother." Options were running through Dodson's mind. Regina took it for reluctance. "That's okay," she said, embarrassed. "I shouldn't have asked."

"Hold up now. I think I can help you out."

"And I won't get fired?"

"No, you won't," Dodson declared. "And you can keep that raise, too."

CHAPTER NINETEEN
Cancer

Tudor was leaving for the day. He stopped at the reception desk, Regina sitting there all prim and proper. It was fun messing with her. He paid her more than he should but it kept her from getting a job someplace else. This morning he asked her to spend the weekend with him in Vegas. He didn't say it like an invitation, he said it like an order, like a command. He was sure she'd give in.

"I made reservations at the Bellagio," he said like it was already decided. "A luxury suite with a Jacuzzi. Ever heard of Penn and Teller? Hard ticket to get, I can tell you."

"I'm sorry, Tudor. I really can't," she said, a hint of fuck-you in her voice.

Enough of this bullshit, he thought. Time to put the screws on.

"Your decision will have consequences," he said, getting official on her. He leaned over the reception desk and gave her his mean look. In a low voice he said, "You have until tomorrow to change your mind. Unemployment insurance won't pay the bills. Believe me, I know." He straightened up, straightened his tie and smiled an arrogant smile. "I'll see you in the morning and we'll discuss your salary."

Tudor took the elevator down to the parking garage, unhappy he had to twist the girl's arm. She doesn't know what's good for her, he thought. She'll change her mind once we're in Vegas. Let her taste the good life. Cozy up in a suite bigger than her mama's house. Stop by Gordon Ramsay's and sip champagne while you snack on osetra caviar at $300 an ounce.

Tudor got off the elevator and walked to his car. He scowled. He couldn't believe it. That scrawny punk Dodson was leaning against the door of his brand-new Mercedes G-Class, more like a white-on-white luxury tank riding on Vossen MX-3 custom wheels at $2,200 apiece.

"The hell are you doing, Dodson? Get off my car!"

"Wha's crackin', Tudor?" Dodson said with that irritating smile. "Nice ride. What'd this thing run you? Eighty, ninety grand?"

"A hundred and forty, thank you very much," Tudor said. "I've got an issue with you talking to my Anita but we'll take that up another time. *Now get off my car.*"

"In a minute. I like it here."

"You *like* it here? Shit. You won't like it when I kick your—" Someone was coming up behind him. Tudor turned around and gasped. It was *Michael Stokeley,* the terror of East Long Beach.

"A hundred and forty, huh?" Stokeley said. His voice was deep and guttural, like there was chain mail wrapped around his tonsils. He knocked on the hood with tattooed knuckles big as walnuts. For a moment, Tudor thought there were dents on the metal.

"He-hello, Stokeley," Tudor stammered. "L-long time no see." Stokeley was with two companions, both inked-up behemoths in wifebeaters and gold chains. The three of them were suddenly surrounding him, standing very close. He could see their scars, their intermittent gold teeth, the folds under their yellowed eyes and the muscles on their massive arms. He felt corralled by three Black buffalo who liked to smoke weed. "Um, s-something I can do for you fellas?"

"Your receptionist, Regina," Stokeley said. "You need to leave her alone."

"Leave her alone? I haven't done anything!" Tudor said, feigning outrage. "What's she been telling you? I should sue her for libel!"

"Gimme your keys," Stokeley said.

"My *car* keys?" Tudor said, shaking his head. "I'm sorry, Stokeley, but nobody drives this car but me."

Stokeley was driving. Dodson in the shotgun seat. Tudor in the back, squeezed between the behemoths. The one called Mako was smoking a joint big as a bouquet of geraniums. It was ridiculous, thought Tudor, like a Cheech and Chong movie. He tried to hold his breath so he wouldn't get high.

"May I ask where we're going?" Tudor asked.

"No, you may not," the other behemoth said. The others called him Do-Right. Mr. Right was rifling Tudor's wallet and generously distributing the cash and twelve credit cards to his colleagues. Then he threw the $650 lambskin Prada Saffiano wallet out the window. Tudor was terrified. The weed and the adrenaline were making him sick. He saw Stokeley put a crowbar in the trunk. What was that for? Prying out his eyeballs? The car came to a stop in front of a tenement building on Desmond Avenue.

"This your place?" Stokeley said.

"Yes, it is. Are you looking for an apartment?" Tudor said.

"Too bad if it burned down."

"Why would it burn down?"

They drove to another of Tudor's properties, a run-down

commercial building on the wrong end of Magnolia Boulevard. "This yours?" Stokeley said.

"Yes, it is. But why are we—"

"Too bad if it burned down."

"Why do you keep saying that?"

They went to three other properties Tudor owned. By now, he was saying "Too bad if it burned down" before Stokeley did. Strangely, they stopped in the middle of an alley. "Get out," Stokeley said. There was nothing noteworthy Tudor could see. Rough pavement, broken glass and dumpsters. Mako had the crowbar.

"Oh no!" Tudor cried. They were going to beat him to death! Instead, the behemoth used it to leverage up a manhole cover. Tudor's eyes went wide. "You're not going to—" Mako dragged Tudor to the edge of the manhole. A mossy sewage smell wafted up. A rusty ladder descended into complete darkness.

"Get in," Stokeley said.

"No, please! I could die down there!" Tudor cried. He tried to wrest himself away but Mako's grip was crushing his bicep.

"I said *get in,*" Stokeley growled. Tudor got on the ladder and went down until his eyes were even with the pavement. The sewage smell was overwhelming.

"Are you gonna fire Regina?" Dodson said.

"No, no! She has a job for life!" Tudor shouted.

"She deserves another raise, don't she?"

"Yes, yes! A good one too—and a better health plan!"

"You gonna 'pologize?" Stokeley said.

"Of course I will. What I did was despicable!" Tudor let out a strangled cry as Mako picked up the manhole cover. They were going to leave him down there!

"Are you crazy? I could die!" he yodeled.

"You won't," Dodson said. "Walk south about what—three miles? It empties into the LA River. Should be pretty shallow this time of year but you never know." The manhole cover descended, Tudor screaming as the darkness swallowed him up. It was warm and humid. He heard trickling water beneath him. *Oh my God, is that raw sewage down there?* He heard his G wagon drive off. He forced himself to descend. He got to the bottom of the ladder and gingerly stepped off. The water was ankle-deep, slimy with moss, things floating in it. He put his hand over his mouth and started walking.

"God save me," he said. He thought about Penn and Teller as he slogged on.

The tickets would go to waste.

Andy Wright sat on a folding chair in his cramped bedroom. The light was off. It was musty in here, like the locker room at school. Nothing was washed, not the sheets, clothes, socks. His mother used to do the laundry. He would take care of it himself, like a lot of other things. They were living on the money she got for selling her car and loans from relatives. That wouldn't last long. Good thing she liked mashed potatoes and mac and cheese from a box. She bought her own booze. Sweet wine that tasted like Hawaiian Punch with sugar in it, the sweet and sour stinking up the house. He hadn't gone to school for weeks. His mom hung up when the school called and she never read the notices because he threw them out. An official-looking lady in a dress came to the door twice and each time, Mom told her to fuck off.

Andy was ashamed of ratting out Isaiah. After he'd set off the Locos' car alarms he hid behind a dumpster and watched them run out of the wrecking yard to check their rides. When they left, he wanted to stay and sleep in the warehouse loft but was afraid TK would be angry with him. The old man knew he was the rat, there was nobody else. He wished he could make up for it. He spent most of his time at the wrecking yard, but now he couldn't go there. He had to face TK.

It was years ago, before Blue Hill and Goliath. Skip was staying at Jessica's for a few days. A slow time, not much work, not much of anything. He went out to score some coke but the guy only had meth. Skip bought a twenty-dollar rock, loaded a vaping pipe and lit up. The high was amazing. *Really amazing*. It clarified everything, like wiping the gunk out of your eyes and seeing what you've been missing. It gave you confidence. It sucked all the noise and negativity out of your head and vaporized it. You felt great. Seriously. You felt fucking great! A goddamn superstar and there was nothing—*nothing* you couldn't do. The shit lasted too. Snort some coke and you were high for what? A half hour? Crack was no more than five or ten minutes. But a meth high lasted six, eight, ten hours, maybe more. You took a second hit thinking, This can't be as good as the first one. But it was! Sex? Christ. You could stay hard for days. A hooker told him, "You're too much for me, stud. Want me to call my girlfriend?"

Another plus, you can focus, like really concentrate. Even on stupid shit. Mostly on stupid shit. He'd been high for three or four days. No food, no sleep. Suddenly starving, he went shopping, running around Vons like a hamster. He spent $140 on six dozen Snickers bars, boxes of donuts, packages of Danish, tubs of ice cream and a bunch of different cookies. He went back to Jessica's, restless, scratching his soul patch, disturbed by its feel, eating Oreos two at a time.

He was watching a show on the MotorTrend channel about changing your gear ratios. He was driving an old Corvette at the time. The ratios were 2.73. He looked them up. He wanted more acceleration, which meant a 3.15 or a 3.42. He didn't know why, but that seemed like something he should know about. He started reading and watching videos. He'd never fixed anything more complicated than a bicycle but he knew for certain he could change the ratios. He believed he was a master mechanic. He believed he could build the space shuttle. A guy at the Chevy dealer told him changing ratios wasn't a DIY project. You needed experience. It was easier to swap out the differential. Many of the articles Skip read said the same thing. But he knew better.

For a week, he was a mad scientist, inhaling information about input shafts, driver gears, countershafts, output shafts, pinion gears and ring gears, filling loose-leaf binders with notes and diagrams. He bought parts, most of which he couldn't identify. He took the differential apart and got confused. He didn't know what went where. The diagrams and instruction manuals had too many lines and arrows and words he didn't know.

He believed he needed the whole picture to complete the project. He needed to see everything at once. He disassembled the drive shaft, the clutch and the transmission. He remembered sitting on the floor, exhausted, sweating, smudged with oil, clothes filthy. Hundreds, maybe thousands, of nuts, screws, springs, O-rings, gears, adaptors, flanges, seals, housings, linkages and assemblies were spread out on the cement in no particular order. Jessica came in, took a look and said, "If you don't get off that shit, you're dumber than a bowl of oatmeal."

That made him angry. That's not how you talk to a man who can build the space shuttle. He felt misunderstood and disrespected. He bought a bottle of tequila and went to the park. He drank while he walked around, talking to himself, yelling at strangers, trying to make them see how amazing he was, telling them he wasn't stupid, *they* were stupid because they didn't understand, because they were ignorant. A wino and a couple of his buddies took offense. They beat him, robbed him and left him unconscious in the azalea bushes. The rain woke him up. He staggered home, sick, bleeding and half drowned. He slept for seventy-two hours. He got up, drank a half gallon of water and went into the garage. He looked around at the carnage and said, "What the fuck happened to my car?" He dumped his stash in the toilet and stomped on his pipe. That was enough of that. But he always remembered the high, that beautiful clarifying high.

Skip was depressed. He guessed that was what you'd call it. His room at the Crest felt like a cave with a bed in it, thoughts of revenge nagged at him constantly, he drank a lot of cheap tequila and watched TV with the sound off. He knew a guy named Kravitz who cooked meth. They met in prison. Kravitz's place was in the industrial zone, a fucked-up house with a tin roof, an abandoned oil derrick on the other side of the barbed-wire fence.

When Skip got there, the house was burned down, the heavy smell of charcoal and burned chemicals in the air. The area was taped off, some guys who were probably arson investigators standing around in the blackened rubble pointing at things.

Skip recalled Kravitz used the "shake and bake" method of making meth. Pseudoephedrine was mixed with water in a big plastic soda bottle. Then lye was added to make the mixture hot. Next, a solvent, which could be anything from acetone and engine starter to drain cleaner and battery acid. The mixture was shaken and a few minutes later, crystals formed. They were poured through a coffee filter to remove the excess liquid and there you have it, easier than making cookies. The problem was that everything but the water was either poisonous or flammable. Make the tiniest mistake, say a heat source too near the fumes or your "shake" container was too small, and you'd get one helluvan explosion. Skip wondered if Kravitz was dead.

He didn't want to return to the motel until he scored. He made a few calls. One guy referred him to another guy who referred him to another guy. Skip didn't like buying dope this way. Dope dealers were fucking ruthless. If you didn't watch yourself they robbed you—if you didn't rob them first.

The dealer called himself Cancer. Do you believe that? thought Skip. *Hi, Cancer, what's up? Want to eat something, Cancer? Let's shoot some hoops, Cancer.* Cancer didn't want to hook up unless Skip was going to buy "some serious points." A point was a tenth of a gram. Skip said he'd buy an ounce for two grand. Cancer didn't argue and gave him a location. A bad sign. Skip never met a dealer who didn't argue the price. He went to the bank, exchanged some twenties for one-dollar bills and stuffed them into an envelope. The meeting place was an alley behind a warehouse.

Skip arrived early. He parked and watched from his car. Two guys were milling around a loading dock. Cancer was probably the skinny one. He was explaining something to a big guy. They argued for a bit, then the big guy crossed the alley to his car. He got in and pulled the sunshade down so you couldn't tell if it was occupied. Cancer looked at his watch, then messed with his phone, glancing around, trying to be casual. A setup, Skip thought. Cancer would come up to your window, occupy you until his buddy came from the passenger side and held a gun in your face.

Skip rolled the windows down and took the silencer off the gun to shorten the length. He held the gun in his left hand, low by the side of the seat. He drove up to the loading dock. Cancer slid off and came to his window.

"You him, huh?" Cancer said. "Lemme see the money."

"Let me see the ice," Skip replied. Cancer produced a Ziploc bag, a handful of aquamarine crystals in there.

"Your turn," Cancer said.

Skip used his right hand and reached inside his shirt and

brought out the envelope. The flap was open, you could see the thick wad of bills. "It's all here," Skip said.

Cancer raised his eyes a bit, looking over the top of the car. That was the go sign. Skip quickly brought the gun up and fired cross-body, putting two holes in the big guy's car. He heard a grunt while he swiveled fast, putting the gun on Cancer. It took two seconds. Cancer didn't have time to react. He put up his hands, dropping the bag of ice at the same time.

"Hey, brutha, ain't no need for all that," Cancer said.

"Pick up the bag and hand it to me or I'll shoot your dick off."

Skip returned to his motel room. He held up the bag of crystals and shook it. At least an ounce, probably more. Not bad for ten minutes' work. He smoked a bowl yesterday, another last night and another this morning. He wasn't using long enough to get skin sores and rotting teeth but he couldn't remember when he'd slept or eaten a meal. He felt good. Ready. Like he could do anything, except there was nothing to do. He neatened up the motel room. Did his laundry, cleaned his gun six times and cleaned the car twice. He showered, clipped his toenails, spent forty-five minutes popping zits on his chest. He didn't like a freckle on his temple and rubbed it until the skin was raw. His phone buzzed. Who was it? Isaiah calling to gloat?

"Yeah?" Skip said.

"You called about the wanted poster," a man said. He sounded Mexican. Skip couldn't believe it.

"Uh, yeah, maybe. Who wants to know?" he said.

"It's my poster," the guy said.

Skip laughed. "No shit? Did you check me out?"

"Vicente said he knows you," the guy said. "He said you were a tough motherfucker for a white boy." Skip was pacing, running his hand through his hair, super excited.

"Yeah, yeah, right," he said. "Vicente was a hard-ass himself."

"He's got tattoos on his stomach," the caller said. "What are they?"

"Two pistols aimed at his crotch," Skip said. There was a pause. He could hear the Mexican breathing. "Call me Skip."

"Uh, call me Arturo."

"Sure, whatever you want, Arturo." There was a pause. Skip took the leap. "We should hook up."

After some back-and-forth they decided to meet in the Vons parking lot at four in the afternoon. No creeping around in the dark. Manzo was early. He drove the Caprice to the far edge of the lot, backed into the space and watched. He was determined to kill Isaiah. What little pride he had left demanded it. Diego's laugh demanded it. Manzo saw someone drive into the lot, turn and then come right toward him. Is that Skip? How the hell did he spot you? Manzo thought. A gun was in his lap. You never know. The driver went past him, backing into a space about five cars away. He turned off the engine and waited. He doesn't know you're here, Manzo thought. He wants to check things out just like you. The boy's got some street smarts. Manzo called him.

"I'm about five cars down from you," he said. Manzo got out of the car, stood and gestured *Come on over.* A skinny white boy appeared and approached cautiously, looking around.

"Get in," Manzo said.

Skip was scrawny and twitchy, wearing a full set of tats and a frayed Levi's jacket with no shirt underneath. He sat upright, like he was trying to see over something. His pupils were dilated, his arms were folded across his chest, hands massaging his arms, then his knees. He smelled like window cleaner. Had to be meth, thought Manzo. Skip was high. Manzo tried meth when he was nineteen, some of the homies were into it. Just like they said, the high was fucking amazing. Manzo smoked for about a week, then he went to Tijuana to do some business. Scoring there was easy but Sinaloa frowned on it. Drug couriers had to have their shit together. By the time Manzo got back to Long Beach he was over it.

"Isaiah pissed you off too, eh?" Manzo said. Skip's jacket was open, a gun tucked into his waistband.

"Yeah, you could say that," Skip said. "Son of a bitch thinks he's so smart, you know? Before I went to the joint, I was doing good. I had my dogs, I'm working—everything was okay. Then along comes Q Fuck."

"Q Fuck?" Manzo said with a chuckle. "That's what you call him?"

"He screwed up my whole game," Skip went on. He was talking fast. "Got me busted, the prick. I lost my house, my dogs, my kennel, I lost every fucking thing! Why should he get away with that? I don't know about you, but I don't let people fuck me over. I don't let people—"

"Okay," Manzo said. "Same as me but—"

Skip talked over him, babbling on about Isaiah and how he messed up his life, and how that bitch Grace disrespected him and how he was going to shoot her too. He was so into it, so keen and enthusiastic, like a kid talking about Disneyland and all the rides he'd go on. Manzo wished some of that energy rubbed off. He was fading. He was tired. The thought of hooking up with this pendejo was depressing.

"If you'd let me get a fucking word in edgewise," Manzo said, interrupting.

"Sure, sure, say what you want, man, it's a free country," Skip said with an exaggerated shrug.

"Maybe this isn't a good idea," Manzo said. "You're high, dude. How are you gonna shoot somebody?"

"I shoot people for a living, asshole," Skip said. "What about you? You look like you're falling asleep, homeboy." He said "homeboy" the same way a cracker would say "nigger." Manzo felt his anger rise but was too detached to do anything. "I mean, are you really up for this?" Skip continued. "Are you gonna stay in the game? Shit, dude, you should be worried about yourself." *Don't push me,* Manzo thought. He wanted to end this but an angry tweaker with a pistol was dangerous.

"Sorry, man, I didn't mean nothing by it," Manzo said. A blob of dullness massed in his brain, his motivation for killing Isaiah—his motivation for doing anything—was melting away. Skip was ranting about Grace now. How she tricked him, how she put him down and what he was going to do to her. Manzo felt trapped, sweat streaming down his neck, the car was getting smaller, the air getting thinner.

"Are you listening?" Skip demanded.

"Yeah, yeah, I'm here," Manzo said.

"What's your problem, dude? You look like you're afraid. You look like you're backing out."

"We don't know where Isaiah is," Manzo said feebly. His last argument.

"I do," Skip said.

"You do? Bullshit."

"No bullshit," said Skip. "Isaiah was at the hospital visiting Grace. I knew he would be. I followed him from there to his hiding place." This is getting real, Manzo thought. Play for time.

"I've gotta get something in the store," he said. Skip was furious.

"What the fuck are you talking about? Are you playing me? Are you a cop?" Manzo thought of something. If he worked it right, Skip could do the killing. Yeah, set the hitman up as a patsy and take credit for the hit. Two birds with one asshole.

"I need a Mountain Dew," Manzo said. "I'm thirsty, aren't you? It's hot in here." Skip licked his dry, chapped lips. You can distract a meth head with anything. "We can talk about the hit in the store. It's got air conditioning," Manzo said.

They went directly to the cookie aisle, Skip opening packages and tasting the cookies until an employee told him to stop. Somewhere between there and the checkout line, they decided to kill Isaiah. Tomorrow night.

"It's a deal then," Skip said, delighted. He did a couple of loud cowboy whoops in the middle of the store. Manzo went home. Now that he'd decided, he felt worse, more confused than when he left the house. The idea of killing Isaiah, of killing anyone seemed laughable. More risk, more danger, more grinding suspense. He wondered if he'd ever relax again. Not likely, not after murdering Isaiah. Manzo's mind was swarming with doubts, trade-offs and the need to escape. It wasn't like him to waffle. He was a leader. He made a decision and that was that. But all he wanted to do now was sleep.

CHAPTER TWENTY
Wanna Pipe Up?

Winnie and Duvall drove back to the station, the tension between them like an eight-hundred-pound gorilla sitting in the backseat.

"I guess you've been snooping around," Duvall said as if it didn't matter.

"No, I haven't," Winnie said. "I promise you, I haven't done anything."

"Bullshit," Duvall said, sneering. He's trying to bait you, Winnie thought. See what you've been up to.

"You have my word, Duvall. No snooping of any kind."

"Oh really? Not even a little? Come on, Winnie, quit fucking around. Who have you told?"

"Have you ever known me to go back on my word?" she shot back. "Have you?" She'd discovered that "giving your word" was somehow less likely to be challenged than other kinds of reassurances. Duvall didn't answer. He drove and nothing else was said. Winnie didn't feel bad about making a promise and giving him her word. She was being truthful as far as it went. What she didn't tell him was what she intended to do.

* * *

Winnie had a feeling. If Duvall stole the cash, it couldn't have been his first time. There must have been other incidents. She remembered a case she'd worked with him the week before. Van Heerdon Diamond Cutters was a shady outfit. Van Heerdon was suspected of dealing in blood diamonds, so named because the revenue went to rebel groups, corrupt governments, state militias and roving gangs of thugs. The people who mined the diamonds were enslaved, tortured, raped and cheated out of their paltry earnings. Van Heerdon had connections in the South African provinces. It was said he smuggled in the diamonds and used the profits to suppress an uprising over political corruption.

Van Heerdon was robbed. A looting gang known as the Kleptos broke into his facility. There was a gunfight. Van Heerdon and his wife were killed. The gang made off with a shopping bag full of diamonds. Some were ready for sale, others were partially processed but most were rough, in their natural state.

Winnie looked into diamonds as a matter of interest. Rough diamonds vary in color from black, ochre and gray to aquamarine, brown and crystalline, like quartz. Their surfaces are cracked and crinkled. There is no sparkle. Your untrained eye would have a difficult time picking them out from the rocks in your backyard.

The prices varied depending on the quality and color. In Van Heerdon's online catalogue, a rough 2.4-carat natural green diamond went for $4,900. A rough 7.32-carat natural champagne diamond was $11,250. A rough 6.74-carat natural champagne diamond went for $20,250. The thieves nearly got away with a fortune.

A car chase ended in a crash on the freeway. Winnie and Duvall were in on the arrest. It was a chaotic scene. The suspects' van collided head-on with an eighteen-wheeler. The truck driver was killed. Two suspects were also killed, one tried to escape on foot, the pursuit covered by the local news stations.

The property room was in a building separate from the station. Its location was kept secret. Winnie used her key card to gain entrance. She gave the supervising officer the case number and what specific evidence she was seeking. Unlike in TV shows, people were not allowed to wander up and down the aisles, pulling things off the shelves.

The officer retrieved the evidence bags and she examined them in a room kept for just that purpose. Several video cameras watched her every move. She looked through the bags one by one, inspecting the diamonds closely, holding the bags up to the light, not knowing what she expected to find. She selected another bag and froze. The stones weren't diamonds, they were ordinary gravel. The bag had been swapped out. Winnie was shocked. How could Duvall be so stupid? He was bound to be caught.

The crash site covered a wide area. Hundreds of diamonds had been scattered all over the freeway and down the ivy-covered incline. Numerous yellow flags marked the locations. Photos were taken to establish what evidence was where. Then the techs collected the diamonds and sealed them into plastic tamper-proof bags. A Post-it with a simple numerical code was applied to the bags. A more detailed label would be printed out later.

A lot of people were there. Uniforms, detectives, supervisors, officials from Caltrans, two forensic teams and medical personnel. Cars were backed up on the freeway, officers and road flares directing them into one lane, helicopters buzzed overhead. Winnie's memory went to work, watching a slo-mo film on the backs of her eyelids. She remembered the bags were collected and put in a cardboard box. The box was set in the cargo bay of a forensics van. The doors were open. No one in particular was watching it but an officer was nearby talking on his phone.

Winnie's slo-mo did not include the actual theft but she could see how it might be done. Duvall places a handful of gravel in an evidence bag. He approaches the officer, says he's needed somewhere else. The officer leaves. Duvall quickly selects a bag, removes the Post-it, sticks it on the ersatz bag and switches them out. It would take three or four seconds.

Winnie began to see Duvall's logic. No one examined the bags again until they were needed for trial. The suspect who survived the crash had a public defender. In the vast majority of these cases, a deal was struck with the prosecutor and there would be no trial. The evidence would remain unexamined. It couldn't be returned to the Van Heerdons—they were dead and no other relatives stepped up to claim it. The diamonds would be held in storage for sixty days. If no one claimed them, they'd be put up for auction, the proceeds going to the city's general fund.

It was an appalling situation, thought Winnie. There was a high probability Duvall stole the diamonds and the theft of Archie's cash only supported her suspicion. There was enough to initiate an investigation. If she was right, Duvall's career was over, and judges tended to go hard on corrupt cops. He'd go to prison for a long time. Winnie imagined the arresting officers appearing at Duvall's front door, snapping on the cuffs in front of his family. It would destroy them all. She decided to confront him. Let him prepare himself, prepare his family.

Isaiah spent the next day at the animal shelter, repairing a stall, hosing down the dog kennels and unloading supplies from a truck and storing them away. It was satisfying work. There was something to do and you got it done. No peril, no bad guys, no nasty loose ends, no jumping from the frying pan to the air fryer. He ordered takeout, listened to Segovia on his phone, changed the bedding on the cot and went to bed early. He was awakened by nightmares. He couldn't remember them, only the fear and an acute sense of loss. He sat on the patio, listening to the animals and feeding the parrot peanuts in their shells. The bird burbled and ruffled its feathers but didn't shriek.

Maybe Harry will let you live here, Isaiah thought. That would be fine. Walking the dogs, playing with the kittens, grooming the horses, feeding the baby hummingbirds, wielding nothing more dangerous than kibble, alfalfa, carrots, birdseed, toy mice and peanuts still in their shells. He imagined there were other people who felt that way.

Isaiah got out of bed. He needed to move, maybe listen to an audiobook so his mind thought about something other than Grace. He slipped on his clothes, put on his earbuds and walked the grounds, listening to *The Other Black Girl.* He was startled when the gate alarm buzzed. He hurried into the office and peeked through the blinds. A silhouette stood outside the gate. He didn't recognize her at first. He'd already written her off as gone forever. *It was Grace.* "I'm coming!" he said. He hurried out of the building to the front gate and fumbled with the padlock.

"Just a sec," he said. He opened the gate. She brushed past him and he followed her inside. No eye contact, expression neutral. She entered reception and stood there a moment. She glanced at the parrot and smiled.

"Are y-you . . . can I—I . . ." Isaiah stuttered.

"Where do you sleep?" she said.

Skip was parked in the Vons lot. He was anxious, squirming around, rubbing the freckle. He checked his gun twenty times, popping the magazine in and out, in and out. Meth got you high, but it also let your anger loose. The need to kill, destroy and avenge was like a jet engine screaming in your face. You have to do something *right fucking now* and nothing on earth can stop you.

Skip did a lot of dumb shit when he was like this. Shit that nearly got him killed. Ease up, cowboy, he thought. Stay in control. He called the Mexican and got no answer—again. Did the guy flake? If he did, he was in trouble. You know what? Skip thought. Fuck it. Kill Isaiah by yourself. Shit, that doesn't work. If you have to run you won't make it. The bad leg. Goddamn Jessica. Shot by his own damn mother.

"The Mexican's setting me up," Skip said, suddenly fearful. He took a closer look around, studying each car and who was in it. "I'm onto you motherfuckers." He racked the slide on the gun. Okay, you're scared, he thought, but not paranoid. Taking precautions was common sense. His view from the car was limited. He slipped the gun into the back of his pants and got out. He tried to seem nonchalant, yawning and stretching, his gaze whipping around from one end of the lot to the other.

"Shit, man, this is bullshit." He was pissed now. Who is this fucking Mexican, holding you up? Who does he think he is? Who does he—? Skip saw an old woman in filthy clothes, babbling as she pushed her shopping cart across the lot. "I know her, I've seen her before," Skip said to himself. At the 7-Eleven. He was sure of it. Was the old woman part of a surveillance team?

The Mexican finally arrived, pulling in next to Skip, going too fast, nearly bumping over the parking block. That was dumb, thought Skip. How about being a little less conspicuous? How 'bout a little tradecraft? How 'bout texting me first? "Where the hell you been?" Skip said as Manzo got out of the car.

"Been?" Manzo said, copping an attitude. "I been where I been, ese, and now I'm here." Manzo didn't look at him, his eyes all over the place, the bulge of a gun under his shirt. His fingernails were dirty. His pupils were—Skip couldn't believe it. *The Mexican was high too!*

"Anybody with you?" Manzo asked.

"No, why would anybody be with me?" Skip said.

"I'm just asking, man, what's with you anyway?" the Mexican said. "If nobody's with you that's all you gotta say. I'm being careful, that's all, just like you."

"Are you high?" Skip said.

"Yeah, I'm high. So are you. The fuck difference does it make? I'll take anybody out, Isaiah ain't nothin' special. Shit. I'll cap that prick in my sleep, you know what I'm saying? I put motherfuckers down my whole life and here I am. You feel me? Do you?"

The Mexican went on ranting—loud, almost shouting and gesturing like a rapper. Do I want to deal with this? Skip thought. He was losing his fire, his mood sliding down a steep hill. Fucking meth. Sometimes it turned on you. The Mexican kept yelling. Somebody from Vons approached. He was wearing a short-sleeve white shirt and tie, his ID badge said MANAGER.

"Um, I'm sorry, you guys, but, uh, you have to leave the property or I'll call the police."

"Go ahead, motherfucker," Manzo said, stepping into the man. "You pick up a phone and I'll come in there and get you." The manager turned swiftly and hurried away.

"Fuck you!" Manzo called after him. He looked at Skip expectantly. "Well? What are we doing?"

"We gotta leave. That guy'll call the cops."

"Fuck the cops and don't gimme no runaround," Manzo said. Skip's mouth was so dry his tongue was stuck to his palate. *"Well?"*

Manzo repeated. In three seconds, this asshole will pull a gun and we'll both be dead, thought Skip.

He said, "Wanna pipe up?"

Skip drove slowly, plagued with tics, twitches and terrible scratching, his deep-fried brain ping-ponging between hyperexcitement and a crazy need to kill. Ugly boils had erupted on his chest. He itched so bad he wanted to tear his skin off. Manzo was in no better shape, wiping his runny nose with his fingers and rubbing the slime off on his pants. It was almost funny. Two geared-up assholes trying to work together.

"Could you maybe hurry up? Drive faster," Manzo said.

"That's just what they want," Skip said. "They pull me over like it's a traffic stop—bang-bang and it's over." Manzo nodded, like he knew who "they" were. Skip parked on the side street next to the animal shelter. The chain link fence was ten feet high, razor wire coiled along the top.

"How the fuck are we gonna climb that?" Manzo said.

"We're not," Skip replied, nearly adding, "you moron."

They got out of the car. Skip kept a pry bar and industrial-size bolt cutters in the trunk. Chain link is tough. Skip hadn't eaten or slept but the drugs stoked his angry energy. He cut link after link, grunting with each cut, his body temp about a million degrees. He could never do this sober. Manzo was antsy, bouncing on the balls of his feet, breathing in sighs, whispering *Come on, man, hurry up, hurry up hurry.* Fuck this guy was irritating.

A few minutes later, there was a four-foot slit in the fence. They pushed and wriggled their way through. They crossed the parking lot to the building. Skip used the pry bar to leverage open the front door. They stood in the doorway, waiting for their eyes to adjust to the dark.

"So what are we doing?" Manzo said like they were still at Vons.

"Keep your voice down," Skip replied.

"Keep my voice down? Who the fuck are you?"

"You're gonna scare Isaiah away. Is that what you want?"

"I want what I want," said Manzo, as if that made sense. "Don't disrespect me, ese. I'll fuck you up."

"Fuck me up how?" Skip said. "If we threw down you wouldn't last a minute." Manzo drew his gun. Skip drew his. From somewhere in the dark, something screeched "NEVERMORE!" Skip jumped. Manzo screamed and ran.

Skip swung his gun back and forth. *What the fuck was that?* He saw the shape of a parrot on a perch. "Goddamn bird!" Skip said. "You scared the shit out of me! Shut up, okay?" And the bird screamed back, "SHUT UP SHUT UP!" Then it took off, flapping over Skip's head and out the door. Skip ducked, tried to shoot but the bird was already gone. Manzo was gone too, the pussy. That's a relief, thought Skip. When this is over, kill that fuck.

Isaiah and Grace made love carefully, their eyes open, radiating joy or great pain whenever they met. They dozed off. Isaiah woke first. Grace was still asleep, covered with a horse blanket, her naked shoulder white and elegant as a swan's. She looked beautiful. She looked blessed. He would never let her go. Never. He was thirsty. When Grace woke up, she'd be thirsty too. Harry kept a case of water under the reception desk. Isaiah slipped on his pants and crept from the room. He was barefoot and shirtless. He went down the hall. He couldn't believe what was happening. Grace was here and in his bed! Were they making up? He was thrilled but frightened too. What if it was sex and nothing else? What if she didn't mean to sleep with him? Maybe she wasn't in her right mind or the pain meds impaired her judgment. He had to get the water and return to fix things. Suddenly, the parrot screeched "NEVERMORE!" Isaiah stopped. Was that random or something else? A moment passed and then, "SHUT UP SHUT UP!" Isaiah drew in a quick breath. Someone was right around the corner in reception. It had to be Skip. His first thought: *Protect Grace.*

Manzo was gone. Skip was still in reception, a few parrot feathers drifting in the air. He was starting to hallucinate, demon shapes were moving around in the dark—and then Isaiah flashed past in the adjacent hallway. "Hey!" Skip shouted. He stepped into the hall, looked right and saw Q Fuck running away. Skip raised the gun and rapid-fired. BLAM BLAM BLAM! He *missed!* The bullets going high, low and sideways. "What the fuck—" He *never* missed.

Isaiah ran, shots zipping past him. A miracle he wasn't hit. *What's wrong with Skip?* Nothing ahead but offices and a conference room, a fire exit at the end. He heard Skip trailing, shouting. "I got you, Q Fuck!" Another salvo, the rounds getting closer. He wouldn't make it to the fire exit. He darted into the conference room and locked the door, knowing it was useless. He'd trapped himself. He heard Skip in the hallway, slowing and stopping, wheezing like he'd run a marathon.

The conference room had no other exit and the windows were wired glass. People thought they were safer but the glass was thin and easy to break. Isaiah picked up a chair and bashed a window repeatedly. It shattered but loose ends of the wires stuck out. They were sharp as fishing hooks. He was shirtless and barefoot. Skip was kicking the door and yelling.

"What's up, genius? Huh? Told you I'd get you!" Skip fired into the door, shredding half of it, the lock blasted to pieces. Isaiah dived under the conference table. Skip was gibbering and cackling, the words slurred and unintelligible. Isaiah had heard this kind of babble before. Skip was high. That would explain why he couldn't shoot straight. And then: BLAM BLAM BLAM! Not Skip's gun, the shots were farther away. *Someone was shooting at Grace!*

Skip kneeled down. They could see each other through the legs of a dozen folding chairs. He was grinning demonically, pouring sweat, skin on his face rubbed raw. Isaiah counted Skip's shots. Three in the first salvo, six in the hallway and three more through the door. Fifteen-shot magazine. Three rounds left.

"Well, here we are, asshole. I'm gonna enjoy this," Skip said. *Don't let him aim, Isaiah, make him shoot in anger.*

"I went to Blue Hill. It was sad, not a dog in sight," Isaiah said. He flattened himself on the floor and rolled. Skip snarled and fired twice, one round ripping the underside of the table, the other obliterating a couple of chair legs. *One round left.* Did he count right?

"They incinerated Goliath, you know," Isaiah said mockingly. "Did they send you the ashes?" Skip made an animal noise. He stood up, tossed aside the chairs and heaved the table over. Isaiah was exposed, but he was already moving. Skip was unsteady on his wounded leg, his gun hand slow to react. Isaiah leapt, tackled him and the gun went off, the bullet shattering a ceiling light. They crashed to the floor. Isaiah was on top, Skip thrashing like a gator in the bottom of the boat, yelling and flailing. Isaiah hit him with a slashing elbow, breaking Skip's nose, blood gushing. Skip roared and threw Isaiah off, blood flying everywhere. They scrambled to their feet. Skip was greasy with sweat, showing his teeth, his deranged eyes like solar flares, his leg wound bleeding through his pants. He was a beast. He was a creature. He was a fucking savage. BLAM BLAM BLAM! Three more distant shots. Was Grace wounded? Was she dead? *You've got to get out of here, Isaiah!*

"I've been waiting for this, asshole. I'm gonna break your neck," Skip said. Isaiah was afraid of Skip's meth-fueled strength and energy. The slashing elbow broke the hitman's nose to no effect. Punch him or knock him down and he'll shrug it off. Skip's body seemed to expand, his rabid face turning purple. "DIE, Q FUCK!" he screamed. He charged. Isaiah took a step to the side, at the same time deflecting Skip's reach with an inside-out forearm. As the killer stormed by him, Isaiah kicked him in his wounded leg. Skip wailed, stumbled and crashed into the wall. Isaiah ran from the room.

The baby dragon flew out of nowhere. It was green with a hooked mouth and big wings, right out of *Game of Thrones.* Manzo ran into the parking lot and watched the dragon fly away. It freaked him out. He wanted to pipe up but a jagged thought came to him. What if the dragon was a setup? What if it was Isaiah's watchdog or something. Be just like him.

"Oh shit," Manzo said. Maybe *Skip* set him up. Why not? He bred all them killer dogs, why not dragons? The fucking hitman wants to kill you! Bullshit, Manzo thought. Skip wasn't no hitman, he was just some white boy with a gun. That prick was giving you orders. Nobody gives the Khan orders! He took the gun out of his pants and went back into the building.

Grace was woken by someone screeching "NEVERMORE!" She opened her eyes and sat up. *Nevermore?* It wasn't a raven, it was a parrot. The bird screeched "SHUT UP! SHUT UP!" Isaiah wasn't there. Something was happening. Alarmed, she opened the door and looked down the hall. She heard a commotion at the very far end. Shouting, furniture thrown around. Skip took away her phone and she hadn't replaced it. *Get to the office phone.* She ran down the hall and turned into reception. She nearly fell down. Manzo coming through the front door.

"It's you, you bitch!" he shouted.

She rushed out the back way and crossed the patio to the kennels. The dogs were barking, out of their minds. She could run down the aisle but there was a tall fence at the end. Manzo would shoot her in the back. She heard him on the patio. There was no place to go.

Manzo went after Grace, following her onto the patio. He caught a glimpse of her turning the corner and she was gone. The dogs were barking, loud, like breaking his fucking eardrums. He laughed. The whole property was enclosed by the same chain link fence Skip cut through with the bolt cutter. Manzo walked slowly, checking his gun, making sure a round was in the chamber. He reached the aisle fronting the kennels. Something weird was happening. The dogs were coming out. The bitch let them loose! Some were wary, some running around, others were fighting. The barking was so loud he couldn't stand it. "SHUT THE FUCK UP!" he thundered. The dogs ignored him.

He saw Grace at the far end of the aisle. She was hunched down, making herself small. He laughed again, walking toward her through the swarming dogs.

He stopped and fired, BLAM! BLAM! BLAM! He missed. The dogs scattered—except for a big black German shepherd. It charged him, snarling, fangs flashing, clamping its jaws on Manzo's gun hand and whipping its head. He screamed, blood spurting from the puncture holes. BLAM! BLAM! BLAM! He fired wildly, the shots were so loud, the flash so fiery, the dog let go, the gun skittering across the cement. Manzo scrambled toward it but stopped. He heard something. He turned to look. He couldn't believe it. Horses! *Demon horses,* galloping straight for him! They were big as freight cars, huge nostrils, big square teeth, burning coals in their eye sockets. Manzo screamed and backed away, hands up to ward them off. He stumbled and fell hard. He tried to get up. The last thing he saw was a blur of hooves and horseshoes.

Isaiah was sitting on the curb, awaiting questioning, hands cuffed behind his back. The police didn't know what role he played in the fiasco. The animal shelter's parking lot was a cacophony of cars, cops, CSIs, paramedics, animal wranglers and ambulances swirling around him. He saw an officer help Grace into a squad car. He called out but she didn't hear him. Or didn't want to. The car was moving away when she looked at him. Nothing registered on her face, eyes unseeing and hard as stones. He might have been invisible.

"Hello, Isaiah," Detective Hando said. She helped him stand and removed the cuffs. "I talked to the detective in charge. Everything's okay."

"Where are they taking Grace?"

"The station or the hospital, I'm not sure which."

"Did you catch Skip?" he said.

"'Fraid not. As far as we can tell he slipped the perimeter." Her partner, a big guy in a bad suit, was standing behind her. He had salsa on his tie and looked pissed. Whether at Isaiah or Hando was hard to tell.

"Detective Duvall. You must be IQ," he said.

"Not anymore," Isaiah replied.

"We have to go. Take care, Isaiah," Hando said. Isaiah watched the detectives move off in separate directions, saying nothing. Something going on there, he thought. He'd see Detective Hando again, he was sure of it. He noticed the parrot, perched on a rain gutter, pacing and swinging its head. He's waiting, Isaiah thought. When the place clears, leave the front door open and let the bird come home.

* * *

When Isaiah fled the conference room, Skip hobbled out of the fire exit, went through the slit in the fence and got to his car. His calf was throbbing, the pain clouding his vision. He was barely able to drive, holding the steering wheel with both hands, using one foot to work the gas and brake. His pant leg, sock and shoe were soaked with blood. His escape kit was at Jessica's house. He nearly crashed a couple of times and almost passed out before he got there. The house lights were off, her car was missing. Someone came and got her, he thought. At least she's not dead in the basement.

He parked in the backyard and left the engine running. He kept the lights off in the kitchen; no reason not to, but he felt exposed. He limped down the familiar hallway to the closet. A small duffel bag held his escape kit. He unzipped it and found a pistol. He racked the slide, put a bullet in the chamber and stuck the gun into the back of his pants. He went back down the hall, entered the kitchen again and stopped. The stove. *One of the burners was on,* the blue flames creepy and startling. "Oh shit," he said.

Jessica stepped out of the darkness. Wavering shadows fell on her half-shaved head, the Frankenstein stitches like welts, like wounds. "Mom?" he croaked. Jess moved very slowly, wincing, teetering, as if she might tip over. She wore one dirty slipper, the sack dress badly stained, dark bruises around her cheekbones, her eye sockets black and empty.

"You left me here to die," she said. She held a gun in one hand, the other hand on the counter to steady herself. He breathed her in, this garbage pile, this freak show, this ugly mess of flab who "raised him" without caring. The blue flames hissed like the life was leaking out of the room. He hated her. His pistol was in the back of his pants. He inched his hand around. "It's too bad the fall didn't finish you off," he said.

"I should have drowned you when you were a baby," she replied.

Yeah, you should have, thought Skip. His life had been nothing but pain, dead bodies and humiliation. Jess was looking at him, probably the way he was looking at her. Not pissed off, more puzzled, more sad, like how did they get here in this fucked-up kitchen with wrecked bodies and the reek of spoiled food in their nostrils and dried blood on their clothes? Jess raised the gun, her finger tightening on the trigger.

"Goodbye, Magnus," she said. He didn't draw the pistol. He didn't even try.

"Goodbye, Jess."

CHAPTER TWENTY-ONE
Go Easy, Q

Andy rode his bike down Dockside. He was scared. Something terrible happened at the house. Too terrible to think about. Thoughts like daggers were ripping holes in his brain. Nothing he could do about that now. He had to see TK. He had to apologize for ratting out Isaiah. He'd talk to Isaiah later, like next week or something. This was enough for now. He hoped the old man was out in the stacks somewhere and not in his office. He rehearsed his apology speech the whole way over but it was too soon. He needed more time.

Andy loved the wrecking yard. Sleeping in the loft, warm in an old blanket, blues from TK's boom box drifting up from his office along with the smells of motor oil, axle grease and hard work. He loved fixing the cars. He thought he'd be a mechanic one day. TK said he was talented, but he might have been acting nice. That was how the old man was. Andy never met anyone so relaxed, so easygoing, so—kind. You hardly ever hear that word anymore.

He approached the yard. It was locked, a chain cinched tight around the two sides of the gate. No one was around. Andy stopped. His heartbeat surged, his throat closed. There was yellow police tape strung across the warehouse door, the office window was broken. "Oh God! Oh no!" He dropped his bike, climbed the fence and ran toward the warehouse. "TK? TK? Are you there? TK?" The door was open, bullet holes were marked with chalk circles. Andy stepped inside and stopped. Crime scene markers were on the cement floor, surrounding a dark stain. Blood. Andy gasped, staggered and nearly fell down. "It can't be," he whispered.

He reversed course, got back on his bike and raced up Dockside and around the corner to Tolbert's machine shop. TK and Tolbert were longtime friends. About the same age, all gristle, grease on their coveralls, wisdom in their eyes. Andy ran inside and found Tolbert looking through some kind of manual.

"Whoa! Ease up, boy," Tolbert said.

"What happened—what happened to—" Andy said, breathless. Tolbert closed the manual.

"You didn't hear?" he said. "TK got shot."

Andy got several calls on his way to Long Beach Memorial. He knew who they were from and didn't answer, didn't even look at the caller ID. TK was in a hospital bed, tubes in his arms. He was watching a TV, mounted on a high wall bracket. Where he'd been hit, Andy couldn't tell. He hoped that meant it was minor.

"Come on in, son," the old man said.

"I'm so sorry, TK, I didn't mean for this to happen, I'm so sorry..." Andy blurted. He stood at the bedside, face in his hands, shaking with sobs.

"Yeah, I know," TK said. His eyes were sad and yellow as old piano keys. His jowls sagged, his wrinkles deep and well earned.

"I'm so sorry—" Andy said again.

"Come here, boy," TK said. He pulled Andy down to him

and held him against his chest. "I ain't mad at you, I ain't even disappointed. You was lookin' out for yourself, your mom too. I know how that is, believe me I do. Hard times make people do things they'd never do otherwise." Andy smelled motor oil and cheap cigarettes. He could hear TK's heartbeat through the hospital gown, steady and strong, as comforting a sound as there ever was.

"I'll pay you back," Andy said desperately. "I'll work for free. I'll come in early, every day, and I won't leave until—"

"You ain't doing none of that," TK said. "Now stand up, stop all this and listen to me." Andy obeyed. "You and me is connected," TK went on. "You know what that means? It means we like brothers. We make all kinds of mistakes, we hurt each other, we don't do the right thing. We might get mad as hell, we might even hate each other, but family is family. No matter what happens, we stick like glue. Do you understand what I'm sayin'?"

Andy wiped his face with his sleeve and nearly smiled. "Yes. Yes, I do, TK."

It was evening. Winnie parked in front of Duvall's house and texted him. *Im outside*. She hated doing this. She hated what she was going to say. Duvall in a Rams sweatshirt and athletic shorts. He sat beside her in the car, his jaw clenched hard, like he was biting through tissue paper, deeper lines on his face. He knew what was coming. He took a breath and so did she. This wouldn't be a quiet conversation.

"I know you switched the diamonds," she said. She started to tell him how she knew but he raised a palm to stop her.

"Come on in," he said evenly.

"You mean—do you really want to do that?"

He didn't answer and got out of the car. They went inside.

Winnie greeted his wife and son, Duvall telling them it was about work. He took her through the house to the screened-in sun porch. It was a warm night. Duvall's daughter Greta was sitting at a picnic table in the backyard, working by the light of a portable lamp. She was typing on her laptop, papers and books at her elbow. Winnie couldn't remember. Was Greta twenty-one? Twenty-two?

"Greta likes to work outside. She gets heat flashes," Duvall said. Strange for someone her age, thought Winnie. Greta was frail, her face flushed, heavy bags under her eyes. "She's going to Stanford, she's home on break," Duvall said, a proud papa. "She's something, she really is." He paused a moment as if to ready himself. "She has multiple myeloma. Those fucking cancer cells get in the bone marrow and crowd out the healthy ones." Winnie was shocked.

"Duvall, I'm—"

"Five years ago, Greta had five years to live," he said. "She's in graduate school now. She wants to finish, she wants to accomplish something before she..." His voice trailed off. He drew in a deep breath as if without it he might collapse. "She got symptomatic in her senior year, her grades dropped and she lost her scholarship." Duvall's loving eyes filled with tears. "I couldn't pay the tuition." He said it like he'd committed a terrible crime. His voice was trembling. "I promised her she'd finish. I *promised* her, Winnie." The strength of his emotions nearly knocked her down. Then, as if one more look at Greta would demolish his soul, Duvall shut his eyes. "You know the way out," he said.

Winnie returned to her car. Even when Ben broke up with her and she fractured her leg in three places and she saw a child run over by a car, she didn't cry. She was crying now, her face in her hands, her body quaking with grief, the tears unable to quench her sorrow. It was as if Greta had already passed. She realized

Duvall wasn't simply an irritating presence with deplorable habits. He was a human being, just like her. She went home, drove into the garage but remained in the car. She didn't know what to do. Turn Duvall in? How could she? Let him go? How could she? She needed to air it out, talk with someone who would understand.

The J & J Ranch was in the Santa Monica Mountains. It was a long drive from Laguna Beach. To access the ranch, you passed through Will Rogers State Historic Park. Will Rogers was born in the Cherokee Nation in 1879. He was an entertainer, radio personality and writer, renowned for his homespun humor and social commentary. In the 1930s, he was the highest-paid actor in Hollywood.

It was dawn when Winnie arrived, the park closed. She parked her car beside the road and walked. Will Rogers knew how to live, she thought. It was a wonderful place. His sprawling house was comfy and charming, set amid mature oaks, surrounded by greenery and flower beds and bordered by large, grassy open space. People would picnic, lie in the sun, read books or do nothing at all, their children happily racing around. The house overlooked an honest-to-goodness polo field, wider and longer than a football field and always beautifully kept. It was so refreshing to see, thought Winnie. Green, open spaces were such a rarity in LA. She walked up the roadway that led to the ranch, tire tracks and hoofprints on the hard-packed earth.

There were beautiful pastures where the horses could mosey instead of standing restlessly in stalls. It was why she stabled Tomoe here. Her dressage partner was eighteen now, getting up there, and Winnie wanted her to be comfortable and content. She saw the horse feeding in a lush green field, enclosed in a white perimeter fence. The sight always gave her heart. Tomoe whinnied and promptly trotted over. She smelled of alfalfa and warm earth. Winnie stroked the horse's neck and fed her an apple.

"Hello, friend," she said. "I've got a problem." They went for a ride. The trail wound through the foothills, Winnie's mind dark and in turmoil. They reached a crest with a view of the Pacific. There was chop on the gray sea, the air was chilly, the horizon bleak. Like the task ahead, she thought. They rode back. Something about the plodding pace and Tomoe's calm, patient manner settled Winnie down. They were nearing the ranch when the idea came to her. "Oh my God!" she said. She couldn't wait and called Duvall from the saddle.

"Did you report me yet?" he said.

"No," Winnie replied. "How much is Greta's tuition?"

"What? What do you want to know?"

"Just tell me, Duvall. How much is it?"

"Fifty-six K, not that it's any of your business."

"I'll loan you the money."

There was a stunned pause. "Are you serious?" Duvall said.

"Yes, I am. I can have it in your bank account by the day after tomorrow."

"But how?"

"I'm a rich bitch, remember?"

"I appreciate this, Winnie, but I can never pay you back."

"Here are the terms," she said sternly. "One percent APR for three hundred sixty months. That's my best and final and I will not negotiate."

"One percent?" Duvall laughed. "And three hundred sixty months is thirty years! I'll be dead by then."

"Then your grandchildren can pay it off," Winnie said. She was embarrassed for him and herself. "I've got to go, Duvall."

"I don't know what to say."

"Me either. I'll see you at the station."

"Winnie?" he said.

"Yes?"

"I still want a new partner."

"So do I," she said, her eyes glassy with tears.

The Big Day. Dodson was at church service. The chapel was full, the congregation excited, abuzz with chatter about the next choir director. It was a hot topic in the neighborhood. Folks argued for their favorite, debated their qualifications and discussed their track records. It was like the deciding game in a championship tournament, winner take all. Isaiah was there, way in the back, of course. Gloria sat next to Dodson.

"I hear you advised the Reverend on this issue," she said disapprovingly. "I can't imagine what you told him. It wasn't about rap music, was it?"

"You mean which one of them old ladies can spit the best?" Dodson said.

"Who said anything about spitting? You are vulgar and odious, Juanell, and I rue the day you met Cherise." Dodson didn't reply. He'd have his moment.

The Reverend came to the pulpit and the room went quiet. The choir was seated below the altar and facing the congregation, elegant in their white robes with gold trim. Elvira and Mrs. Yakashima were on opposite ends of the first row. Cherise was in the row above them, a lily among dandelions in Dodson's eyes.

The Reverend was irate. "There has been some controversy surrounding the appointment of a new choir director," he said, his voice filling the chapel. "And I must tell you, what I've seen in the last few weeks was, frankly, disgusting." The congregation was still, only the rustling of clothing and nervous stirring. A few of the self-righteous were shaking their heads.

"This church is a holy place, a place of worship, a place of love," the Reverend said. "This isn't a petri dish for petty grievances. People have actually taken sides in this matter! And I'm sad to say, conflict, arrogance and unacceptable behavior have been the result." Elvira and Mrs. Yakashima seemed to disappear into their robes. "Unfortunately, I myself unwittingly encouraged this woeful situation," the Reverend went on. "I am thoroughly ashamed and I'll ask God's forgiveness and if you have participated in this nonsense I suggest you do the same. Now for the announcement."

The Reverend paused, took a sip of water and cleared his throat. He's working the crowd and he's doing a good job, thought Dodson. The suspense made the congregation sit up straighter. Someone coughed. "Our new choir director is... Cherise Johnson." Johnson was her maiden name and Dodson was glad she kept it. She needed her own name. She deserved her own name. There were gasps and wide smiles and then an outpouring of gladness. Somebody said, "Bless you, Reverend." Somebody else said, "You're a wise man, Reverend." And by Dodson's reckoning everyone agreed. Cherise was astonished, her hand over her mouth. Elvira and Mrs. Yakashima bowed their heads, maybe in prayer, maybe in relief. "Can I get an amen?" the Reverend said.

And the thunderous answer came, "AMEN!"

The service ended, people filing out of the chapel, chatting happily, laughing like they knew it all along. Reverend Arnall at the door, hugging, shaking hands, thanking them for coming. Dodson was still seated and so was Gloria.

"What d'you think?" Dodson said.

"I think that's the best thing you've done in your entire life," Gloria said. She rose and moved off in a huff. Isaiah was already gone.

"Well done, Juanell," the Reverend said when they were alone. "We might recruit you yet. You know, it just occurred to me that I took credit for your brilliant idea. I'll correct that at the next service."

"Don't worry 'bout it, Reverend," Dodson said. "There's only one person I need credit from." He went outside. Elvira and Mrs. Yakashima had left. Someone said they were going to shake hands but couldn't do it. A group was gathered around Cherise, congratulating her, telling her that Jesus guided the Reverend's decision and the choir was sure to be better. Dodson caught Cherise's eye and she smiled like the sunrise, lighting up the sky, making shadows of everyone else. He breathed in and the air felt cool and good, and he was joyful for the first time in a long time.

Isaiah called Grace repeatedly but she wouldn't answer. He couldn't stand it. Despite Deronda's warning, he went to her house. Deronda opened the door but didn't invite him in.

"Grace is gone, Isaiah," Deronda said. "Left early this morning." He was dazed a moment.

"Did she—"

"Leave a note? Say where she was going? No, she didn't. And she's not coming back."

"I didn't mean for any of this—"

"I know, Isaiah, and Grace knows too," Deronda said. "You never intended for this to happen, you wanted the best for her and if you could do it all over again you would. But that don't matter now. She's out of your life and you better get used to it." Deronda kissed him on the cheek and closed the door.

The animal shelter was in shambles so Isaiah went to the wrecking yard. TK was with a customer. Andy was there, unbolting the bumper off an old school bus. It was hot. Isaiah went into the warehouse to find some shade. It didn't register at first. In the very back, the blue tarp covering Grace's Mustang was on the ground.

The car was gone. Isaiah's spirits sank to the bottom of the sea. You shouldn't be surprised, he thought. She only took what was hers in the first place.

Dodson came by and they walked the grounds together. It felt like a graveyard. Crows circling, cars with broken headlights stacked like the eyeless dead.

"I know you're not all right so I'm not gonna ask," Dodson said, "and I know you don't have plans or any idea what you gonna do next so I'm not gonna ask you about that either. You're in a sad way, Q. You don't have a job, your ol' lady left you and you've got PTSD."

"Are you trying to cheer me up?" Isaiah said.

"Not possible," Dodson replied. "It's gonna be a long damn time before you cheerful again, not that you was before, and by the way, I don't have any advice either. You on your own, Q."

"That's it? I'm at the lowest point in my life and your response is 'You on your own, Q'?"

"I'm just bein' real," Dodson said. "What was you expecting? A pep talk? That shit don't make nobody feel better."

"True enough," Isaiah said. "But being real is worse."

Dodson's phone buzzed. "It's Cherise." He turned away. "What's that, baby? How's your hero? He's like he always is, the coolest brutha in the hood." The conversation continued. Cherise was planning a birthday party for Micah. She thought he was too young for a PlayStation and Dodson agreed. "He'll be too young till he gets a job. Them things cost six, seven hundred dollars." Cherise said there was a parent-teacher conference on Thursday and Reverend Arnall had invited them over for dinner. She wanted Dodson to stop and pick up a bottle of wine.

"I don't know nothin' about wine," he said. They talked some more about small things, Isaiah's envy sharp and penetrating.

Dodson had a family to fill up his life. Isaiah had nothing. The call ended.

"I gotta go," Dodson said.

"Well, thanks for coming by. I feel so much better now," Isaiah said.

Their eyes met, so fleeting it might not have happened at all, so meaningful it would stay in Isaiah's memory forever. Dodson walked off, calling over his shoulder,

"Go easy, Q."

"I'll try."

Isaiah sat in TK's office chair, turning back and forth, the creaking a metronome for his headache. He'd reduced himself to a bad memory, an experience people would tell Grace to forget. She would remember him when he wanted to be erased. She took his love and he would never get it back.

"Mr. Quintabe?" Andy said. He was standing in the doorway.

"What is it, Andy?" The boy was tongue-tied with fear and indecision. "It's okay," Isaiah said. "You don't have to apologize."

"It's not that. It's something else."

"It's not really a good time for me, Andy."

"It's sort of important."

"Everybody's problems are important, but not to me," Isaiah sighed. "Not anymore."

"Yeah, but this is *very* important," Andy said. Isaiah heard it, like the rumble of a distant storm. The kid was going to ask for help.

"I need help," Andy said.

"I'm sorry, but I'm retired from the helping business. I'm not taking on any more work for you or anybody else."

Andy was devastated but held it in. "Oh, okay," he said. He left and came right back.

"Mr. Quintabe?" Isaiah felt his hackles rise.

"Andy, I just *said* I wasn't—"

"Somebody's trying to kill my mother," Andy said. The air was thick and motionless, the kid waiting, eyes urgent, hands together as if in prayer, pleading with his whole self. *Stay strong, Isaiah. Tell the boy to leave or you'll be right back in the sewer. Right back with the killers, crazies, gangbangers and pedophiles.*

"Sit down, Andy," Isaiah said. "Tell me about it."

Acknowledgments

My thanks to Brian Gantwerker, Sandra Ho, Andrew Leuchter, Thierno Diallo, Pat Kelly and my wife, Diane, without whom I'd be a puddle on the floor.

EXPLORE JOE IDE'S IQ SERIES . . .

'The best new discovery I've come across in a long time'
Michael Connelly

'Writing so sharp you may cut your fingers on the pages'
Attica Locke

'The best thing to happen to mystery writing in a very long time'
New York Times

'The Holmes of the 21st century'
Daily Mail

'Conan Doyle's characterisation and Raymond Chandler's phrase-making'
Guardian

'An electrifying combination of Holmesian mystery and SoCal grit'
Time

'Truly feels like an heir to Elmore Leonard'
Daily Telegraph